I0776980

Hierophant Trilogy:

THE

A S C

N

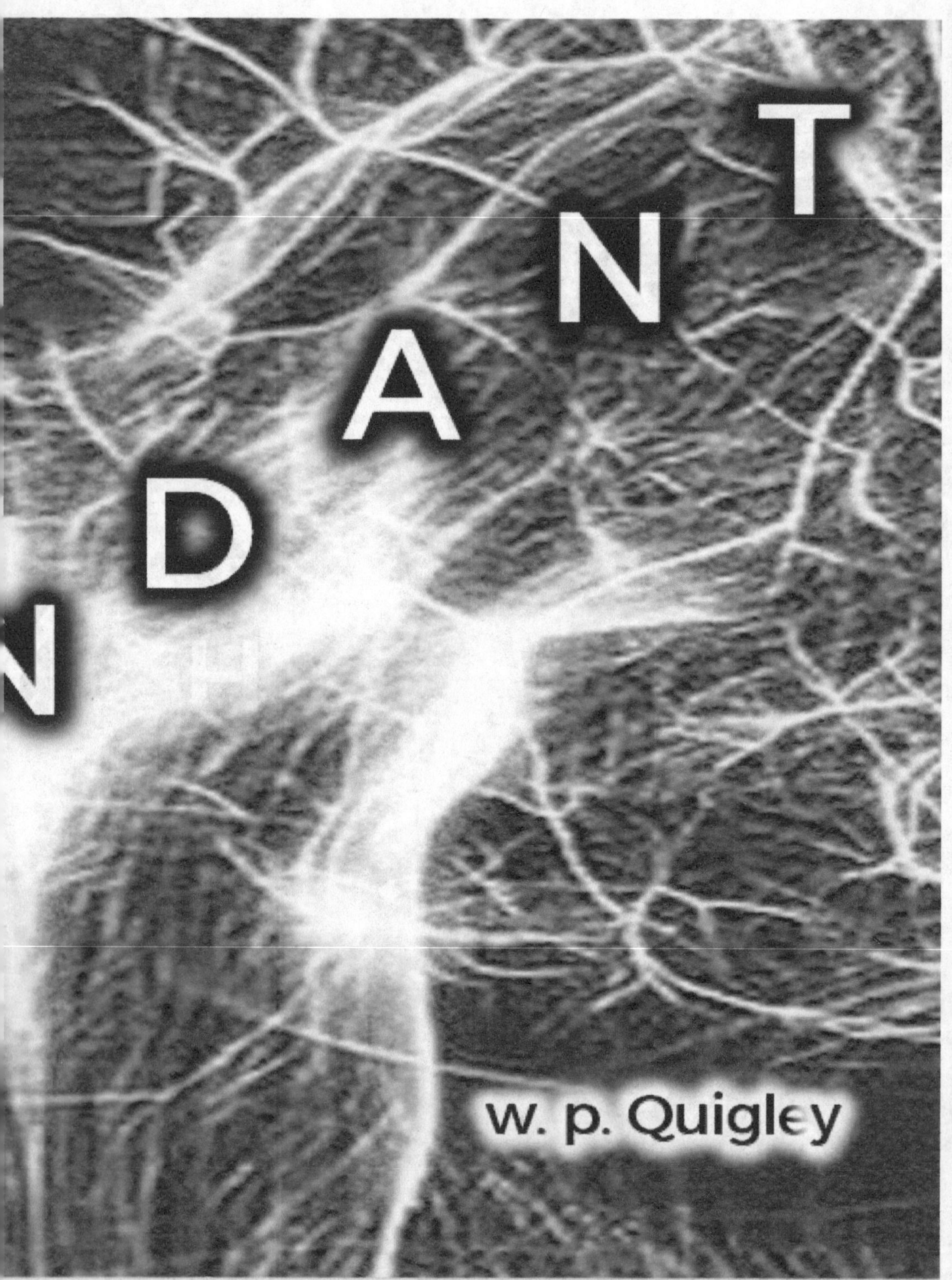
N D A N T
N
D
w. p. Quigley

ASCENDENT PUBLISHING, 1640 WORCESTER AVENUE D613, FRAMINGHAM, MA 01702

SECOND EDITION

Foreward by Lucienne LeBeau, editor, © 2023 Silver Hollow Stories and Lucienne LeBeau.

ISBN: **978-1-963970-01-2**

F O R E W A R D

When you live through what we've lived through, drawing out words is a necessary step in recovering.

He's a mad scientist in real life. No joke. When I met Mr. Quigley, it was in a Facebook group that he and his former paramour built together. I was on his podcast as a guest (under the name Anne Hogue-Boucher) talking about psychology and horror. I talked about my books and Wally gave me his time and interest. We connected as friends. As a couple of whacky, neurodivergent people who just didn't seem to fit in anywhere, nor did we want to. I've now been lucky enough to say I've met him in the meatspace as well, and it was like meeting a long-lost brother.

I watched him grow as a person and now as a writer. I was with him during some of his more trying times—and I lost touch with him when those times tried to swallow him into the void. Yet he returned. And he got stronger.

As the editor to this behemoth trilogy, I'm really proud to see how far he's come and how fast, too. His work will only get better with time and resolve. He knows, like any good writer, that he needs to get his million words out in order to begin to master the craft.

His first contribution towards that goal was the short story collection *ChaoS/HeaveN*, a collection of poems and prose. Here's the second...the opening volume in what he's calling his Hierophant Trilogy... THE ASCENDANT.

Nothing Walter writes is for the timid. He writes from a culmination of knowledge, experience, and feeling. Whether it's his contribution to Double Feature Magazine DVD EXTRAS or what you're about to read, everything he writes serves a purpose.

Tell the story.

And boy, does he ever. Without flinching.
It's my honor and privilege on behalf of Ascendent Publishing to present THE ASCENDANT, by Mr. W.P. Quigley.

-Lucienne LeBeau, Editor

PREFACE

I totally had to re-write this preface a couple of times before I finally settled on the one you're reading right now. The book itself? Feels like I went through a hundred iterations of the text until at last I was satisfied it had reached its final evolution – but in reality, it was only four.

However - the prologue never changed a single iota throughout the entire writing process, and if one considers it as the proverbial solid foundation upon which the house was built, hey, maybe all the second-guessing I did of myself along the way will be worth it.

The first preface was meant to be a discourse on what is now known as neurodivergence – its history, manifestations, current medical and societal understanding, etc. It was pandering and silly and faux-intellectual in tone, and when I realized this out it went. There were really just a couple of worthwhile takeaways. The first was that it's not a recent phenomenon and there hasn't been some drastic boom or uptick in sheer numbers just because our collective knowledge base and understanding has greatly increased in recent years. The second – pure conjecture – was that there's a pretty decent chance that a good many of people labeled as mystics, holy men, shamans, witches, and the like were neurodivergent because of their attendant, characteristic "different" way of perceiving the world and the way in which we interact with it as well as the people therein.

Yes, I said 'we' there.

Aside from that all of that business, I came to realize what it was that I really wanted to say here, at the beginning of all things:

The importance of meeting the basic and essential human need for connection with and to others cannot be understated in any conceivable context. There are so very many of us that struggle daily to do so through no fault of their own. And we as a species, down through the social strata from nations to cultures, cities, towns, communities, all the way down to within families and lastly to individual interactionss generally fail at adequately compensating for our fellow humans' shortcomings and deficiencies.

This fact of our existence doesn't just apply to neurodivergent people, but any number of sub-groups that bear a diminshed capability to feel at least some form of that vital connection to others. Any organism, regardless of species, that has been the victim of abuse or neglect suffer a greatly damaged ability to make any kind of healthy connection with essentially anything else living.

The further we drift from ourselves, from each other, and society writ large, the worse off we become. Our chances for survival are worse. The more likely we will destroy ourselves. Love thy neighbor, asshole, or we're all fucked.

Each day, in one way or another, we're told, shown, or reminded of how we are different from each other. We're sorted, categorized, and delineated, but not in such a way as to celebrate uniqueness and the majesty of our awesome and remarkable diversity, but rather to draw lines in the sand, pick sides, and make one thing better than the other.

And that's when we start going at each other.

We abuse the shit out of each other.

Eventually and inevitably, that abuse reaches an endpoint – those sections of our population that are not only too weak to defend themselves, but instead look to others for the support necessary for their very survival.

By definition, they're the easiest targets. It's like a warped, distorted version of the food chain.

So while you're reading this book, and really anytime thereafter, try to remember and/or keep it in the front room so to speak, to make it a point to find someone you are much, much different than in some glaringly obvious way or ways…but then do the unthinkable - look deeper for the ways you and that person are exactly alike, even one in the same.

That's always a beautiful thing, really, when you can make a connection between things that are fundamentally unlike. A kind of magic happens there, where a hidden and secret truth becomes obvious, and suddenly the world doesn't seem quite so random, chaotic, and disordered. Define the difficult to define. Let go of the easy. There is connection inherent in all things and in all people, it's all a matter of finding it.

The more a connection demands it be searched for, the more rewarding it is – without exception, I've found.

We, as a species, will never grow past our limits and evolve until we all can begin to pull closer to each other instead of pulling apart. Again, that begins with connection.

The Hierophant Trilogy, the first novel of which you hold in your hands, is set in motion by the drastic actions taken by a person who, ostensibly, could be considered a modern take on the 'mad scientist' trope. He's driven by one simple motivation - to make it possible for him to connect to people, even if his efforts only succeed with just one other person it still is far better than zero.

In this way, our 'mad' scientist plays the roles of *both* Dr. Frankenstein and his monster. His alienation, sense of abandonment, and unending loneliness drives him first to that most desperate, stigmatized of actions…and when he fails to do even that, our subject turns it up to eleven. And who could blame a person for attempting the impossible – given adequate resources and the intelligence to devise a methodology for doing such a thing?

Because there really isn't anything more horrible, more painful, or more tragic than the human soul who is entirely deprived of the meeting of that need for acceptance and for love for virtually their entire lives.

We would all do well to look out for one another to ensure that never occurs to anyone in our orbits….

…because terrible things can result from that pain.
The most terrible, terrible of things.

And they all come from a place that doesn't actually exist –
shouldn't exist -
and yet…
you can feel it;
you can sense it;
and therefore
you know
that
even in absence…

that it most certainly does.

Table of Contents

No one should deny the danger of the descent,

but it can be risked. No one need risk it, but it is certain someone will.

And let those who go down the sunset way do so with open eyes, for it is a sacrifice which daunts even the gods.

Yet every DESCENT is followed by an ASCENT.

the vanishing shapes are shaped anew,

and a truth is only valid in the end only if it suffers change and bears witness

in new images, in new tongues like a new wine that is put into new bottles.

-   Carl Jung

P R O L O G U E
D e s c e n t

Dr. David Keating laid back onto the metal gurney in his laboratory and took a deep breath, in through his nose and out through his mouth. On the exhale, he could taste the unnatural tang the vapors that had been produced by the organic solvents present in the lab - the very same ones that permeated every millimeter of his sinuses. Ethylene glycol, ammonium nitrate, and benzyl alcohol combined in the air to form a ubiquitous and pungent aroma so toxic, so powerful that Caleb and Sarah had to step outside the lab every thirty minutes or so. Keating however, had no need to do the same.

A moment later Caleb West, one of his two lab assistants, began applying the restraints that were likely necessary given what Keating and his team were about to do in just a few minutes. Keating felt the leather straps being wrapped around each of his wrists, then his ankles, as each extremity was secured in place. Four-point restraints were likely required - once the final dosing of the enzyme was administered.

Dr. David Keating, tenured professor of six years at Gordon University, with doctorates in biochemistry and genetics and winner of the Eli Lilly Award in Biological Chemistry in 2009…was unsure of what would happen that day. Neither of his two assistants had any idea either, the other of the two being Sarah Fischer, the teams' medical expert.

Almost none of the extraordinary events and phenomena that had occurred in the days and weeks prior that day had been regarded by the team as anything else other than impossible - at least outside of a science fiction or a horror movie.

And yet, these events, these phenomena, had all happened regardless of their likelihood, probability, or whether anyone 'believed' they were possible.

Not all of them were good.

Ergo, the restraints.

Dr. Keating closed his eyes and tried to relax as well as he could. Taking another breath, deep and deliberate, he attempted to clear his mind - but failed to do so. He could not silence the chattering, nervous thoughts of Caleb and Sarah that he could hear just as clearly and easily as if they were spoken aloud. Keating's recent telepathy was just one of the phenomena that had occurred during the past few months. There was no controlling this ability, so Keating could only listen - and wait for the final stage of the experiment to begin.

Caleb was thinking about what he would say to the university, as well as to any authorities, should the worst happen that day.

What am I going to tell them if David dies?

Death was a possibility that Keating had never considered for more than a fleeting moment or two, dismissing that outcome almost as quickly as it surfaced in his mind. It was a necessary risk, and besides - if his experimentation failed to fix his conditions, he had no intention of continuing his existence afterwards, regardless of any positive changes that may have occurred.

Keating had accepted that he was either going to change or die. He might as well die trying to save himself from the conditions that plagued him throughout his life.

"Caleb, can you loosen the straps just a little? The feel of them right now is bothering me." Keating's sensory issues, specifically those around physical contact and being touched, had been alleviated somewhat thus far; months before he wouldn't have been able to tolerate the straps' presence even for a moment.

As Caleb adjusted the straps, Keating reached into Caleb's mind further, to discover that he had never at any time abandoned the consideration that their ongoing experimentation could kill his mentor and friend. Keating admired him at that moment. Caleb had been quite brave in that regard.

But then Keating considered that maybe Caleb had been weak for not standing up to him and putting a stop to things. He still admired Caleb despite this last notion.

Sarah, on the other hand, was filled with anger and resentment - had been for quite some time. It was disconcerting, having to hear the amount of vitriol and resentment she'd stored up for both he and Caleb, then reaching a crescendo for the proceedings that day. Keating heard her in her mind go over her plans to disappear that evening, regardless of what occurred. This was acceptable to Keating. Sarah had fulfilled her purpose.

His assistants had never been, nor would be able to fully understand his motivations for doing what he had done to himself. Keating simply could not bear to live another day with himself as he was.

He was no longer able to remain a prisoner in his own mind.

That he had already begun to expand well beyond his handicaps, his mental illness, and his isolation was the truest sign that he was on the right path.

He felt Caleb's fingers probe the flesh near the top of his spinal column, just between the C4 and C5 cervical vertebrae. He felt a finger locate the spot, and then:

"Ready?" said Caleb.

"Yes," Keating replied.

Caleb first applied a generous portion of lidocaine to the area. Then, tiny pin pricks of Novocain, just under the skin in several spots to numb the area below the surface.

And then, the injection.

The needle pierced the skin with a finality - and then into the spinal column itself. The enzyme had to be injected there, as it was too large a molecule to pass the blood-brain barrier. Dr. Keating felt the needle inside and the warm, clear, viscous liquid as it flooded his central nervous system.

Any moment and....

His next experience was the feeling of rending, splitting, and fracturing - but not of any physical object in the room and not any specific part of his anatomy. It was his consciousness, his awareness, his essence that bore this instantaneous torture. What was once singular had now begun to somehow replicate, like individual cells inside of an organism. Each split was another copy of his own sentience, fully aware of itself and of the others at the same time, but each new generation was composed of raw, pure, unchecked electrical energy. His senses were overwhelmed, and he could not control what was happening to him.

He felt himself traveling through the air, through wires and cables and then, he felt himself coursing through...other people. He was hurting them. Killing them, somehow. He could feel their last moments of agony. Dr. David Keating experienced what it was like to die, except that the death he experienced was not his own.

This sensation, at the last, was too much to handle. If he continued to allow the expansion, he wasn't sure that it would ever stop. Or how many people would be hurt or worse.

He exerted his will - his primary will to bring the reaction under some kind of control. There was a feeling of simultaneous dissociation from the infinite versions of himself that had been generated that was like tearing off as many bandages from as many wounds all at once. Then, a separation. He felt reality slip away.

And then he began to descend.

Deeper and deeper, lower and lower, all those fractions of himself spinning and turning in an ever- narrowing gyre until they all merged, slamming into each other all at once at the nadir of the cone.

Darkness. Unending, unrelenting, and suffocating. Moments earlier, he'd been conscious and aware of the thoughts of not only himself, but the people in the room with him. Now, there was nothing. No sound, no light, only...him.

Darkness and silence.

He had spent his entire life as separate, isolated, and alone. Every conversation, even ones Keating engaged in with people he'd known for years, felt like tests of his ability to control his anxiety. Stumbling over words. Inability to make eye contact with another person for more than a second or two.

Unable to connect in any kind of meaningful way with any other human being. And now he had only succeeded in taking that state and bringing it to an exponentially worse extreme. He was truly alone.

Or was he? His own will had brought him down to this void, this netherworld where nothing existed - no time, no space, with no beginning and no end to it all. He knew that he wasn't dead. Could he reach out? To find someone - anyone? What was left of himself here in this place?

Keating concentrated. He needed a focus - a person that he could reach out to. He first tried Caleb, then Sarah. He found that he couldn't even picture their faces, let alone connect to their consciousnesses. How could he not remember their faces? He began to panic, trying to picture the face of someone, anyone he knew - but he found that he could not recall a single person's countenance.

And then - as if by chance, he thought of the woman. Her face appeared in his mind as clear as day, with no difficulty at all. He considered this for just a moment, and quickly deduced the reason why he could see her. They had...things in common. They were very much the same in their makeup, neurologically speaking. That had made it possible for Keating to reach out to her.

Magdalena was her name.

And he also admired her from afar. It seemed so unlikely to him that there could be another person as uniquely damaged or 'special' as he was. Their overlap, their mutual shared experiences were so closely aligned that it seemed even more impossible that two people could be that alike than the idea that he'd somehow developed the ability to hear another person's thoughts.

Was it love? He couldn't tell, simply because he had never actually been in love with anyone before.

No. It couldn't be.

Love was never meant for a person such as he was. Besides, he'd never met this person in his life, and you couldn't fall in love with a person you'd never been face-to-face with.

But none of that was important, however. What was important was that she was there, in his thoughts, and so it might be possible to reach her. He bore down with the considerable force of his mind and pushed his consciousness upwards through the void to wherever she was.

In what could have been seconds, minutes, or hours, he felt her. Her mind was in a dormant state. She was probably sleeping. This was strangely fortunate, for it was unclear as to whether he would have been able to reach her if she had been awake. He extended himself further outwards and could then feel her presence fully. He called to her….

Magdalena…

Magdalena...

please….help me….please……

Magdalena…

it's David…

part ONE:

THE EXPERIMENT

Magdalena was out on the back porch, arms folded, taking in the view for what had to be the hundred-thousandth time since she'd lived there in that house. Each time she had done this, she'd become disappointed and dissatisfied with both her existence and that of all she surveyed. She partook of this ritual of dismay anywhere from five to fifteen times a night, when she'd scan the streets outside, the humidity-worn and hurricane-beaten houses in her neighborhood, and the skies above for any kind of change or disturbance.

And in making each of those hundred-thousand trips out to the back porch over the years that she shared that miserable dump with her sister, there had never been so much as a single deviation, blip on the radar, or even just a single thing out of place.

And the feelings she experienced when she made those miniature excursions were inevitably the same.

Well, the same until recently.

The usual suspects:

Boredom.

Impatience.

Anxiety.

Dread.

But lately, in just the past year, a new feeling had arisen among those usual suspects, so to speak. This new feeling started off as just a whisper, a hint, a pencil sketch of an emotion. In the interim, it grew and took on more and more definition with each passing day.

On that evening, this newcomer had finally reached a shout, an incantation, an entire gallery of finished oil paintings with each one illustrating a different aspect or facet of it.

The feeling was despair.

Magdalena's life was passing her by, and she was absolutely certain there was nothing she could possibly do to stop it from doing so.

A person's forties were supposed to be when one starts to reap one or more of the benefits of a life well-lived - a rewarding career, a home, happiness, and fulfillment. Any one of these would have been fine. Magdalena had none of these. She turned forty-three last week.

She looked to her left and watched as a beat-up Subaru struggled down the nearby highway, trailing fumes of both exhaust and failure behind it in equal measures of each. She shook her head in disgust at the sight. The parallels that could be drawn between the dilapidated auto making its way down the road and the course her life had taken were apparent, almost blatant.

She thought:

Despair is what a person feels when they know that their both their life and destiny are doomed to be utterly pointless – and this result was as inevitable as it was inescapable.

She walked back into the house and sat down on the living room couch. She'd been watching a Lars Von Trier movie - but one of the far too pretentious to handle ones and not one of his better offerings .

"Melancholia", it was called. Melancholia was what one felt after having wasted three hours of their life watching it.

"How the fuck did Kirsten Dunst get a part in this movie?" asked Magdalena, to no one in particular, yet she still expected an answer. This was a mediocre actress whose biggest career highlight had been an upside-down kiss with the second-best Spider-Man. Two years later, she landed a lead role in an art house film with a director like Von Trier. Magdalena felt that this fact deserved justification. As she was wont to do, she answered her own question in her head in the same voice but from another part of her mind.

"She was fucking the director," she said, again addressing no one in particular. This was one of the common manifestations of her own unique brand of ADHD. She'd run full-blown conversations with herself, complete with questions, answers, and lively discourse.

She finished the brief dialogue.

"Yeah, you're probably right, Mags. What a skeeve."

She stopped the movie and began flipping channels. Once in this mode, she never watched anything for more than two seconds, and never ended up settling on anything to watch. This was also a ritual unto itself, but unlike her forays out onto the porch, this one elicited no emotion whatsoever. It was yet another of her oft discussed and well-catalogued ADHD behaviors, one that also erased any emotions that she may have been experiencing just prior to engaging in it.

Despite that the fact that she and her sisters' television only had twenty or so stations to watch, Magdalena would keep clicking between them regardless of the fewer number of channels to oscillate between. Eventually, after an indeterminate number of laps around the tiny oval track of free-to-view network channels Magdalena would announce to exactly no one:

"Fuck it."

Because there was nothing else to do but go to sleep.

Except, she wasn't going to fall asleep, at least anytime soon. The announcement was to herald her going to lay down in bed, but not to get any sort of restful slumber. She could put on pajamas, take a hot shower, or go so far as to take a Trazadone, but in the back of her mind she knew that all this treacle was futile, and sleep would remain as elusive as ever for yet another night.

What was then going to happen was this (yet another ritual):

She would first crank the air conditioning, then shut off the lights, and at last get under her comforter. After ten minutes in restless darkness, she'd pull out her cellphone, surf her social media accounts, watch random YouTube videos, and disappear down Wikipedia holes and online web pages until four o' clock in the morning. Insomnia and ADHD are the Waldorf and Statler of neurological diagnoses; neither really had anything to contribute other than unneeded and unasked for commentaries, insulting in their intent, if one imagined them running one's mind into madness from their lofty Muppet Show private viewing booth.

For whatever reason, or maybe no reason, those feelings of emptiness, meaninglessness, and futility she'd felt outside on the porch had followed her inside and into bed. The channel clicking ritual had failed to erase the despair.   To have it remain in her head, follow her around and continue to torment her was not a tenable situation.

Now the dread followed her and carried those other feelings with it, and they all grew. They festered and mutated and fused together into something much worse. What would arise out of that morass?

Loneliness, perhaps. Inescapable, paralyzing, and overwhelming loneliness - that undeniable feeling that in her predetermined and meaningless life, there would never be anyone to at least make it somewhat worth continuing with life.

Loneliness starts out as a few words quietly spoken into the ear, or a tug on a loose thread of a sweater. The words repeat over and

over again and amplify inside the mind; the sweater unravels into a
mess of disheveled, ruined threads. Whichever metaphor one preferred,
loneliness always comes to a terrible zenith where it becomes painful
simply just to exist.

And when you feel that kind of loneliness, you're convinced
that *you will always be alone.*

Loneliness is a motherfucker.

Magdalena had laid in her bed for only just a few moments
before that loneliness was there, sitting in her head and in her body.

And while she lay there, flipping through Facebook feeds and
Instagram stories, that awful alchemy continued in her background
thoughts. Despite continuing at 3 o' clock in the morning, there was a
palliative.

She'd ask the social media world if being alone was to be her
fate - and in doing so, she hoped for either sympathy, reassurance, or
any response at all to let her know that someone was listening. That
someone gave a fuck. She posted:

Magdalena Christie
Is this all there is? Am I doomed to be alone forever? Why even
bother.

Magdalena's post elicited the responses she wanted to see and
read, even at the typically advanced time of night when she'd made it.
The comments read:

"I'm always here for you"

"Call me tomorrow"

"You good? DM me now!"

And so on. Some of the names she recognized, some she
didn't. The ones she didn't were all from groups she was a member of
and participated in - like ones that pertained to her interests - horror
movies, activism (anarchist action to black lives matter to climate
change), and ones that were for those that shared some of the same
disabilities she possessed.

Likes were likes though, and the more received made her feel
better.

She thought to herself: *I'll talk to a couple of people tomorrow. It'll be*
alright. And maybe she would, for a time.

But the anguish always came around again.

It was almost four.   Magdalena was finally tired enough to
drop off to sleep. She put away her phone and began to drift off. The
last thing she remembered before she did completely were the lighter
purples and violets that seeped through the blinds that hung over her
windows, those softer hues produced as the last darker shades of night
faded and then disappeared.

First, there was falling. Not like the kind you felt while experiencing a hypnic jerk. Those woke you up. Then it stopped. There was no sensation of landing to accompany the stopping.

Then, there was darkness. Deep and profound. Endless.

It felt like death at first. Was this what death was like? It could be, and it also could not be.

This must be a dream.

It couldn't be that either. Her dreams were never this dark. Neither were her nightmares.

This was not a dream.

This was not a nightmare.

This was new. This was different.

This was alien.

From a no-place, somewhere in the darkness:

A voice. A male voice. Afraid.

"H-h-hello?" he said. He kept saying it.

"Hello?"

"H-h-hello?"

She found she could walk. She followed the sound of the man's voice. She couldn't be sure of where exactly the calls came from. She could only move in a general direction.

The darkness was total, but it wasn't that there wasn't any light to be had – anywhere. Rather, there was nothing to see.

Absence. Of everything. A black reality.

And then, a light?

Tiny at first. Pinpoint, as if on a hidden horizon - like a Christmas star on a tree in a living room window, but the house was a thousand miles away. It was strange and haunting. It was purple, indigo, and blue, shifting between those colder shades at equal intervals.

The voice again. Whispering, low-pitched, but still far-off. How could you hear a whisper from far away?

Magdalena could tell the voice emanated from the light. It called her, not by name, but by her presence. Summoning her.

"Come. See."

Fear began to take her. She willed herself closer.

Before long, she could make out a vague shape. A moment more, and then - the shape of a man. She saw the source of the light –

but what that source was…it was impossible.

The then cobalt light shone from within the man's head. It was difficult, but she thought she could make out his features. He was her age - maybe a little bit older. Balding – but light brown hair on the sides. She could see there was some gray there too.

He saw her. No - he became aware of her presence. And his eyes fell onto her, looking at her. She drew near. A few feet? Yards?

He stood there, stark against the void that surrounded him. She peered closer, and when she did, she saw he was in pain. The light was burning him from inside.

He was in desperate pain. And yet - he smiled at her, despite the visible agony he was in.

This was not a dream. She had to help him. He was trapped, somehow.

She held out her hands to him, as if to beckon him closer.

"Your eyes," he said.

What was he talking about?

"My eyes?" she replied.

"Your eyes are like black stars. They are the gates. What burns me could be shared and enter thus."

Gates? What did he mean? To where?

"Gates to where? To what?" she asked.

He said the word - and when he did, something opened inside her mind.

The word was what could be.

The word was what they were.

The word was a people.

The word was beautiful. And then - she had forgotten it. But did she ever know it?

Then, something else. Someone else. They were being watched. Unseen eyes in the darkness. An observer who shouldn't be there with them. A person? A person that had stowed away with this man. This person was not there in the darkness with them, he could only just see them.

How was this possible?

Magdalena said: "someone's here."

The man paused, and then, as if to acknowledge this, turned his mind elsewhere. When he did, the pain inside him intensified, as the light inside him grew even brighter. His focus upon himself must have been what kept his suffering from consuming him. Magdalena felt the presence banished at once. Then, it was as if it was never there.

The man seemed to cry out in fresh agony, but there was no sound when he did.

The man reached out for her.

"They are coming."

"Who is coming?" she asked.

"*der Geistlos*. I don't even know what they are. I don't know why I know that. I just know that they're…" he replied.

"I don't know what that word…"

She reached out for his hands, but before she could take his hands the light tripled in intensity. It was burning its way out from within him.

"They're afraid of the light, but even this light will dim in this place."

"How can you know that they're afraid when you don't even know what they are?"

Just then, his skull appeared to expand, splitting, and fracturing his skull in jagged fault lines of bone and flesh instead of rock and earth. At the most severe points, the light poured out, brighter than the sun. How could he have held that light in his mind?

She saw blood seeping out of the cracks now, at first small rivulets, now becoming constant streams. He was dying in front of her.

She reached out her hands again and managed to find his.

"Don't think about that what you see - I can fix myself. But first, let me show you where," he said.

In that instant, she saw.

She was out of the dark. She was in a laboratory. There had been an explosion. There was fire everywhere. There were electronics and instruments - all haywire. The man in the darkness was there, lying on a gurney. His body, anyway. The eyes were rolled to the whites. He looked weak, debilitated, barely alive and yet…he was speaking.

There was another man, younger, hunched down close to him. The younger man listened as he spoke - but the words were unintelligible.

There was a third person in the bedlam - a woman. She was running around with a fire extinguisher, putting out the biggest of the fires. The extinguisher ran out.

Magdalena could hear fire alarms.

Then, the younger man stood up and turned his gaze to her.

But - he couldn't see her.

Magdalena knew that to be true. The man on the gurney, the same man who shone with blue light from his mind could see her, through just the whites. He smiled at her. And this warm, inviting face was the same as it was in the darkness where she'd first seen him. It was a smile as genuine and real as she'd ever seen. Yet still in unimaginable agony.

The man had called to her, and she had answered.

He was familiar. She almost recognized him, but not quite. But from the darkness where part of him stood trapped and from the fire in which the rest of him lay, he saw her and he looked...relieved. He spoke that word to her one more time.

Then, like a film that had been cut short, the dream, vision, astral projection - whatever it was - was over.

Magdalena opened her eyes.

She was back in her bed. The sun had pierced its way through the blinds in her room, and a single beam was projecting onto her cheek, warming it.

That couldn't have been real, she thought. Reaction to one of her medications? Not likely. Her meds hadn't changed in four months, the longest stretch for which she could make that claim in years.

Sleep habits? Those had always been fucked from the time she was a teenager. Her crippling insomnia had been going for almost thirty years strong.

There were no immediate explanations for what she had just experienced.

Magdalena sat up in bed and got to her feet. As she did, a searing bolt of pain rocketed through her skull, starting at the soft spot of cartilage at the bridge of her nose between her eyes. It ended at the base of her neck, where skull met spine. Aftershocks and echoes of the pain ping-ponged around inside her head.

It felt like what an orbitoclast might feel like when first jammed into a person's eye socket, then wiggled around inside to ensure every bit of frontal cortex had been sufficiently scrambled. She immediately dropped to one knee.

"What the fuck!?" Magdalena half-shouted, and half-cried. The pain lasted for no less than ten minutes. In that time, Magdalena could only manage to prop herself up on her knees, face pointed down at the ground, hands on her temples.

And then, as quickly as it had arrived, it was gone. Poof. Like the dream that wasn't a dream. The vision.

She slowly got to her feet and began thinking about getting herself to an emergency room. Or at the very least, a walk-in clinic.

But the pain was gone. *Fuck it*, thought Magdalena. She instead tied her hair up in an elastic, put on her glasses, and went downstairs to the kitchen.

Cereal. Maybe she just needed to eat something. There were Apple Jacks, still her favorite. She grabbed the box, the milk from the fridge and a spoon. She wolfed down three heaping spoons of the sugary red and green O's. She unlocked her cell phone.

It was...four fucking thirty in the afternoon? Jesus. She hadn't fallen asleep until four a.m., but that didn't explain sleeping away almost the entire day. She'd sleep twelve hours occasionally, but only if her and Amy had an edible or two the night before.

Magdalena was properly freaked out. Her mind reacted in predictable fashion, by splitting into 38 directions all at once. Grounding. She needed a grounding activity, like her therapist had taught her. Performing a routine task or tasks was one. Magdalena glanced at a nearby spot on the table. There was a bunch of mail on the table for her, so she decided to wade through that.

She went through a stack of bills - or least she thought she did. It was more like shuffling a deck of cards. Here was her cell phone bill. Here was an insurance statement. Here was a Target catalog. None of these were even remotely distracting enough to pull her mind away from the thought of that man, alone in the darkness.

It was no use. Magdalena couldn't shake the experience from the night before.

She finished her cereal, she kicked the tv on, and began to do her flipping again…..and then stopped on a channel. She'd actually stopped on a channel.

It was CNN.

And on the screen was the laboratory she'd just seen during the night. The fucking laboratory was on fucking CNN.

"...it is unclear how many injured and or dead there are on campus, as several explosions occurred in buildings throughout Gordon University. Ah, these explosions were not confined to one area of the property as well…the initial - and largest - explosion came from the laboratory of this man - "

The television then flashed a picture of the man from the darkness.

"Dr. David Keating, of Manchester, New Hampshire, a biochemistry researcher and professor… formerly of M.I.T. It's worth noting at this time that Dr. Keating was terminated from his position there for undisclosed reasons. We have not reached out to…"

Magdalena felt her knees buckle as the living room began to spin. She felt faint, overcome by what she'd just seen. A moment later, the remote control for the television remote control slipped out of her hands, as Magdalena could no longer feel her extremities. The remote's battery cover snapped off when it struck the ground and flew up at an arc towards the television screen. By watching the cover the entire duration of its truncated flight path as it first struck the monitor and then fell to the floor a few inches from her feet, Magdalena managed to snap out of the combination fainting spell/panic attack. She sat down on the couch.

Magdalena recognized him. She did know him…but not personally. They'd never met - but she knew that she had to go to him.

What was the word he had said to her?

Magdalena found that she could remember, quite easily in fact. She sighed and said the word.

"Ascendant."

Chapter Three

FROM: CWest@nephrilium.onion.tor
SENT: **Monday, November 28th, 2023 11:05 PM EST**
TO: SFischer@nephrilium.onion.tor
SUBJECT: David's Journal

Hey.
Hard to believe it's been almost two weeks since the explosion Sarah. Hard to believe it even happened, especially while I've been on this wild goose chase in Nowhere, Germany. The distance from Boston makes it all seem like it was a bad dream. You're still there, though, and you and I have to stick together - no matter what. I don't want to spend the rest of my life in jail, and neither do you.

But good news - I've succeeded. I still don't buy the reason why Moretti sent me instead of you in the first place, but let's face it. If it wasn't for him, we'd both be in prison by now. He'll get what he wants, and the two of us can move on with our lives.
I got a hold of Keating's journal. Turns out he'd sent it here, to Germany, the night before the last day in the lab. He knew something big was going to happen, but did he know how big? No way to tell.
Or maybe he did. I suppose it doesn't matter either way.

Also:
*I know how uncomfortable you are using the dark web - I'm uncomfortable using it too. But it's the only way we can guarantee nobody's intercepting our communications. It's for the best. Moretti won't know about these communications — so just remember that in case he shows up on your doorstep before I get back. Just ensure you're on the TOR browser and use the email application & url I sent you and **don't** use it for anything else. Period.*
Right. The journal. I'm sending you the important entries now, ahead of time, so there's nothing in there that might catch you off guard. I have the physical copy sitting right next to me in my carry-all. It took me a couple of days to convince David's cousins Heinrich and Karl to turn the thing over to me. They weren't as...peculiar as David, but they were suspicious of my intentions. Thought I was a fucking CIA agent or something — so maybe that explains David's constant paranoia. Or maybe it was just his laundry list of issues. And these guys — Heinrich and Karl? The mere mention of David's name seemed to just piss them both right the fuck off.
Anyways.

Read all these entries before I get there. I'll be boarding any second now, which puts me back home tomorrow afternoon. Can't wait to get the fuck out of here. Between the journal and those videotapes, we should be able to avoid having our lives destroyed. Which is probably more than we deserve.

I see that I was wrong now, Sarah, and I'm sorry I didn't take your side and at least try to put a stop to it at the end. I guess that once we started making those breakthroughs - I lost sight of the important things for getting our name in lights. So I'm doing everything I can to get us out of this.

There are four journal entries attached that I scanned direct from his texts. They explain the most about where his idea for all of this got started, his thoughts behind what was going on, etc. There's shit in here he didn't even tell us, Sarah. I don't think Keating really trusted anyone, including us. You'll see. Better if you read it, coming from him, rather than me just telling you. The man was in serious, serious pain.

There's a contact in it too - a colleague of his at the University of Texas, although I don't recall offhand what her name was. Moretti, or whoever it is that he works for, will have enough to recreate the experiment. Worst case, they track her down maybe, and get whatever else they need from her. Why anyone would try to do that is beyond me. Some frontiers were never meant to be explored — and the three of us certainly didn't hesitate to break that rule.

I didn't find anything relevant on his secondary laptop - you know the one we saw floating around his office a few months ago. It's only been used a couple of times, and from its browser history, it was only just to logon to his Facebook account - of all things. Can you believe that? Dr. David Keating, PhD, formerly one of the world's leading molecular biologists - and not only did he have a FB profile, but he kept it on a separate computer like it was porn or something.

I gotta warn you about these scans though — there's a LOT of long-winded philosophizing - complete with a lot of big words strung together to say absolutely nothing. But that was the man in a nutshell, wasn't it? Whatever it was that made him so special and so brilliant was also what made knowing the man so tragic. You, me, hell everyone just accepted it as his normal. That whole thing about brilliance and madness being connected...but who knew the guy who could recite the entire primary amino acid sequence of Human Cytochrome C from memory had a secret romantic and contemplative side...I think he may have been the loneliest man on the planet Sarah.

Agent Moretti told me before I left that he'd know if I was lying or hiding something. We'll see about that. He said he didn't have any reason to contact you, if you stayed put and did what you were told. But make no mistake - you're probably being watched every second of the day. As far as I am concerned, he hasn't earned our full trust. Not even close.

Makes me wonder just how connected Moretti really is. And to whom, or what.

Lastly:
Remember how stunned we were when Magdalena just showed up, out of nowhere, four days after all hell broke loose like she'd walked out of a dream? "Her eyes are like black stars, they are the gates" was what he said to me in the lab. And then he described her to me. The last word was he spoke was her name. I'm praying that nobody knows a thing about her. And that's she stayed right where we stashed her.

Jesus.
This all can't be real. But it is.

Sitting in her living room thousands of miles away, Sarah Fischer finished reading Caleb's email mere minutes after he'd sent it. She'd almost instantly become aware of its presence in her inbox because she had been impatiently watching the display on her laptop for hours, ready to pounce the instant it arrived. When she finished with Caleb's stupid little *'Mission: Impossible'* I'm-doing-this-for-us routine in the body of the message, she didn't hesitate. Sarah forwarded it to the email she'd been instructed to by the man on her phone. Moments after it left her outbox indicating that message had been passed on, her phone rang.

She answered it on the second ring.

"Hello?"

"Well done, Ms. Fischer. CRUCIBLE thanks you for your assistance," said the man on the other end of the line. The non-human sound of his voice would have frightened a serial killer.

It was far too low in pitch. So low that it was barely audible. Normal human beings didn't – couldn't sound like that.

"Am I done now?" she asked.

"No." The line disconnected.

"*Goddamnit,*" she whispered under her breath. Her thoughts turned directly to the bottle of Jack Daniels in the cupboard. The liquid within screamed to her in that moment.

She shook it off. If only for now.

She instead opened the four attachments to Caleb's email and began to read Keating's journal entries.

She had to know what she had just turned over… without even so much as blinking.

Chapter Five

Journal entries of Dr. David Keating, Ph.D.

January 14th, 2022

I think that I have noticed, or rather, become keenly aware of a default setting in my approach to writing in my personal journals.

I feel that I must reach back, all the way into the furthest corners and shadows in my mind and pull those thoughts and notions out from their depths so that I can set a kind of external order to them. They appear then, to me, as monoliths and obelisks of colors outside and beyond the visible spectrum.

I reach all the way into my soul to pull those emotions out to sit uncomfortably on a wooden bench in an empty room.

And I reach into my heart… where you can watch the same singularity of sadness and sorrow fold in on itself to a single point, supernova, expand to infinity, and then begin to collapse again and again.

Those are my best metaphors for what I am, if I am to be split into those three widely accepted conceptualizations of the metaphysical makeup of a person. Nothing amuses me more than to consider the possibility that our idea of a mind, a soul, and a spirit may not even be tangentially accurate as to what constitutes the individual , but for our conversation it is convenient to use these old philosophical currencies.

These ideas stir me to ponder what I consider to be the most basic and elemental of human emotions - that of loneliness – as I look over to the right side of my desk and see the now half empty bottle of pills next to my desk phone and stapler.

I may have as little as a half-hour to finish this journal entry, so I must be brief.

This will not be some adolescent diatribe on how sad and unloved I feel as though I am. It is my firm conviction that we are all patently alone simply because of 'the rules of the game' as it were. This level of existence has been constructed on a foundation of single-ness, wherein an array of senses is hardwired to a central 'perceiver'. You are the only one who sees and perceives the world the way that you do, your reality has a population of one and that is the way it will always be until the moment that reality ceases to exist – or rather, ceases to exist in the way that it has for however how long you've lived until that death/transition occurs. Before I go any further on any subject of weight or significance, I want to absolutely share with you this paralyzing fear that overtakes me for at least a few seconds every single day:

I am terrified of dying alone.

I will face this fear now as I write.

I can feel the drug taking effect.

Anyone who has ever said that they weren't afraid of dying is or was a bald-faced liar. Everyone is afraid. And because of our hardwired, biological single-ness, all of us will each die alone, and our deaths will be only ours to know. It is the most terrible aspect of human existence.

I have spent countless days and nights, both at home and in my laboratory experimenting with consciousness with the hopes of uncovering something… anything heretofore unknown about its true nature. In doing so, I became even more detached from reality than I am simply by existing.

Despite this separation from the course of events and the so-called physical world, I could only draw two conclusions:

I could never fully escape my recurring thoughts of my own death.

There were still limits to what could be unlocked and expanded upon, insofar the nature of the relationship between consciousness and reality. Such is the irony and the tragedy of "being", one supposes.

Can barely type. Must finish.

I thought of the altered biochemistry and neurology of the addict – my father and older brother were such poor, cursed souls afflicted with compulsions to one substance or another. They never seemed to live in the same world as anyone else, even next to the individuals that shared an identical addictive condition – alcohol, heroin, etc.

It occurred to me that every person is an addict. We *are* all addicts but in a different kind of sense, to "being" - the continued stream of input through our senses that is focused by an internal lens, interpreted by a neurobiological machine that associates meaning, and then is added to pre-existing software. We are that ever evolving matrix and machine and the product thereof. So, we simply must always be solitary as a condition of being.

Loneliness is hardwired into us as a prerequisite for even existing at all. The fear of death arises from the certainty that we will no longer receive our 'fix'.

I don't think that I can contin----

March 3rd, 2022.

And so I continue.

I was told that a janitor, performing his nightly cleanings of the Science Building here at the university, discovered my unconscious body a few hours after I'd fallen into a state of unresponsiveness.

Rushed to a nearby hospital.

Kept in a medically induced coma for a little under two weeks. The drug was tapered off, and a team of physicians and nurses waited to see if I would return to this appalling world.

And so I continue.

I have spent the past week in the private laboratory afforded to me by my benefactors at Gordon. The arrangement was that I would run their Molecular Biology program, and they in turn would leave me alone to my work. The suicide attempt has altered the latter part of that arrangement, such that I'm monitored now by the University board of trustees. It is frustrating, but it's to be expected.

No one outside of the University and myself have the knowledge of the attempt, thankfully.

After reading my last journal entry, back in January, I've been galvanized to continue my investigation into a molecule I have named 'operamine', a neurotransmitter I had previously discovered and isolated from the brain of the common honeybee. This remarkable compound forms the basis of most, if not all signaling cascades throughout the honeybee nervous system. It is, for lack of a better term, a master molecule for that particular species.

The existence of this neurotransmitter had only been theorized to exist, even by top zoologists and entomologists…until my work. No researcher or scientist had approached the question from biochemical analytic methodologies, a ponderance best left for those that would question the grand motives of the scientific community writ large.

Conspiracy theorists, religious zealots, and the average American citizen, essentially.

Oversight notwithstanding, it is my contention that operamine is the key to unlocking the unlimited potential of the honeybee's defining characteristic - the trait which has served as their distinct evolutionary advantage over many other species of insects. It has allowed them to flourish, mankind's detrimental impact aside. Were it to be that, somehow, *homo sapiens* were to make use of this trait or at least incorporate a fraction of its potential, it could unlock aspects of consciousness and alter our concept of 'being'.

Consider a world where no one was ever truly alone.

Trauma to one could be trauma to all.

It would follow then, that mental illness in all its forms could become a thing of the past.

I kept my work with operamine to myself, because of these very reasons. The compound could be used for great good, but also could be used for immoral, even evil purposes. One shudders to think of any government getting their claws into this work. It does not belong to one group of people. It belongs to humanity. I will ensure it stays that way.

To that end, the exact nature and purpose of my studies were known only to me and my assistants, Caleb West and Sarah Fischer. Both were exemplary graduate students at M.I.T. in my tenure there, and both have earned my trust and admiration. They are the closest to being actual friends that I ever have been able to say about anyone in my life.

They were the only bright spot in my time at that institution.

Professor Emeritus, indeed. M.I.T., that pillar of scientific study and knowledge throughout the academic world, with its contributions to society and laundry list of scholars, geniuses, and luminaries – a sham! It was and still is limited in the kinds of research it chooses to associate its pristine reputation. After all, it must maintain its status as a beacon of respectability above all else. When it became known that I'd devoted my studies and their resources towards reversing the aberrant neurobiology of PTSD and cPTSD sufferers they grew wary. "Pathologies best left to psychology and sociology," was what I was told. When I began my first trials, I was summarily dismissed. Their version of events incorporated a physical altercation, exaggerated to ensure my disgrace was total and complete. I was forced to abandon the project as well.

Gordon, however, was not quite so limited and/or dogmatic in its approach or oversight. At least until now, that is.

Ostensibly, Gordon is under the notion that the crux of my research to be into imaginary correlations between levels of that molecule in honeybee brains and failure/decay of nascent honeybee hives. The decline in honeybee populations throughout the world is of concern in many circles for the potential impact to global environments. Thus, it became easy to delve into the discovery and application of operamine with little or no interference. The molecule itself is quite remarkable.

In layman's terms, operamine is what those of a lesser understanding of biochemistry would consider as a 'thinking' molecule - meaning that it carries out tasks within the sympathetic and parasympathetic nervous systems independently of direction by the organism's cerebral cortex or endocrine systems.
Operamine functions as a kind of self-regulating, secondary nervous system, wholly separate from the rest of the organisms' functions.

Yet to date, I have not been able to ascertain what, or how it responds to the external environment of the honeybee. It is a complete mystery. One I intend to solve.

It is cultivated and purified through standard and widely accepted cell culture, fermentation, and chromatographic methods, the details of which can be found in the **" Method for Operamine Purification"** appendix of this journal, pages **47 - 86**. These methodologies are no different in practice than what is used by both public and private pharmaceutical companies in their production facilities, save for the usage of our proprietary Tertiary chromatographic resins, designed by Caleb West only three years ago. Quite remarkable, that boy. The patent on his design for the resin would set him up for life, and yet he chooses to keep knowledge of its existence to our team, so that we may continue our pursuits without distraction.

It will take anywhere from 4 - 6 months to complete a single human trial. I will submit myself as the first to undergo this treatment. The possible detrimental side effects can be no worse than what I have endured these past two months.

I fear death, but I fear life more.

There are other considerations to make; certain...physical modifications must be made to my own brain to allow for **it** to be able to take its full effect. Sarah Fischer will handle these anatomical modifications. Her experience with surgical techniques, although incomplete, will suffice. Six weeks of recovery is required, after which the administration of operamine will commence. This will ensure there is no "shock" as it were, and should minimize any type of immune system response.

I am already ecstatic to be both a pilgrim and explorer on this new frontier. This new territory shall be where biology, chemistry, psychology, and sociology will finally intersect in a meaningful, significant, paradigm-shifting way.

And if there is any mercy to be had for me in this world, I will be made whole again.

Sarah rubbed her eyes. She was exhausted but knew that she'd never be able to sleep.

Again, the whiskey called to her.

Again, she did not answer.

She had asked herself so many times over the course of the past year why she kept the bottle in the first place. It was temptation. It begged her failure to maintain her sobriety. Each time she'd done this, she knew the answer but could never bring herself to think it.

She did so at that moment.

"Because you're not actually sober, Sarah," she said aloud.

Keating had attempted suicide in January, something that neither she nor Caleb had any knowledge of happening. Same for the coma, and the recovery thereafter. They were told by university staff he'd left to attend to a dying relative of his. Sarah had known it was utter bullshit, but never investigated the matter further. She really didn't care either way.

It made perfect sense, however. Keating's willingness to have his brain sliced up, injecting himself with a drug that could have killed him, all of it. The man was in the throes of utter desperation. Sarah knew the feeling well.

The whiskey called to her again. Not long now before her will would break.

She tied her shoulder length dirty blonde hair up into a ponytail, sighed, and continued to read Keating's journal.

"Where is Magdalena in all of this, Keating," she asked her laptop.

Chapter Seven

March 17th, 2022

Continuing on my thoughts from Jan 14 entry.

Are we as individuals, truly individuals? Or are we amalgamations of things hitherto undreamed of? We assume that each one of us, in being a human, is a singular person or entity. Is it possible that this is an erroneous assumption? Is our perception as a human being a kind of gestalt illusion, generated by colliding sensory inputs and transient thought patterns? These are the questions I've asked myself so many times, on so many lonely nights.

There are the things that define us that the world never knows - the internal, those dark secrets that we don't share. Carl Jung referred to this side of the individual as 'the shadow'. His theories are likely the closest to its true nature.

Would this 'shadow' self then be an amalgamation of our traumas, our faults, and defects?

I've sought others out that might be like me, people that suffer with the same afflictions and mental illnesses. To light the darkness within me, as it were. In that endeavor, only one person has stood out to me, but I share nothing in common with her save for our accumulated diagnoses. Still, I've looked forward to our interactions. The way we communicate with each other, the 'knowing' of what it feels like to be constituted such as we are...I feel safe, connected when we talk. I think that we shall never meet in person, however.

It is unfortunate that this is so. For those fleeting moments, I did not feel so alone.

I digress. The idea that who we are is as a sum of parts, a gestalt is accepted as truth. But can those parts be broken down into various independently operating components? Is that what operamine could represent? An actual, tangible physical component, and not another nebulous and difficult to define aspect of the greater whole?

I had to know more about the honeybee itself, for context. I sought out my colleague, Dr. Mary Ashcroft, whose work in zoology and proteomics dealt primarily with the honeybee. Ashcroft devoted her considerable acumen towards broader, fuller studies of the creature than I, so her insight would prove invaluable. I phoned her yesterday morning.

"Well, hello there, bee girl," I began.

"That's bee *woman* to you, mister," she answered.

I always feel like I offend somebody before I can even say a single thing. I heard an audible sigh from the other end of the line from her.

"Typical David Keating," she answered. "Contacting me out of nowhere, sounding like his laboratory had exploded and was on fire, and then sounding positively jovial and poking fun when I actually get to speak to him. I'll never understand you, David, nor do I think anyone ever will. To what end do I owe this pleasure?"

"I felt it was important to state on the record that mental illnesses were not causalities of unusually high intelligence, or in any way enhanced them."

"Hunh?" she replied.

"A joke, Mary."

"It was?"

"Yes. I know the rumors fly in our circles, and I thought that by making…"

"There's nothing wrong with you, David. I know you think that, but its' not the case. Please tell me you've been seeing a therapist."

"I have not."

Mary sighed, and then changed the subject quickly. "Well, what then, can I help you with today?"

"Tell me all you can about the hive behavior of the honeybee. Leave no stone unturned, madam, for it bears great significance to my current research."

"What are…you. Uh, okay. I'm not going to even ask you what it is that you're doing. I feel like if I know, I'd be obligated to inform some manner of authorities."

There was much that I didn't know about the organism - my focus had always been on atoms and molecules, interactions at unseen scales. Mary's talents lay on far more macro scales - with whole organisms. This probably explained my unrelenting notions of trying to break down the human consciousness into subunits. I just could never understand the individual.

She began.

"Those of us that specialize in the honeybee don't really regard then as individual organisms – you gain a better understanding of them at the hive level. As the hive goes, so do the members of that hive.

When the hive dies, all of the honeybees follow suit."

"So the hive of the honeybee can be thought of as a singular organism. Within that organism, there are well defined roles, worker, drone, queen, and so on. Each bee serves a purpose in maintaining the survival and health of the hive, or larger organism.

Each 'class' of bee performs an essential function, such that one can make the obvious connection to the various systems that sustain other species, respiratory, digestive, but on an external, macro scale. Some of this is coordinated by pheromones, but other facets remain unexplained. I'm convinced there's a means of communication we have yet to elucidate. What connects them so? Even I don't have the answer for that. Did you know that the brain of a honeybee can perform calculations faster than the world's most powerful supercomputers? What could possibly have augmented their brains in such a manner you would ask."

I already knew the answer.

"Thank you, Mary. Have a pleasant day."

"But Dav-"

I hung up before she could continue.

I know what you're probably thinking so far Sarah - because I thought the same things. One, his journal is just as all over the place as the man was. It was always so difficult to follow him and his train of thought in real life; for that first year we thought it was just his genius, but there was way more to it than that. Moretti told me straight up that he'd been diagnosed with severe ADHD - as well as a few other things, but he didn't specify what those were. But, in retrospect, it doesn't really come as any kind of surprise. ADHD isn't enough to explain it all, not by a long shot. The suicide attempt did shock me though. There's always baggage that seems to come with genius I suppose. David was a very sick man, Sarah.

We're the closest thing the guy has to actual friends, Sarah, and look at all the things that he kept from us. This experiment wasn't motivated by the gain of knowledge for knowledge' sake, or to improve the lot of mankind - he was trying to save himself. Maybe others that are like him.

What does this mean for us? I think this proves we save as much of his work as we can. Maybe we can save him. Doubtful, but possible.

Magdalena is the key, but why her remains to be seen.   We still need all the information we can muster. There's one more journal entry — the synthesis he mentioned in the second entry. You'll need to read it.

Appendix 1:   " Method for Operamine Purification"

The novel enzyme I have given the name 'operamine' can be produced at small scale, ten-liter bioreactor capacity utilizing Bovine Serum as a growth medium, with fresh media added 2x per day. The cell culture is then….

Sarah skipped all the biochemistry nonsense that David and Caleb loved to bore the shit out of people with. She lasted a full paragraph on this go-around, but even what was ostensibly the highly specific metholodgy for producing what everyone seemed to be after wasn't enough to keep Sarah interested.

And as if they had known the moment her attention span vanished, Sarah's phone rang. What more could CRUCIBLE possibly want? She was giving them the store, and actually had it to give now.

"Hello?"

The man with the deep, monotone voice spoke.

"Who is Magdalena, and where is she now?"

Sarah cleared her throat after digging it out of her feet. They were so many steps ahead of them, seemingly all of the time without fail or falter. She began speaking.

"She's not from around here. She came from Florida…started coming up the day of the explosion. But she's here now, though. I mean – not *here*, here – in Boston."

"Continue."

Sarah went on babbling for another ten minutes. Most of it was incoherent nonsense, and to make matters worse, Sarah knew it was incoherent nonsense she was spewing. At no time could she stop herself from sounding like an idiot.

Fear of a fate worse than imprisonment or death will do that a person.

When she had finished, the man on the other end had only one word to say before disconnecting.

"Fascinating."

Magdalena continued watching the news for about another hour, scouring the national news networks for any more details about the explosion. She didn't get much more than what she had gleaned in those two minutes when she first stumbled upon the story, but what she did learn would be useful.

David had two assistants working with him in the lab, but she already knew that part. She'd seen them both.

The fact that they had survived, completely unharmed, she did not know. Magdalena decided that when she did get to Massachusetts, she'd seek them out first. She supposed they were what detectives would call a 'lead'.

But, despite the seemingly miraculous fate of David's underlings, there were fatalities – at least three, as reported by MSNBC. Dozens of injuries.

"What were you and your cronies fucking doing, David?" Magdalena asked the television screen. She changed the channel, this time to FOX News.

Magdalena sat and watched as FOX's afternoon anchor, a blonde-haired, blue-eyed woman straight out of *Ubermensch* casting, started spinning the event as a false flag operation staged by the radical left wing deep state. And so it answered her question by proposing there that there hadn't been any explosion at all, David and team had likely only been playing with their beakers and test tubes that day.

"Oh, fuck this," she said as stood up from the couch. Magdalena pulled her phone out of her back pocket when she reached her feet and pulled up her social media. She lost herself in the application, her resolve to 'fuck this' vanishing with the swipe of a finger. She sat back down in the same spot on the couch.

For another hour, she read through all of her interactions with David on that platform, from DM's to their shared comments on posts in the "ADHDistic Community" group of which they were both members.

"Why did you pick me, David?" The television would not have any answer for that question, however.

The shadows grew long in the living room while she sat, eventually reaching a critical mass of darkness that snapped her out of the digital trance that locked Magdalena in place.

"Shit," she said aloud and then finally followed through on her 'fuck this' imprimatur from an hour earlier.

Magdalena then spent the better part of the evening rounding up belongings for the trip north, to Boston. Distracted and mostly out of sorts, the task took far longer for Magdalena than it would a person who suffered no neurodivergent conditions or maladies. She placed what she thought she'd need on the part of her bed that stayed made throughout the previous night's vision quest.

Now what, she thought.

She thought of her favorite, worn red backpack as a viable form of luggage. What she had gathered didn't amount to very much at all: just a few changes of clothes, socks and underwear, a phone charger, toiletries, and a diary. Before she stuffed the journal in, she decided to make a quick initial entry for the day. It simply read:

November 15th, 2022. Today, my life changed. I don't know if it'll be for the best, or if it will cause more problems than I already have.
And I don't care if it does make my life worse,
Anything is better than here, waiting to grow old and die.

She was going to write more, obviously, but she'd do that later. She had started packing around seven. She'd made the journal entry at eight. The entire process of packing just the few items had taken her fucking four hours.

This realization left her full of doubt. What the hell did she think she was doing?

And then, as if to pile on, came another realization.

She hadn't even thought to check her bank account. Travel costs money - and it would cost even more due to the spur of the moment aspect of her newly planned journey northward. Her reality was that her finances only got into four-digit territory for a few hours every other Friday - just after midnight when her direct deposit hit her bank account. A few hours later, on those same Fridays, Magdalena would wake up and spend her first moments paying overdue bills in order of urgency and/or amounts until all that was left was her survival money for the next thirteen days. This meager sum ended up in the 150-to-200-dollar range - on a good pay cycle - for the thirteen days that would follow.

Today was Tuesday. She wasn't due to be paid for another four days. Magdalena already knew that petty cash was going to prove anemic at best.

She opened her banking app on her phone, and she found that she had three hundred bucks - somehow. There was hope, then!

With newfound optimism and the anxiety that came whether events looked up or down (it never mattered) she looked up one-way flights to Boston for the slim prospect that maybe, just maybe she'd be able to get a seat on one of those economy, super cheap, take-your-life-in-your-own-hands airlines. *Spirit*, or some other such company that sends rubber-band powered aircraft into the sky with actual humans upon them.

Even among those airlines-with-an-asterisk, there was nothing that left Tampa Airport cheaper than two hundred eighty dollars that night, and it didn't get any better for the rest of the week.

Not that she could wait for something cheaper anyway.

And that two-eighty was for a one-way ticket only. There was no way she'd be able to afford a round-trip.
Magdalena looked up at the ceiling in frustration, realizing that traveling by air at the last second was not a thing people living paycheck-to-paycheck could do. At least not without some kind of help. Unfortunately, people living paycheck to paycheck were the only economic class of people she knew or associated with in her life. Magdalena's parents weren't in the picture, and neither was any other family other than her sister Amy. Asking someone to help her was out of the picture.

Driving was also not an option, either. There was only one car for the household she lived in, that her and Amy shared. Their car was for Amy and Magdalena to get to and from and their jobs first and foremost, so just popping off with their shitbox for who knew how long was not feasible. Magdalena had no idea when she was going to come back, and so there was no way she could take the car.
Discouraged, she looked over at her backpack. Maybe she should spend the next three hours unpacking instead?

No. She had to go. There were other ways to get to Massachusetts. Not as convenient, in fact, downright risky, but it had to be done.

She was going to have to take a bus.

Hey, maybe that adds an air of adventure to it! she thought.

"Bullshit, Mags. It's a Greyhound bus," she said to her empty living room.

She looked back to her phone. After a quick search, then an entry of her atm card number, expiration date, and security code, she secured roundtrip seats to Boston on a few of Greyhound's silver boxes of rolling lumbar displacement and forced insomnia…all for the low cost of 79 dollars. She could go anytime she liked. Buses left on the hour.

Well then, Mags. No time like the present. She grabbed her things and made for the living room to wait for Amy to get home from her shift at Friday's. Magdalena took one last look back at her room, and the bed she'd slept in for the past twelve years. It looked as welcoming and as cozy as it ever had, maybe even more with the knowledge that she'd be traveling so far away from it.

And that was the problem, then, wasn't it?

Her sister and roommate Amy got home from work around nine.

Magdalena wasted little time to tell her that she was going away for a few days. and needed a ride to the Greyhound station twenty miles away.

Surprisingly, Amy didn't even ask where she was going. Amy didn't even ask her about what she was going to do about work for those days she was going to be away.

Amy just smiled at her, and replied with:

'Okay, gimme a second, I need a shower."

Magdalena continued to sit in the living room, waiting and listening to her Spotify, trying to lose herself in her music. Before she could even get to a third song, she felt Amy give her a tap on the shoulder. Amy had delivered it in passing right past where Magdalena sat, without even so much as a look back as Amy exited the house. Magdalena pulled off her headphones. She heard Amy start up their Tercel, then crank up Tame Impala to a volume loud enough for her to hear it from inside.

Amy always did that instead of beeping the horn to let her know she was ready to drive wherever it was that they needed to go.

"Bitch is turning that shit down when I get in the car," she said. "Tame Impala fucking sucks."

Magdalena smiled and grabbed her backpack to jump out the door.

She thought to herself as she stopped dead in her tracks after taking just two steps, her mind already venturing off from the here and now yet again:

Even if I can get there, what the hell am I expecting? How do I even find those other two that were there?

And then she thought:

What if this is some kind of weird coincidence, and not a calling to go save this guy?

Then came more and more intrusive thoughts, each one more fatalistic than the one before.

Before she knew it, Amy was standing by the open front door. Magdalena had no idea how long she'd been standing there lost in her own head.

"You haven't taken your meds today, have you? I've been out there waiting ten minutes."

"Uh, no." Ten minutes?

"I bet you didn't even pack them, did you?"

"Ah, I got distracted."

Amy sighed. She'd grown her hair out long just to contrast to Magdalena's dyed blue mohawk, and in her mild impatience with her sister began tying it up into a ponytail.

"I'm not going to stop you from going on this trip – wherever it is Mags. Frankly, I've stopped trying to keep you from doing *anything*, but I'm just gonna say two things. One, you know I can always tell when you haven't been taking your meds. I took one look at you when I got in and you look as if you've been all over the place all friggin' day."

If you only knew, big sis, thought Magdalena.

"Before we go anywhere, you take your meds, and then I make sure you've packed them."

Magdalena hadn't forgotten about her medications, so much as she had been preoccupied with much larger concerns for the duration of the day. She did think of her scripts at least 3 or 4 times but was distracted seconds later each time. So, she never took them and hadn't packed them.

But Magdalena wasn't about to tell her sister why she hadn't taken them - the not-dream that was beamed into her head straight from purgatory, the subsequent minor cerebral hemorrhage, and then seeing the whole thing play out on cable news before she could even settle into her day. She was afraid that Amy would try to stop her from going if she did.

"Yeah, you're right. Be right back." She walked into the bathroom and unslung her backpack. She sighed, loud enough so that Amy heard her.

Amy yelled from the living room.

"Don't get all down on yourself again, Mags. It's just medication, you didn't forget to keep living!"

Whatever the hell that was supposed to mean. That was Amy's go-to phrase, no matter what minor transgression on Magdalena's treatment had occurred.

Forgot to pick her up at work on time?

You didn't forget to keep living.

Forgot to eat something for the entire day?

You didn't forget to keep living.

Didn't drink any water?

And so on.

As if 'forget to keep living' was something a person could do, even with Magdalena's laundry list of conditions.

"Speaking of which," Magdalena said as she opened the medicine cabinet. She was met with the usual complement of small orange, plastic containers with screw-on white tops lined up in military formation style on the shelves.

To the left was escalitopram, 20 mg, the maximum dose a person can take in a day. The rest of the world knew this drug as Lexapro, not the Harry Potter incantation printed on the bottle. This was her major depressive disorder medication.

Next to that were amphetamine salts or good ol' Adderall. Also 20 mg, for ADHD.

Next to that was Hydroxyzine, 50 mg. This was a repurposed drug, a member of the same family as Dramamine and Benadryl, recently discovered to have anti-anxiety effects. It also assisted with PTSD symptoms as well. She took one of each in her hand, threw them in her mouth like they were peanuts, and then finally gulped all three with a glass of water. She took the pill bottles and moved them into the front pouch of her backpack.

She walked back into the living room, where Amy was sitting in the recliner looking at her phone.

Magdalena could tell at-a-glance that her sister was scrolling through social media. Amy looked up at her.

"I'm sorry I just jumped in the car ahead of you, Mags. Should have waited," Amy said.

"I should be able to manage myself without taking them for a few hours, Amy. I don't need a fucking escort." Magdalena walked over to stand in front of Amy and kicked her sneaker.

Amy stood up and dropped her phone into her pocket.

"Keep telling you that you shouldn't set an expectation for yourself that you're always going to remember."

"I don't have dementia, Amy."

"I know. That's not what I meant."

The two of them walked back out to the car, which was still running and still blasting Tame Impala.

"Tame Impala sucks, Amy."

"I know. That's why I picked it,"

The two of them got in, Magdalena immediately turning the radio off. Being in that small an enclosed space with music that loud was instant sensory overload.

They drove in silence for a few minutes, which neither could handle for any longer than that. Amy pulled the trigger first.

"When was the last time you forgot your meds anyway? It's been a pretty long time."

"Thirty-nine days," said Magdalena.

Amy smiled at this response. Of course she knew that number. But it was those odd, superhuman-like feats of recall and memory she could never tell came from the ADHD, or Type I ASD she also had to contend with.

Amy remembered that one time, when they were in history class together, their teacher started quizzing the students on dates and names associated with the American Civil War. The teacher, Mr. Marks, kept reeling them off and nobody had an answer for any of the questions, except, of course, for Magdalena. She just kept raising her hand, not looking up from her book, as she breathed July 1, 1863 for the Battle of Gettysburg, April 9, 1865 for the Treaty of Appomattox, and so on like all that information was written on the page of the book she was looking at.

Chad Sims, perpetual douchebag and varsity sportsball player leaned into her ear from his seat behind her and said the word "freak", which everyone in the class heard. Amy saw her sisters' face turn beet red with embarrassment, and for that, Amy later broke into Chad's locker and dumped a repurposed 20 oz. Coke bottle of soiled toilet water all over his shit. For all of the other crap that Mags had to contend with, mockery at the hands of others was not something she ever tolerated or allowed. Chad learned his lesson, and that was that.

It was recalling shit like the last time she'd forgotten her medication and the date Grant accepted the south's bullshit surrender seemingly from the same space in her mind and straight off the top of her head that made Amy regard her sister not as somehow disabled, but as a unique-minded individual that society needed to keep up with. Not the other way around.

"No shit?" Amy knew she wasn't lying, but feigned disbelief was a good way to instill a sense of accomplishment when there wasn't one present.

"Ya. No shit." Amy's plan did not work.

"Well, it must have been something pretty crazy to cause you to miss them. Did something happen?"

Magdalena chuckled. "Yeah, something happened."

"What?" asked Amy.

"You wouldn't believe me if I told you."

"Try me."

"The long version or the short, Amy."

"Long. We've got another 25 minutes until we get there. Plus, I'm sure whatever it was is the reason why you're about to get on a fucking bus to wherever. You're not going to meet some guy, are you?"

"Amy, I already told you I'm done with guys for a long time. But it is meeting a guy, though. He's a college professor, or a scientist, or both."

"Okay, so what happened?"

They were in the car and on their way. Magdalena decided that it was safe to give her the rundown.

Amy sat quietly and listened to the first half of her sister's outlandish story without comment or expression. Magdalena paused at having Apple Jacks in the kitchen and waited for an initial reaction.

"Go on," was all Amy said. Emotionless.

And then it was on to the news story on television, the explosion, and then finding out that what she'd seen in her vision had really happened, albeit a thousand miles away. Amy continued her poker-faced attention, and when Magdalena finished everything that she had to say, a solid five minutes of silence in its wake.

Amy then asked:

"What in the actual fuck are you even going to do when you get up there Mags? Track down his home address from the college and knock on his door? Go up to this guy and say 'hey, you rang? How can I help you?'"

"I don't think it's going to be that simple, Amy. Pretty sure he's in some kind of coma…" Magdalena trailed off at the end, partly because she was unsure of that last statement, partly because it might have alarmed Amy to the point where she'd turn the car right around and go back home. Magdalena managed to lower her voice enough such that the last word, coma, was almost inaudible.

"He's in a what?"

"Nothing, Amy. Jesus. Look, I don't know what I'm going to do. I mean, I do. I know the names of his two assistants, the ones I saw in the lab with him. I plan on finding them when I get there."

"Great plan. They're probably in fucking jail, Mags."

"Amy, the guy's in trouble, like, *real* trouble, and he needs my help because of whatever the hell it was they did in that lab. He reached out to me."

"Yeah, but why do you care? Never met this person, never been to New England, and you don't even know what to expect when you get there. This is already totally fucked, Mags."

"He's like me, Amy. Up here," Magdalena pointed to her head. "I can't put my finger on it, but when I was in that dream with him, I've never felt that connected to someone ever in my life."

"Was he at least…"

"He was okay, Amy. But not my type though. Too bald. Stupid question, by the way. I'm not doing this so I can get laid, jerk."

"What am I telling everyone at work, Mags?"

"I'll leave Cam a message. Don't worry about it."

"Well what are you gonna say, in case someone calls you and asks?"

"Just say I'm in the hospital and then none of your business."

"Fine."

At last, they pulled up in front of the Greyhound station. From the outside, it looked like any of the other businesses around it, except for the fact that it looked as if it hadn't seen any kind of building maintenance in decades.

.Magdalena reached into the backseat and grabbed her stuff.

"Okay, I'm off." She opened the passenger side door. As she did, she felt Amy's hand slip around her left bicep.

"Mags?"

Magdalena stopped and turned to her sister.

"Yeah?"

"Why are you really doing this? Yeah, go save the mad scientist. But really, why?"

Magdalena turned her head and looked down at her feet.

"Because I'm sick of walking out to our porch twenty fuckin times a night to mark the hours while the rest of my life disappears. I go out there, and watch cars drive by, waiting for something to happen, like it's gonna leap out at me or some shit."

"Kinda did, Mags. I mean, not out of the street, but in your dreamsss!" Amy said this last by waving her hands around and speaking in a goofy, spooky way in both affectations.

Mags punched her shoulder, just hard enough to get her to stop her pantomime.

"Seriously, Amy. I want my life to mean something. Not just going to work and paying bills and keeping my head above water. I'm afraid it won't be too much longer before it'll be too late, and I'll just be left with winding my days away until I'm dead."

Amy sighed and said: "Ok. Fair enough. Go save your prince. Fucking call me in a couple of hours. I'm serious."

Magdalena turned back to her sister. She smiled at Amy, a bittersweet grin, marked by a single tear that ran from her left eye as if it were on a prison escape.

Amy gave her the same grin. They embraced each other for a few seconds in real time, for hours in the timekeeping of emotions.

"Stay safe, kid," Amy said.

They released each other, and Magdalena stepped out of the car. She closed the car door and watched as her sister drove off into the night.

At that moment, Magdalena felt the absolute certainty she would never see her sister again.

Chapter Ten

It was morning. Sarah had long since abandoned her laptop and her desk in her living room from the night before and had been staring at the digital alarm clock on her nightstand for hours. She simply laid there and watched the numbers and the time roll by.

The sky eventually lightened through her partially drawn blinds, but not enough to shake her from her fixation on the glowing red digits, still the brightest thing in the room.

11-29-22. 7:15 am. A crimson dot glowed to the right of the bottom half of the five, indicating that it was A.M. Time, at this time of year in New England, took on an ephemeral aspect that made one constantly feel as if they'd died and awoken in a slate-colored purgatory.

At last, she rolled over from her side onto her back. A single crack ran in the ceiling from one corner of her bedroom to the one diagonally opposite. Just seconds after Sarah had turned her gaze upward, that same crack leaked a few tiny chunks of plaster into her face.

"Okay, I get it. The fucking videotapes."

Sarah sat up and pulled herself forward to sit on the edge of her unmade bed. The ponytail she'd pulled her hair up into hours before was fucked up from her laying down for basically hours, so she yanked it out. Her hair was all over the place. She didn't care.

"We're all going to fucking die," she said, and then looked over at the nondescript cardboard box on the floor by her television.

"We should all already be dead."

All four top flaps were open on the cardboard box, and each skewed at their own unique and bizarre angle from the vertical sides they were attached to, as if a child had frantically ripped open the box, looking for some last-second Christmas present. She couldn't see the contents of the box from where she sat, but each of the numerous VHS cassettes within might as well have been screaming, an analog cacophony alerting her to their presence.

They'd been shouting ever since she'd entered the room. Staring at her alarm clock had quieted them. At that moment, she considered what was on the collection. Each one had their own discrete amount and proportionate level of horror. Sarah thought that by viewing them sequentially, she might reduce the terror she'd experience by revisiting the traumas of the last several months.

She'd promised Caleb that she'd round up the ones that Moretti should see, or the ones he thought would be enough for that strange man to leave them alone. They – the local and state police, that is - hadn't searched her apartment. At least not yet anyway. Caleb told her, before he got on the plane to go on his little quest in Europe, that they'd have a warrant sooner rather than later, and then the Commonwealth of Massachusetts and the city of Boston would come for as much evidence they could tear out of her apartment. Moretti confirmed this with her as well, standing, grunting, and nodding just behind Caleb at the flight gate.

Sarah shook her head. Caleb had it in his head, even before getting on that plane, that for some reason he was under the misguided notion that his jaunt was the equivalent of jumping on a grenade for them both. She was the one that had to stay in Boston. She was the proverbial frog, sitting in the water, dimly unaware of its heating up to boiling until it was far too late.

And she was the one that wanted out of this shitshow as far back as September. It was at that moment that Sarah remembered why it was she'd gone in with the alien robot-voiced man and whom and whatever else from CRUCIBLE in the first place.

Because fuck David, fuck Caleb, fuck Maroni or Moretti or whatever the fuck his name was. And especially fuck Magdalena. Whoever she really was. Fucking scam artist.

Eleven days.

Eleven days since they blew up half of a university and accidentally killed a bunch of people. Parsing the past few months through the magic of video - VHS video no less - was the absolute last thing she wanted to do. The last thing she deserved to have to do.

Eleven days, she'd known she had to perform this worthless, pointless chore, hopefully only just to keep up appearances with Caleb. She'd likely would have just bullshit her way through it, picked a couple of tapes at random, if it weren't for the cold truth that she had no idea if she could really trust CRUCIBLE. The answer was likely no.

Eleven days Sarah had sat in her own crucible.

Eleven days she'd been well and truly alone.

And on this morning, at that moment, it had finally become far, far too much for her.

She stood up and strode to the kitchen, moving faster than she had even during the day of the final dosing, the last day of the experiment. She pulled open the cabinet door, the one above the sink and almost too high for her reach without the aid of a stepstool. The bottle of Jack Daniels was there, full, and waiting for her to crack it open like a newly acquired horror novel still smelling of the bookstore from which it was purchased. She filled a half a coffee mug with the brown liquor and gulped it down in the span of seconds.

In the span of a few more seconds, the three, possibly four ounces of ethanol began polluting Sarah's bloodstream and corrupting her higher brain functions. She closed her eyes and cast her mind back, away from the present.

She remembered back in September, David and Caleb insisted on continuing despite her protests. She continued to help them. By then, really, it was far too late to back out. Sarah wondered why she'd even bothered to say anything by that point.

Sarah cast her mind back further, searching for the moment when she could have – should have backed out of the whole mess. All the way back, to the beginning.

April. The beginning for her, anyway.

Sarah remembered her reticence upon reading Keating's proposals and his research, on April Fools' Day. *How fitting*, she'd thought then. *How fitting*, she thought standing at the sink albeit in a different context and with far less irony. Was that the moment when she should have said no to it all?

Yes.

But would she have done so, ever have done so, if presented with the choice another hundred times?

No.

His ideas were borderline insane, but Keating was a genius. And he was never wrong. Ever. And then, there was the last five pages of his proposal – the carefully crafted legal consent he'd already bestowed upon both her and Caleb.

Sarah opened her eyes. The kitchen swam around her. She felt dizzy. She regretted agreeing to participate in this ghastly experiment almost as soon as she called David to say yes, but what was done was done. At least now she remembered why it was - what it really was – that caused her to say yes to the whole thing. Why she'd chosen to help this man, David fucking Keating.

This man, who'd taken her in after her final disgrace at med school, looked the other way as she'd go on to relapse another three or four times in her first year as a PhD candidate under his tutelage, who'd accepted Sarah regardless of her addiction. He was trying to fix himself. Something she'd been trying to do as well.

She sympathized. She understood. And most of all, and probably the most terrible of all the reasons - she felt obligated.

Could she have ever told him no? Could she have ever backed out? Probably not.

So, there was nothing left but to try to recover what could be recovered of her life. To save what was left of her soul. As it stood, she was a part of this forever. Otherwise, she would have just dropped everything and fled across the country for all anyone else cared.

When she finished reading the email with journal entries that Caleb had sent her, she did feel somewhat relieved. Keating likely had been surreptitiously giving himself the enzyme with no supervision and without notifying either her or Caleb. That, she felt, absolved her somewhat of the disastrous outcome of the experiment. The explosion in the lab, Keating's coma, the collateral damage and human cost would have happened with or without her participation.

The cell phone in her pocket rang and vibrated. It was not the one her shadowy liaison used, but rather her regular iPhone with its contact lists and useful apps and photos and the like. Caleb had told her that he'd call her on it when he'd arrived back in the states. Had to act as if his trip had been planned all along, and leaving obvious breadcrumbs was necessary. She was still surprised he was allowed to leave the country - but Caleb had explained that they likely *wanted* him to go there to obtain more information about what had happened to Keating. Moretti had likely greased that wheel as well – which only made her more suspicious of Moretti's motivation. Why was he so keen to help them, when his law enforcement colleagues seemed far more bent on wrapping this up as speedily and as quietly as possible? Why would the FBI even be interested in the scientific details of their work in the first place? Caleb must have considered this as well. Unless he knew something she didn't.

"Caleb?"

"Hi Sarah."

"You're here already?"

"No, obviously not. Waiting for my connecting flight in London."

"So why are you calling now, dude? Thought the plan was…"

"Did you finish going through all the videos?"

"No, not yet. Still working on it." Wasn't about to tell him she hadn't even started.

"Finish, Sarah. You only have a few hours left until I get there."

"Are you coming here with Moretti?"

"No, not at first. I'm going to contact him when I land at Logan. I'm hoping I can get at least an hour with you and Magdalena alone before he shows up…so we can get our stories straight. Where is she?"

Magdalena had been holed up at a hotel that Caleb and Sarah had booked using a fake name and a bogus credit card Caleb had kept on him that belonged to an ex-girlfriend. Kind of a scumbag move on Caleb's part, but it was what it was. Sarah didn't bother to ask why he'd kept this girl's credit card, and frankly didn't care. They'd stashed Magdalena there not long after she showed up in their office a couple of days after the explosion.

"Same place. She's been waiting there, being a good little doggie. Didn't go anywhere. Did what she was told."

"You really don't like her, do you? Jealous?"

"Fuck you Caleb."

"Magdalena. Still can't get over that name. Has she tried to contact you at all at least?"

"Nope. And yeah, fucking weird name. But whatever Caleb. Are you coming straight here from Logan?"

"Have to make a stop at my house first, and then I'll come there. Get a hold of little miss bluehair and tell her to come to your place as soon as possible."

Sarah knew he'd be followed the second he stepped off the plane. Magdalena too. By whom, and how many different interested parties, she didn't dare to consider. She supposed none of it really mattered anyway.

"Okay, *boss*."

"Oh, I'm sorry. Allow me to rephrase. Will you *please* ask her to go to your place?" His tone of sheer mockery and contempt leapt out of the phone.

"You don't have to be an asshole about it, either Caleb."

"Sarah, we don't really have time to be working through our communication difficulties at the present. I'm literally looking at two scary, black bag-looking guys who just happened to be waiting in the same gate for the same flight as I'm supposed to take. Who the fuck knows who they are? FBI? Who's to say. NSA? Who's to say?

Probably CRUCIBLE, dickhead, but you wouldn't know about that, would you, thought Sarah.

"Some other mystery alphabet agency? WHO'S TO SAY?"

"Don't have to yell, Caleb. I get it."

"They could be getting ready to either arrest me again as soon as they're able, or follow me wherever, or maybe I'm just being paranoid, and they're just *really* well dressed in their matching black suits." There was a pause. Then a sigh. "I'm sorry if I sound short."

But he did have a point.

"I'm fucking stressed out, too, Caleb. I still don't think we should just be handing these tapes over to Moretti. I don't trust him as much as you do."

Another pause. Longer this time. "I don't trust him at all either, Sarah. But since the fire, nobody - not the university, not the cops, *nobody* has helped us in even the tiniest of ways. And we have to see Keating at least once. I think the only way that happens is by giving Moretti what he wants."

"I just don't know if I can go through it all again. Watching that last tape…"

"I know it's hard. But you've gotta do it."

"Okay, fine." Frustrated, she hung up without another word.

Sarah's intention was to sort through the cassettes as Caleb asked, but not to hand over anything that would implicate her any more than she was already culpable. This part of the record of the experiment would be made up of what she and she alone would allow Moretti to see.

She returned to her bedroom. She looked over at the box. She'd have to go through them all to pick out which ones she'd bring. The others, she'd destroy. This notion served to both unsettle and reassure her simultaneously. She went back to the kitchen, grabbed the bottle and the coffee mug she'd just used, and set herself to the task.

There was no need to tiptoe around relenting her sobriety while she watched. She'd given in, so there was no reason not to keep the booze handy. Four years of sobriety down the drain. But it wasn't her fault. She was pushed into it.

The last time she drank, Sarah got behind the wheel of a car to drive home. Halfway there, she ended up hitting a pedestrian on a bicycle while running a red light. The cyclist was unhurt, but the overall damage had been done.

The arrest, losing her license, hitting that kid on his bike, was enough to keep her sober for the interim years. She would tell herself several times over the next few hours that the months-long illegal human experimentation, the explosion, and the deaths were enough to allow a slip – but then all that followed in their collective wake practically insisted on it.

Sarah was well-buzzed by that first elephant-sized belt of whiskey; her tolerance having been reduced to zero by the years of abstaining. The newly felt liquid courage she'd acquired caused her to practically tear the first video tape out of the cardboard box, like a modern-day Arthur pulling Excalibur from the stone.

She regarded the single word written in red cursive sharpie on the label on the top side of it. She hadn't written that word, but it indicated that this was her star moment in the entire endeavor.

The word was "operation".

She pushed the tape into the VHS player she'd found at a yard sale a week before. She laughed out loud at the irony - here she was, simultaneously responsible for one of the most egregious disregards for scientific and medical ethics in recent memory (consent be damned) as well as what was likely the greatest breakthrough in neurobiology in history.

And she was about to review the video documentation of it on technology from fucking eighties.

Fucking Keating and his idiosyncrasies. The man had so many issues. Issues never really dealt with or addressed properly.

Caleb liked to pretend to his boss that he was just that kind of eccentric that came with being a genius of Keating's level.

There was a moment or two of static, and then the action began on the tape. Sarah just started laughing to herself as began to watch the records from the past few months come to life on her tv.

"Issues, issues, issues ishewwwwwws," she muttered between the laughs. "Oh boy, did Davey have some ISH-EWWS!!!!"

She dimly thought, amid the growing haze of intoxication, she had some of her own as well.

"OPERATION - September 18th, 2022" (VCR Analog Recording):

From the onset, it's obvious to the viewer that the camera isn't mounted or fixed in a single position. When the static that appears at the very beginning of a VCR tape rolls up to the top of the screen, revealing at first a black screen underneath and then the first few camera shots, the camera angle wildly moves about the room. The floor is the first thing that shows up on a television, followed by the ceiling, then the lens is pointed at Keating's face in extreme close-up, and lastly falls upon Sarah's back – albeit incredibly out of focus. The first sixty or so seconds of the tape would have been the beginning of the most poorly shot found footage horror movie in history, were it filmed for that purpose.

The camera finally stabilizes, and the cameraman identifies himself. For this clip, this was Caleb.

"I still don't understand why we're not recording this with something invented in this century David," Caleb complains. His voice so close to the microphone mounted on top of the camera that even at a conversational volume, the sound of his speech overloads the speaker. It's as if he's speaking into a megaphone positioned just a few inches from someone's face.

The camera view swings around again in a blur, returning to the fourth-rate *Blair Witch Project* filming technique that marks the beginning of the recording. The last thing anyone watching would think this footage would be is the visual documenting of advanced biochemical and physiological research.

But then the angle and the lens settle, at last. The view stops on Sarah, this time facing the camera directly, and well in focus. She is dressed in surgeon's attire – sterile blue gowning, hair cap, face mask & shield, sterile sleeves and latex gloves. Only her eyes are visible, staring dead into the camera with purpose.

It's clear at this point that Caleb, Sarah, and Keating are in a makeshift operating theater, likely in or on the Gordon Medical School campus -a facility about three miles down the road from the main campus. The main campus is where their shared lab is located.

Sarah's features turn into a grin, the edges of which can be seen just outside the parts of her face that are covered by the mask.

"Aw, is someone spooked out by a day working in Uncle Herbie's old stomping grounds?"

"Fuck you, Sarah," replies Caleb.

Satisfied with taking a dig, Sarah begins her dialogue.

"September 18th, 2022, ten-fifteen a.m. Today, we will be conducting the cerebral surgery that Dr. Keating has detailed in the Ascendant Experiment abstract. Also included in the abstract is Dr. Keating's legal consent to this operation."

Those watching the tape would notice Sarah's eyes diminish in intensity here. It conveys a moment of doubt and worry on her part. She steels herself and continues. The intensity returns.

"Specifically, we will be physically altering the midbrain structure to align with and physically resemble that of the common honeybee. It has been previously established through extensive experimentation and research that the honeybee brain's computational potential far exceeds that of its human counterpart. This ability owes much to the physical structure of the brain, enabling even a 'worker' or 'drone' to make computations that rival the world's most powerful supercomputers. It is believed that the sophisticated neural network that is established within the brain is due largely to sub-organs called "mushroom bodies". In order for the novel and proprietary neurotransmitter operamine to actuate its function within a human central nervous system, alterations must be made to the organ such that analogous structures to the aforementioned 'mushroom bodies' are present."

The camera pans down to the shaved top of Keatings's head, bald and exposed.

Sarah makes one final statement.

"The patient has been anesthetized using standard and accepted procedures." She steps to her left, revealing a large blue cloth divider with a circular aperture towards the bottom. Protruding from the aperture is the top of Keating's head, shaved clean of hair. The light just above the operating table catches his skull in such a way as to produce glare in the camera lens. The rest of his body cannot be seen.

Sarah reaches to a table even further to her left and produces an electronic bone saw, a small, cruel looking device that looks as if it was stolen from a woodworker's bench. Sarah flips a switch, and the machine springs to life, emitting a high-pitched whirring sound. She begins cutting away at the flesh and bone of Keating's skull. The pitch of the bone saw's sound drops a full register as it does its work.

There is a break here, as the recording stops and a wall of static rolls up from the bottom of the screen.

Watching the video, Sarah sat quietly for a moment, but then began to laugh hysterically. She paused the tape. After almost a full five minutes, Sarah managed to cease her cackling.

"Motherfucker had to stop to go throw up. What a sissy."

Sarah hit play on the tape and resumed watching.

The video starts again, and Sarah is busy with a scalpel, making cuts inside of Keating's head. Caleb begins to speak.

"In 1929, Hans Berger, a renowned German scientist, discovered the existence of alpha waves in human brain function. Alpha waves are oscillations that have been connected to primary and higher brain functions as memory, attention, and above all - consciousness. The honeybee brain also produces these alpha waves, albeit at a different frequency. The human alpha waves oscillate at 10 Hz. the honeybee at 18. What is most fascinating is-"

Sarah cuts him off. "Hey Caleb?"

"Yeah?"

"Can you shut the fuck up? Kinda might be giving Dr. Keating permanent brain damage here. Need to concentrate."

"Sorry."

The tape goes on for another vivid and graphic thirty minutes before it cuts off. Sarah announces each specific operation as it is performed - most are removal of parts of Keating's cerebrum. There is one significant outlier from this trend, which occurs at the very conclusion of the procedure.

Sarah: "After having removed tissue here," she points to one side of Keating's brain "and here," we will then splice Brodmann areas three through fourteen into the hippocampal region. By doing so, we mimic the aforementioned "mushroom bodies" present within the honeybee brain with one augmented structure in Keating's human brain."

Sarah performs the action, and leans back, satisfied.

"Let's put him back together."

The tape cuts out.

Sarah pulled the cassette labeled **"Operation"** out of the VCR, dropped it flat on the ground, and violently stepped on it several times, smashing it to pieces. Sarah swept up the black, brown, and clear plastic shards from the tape casing and the tape itself into both hands. She marched into the kitchen, scanned the room, and spotted her mop bucket in the far corner near her pantry. She dropped the remains of **"Operation"** into the bucket. Sarah then darted into the bathroom and located all the nail polish remover she could find, three bottles worth. She returned to the tape and dumped all the cosmetic cleaning chemical into the bucket and swished it around. The acetone did its work within seconds, destroying any chance of recovering even a second of Sarah's work on film.

She'd decided the second the bone saw made its appearance that this recording was never going to be seen by another living soul. It was irrefutable proof of the worst aspect of her involvement in the experiment, and once destroyed, she concluded, she'd stand a far better chance of not going to prison for the rest of her life.

Or worse.

This video was never going to be seen by anyone else ever again, period. Sarah had learned through a lawyer friend of hers that she could still be held criminally liable for performing the operation, consent or no – despite what she'd been reassured by Caleb and Keating as that not being the case. They'd emphasized that because the surgery was part of an established scientific experiment under controlled conditions, the whole 'practicing unlicensed medicine' thing could be skirted.

Not so. The two of them were full of shit from the get-go.

And this had enraged Sarah.

And maybe that was the biggest reason why she answered CRUCIBLE's call. It was at least one of the reasons, regardless.

The tape was as-damning-as-it-gets evidence of a crime – a felony- on her part. It wasn't just unethical - without any kind of licensure, Sarah's actions may have sophisticated neurosurgery in one context, but it was aggravated assault in another.

That mystery agent Moretti must have known knew surgery was part of the experiment and had therefore also known she'd carried it out, but for unknown reasons never mentioned it once. He'd likely deduced it on his own, but even if he hadn't, Caleb would have spilled the beans to him when she and him had been brought in for questioning days before.

Sarah, however, did not possess the same inclination towards being as transparent as possible with the authorities. So fucking bye-bye "**OPERATION**" They - meaning the academic staff of CM University, the cops, and Moretti – probably needed the tape regardless of whatever Caleb told local cops or Moretti for that matter.

And they were never, ever going to get it.

Caleb watched the two men from Men in Black central casting for the entire time he sat at the gate waiting for his flight home to Boston.

Those same men sat and watched Caleb.

Neither party made a move to approach to parley with the other, even after each was aware of the other's presence.

Caleb first noticed them a few short minutes before taking a seat near the American Airlines desk just to the left of the doorway where his plane would eventually connect. They stuck out to everyone who caught sight of them, like they were cosplaying evil government agents, but no one really seemed to care, barely acknowledging their presence.

But Caleb wasn't just aware, but thoroughly alarmed. His adrenaline levels felt as if they steadily increased for the duration of the standoff.

He could only speculate as to how long they'd been trailing him. Grasping for a thought, *any* thought as to who or what agency they might be from and coming up with nada, no dice, not even the faintest clue, panic began to set in.

All at once, Caleb decided to call Sarah. Ostensibly, to ensure she knew what his plan was when he was due to touch down in Boston that afternoon – and to remind her of what she needed to have done.

He wasn't surprised she hadn't reviewed any of the tapes. He was surprised that she hadn't out-and-out just destroyed them all the second he left for Germany. The phone call didn't last long and if one was being generous, it was also decidedly antagonistic in tone. Still, the impromptu chat served its purpose. Going over the plan with a person who was on your side was reassuring enough.

But when he disconnected the call from Sarah, Caleb glanced over at Heckyll and Jeckyll. Still just sitting there, watching him.

And then it dawned on him. Of course! Why didn't he think of it before? These two were probably working for the same agency, group, or organization Moretti did. He'd sent them to the gate to make sure he got on his flight, which explained why they didn't approach themselves.

The American Airlines customer service rep picked up that weird CB/microphone thing they kept behind their desk. She clicked a button on it.

"American Airlines flight 1071 to Boston Logan airport will begin boarding in five minutes." She clicked the button, and the area returned to its relative silence.

Might as well just introduce myself then, thought Caleb. He was, after all, indirectly working with them as well. Maybe that's what they were waiting for, was for him to approach them to speak.

Caleb got up and began to walk towards them.

But as soon as he did so, the two men also got up and walked towards Caleb.

Their action and movement did not feel right to Caleb in the slightest bit. After just a few seconds, they were face to face. Caleb spoke first.

"Uh, hey guys…um, I guess you guys work with Agent Moretti. So, I just wanted to say that-"

One of the G-men interrupted him mid-sentence.

"Dr. West, if you see, speak, or interact with Agent Moretti in any form, we'd ask that you contact us immediately."

If Caleb was alarmed before, he found himself now completely terrified.

The other man produced a card from his suitcoat pocket and handed it to Caleb.

The man who'd interrupted Caleb continued once he'd taken the card from his counterpart.

"We look forward to your anticipated cooperation, Dr. West. It is in your -and his- best interests that you contact us immediately." And without another word, the two black baggers strode away.

Caleb found himself in a constant, unrelenting state of vertigo and shock from that moment up until the time he took his seat on the plane. There were government agents…*looking for Moretti?* None of it made any sense anymore. If Moretti wasn't working for whoever the fuck those guys were, then who's side was he really on? What were the sides anyway?

Caleb West, graduate of M.I.T. and one of the smartest minds of his generation, could not control his racing thoughts. At last, he looked at the card the silent one had handed to him. There was a phone number and a single word. The phone number was unremarkable. The word was not. It simply read, in bold Arial font:

"CRUCIBLE"

Chapter Twelve

"RECOVERY - September 20th – October 13th, 2022" (VCR Analog Recording 2):

Sarah returned to her bedroom after destroying the first tape and rewarded herself with a quick, smaller slug from the bottle of whiskey. She chased it back with her bottle of cola. She felt the warmth of the alcohol heat her cheeks, her chest, her arms, and her legs. The feeling didn't last as long as it had earlier when she first drank from the bottle. She felt cold, and sick again in mere moments. She lurched over to the box of analog horrors, and pulled out the second tape, entitled **"RECOVERY"**.

Sarah was unsure of the exact contents of it, unlike the first cassette. This second tape in the full visual record of the experiment, **"RECOVERY"** was recorded over the three weeks following Keating's operation. It consisted of Keating's immediate, physical return to coherence from the surgery. Sarah lay flat on her back in her bed. She turned the cassette this way and that, as if just looking at the tape would reveal some of its contents to her. And after a few seconds of this, it did.

Sarah scowled at the tape. Keating, just two days after having his head cut open and, in his painkiller-addled delirium, revealed to her and Caleb he'd deviated from the procedure and administered an injection of operamine, small, just twenty CC's, but significant, nonetheless.

What he'd done, essentially, is ruin the experiment altogether. He then purposely kept the information from his assistants because he knew that if he had shared what he had done, they would have bailed out on him immediately.

The original design was to use Keating as both the experimental and the control group; but each 'grouping' was based on his cerebral activity and responses at different stages, or points of time during the study. The control portion was to be made up of his baseline brain function after the operation and his recovery, free from any kind of operamine dosing. The exact effects the of physical modifications to his cerebrum and cerebellum could be ascertained, as well as his suitability to continue with the experiment.

If Sarah had given the professor fucking brain damage during the operation, there was certainly no point in continuing with the remainder of the protocol.

Once this baseline had been established, dosing with the operamine enzyme was to proceed, thus creating the 'experimental' portion of the study.

But shithead had dosed himself prior to the surgery, just so he could feel 'normal' quicker, at least according to him. That's what he ended up mumbling in the video. The 'control' group aspect of the experiment was already blown to shit but for that simple, selfish act. At that point, who could tell what was Keating, what was Keating with just the surgery, and what was Keating with surgery and enzyme? No way to be certain.

Keating drops a hit of bee-zyme into his brain prior to the surgery. If anything was ever going to be repeated, whomever undergoing the treatment would have to undergo an initial dosage as well. Or maybe…

Son of a bitch, thought Sarah. Even in her whiskey-addled train of thought, she was able to pull a separate motivation for Keating's self-dosing, one that hadn't been openly shared with her and Caleb, and one that wasn't immediately obvious at the time.

Maybe Keating never intended for the experiment to ever be repeated. He likely concluded that if this whole thing didn't work, he'd either be dead or a vegetable. Maybe…that as a fallback, this was a second suicide attempt, under the surface of it all. Normal human being or bust, as it were. And he had no problem dragging her and Caleb down with him if things went bad.

Sarah found herself hating Keating even more as she pushed the tape into the VCR.

The footage begins, and the camera is stationary and positioned at the foot of a hospital bed. The room is not in a hospital, but rather in a master bedroom. The area is well-lit, with mid-day sunlight streaming in through several open windows. The camera is set to a location in the room that takes advantage of this lighting. Keating is laying on the bed, with bandages wrapped around his head but smiling. Sarah is sitting off to one side, legs crossed and relaxed. Caleb is on the other side of the bed, with a clipboard and pen in hand. Sarah begins speaking first.

"Good afternoon, I'm Sarah Fischer, to my left is Caleb West, and the man who lay in front of you is Dr. David Keating. It's September 20th, two days since the operation, and Dr. Keating has awoken and is fully conscious for the first time. After an initial round of physical checks, Dr. Keating has stated he is ready for some baseline questions and tests to check for any potential cognitive difficulties that may have resulted from the operation. We will perform these now as part of our first data set to ascertain this, and whether it is safe to proceed with administration of the enzyme. Caleb, David, are we ready?"

Caleb: "Sure am."

Keating: "Go ahead and get started guys."

Caleb flips over the top page and begins to read.

"Can we have your full name and birthdate for the record?"

"My name is David Herbert Keating. Born January 15th, 1976, at 6:28 am, Berlin, Germany. My parents' names are Emil Neumann and Catherine Keating. Their birthdates are…"

Caleb cuts him off. "That's okay David - just need the name and birthday, sailor. That's it."

"Caleb, by recalling my parents' names as well I can further show that unequivocally there's no damage to my long-term memory."

Caleb smiles. "Let's just stick to the script, boss. Next question. Where are you, what's the date, and what time of day is it?"

"It's 12:30, Caleb, on September 24th, and we are in Arkham, Massachusetts on the campus of Gordon University. Harding Science Building."

Caleb jots down a quick note and checks a box.

Keating sits up and looks over to Sarah with concern.

"Lean back, David," Sarah says. "he's not writing anything bad about you." Keating looks back into the camera, and then appears to relax somewhat by leaning back against the mattress. It's clear that Sarah is satisfied with his movement back to his original position.

The camera, however, shows his eyes darting back and forth between her and Caleb.

Caleb flips the page over and is just about to begin again when Keating coughs, rubs his eyes, and starts blurting out random facts.

"Jamaica Plain, Massachusetts. Manchester, New Hampshire, Unmarried. I do not have any kids. The experiment is to study the novel enzyme operamine and its significant effects on both the perception of reality within conscious individual and social constructs as well as subconscious domains."

And then, at the last - "Red. Four hundred forty-one."

Caleb's countenance flips from a look of half-serious inquiry to having been tasered with a stun gun. Caleb stands up immediately and walks over the camera. The entire picture is blocked by his midsection and stops abruptly.

The recording starts again, this time inside of the laboratory. Sarah is holding the camera, the view unsteady. Caleb is in full view. It's a close-up shot. Caleb's pale cobalt eyes keep looking at a point that's off camera. He brushes his sandy-blonde hair out of his face, since having pulled the man bun elastic out of his locks. He is nervously pulling the same elastic back and forth, stretching it out in a near panic.

"So say that again, Caleb." she tells him.
Caleb beings to whisper. "Those things he was blurting out, Sarah. All the way down to red, and four forty-one. Those are the answers to questions I hadn't asked yet, Sarah," he whispered.

"Why are you whispering Caleb?"

"I - I don't know Sarah."

"So what? Maybe he'd memorized them whenever we wrote these questions up. I mean, it's not like they're difficult or unusual questions."

Caleb shakes his head back and forth, almost violently.

"You're not getting me, Sarah."

"What, Caleb. What? What don't I get?'

"Those last two answers? Red? Four hundred forty-one?"

"Yeah?"

"Yeah, those were supposed to be first a simple visual test identifying colors, and then and multiplication. A picture with the color red on it, and then twenty-one squared."

"So the fuck what?"

"Don't swear on camera Sarah. And there's no way he could have known those answers.

"Why?"

"Because when he and I were working on this battery of questions a month ago, we specifically decided that on those two questions at the end that I would make them up the day of the testing…so he couldn't memorize the answers. Plus, the questions were supposed to be asked in a random order - and he still somehow knew that too."

"So how could he have…."

The recording stops again.

It starts again, back in Keating's recovery room. Keating is sitting up when it starts, again, smiling. Only he is visible.

Caleb walks in a second or two later. He sits down, puts his hair back in a ponytail, rubs his face twice with both hands as if he were washing, and then sighs.

"How did you do it, David? How could you have known about the questions?"

Sarah zooms the camera in on Keating's face to detect any type of irregularity or abnormal facial expression. Aside from the bandages covering his forehead and the raccoon-eyes he'd received from undergone cranial surgery, there was nothing about Keating's appearance that appeared irregular. At least, for his current situation.

"This may be difficult for you to accept, Caleb, but I could hear the questions appear inside your head. They made a ringing noise, quite pleasant actually. Like a dinner bell, almost. It wasn't like mind-reading, though.

As in, I couldn't hear them unless they pertained to me. It's because they were directed towards me, you were thinking about me. I think since I was already present within your mind, it made it so I could see the questions."

Again, Keating smiles. At first the smile would appear hopeful, even cheerful to the viewer. At this point, it is both weird and creepy to behold.

Sarah puts a stop to it.

"David - stop smiling. Kinda inappropriate."

The camera zooms back out, and Caleb is shaking his head back and forth and looks at Sarah with full a full 'what the fuck' look.

Sarah hit the pause button. The moment wasn't nearly as shocking now as it was when she and Caleb had experienced it back in September. In the recording, they'd find out in moments what he'd done, taking the twenty CCs of operamine prior to the surgery. Keating's first display of his elevated consciousness had alarmed, even frightened her and Caleb.

Now, that part of the recording made perfect sense.

Sarah decided that she'd hand this tape over to Moretti. If Moretti thought that what was going on was more on Keating, and not on her, than all the better. Sarah decided to scan the rest of the tape. Covering three weeks, the full recording was over two hours. She fast-forwarded past the revelation that Keating made moments later to the two of them. No sense in making herself even angrier about the whole business. Sarah released the fast forward button and allowed the tape to continue.

The video static disappears, and the video resumes. There's a short blip – but then it appears as if only a few hours have passed since the beginning of the recording. The windows are no longer opened, and the blinds have since been drawn. No light is coming through the part of the windows the blinds do not cover, and a lamp is on, but it's located somewhere off camera to not interfere with the shot. It is nighttime.

Sarah is sitting next to Keating, facing him. She places the video camera remote on the table, and only half turns to the camera.

"Same date, September 24th. I am interviewing Dr. David Keating, following up on the extraordinary events from September 20th," Sarah fully turns to David.

"Dr. Keating and I have been discussing what he experienced while under anesthesia and unconscious during the actual surgery and he displayed on September 20th. In my estimation, I believe they are related."

David bears the look of a child who has been caught with his hand in the cookie jar.

"David - what did you see, while you under?"

David begins: "Sarah, as I've mentioned before, this is my third surgery. The first was for a tonsillectomy, the second for a spinal fusion. Both times, the sleep was dreamless. Conventional anesthetic prevents dreaming I think, in most patients, but that's not always the case. It did for me, however, on both of those occasions."

"But this time, it was different. What did you see, David?"

"It was cloudy at first, almost like I was underwater, but at night - there was no light to see above the surface. All sound was muffled. And then, the operating room swam into focus, wave-like, however. It was as if veils were being lifted one by one from my eyes, and then at last I saw the operating room quite clearly. But through your eyes. I could see you, operating on me."

Sarah turns toward the camera. "The inference here is that the operation has allowed you to connect with whomever is thinking of you or about you, then."

"It would appear that way, Ms. Fischer."

"I don't know what to do now, David. You – we – didn't anticipate any of this."

Keating takes her hand. Sarah looks at him, and he returns this with an expression of reassurance.

"I'm sorry, Sarah. I truly am. I shouldn't have taken that dose. But we need to carry on. This is important."

Sarah appears caught off guard. This gesture of…empathy…was one she'd never experienced coming from Keating. Ever.

"So if I'm to make a suggestion, we stick to the same dosage plan, but in a couple of weeks, let's set up an EEG, and an alpha wave apparatus. We'll conduct some tests there to get a better picture of what's happening.

"Agreed," says Sarah. "You want to say anything else for this record, Dr. Keating?"

He smiles, and then turns directly to the camera, making eye contact with the viewer. "I, Dr. David Hebert Keating, may have made the first real breakthrough in establishing the biochemical basis for a kind of induced telepathy. This is of course, subject to further testing, but the operation could be considered to be at this stage…a success," Keating lets go of Sarah's hand with his own and places it on Sarah's shoulder, "thanks to the brilliance and skill of my team. Our initial results, although unexpected, have shown that enzyme operamine could have the potential to unlock so much of the human potential that we, as a species, have only dreamed of."

The tape cuts out

Sarah considered that, yes, he did unlock something within himself, although what that was still wasn't clear. It all looked so hopeful then - as if just the operation itself had broken down fundamental barriers in the human experience. It really hadn't though. Just for him.

Sarah watched the rest of **"RECOVERY"** play out. She wanted to blame Keating for everything. She couldn't though - she had come willingly down the path, along with Caleb. Was it partly out of a sense of obligation to the man that had helped turn her life around? Had helped her get sober all those years ago? It was, but there were more to her motivations.

What Sarah really wanted to do was stick it to the people who'd given up on her. She may not have been able to cut it as a doctor, but she knew could make an impact as a researcher and a scientist. And Keating was her quickest way to doing that. So, of course she was on board, at least at first, with Keating's foray into science fiction.

The booze was really starting to kick in at that point. Not the immediate physical sensations, or disordered thought. She was losing her sense of time. Sarah thought that she'd go through another couple of tapes, and then give Magdalena a call to have her come to Sarah's apartment.

Sarah didn't trust her, either. Hell, for all she knew, the girl could have been some kind of scam artist. It was extremely doubtful, but possible.

Sarah was short on trust these days.

And a mean drunk, as well. Somewhere in the back of her mind, the last semblances of her common sense were screaming at her to stop drinking then and now.

Wasn't going to happen, though. Once she started, it usually took something dramatic for her to stop, or be stopped.

Sarah half stumbled over to the television. She hit eject, and then yanked the tape out before it was fully out of the player, nearly ruining it. She tossed the tape onto her bed, next to a carry-all bag she'd prepared yesterday. She was leaving her apartment at some point that day, and when -if- she'd be back she had no idea.

Back over to the collection of videotapes. She leaned over, almost going ass over teakettle fishing out **"Alpha Waves/EEG"**.

"Let's watch some fucking alpha waves, boys and girls!" she shouted to her empty bedroom. She jammed the cassette in, almost breaking *that* one. Sarah got underneath her covers, pulled the blankets up to her eyes, and waited for the video to start.

The second before it could, however, the "burner" phone started to ring. There were only two people who knew the number - and Caleb had already called today. It had to have been Magdalena, calling from the hotel.

*Speak of the devil…*thought Sarah.

"Hello?"

"Hey, it's, uh, Magdalena."

"Hey, it's uh, Sarah," she mockingly replied.

"Didn't you mention that there was a video of that last day in the lab? When the explosions happened?"

Sarah sighed. "Yeah, there is. He even says your name out loud in the video. The whole thing is completely crazy. But you knew that already. Listen, I was gonna call you anyway. Head on over. Caleb will be here this afternoon sometime."

"Uh, okay. But can I look at that video real quick?. I know it's short notice, but there's just something I want to check."

"Magdalen-" Sarah was aggravated just hearing her voice.

"There's something bothering me from that day. I need to see that video."

Sarah jumped out of her bed and punched the wall. Hard.

"What was that?" asked Magdalena.

"I dropped something. Look, Mags…why didn't you ask me this before today, of all days?"

"I told you. Please don't call me Mags. My sister is the only one who call me…"

"Whatever. You literally waited days to ask me this shit. Couldn't have done this any time in the past week, maybe? Kinda tough setting up a private screening of the day of meeting Caleb and possibly Detective Moretti again."

Sarah knee she'd have to watch the last video again that day..and soon as a matter of fact. It didn't stop her from seizing a chance to berate the woman.

"Yeah, I thought it might be too much to ask. I'm sorry I didn't think of it sooner," replied Magdalena.

Sarah held the phone to one side for a second, but then brought it back to her ear. "Address is 43 Waterfall Lane, Somerville, MA. Get an uber. The ride over shouldn't take any more than forty minutes."

"Oh, thanks Sarah," said Magdalena. Be there as soon as I…" Sarah didn't wait for her to finish her sentence. She pushed the 'end' button.

"See ya in a bit, sweetheart," said Sarah to her empty bedroom.

Ever since that day when Magdalena walked into their somehow still-intact office at the university, like some mystical figure from a high fantasy flick with sorcerers and goblins and warriors and wizards, Caleb and Sarah were both dodgy and obtuse that final tape around Magdalena.

They had their reasons.

Chapter Thirteen

Maybe taking a Greyhound bus wasn't such a great idea, was Magdalena's first thought upon entering the Tampa Greyhound bus station. Somehow, in her mind, she'd pictured it as a place that at least partially resembled its transportation counterpart's: vis-a-vis train stations, airports, or even public transportation locales. There were certain accoutrements, aspects, creature comforts for travelers that one expected of such places. The Tampa Greyhound station bore exactly zero of these creature comforts.

For starters, there could have been at least one, possibly even two food vendors available to provide some manner of grotesque, yet edible and/or nourishing food for the traveler at large. One of these would likely either be a McDonald's, or a Dunkin' Donuts, or even just a convenience store-like booth. No dice, however, inside the Tampa Greyhound bus station.

There were, however, two vending machines – yet even they had been pillaged of any and every item that could be considered viable as either edible or as a beverage. French onion sun chips and Diet Mr. Pibb was the best these machines had to offer. Magdalena glanced at the machines and immediately passed on both options.

Next, Magdalena expected that there be information booth or at least, an employee of Greyhound to assist or direct people on where they needed to go or what they needed to do to get where they were going.

That was also a no. There were only two people visible inside the station when Magdalena walked in - and neither appeared to be affiliated with the eponymous transit line. One was a legitimate customer - a man of about forty-five, glasses, and a black winter hat. A bit odd for Tampa, but maybe he was headed north too.

Maybe he also had a dream about a mad scientist begging for help from some netherworld too? Maybe not.

The man had a backpack jammed so full that it looked as if the zippers were going to give up and burst in protest at any moment, having been asked to work beyond their job requirements for the very last time. Magdalena imagined the contents flying everywhere as celebratory streamers fell from the bus station ceiling. *Headlines: 'zipper unions win the right to spend their weekends unzipped, free from struggling to keep an entire dresser inside of a single backpack. We now go live to Tampa to the live victory party'.*

Magdalena caught herself lost in her thoughts, oblivious to her surroundings, staring at the man and laughing to herself. He looked back at Magdalena, meeting her gaze, and visibly frightened of the strange girl giggling at him like a serial killer. How she must appear to him! She averted her gaze and ceased her giggling. The man clutched at his pack as if it were the last parachute on a doomed airplane as Magdalena strode past.

The other individual in the station was homeless; a poor, forgotten woman of fifty (she appeared as if she was sixty) sleeping with her chin on her chest. Whatever alcohol she'd been recently imbibing permeated the air inside the station, so that the only detectable odor inside was that awful approximation of paint thinner she'd been imbibing – and the smell of industrial cleaner that had been used on the decades-old benches and floors in the station.

The station was a single room then, with the double doors on East Polk Street by which Magdalena had entered and three separate doorways opposite that entrance as means of egress. The letters "A", "B", and "C", each painted on placards, hung above its respective passage, ostensibly marking them as 'gates'.

At least these gates vaguely resembled something that could be found in a train station.

To the north end of the bus station were the ticket windows, of which there appeared to be four. Four windows built presumably to service a greater demand for the services of America's largest bus transportation service. As it stood now, only one was open, and one barely visible individual, masked, face-shielded, and gloved to protect herself from a potential COVID infection, sat in one window. She idly read a paperback.

This is the most depressing place in the universe, thought Magdalena.

She walked over to the window and bought her ticket.

Magdalena had never taken a bus anywhere ever in her life, other than those of the obnoxious yellow variety that ferried her to and from grade school when she was younger. Magdalena was a bit surprised when the woman slid a stack of tickets in a little envelope through the window to her. She'd assumed it would have been one, maybe two slices of paper. Magdalena apparently had four and thirty-eight connecting buses for her journey.

She took the manifesto-sized booklet and sat down on one of the metal benches.

Fortunately, she wasn't in the most depressing place in the universe for very long. After a matter of only a few minutes, a man dressed in a ridiculous blue uniform pushed open door (gate) C halfway. He announced to the room: "all points north, five minutes," as if the station was full of people waiting on his appearance, and then disappeared from whence he came. Magdalena found herself wondering as to whether that meant her, despite her destination residing in the direction the uniformed man had just proclaimed.

Fortunately, she wasn't in the most depressing place in the universe for very long. After a matter of only a few minutes, a man dressed in a ridiculous blue uniform pushed open door (gate) C halfway. He announced to the room: "all points north, five minutes," as if the station was full of people waiting on his appearance, and then disappeared from whence he came. Magdalena found herself wondering as to whether that meant her, despite her destination residing in the direction the uniformed man had just proclaimed. She stood up and walked towards the ticket window, and the woman sitting there looked up from her paperback (a horror novel called "Dollface", so whatever the hell that was about) to nod, lean over, and say into her little microphone the words "yes, that's you".

Magdalena made her way to 'gate C'.

By the time she'd boarded, got settled, and the bus had left Tampa's city limits, it was eleven o' clock and Magdalena was mentally and physically exhausted. But neither of these states of being meant a thing to Magdalena as far as actually being able to get some rest went. She knew that sleep, the restful kind anyway, was going to come at a premium on this little epic journey of hers. It was a hard enough time getting rest in optimal circumstances such as being at home in her comfy bed.

And at that moment, she was alone in the dark on a bus in an unforgiving seat that felt like it had been set to "lumbar torture". Which was to say nothing for being alone, exposed, and riding in a decidedly unsafe mode of transportation as it were.

After some finagling, Magdalena managed to adjust her seat to "non-consensual spinal adjustment". She then took her evening meds and did her best to wind down.

Magdalena pulled her journal out of her things and clicked on the small light above her head.

She opened it to the entry she had started earlier that day.

November 15th, 2020. Today, my life changed. I don't know if it'll be for the best, or if it will cause more problems than I already have.

And I don't care if it does make my life worse. Anything is better than here, waiting to grow old and die.

What was she going to write after that, other than stuff a person suffering a severe psychotic break would write? Okay, maybe 'psychotic break' was a bit of an exaggeration to her mental state, but should she ever run afoul of...well, run afoul of anything, and if interested parties began poking around through her stuff…and they ended up finding the handwritten pages of a person in search of a dying mad scientist from Boston…and then discovered her laundry list of neurodivergences…

Magdalena's train of thought was off, ruminating over any number of fatalistic endings to her quest. There was this ending, where she ended up dead in a ditch. There was another where she somehow had psychic abilities. And there was still another…

Magdalena never wrote a word. She fell asleep with the book open and the light on.

It happened that way sometimes.

She was awakened in the early morning by the fleeting, ghostly blue light that exists only in the minutes just before sunrise. It poured its way in through the bus windows like a cobalt-colored fog. There was a moment before she fully came to her senses, feeling the obscene stiffness in her neck before she felt an elbow to her side as a stranger ruffled through her backpack.

A split second followed, and then full panic flicked through her body like a bolt of lightning in a hazy sky during a summer thunderstorm. Vivid. Chaotic. The panic burned an afterimage into every cell in her body.

If she'd awoken from another vision instead of the dreamless sleep in which she'd just been immersed, there would have been no way she would have reacted in time to the attack - it would have taken her a solid ten minutes just to have been able to move. She hadn't had one though, and that was fortunate.

She twisted to her left as if she had been smacked. In the seat next to her was a black-haired, pock-marked man. He had one arm fully rummaging through her things as if they were his, his other hand off to the side. In that other hand, the motherfucker was clutching two of her medications. The motherfucker had her Adderall pill bottle opened and had likely already helped himself. The other was her anti-anxiety meds.

Scumbag noticed she had awoken. Instead of bailing immediately and moving away, he smiled right in her face.

"Hey there! Don't worry. You're still on the right bus," he volunteered.

Magdalena grabbed at her prescriptions.

"I need those!"

The man pulled that hand back, deftly winning that impromptu round of 'keep away'. He pulled his other arm out of her bag, placed the hand attached to the end of it against her face like a schoolyard bully, and pushed her head against the window - neutralizing any kind of leverage that she had to continue wrestling with him.

"Oh yeah? Well, *I need them more, cunt*," he whispered. He bared his teeth after his declaration, which bore the twisted, blackened trademarks of a seasoned crystal meth addict.

Magdalena was helpless and frightened into near paralysis. All she could muster then was a muted "mmmmmnnhhh" sound.

The man turned towards the front of the bus and yelled towards the driver.

"Sir! This woman just tried to assault me. Please help. She's trying to steal my heart medication!"

The driver noticed the melee at Scumbag's warning, and immediately began to slow the bus down. The driver made it as if he was going to pull over on the side of the highway as soon as he was able.

The man turned to her and smiled again. The smile said:

"I'm taking from you, I'm violating your space, and I'm going to get away with it. I'm even going to make you look like the villain."

This second, mocking smile set something off deep within Magdalena. All the fear and panic and helplessness distributed throughout her body gathered up into a ball, like so much yarn. It then spun itself into steel and copper and iron cables. The cables twisted around themselves and became circuits, which connected themselves into her nervous system. A transmitter had assembled itself in her mind. All that was left was to turn it on.

Magdalena thought:

"Fuck this guy."

And then, she flipped the transmitter switch to 'on'.

The volume of the outside world fell away in her ears, replaced by only a single, deafening drone. She knew she was the only one who could hear it on the bus, but somehow, she knew that there was one other who'd be able to hear it as well. Hopefully, he'd be able to respond.

The sound was the angry, robotic, and vibrato hum of one very pissed and very stressed queen bee.

In a secure hospital room hundreds of miles away in Boston, David Keating's eyes popped open. He sat up in his bed. Nurses, doctors, and two FBI agents ping-ponged around the room, frantically making calls on cell phones, alerting other hospital staff, and preparing emergency treatment.

He spoke. And after he spoke, his eyes closed, and he fell unconscious once more.

"Show him what it's like to be you," was all he said.

CRUCIBLE took note of this event as well, as they monitored both Dr. Keating in Boston, and the focal point of his alpha wave transmission, a few hundred miles to the South…

With her right arm, Magdalena calmly and deliberately brought her right hand up and gently covered Scumbag's – the one that pinned her head against the window. She did not grasp or hold his hand. She made as much contact with her palm on the back of his hand as she could.

And once she had achieved enough skin-to-skin contact to enter his mind, her anger, silent and cold, took over. Her eyes rolled to the whites. Scumbag noticed this but had no time to react. Even if did have a second to pull his hand away, he wouldn't have been able to regardless.

The outside world vanished from Magdalena's sight. It was replaced with an image that snapped into focus, like a television set had been turned on. There, in her mind's eyewas a skyscraper. It was like any other one would find in any major city, except there were only doors, countless doors where all the windows should have been. They were numbered beyond counting. And the skyscraper was a bright, magnificent silver. Not stone, or brick, or other conventional building material. Beautiful…unmarred…smooth…silver.

Each door looked as if it were made of some black, alien metal, and upon each was a cartoonish, shiny red doorknob. The building itself stretched upwards into infinity, level upon level. And, on each level it was nothing but these surreal-looking portals, one after another in horizontal succession.

As she watched, one door would open, stayed open for a moment, and then closed. Another door would open at the exact same time one closed, so that one door was always open. From inside the building, a white, uniform light shone from within.

Magdalena considered this structure for a second and knew almost immediately what the building and its doors symbolized.

The building was Scumbag's mind, a representation of his conscious train of thought. The doors were possible points of interaction with the outside world, and whichever one was ajar was his mind's point of focus.

Magdalena briefly thought of what her "skyscraper" must look like. It probably had multiple doors open all over the place, with no rhythm or reason to its operations. Opening at random, closing at random, any number of doors open at once.

Keating had said 'show him what it's like to be you'. She thought, no. That wouldn't be enough. She would show him what it was like to be her, *times a thousand*.

So she did. Magdalena, with a simple exertion of will, opened all of the doors in his 'skyscraper' at once.

Magdalena inserted herself through every portal - and found herself able to control and manipulate every neuron, every synapse, and every gland in his mind like they all were her own. She began to drain from them, pulling, *withdrawing* from each like a syringe.

In the 'real' world, Scumbag stopped wrestling with her at once and became still. His eyes rolled in their sockets to the whites as well. He began to mumble but could only muster feeble vowel sounds. Words formed after a few seconds.

"I'll have the turkey club please, ma'am," he said.

At that moment, clear fluid began spitting from his ears. Then yellowish, then pink. Then rivulets, then like a weak tap, and then - like unrefined syrup, leaking out of a maple tree.

Scumbag's hand slipped out from between Magdalena's face and hand. He dropped her medications onto the ground with the other.

Magdalena slipped back into reality and saw what she had wrought. Magdalena smiled.

He stuck his left index finger up after dropping the pills on the ground, as if asking her for a minute to gather himself. Or, alternatively, to insist upon the turkey club he'd just ordered. He held it aloft for a second, then took the finger and pushed it into his right eye. He did not stop, even after the orb had popped, until he reached the back of the socket. He began to wriggle it around, as if he were trying to dig the last bits of peanut butter out of a jar.

"This eye is really iittttttttcheeeeee" Scumbag said and began to mindlessly giggle.

Across the aisle, a half-drunk middle-aged woman watched with horror as Scumbag performed his crude strabotomy with an index finger. After a few more seconds, he managed to dig out all that pesky, itchy eyeball. The woman then promptly stood up and let out a piercing, sustained wail. The shriek alerted the rest of the passengers on the bus to the abject horror occurring across from her.

The bus at last came to a stop on the highway shoulder, which jolted Magdalena out of the joyful schadenfreude she experienced in watching her attacker (a) lose control of his mind, and (b) blind himself in one eye. The bus erupted into complete chaos. This was in no way part of the plan, and it certainly was an untenable situation. Magdalena knew at that second she had to disappear - and disappear quickly.

She looked over the seat and saw the bus driver speaking frantically into a cell phone. She stuffed everything she could into her bag. She stood up. She stepped deftly around Scumbag seated next to her and into the aisle.

"Heeyyyyyyy….what about my sandwich," he protested, like a hippie at a music festival who'd been passed over for his turn on the joint being smoked. Magdalena made for the front of the bus.

She only had to negotiate a couple of rows before she was at the very front. The bus driver had his back turned for the moment. It was her chance to get off unscathed. The doors, down a couple of stairs to her right, were closed. Magdalena quickly scanned the bus driver's controls, and easily found the 'door open/close' button. It could not have been marked more clearly.

Bus driving school must be super easy, thought Magdalena.

She pushed the button, and the doors flipped open. She made her move and bolted for the outside. There was no time to worry whether the driver in the ridiculous uniform would have reflexes quick enough to close them again before she made the doors. Magdalena got to the first step of the stairs, and jumped…

"Well, I guess it all kinda worked out," Sarah said out loud while she idly played a cell phone game, "Merge Dragons". The game was her go-to stalling tactic for just about anything she didn't want to do, at least immediately.

She put the game down a second later and began to do half-drunk logistics in her head. This was a slightly more productive use of her time. In the background, the **"Alpha Waves/EEG"** recording played. Sarah had stopped paying attention quite a while before her procrastination began in earnest.

If it Magdalena took fifteen minutes to get her shit together from when they'd just hung up with each other (actually, Sarah had just hung up on Magdalena, no mutual farewell at all), and then another forty, fifty to get from the hotel they'd stashed her at in Southie to her place in Somerville, that left her about an hour or so to get through the rest of the tapes.

Caleb had advised Sarah - bullied, more like - into making sure Sarah reviewed everything they had on video, and then to destroy whatever could be used to recreate their work. It didn't look as if she'd be able to get through them all, but most of them were just observations of Keating as he progressed through his metamorphosis into whatever he was anyway. Sarah put her phone down and grabbed tapes four through seven and put them next to **RECOVERY** on her bed.

As far Magdalena's knowledge, who gave a shit? thought Sarah.

She laughed at loud at this notion. Fuck the blue-haired girl from Miami. Or Tampa. Wherever. Sarah had told her all about the experiment the day she arrived, at least the parts Mags needed to know. How could she not at least

give her some iota of what she, Caleb, and Keating had been up to? Sarah had thought then, before Magdalena had even shown up, then that somehow Keating had been keeping something from them all along, something other than that initial dosing. And after Sarah had given her the rundown, the dumbed-down version, Magdalena had very emphatically stated the only thing that she knew was that Keating had 'touched' her somehow. At that moment, Sarah had regretted the decision to let her in on a few of their secrets almost immediately.

She mused that it was a miracle that Mags had sat tight and maintained radio silence up until today. That woman didn't have to wait around any longer though – she'd made it clear she wanted to see what happened the day of the accident on their end, so to speak. And Magdalena had probably concluded that Sarah (and by extension, Caleb) planned on keeping the exact details of that final day from her. Magdalena was correct on that score and knowing that made Sarah dislike her even more than she already had.

It was also safe to say that Sarah didn't like Magdalena from the second they'd met. But in one sense, Sarah did feel a certain kinship with Magdalena - they'd both been dragged into the machinations of the same idiot men. Didn't matter how many degrees Caleb and Keating had – they were still blinded by glory, advancement, all that macho bullshit.

Sarah felt obligated to Keating because he'd given her a lifeline from her failed medical career into pure biomedical research…his research. That's where it ended for Sarah. She wondered what it was that roped Magdalena in. It couldn't have just been the 'vision', as Magdalena had described her experience.

Sarah glanced back to the television. Fucking telepathy. That's what she'd decided to write on the label, except…was it really telepathy? ESP? Or, as Caleb and Keating had put it at one point - the next stage in human evolution? Fucking guy thought he'd become Professor X. Instead, he'd become a vegetable, as far as she knew. This wasn't the goddamn X-Men. Sarah paid attention to the recording again.

Alpha Wave Measurements/EEG (November 2nd, 2022) (VCR Analog Recording 3):

Keating is alone at this part of the recording.

There is no sign of Sarah, nor Caleb.

He is sitting comfortably in a chair, with a number of electrodes and wires running from a black headband wrapped around his forehead. The headband is wired to a grey, primitive-looking machine perched close by on a table next to him. The machine has several switches, dials, and commensurate readouts for all upon its face. It looks more like something out of a cautionary electric safety video rather than a sophisticated piece of equipment.

"I've given Caleb and Sarah the next few days off so that they can gather themselves for the extensive work we have ahead of us. They've been outstanding…both of them. None of this is even remotely possible without being able to produce three kilograms of purified operamine to work with as well as the surgical skills displayed during the operation…" Keating shakes his head in disbelief.

"I'm truly lucky to have them." Keating looks into the camera, knowing that Caleb and Sarah would eventually watch the video. He gives the camera a look of genuine appreciation, even affection. One can tell immediately that expressing that emotion is something new to Keating, as his features look unsure, even in their softness.

"Anyway," he says, "no time like the present. Let's see what the EEG has to say about my so-called telepathy."

Keating flips a couple of switches on the outdated, but since-identified EEG machine to his left. A soft, regular beeping sound begins emanating from the machine, as well as a glowing pulse on one of the digital displays that read his real-time brainwave patterns. The machine he uses is now painfully obsolete to the viewer, regardless of their knowledge of what's used in hospitals in 2022.

Keating reaches over and grabs a small remote with his left hand. It's the camera remote – Keating zooms in with the camera lens to close-up of his face. The lens moves to the left, over from Keating and to the front panel of the EEG. It focuses in, until there's nothing on-screen except for the single digital pulse of light bouncing its way from one side of the screen to the other. Nothing appears to be out of the ordinary, except for the frequency of the pulses, which Keating points out.

"The average frequency of the human alpha wave is around 10 hertz. That of the honeybee is 18 hertz. Caleb had begun to go into more detail on that regard during the surgery but was cut off by Sarah. She was right to do so – but back then, I had no regard for the appropriate and the inappropriate, as I do now."

"As you can see from the readout, my measured alpha wave output has normalized at 14 hertz. The collected data from this machine will of course be published with the rest of the findings, but this data point is the clearest, simplest, and most reproducible as evidence that the most basic functionality of my brain has been fundamentally altered. Undoubtedly, there will be those who doubt, even dismiss outright the visual evidence of induced telepathy and even ESP in the two previous recordings."

Keating closes his eyes.

"Colleagues, whether you believe it or not, I have acquired a kind of sixth sense. I can reach out to those individuals who are thinking of me or have me in their thoughts. They make themselves "open" to me when they meet that pre-condition. Now, I will show you how further treatment with operamine and exercises on my behalf have further expanded this ability."

Keating inhales, then exhales, as if meditating. He appears to concentrate, as the circular shapes of his pupils can be seen darting back and forth underneath the eyelids. The overhead lights and lamp begin to flicker on and off, and then shut off altogether. The only thing left illuminating the recording is the EEG display. The beeping noise emanating from the device speeds. The waveform on the display tightens.

Keating speaks again, only what emerges from the darkened screen is no longer his normal voice. It sounds as if there are multiple voices speaking all as one...but in lower pitches. It is hostile sounding, regardless of whether the message was threatening or not. The voices sound similar to a drone.

"I have even been able to interact with nearby electric currents and circuits in such a way that I am able to affect the energy itself…to reduce or increase the amount of voltage present in the source. I have yet been able to engineer a solid, quantifiable, and reproducible test for that."

Sarah laughed out loud. While the first part of this segment played, she downed another small shot, just to maintain. Her metabolism processed ethanol like it was nobody's business, and Sarah had already started feeling the effects of a hangover start to build. Once she'd finished the top-up, she thought:

How the hell would you were going to measure how much you could fuck with mother nature with just your mind, David? Hold up a blacklight lamp so maybe they could see David's magic electric mind waves?

The Keating-drone begins to speak again, in that unholy cacophony of darkened voices - one on top of each other.

"The accompanying increase in frequency of recorded alpha waves – now at approximately 53 hertz, obviously cannot be used to provide proof of the existence of a 'controlling force' emanating within my mind; this is coincidental evidence. It *is*, however," The voices drop even lower, sounding like so many demons broadcasting straight from the seventh layer of the abyss.

"QUITE COMPELLING."

This last statement seems unintentionally ironic as within less than a second, the frequency of beeping on the EEG slows down, the digital read-out spreads out, Keating opens his eyes, and the lights in the room turn back on. Watching it unfold is disorienting to the viewer.

The tape ends.

Sarah made no attempt to get up and shut off the tape. She had to really think then – or at least attempt to think. Sarah needed silence when she really needed to plan, even while sober. With nothing left on the "alpha waves" tape to show, no sound came from television, only static on the screen. Sarah closed her eyes.

Would two through seven be enough for Moretti? Probably not. So far she'd already smashed the operation video. Moretti would ask for it and she was going to have to say she had no idea what happened to it. No way he'd buy He'd know that she'd destroyed it.

So she had to give him something worthwhile, otherwise she thought she may actually be looking at jail time. Obstruction of justice, or whatever that was called.

And somehow, she knew that CRUCIBLE would not be there, nor even care to rescue her or bail her out from Moretti's authority.

She knew then that one of the videos had to be of the final day - the day of the explosions and the deaths, the fire, and the chaos. The eighth and final tape.

Her pulse began to race.

And whenever she thought of that day, the final day of the experiment, and to the human toll that the experiment ended up exacting, she became paralyzed with fear, guilt, and unmitigated panic. It felt as if an entire planet had somehow fallen to earth and crushed you where you stood.

Sarah unconsciously began to sweat. In that moment of pure dread and fright felt in equal and awful measures, Sarah re-discovered that she'd so deeply wished to never have to watch the tape marked "The Final Day" ever again. She began to debate destroying the tape before Magdalena could show up to say otherwise. She began to debate destroying the tape, to hell with whatever consequences or punishment Moretti could heap upon her.

Sarah began to weep.

It had been a full two days since the encounter on the Greyhound bus. During that time, Magdalena had only been able to utilize the single mode of travel that remained at her disposal to press on in her northward journey: hitchhiking.

And in that span of forty-eight disheartening, cold, sometimes light, sometimes dark hours, she met with predictably horrid results. Which, she supposed, was pretty much all she could hope for. Maybe even deserved. Scumbag was an addict, just trying to get high. Magdalena had turned him into a one-eyed moron for his troubles.

Thus, on top of the anxiety of relying on a mode of transportation that ceased being remotely pragmatic for decades, Magdalena carried with her the guilt of taking retaliation much too far with her attacker on the bus.

She worried about what could happen were she to catch a ride with an individual who had far more sinister and violent purposes in mind.

But she worried not for herself. She worried for whomever would attempt something more injurious than ripping her off for a few prescription pills out of her backpack.

Magdalena considered that possibility, and then thought:

Maybe they'd deserve what they *got.*

The very notion of hitchhiking became obsolete the instant one ahead-of-the-curve psychopath made the realization that hitchhikers were all essentially pre-disappeared potential victims. And yet, here Magdalena was, rolling the dice every time she stuck her thumb out.

Did she fucking want someone to die?

Physical and psychic violence notwithstanding, there was also the matter of state and local authorities potentially being on the lookout for a tattooed, pierced, blue-haired woman (kinda hard to miss) that may or may not have convinced a meth-head to scoop out one of his eyes with his own index finger.

Every second Magdalena spent walking alongside the road, a psychic timebomb disguised as easy prey, she felt as if she'd collapse to her knees and simply give up under the weight of it all.

And yet, Magdalena did no such thing.

Despite catching only one ride in those forty-eight hours, that took her only a half-hour drive further north. She'd walked nearly as far since leaping from the Greyhound bus doors onto the highway.

She simply just kept going.

Two days earlier, when she'd leapt from the bus like an drunken Wonder Woman, she was fortunate to hit grass in the most awkward way possible, instead of pavement. That it was grass, a patch on the forgiving side as well, was sheer luck - if it had been pavement there to break her fall, she'd have easily broken a bone or two. Her journey into Mordor, i.e., Massachusetts, would have ended on the side of an interstate somewhere in South Carolina.

Also fortuitous was a nearby tree line, that consisted mostly of conifers still green and still able to provide cover into which she could disappear. Once she gathered enough of herself to be able to stand upright, Magdalena bolted for the woods.

Odd: as she ran for those trees, she was certain the bus driver never yelled after her, or even called for her to stop.

Magdalena's brief run of good bounces ended after finding a connecting road, not one of the lesser-traveled, backwoods kind, but one that did see some regular traffic, after only a couple of miles straight into that wooded area. Magdalena followed that to a connecting state highway. The state highway even ran North-South. At least then it had seemed that the gods were acting directly in her favor.

After three hours of walking, Magdalena's hitchhiking began at the same as when her feet began to ache. A Honda Civic pulled over not more than ten minutes after she'd stuck her thumb out to the road for the first time in her life.

That first ride she hitched — the only ride she'd taken since she'd broken Scumbag's brain so thoroughly so as to induce self-inflicted eye-gouging - was with an overweight line cook from Bradenton, Florida named Vic.

He pulled over to the side of the road just ahead of Magdalena and yelled back to her from his drivers' side window. He offered her a ride before she'd really committed to the whole "catching rides with strangers who could be complete psychopaths" approach to getting North.

Vic seemed harmless enough at the start, but then again, all psychopaths probably at least project benevolence at first. It's not like maniacs walked around with a sign around their neck or a drove a car with a bumper sticker that said: "I'm going to either kill or rape you the first chance I get", regardless of how helpful either would have proven to be for the would-be passenger slash victim.

But it took Vic just twenty minutes before he became interested in other, more intimate forms of payment, when signs started appearing for the North Carolina border.

"How far were you planning on riding with me, angel," said Vic, trying to sound suave and instead coming off like a higher-pitched, non-cartoonish, and evil version of Quagmire from the cartoon *Family Guy*. He might as well have been screaming to the entire world 'hard-up horny asshole through a loudspeaker here'

"I know you said you were going up to New England, but heh, I ain't going that far."

Magdalena sensed trouble immediately, and that sense had nothing to do with any *Scanners*-like powers Keating might have bestowed upon her.

"You know, you can actually drop me at this next exit. Think I'm gonna rest here for the night. Gotta be a hotel or something near the offramp."

Vic, who had been slouching in the driver's seat, sat up at attention at Magdalena's ultimatum. He knew that whatever he was going to try, he was going to have to try it in the next few minutes.

"Honey, if you really need a ride right to New England and don't wanna get back out on the road like I found y'all, there's probably something we can arrange between us to get you all the way there…"

And then Vic put his hand right into Magdalena's crotch.

The high-alert state hadn't nearly subsided from that morning, so Magdalena formulated an escape within an instant.

Vic drove a stick shift. Magdalena spotted it as Vic's fingers began to spread across the breadth of her genitals. Because the prick had leaned over so far to his left to get a handful of the good stuff so quickly, he was in no position to be able to even come close to stopping her if she made for the stick.

There would be no repeat of the Greyhound bus, at least this time. All that it would take to dispose of Vic TinyDick was jacking his late model Civic into park, fucking the vehicle's transmission way up and causing the vehicle to first make an unbearably painful squealing sound, followed by its engine stuttering to a complete stop.

It was a good thing fuckface drove a late model. If it had been a newer car, Magdalena knew she wouldn't have been able to jam his shitboxes' transmission into park. She also thought, *fucking his car up isn't enough of comeuppance for him. Think I've got something extra for him.*

Maybe they'd deserved what they got.

"Vic, I'm so glad I dated a mechanic in my twenties. Now that dude could fuck," she said aloud just before she thrust her left elbow dead into the soft spot of his right temple.

The elbow stunned Vic into a half-concussed stupor instantaneously. Magdalena used every ounce of her strength to then slam the stick from fourth gear into park.

Cue horrible noise.

Cue Honda Civic stuttering to a full stop.

Vic couldn't even try to chase her. She was gone from his sight before he could recoup his senses.

Magdalena ran flat to the next off-ramp, down it, and listened for his ruined transmission to rankle by to be sure that she was safe.

Magdalena kept going. She made her way back onto another state road, this time in North Carolina, and pressed on. She'd been pushed into her very own berserker-like mode.

Which was nothing more than a distant memory as of the morning of November 18th. It had been seventy-two hours since the vision.

Magdalena had just about lost hope of getting to Boston in time to do much of anything for Keating. She'd almost given up even making it to Boston.

Lost somewhere still south of the Mason-Dixon line, it looked as if it was time to contact Amy.

Time for the rescue.

Hateful thought.

As Magdalena pulled out her cell phone and started dialing her sister, an almost decrepit station wagon pulled up alongside her and stopped. The thing was so old, its oddly-shaped, oversized, and sickly green-colored relic bore that iconic, cheesy not-wood wood paneling. The stuff that adorned the side doors and rear of seemingly every station wagon made prior to 1987. How this thing could possibly still be running…

Magdalena prepared herself for the next interstate villain, making sure she was ready for anything, until one of the passenger-side rolled down (manually) and the man driving the car yelled for her to jump into the backseat.

Despite all that had happened the past few days, she did as she was bade. There was something…innocent about all of this.

And that is when Magdalena Christie met Sam and Roger Melanson.

Magdalena strode towards the vehicle, and the man driving chirped another friendly imperative.

"You mind hopping in the backseat? Sam's the one that wanted some road trip company."

She opened the door and hopped in, seeing a child strapped into a car seat on the opposite side.

He was a boy of no more than ten or eleven, but it was clear at first regard that he'd been born with a more severe form of autism. The boy's left hand was opened flat and pressed so firmly into his forehead at the wrist that it was painful for Magdalena even to watch. The fingers on the hand were all cocked in different directions, as if each were trying to escape from the hand itself and shoot off into the night. At once, she realized that the boy appeared to be hiding his face from her, wearing a face that was equal parts pain, shyness, and glee. His legs were kicking incessantly, back and forth with no discernable pattern or rhythm, in circles and back and forth.

Magdalena looked to the driver. He was a hopelessly average looking man in his mid-forties, brown hair neatly parted to one side and wearing a very mild-mannered yet appealing cashmere sweater. He turned, and nervously smiled.

Magdalena found herself wishing this man was a lost uncle or at least relative. The first set of wrinkles on his face spoke of both unceasing kindness…and unimaginable sadness as well.

He said to her:

"You're not going to rob us, are you? I'll have to warn you then, if you do try any funny business, Sam here might get very upset with you," and nodded to his charge in
the backseat. There was an awkward moment of silence, before both he and Magdalena shared a laugh.

And then Magdalena broke. It was ten full minutes of sobbing. Neither Roger nor Sam said a word, only waited. When Magdalena quieted, she heard the kindness she'd seen on the man's face in his next words.

"Looks like Sam and I are taking you right to wherever you need to be, young lady. Right Sam?"

Sam's head jerked up and down in agreement.

"Came just in time…?"

"Oh, it's uh…sorry. Magdalena. Magdalena Christie."

"Magdalena? Whoa. That's a beautiful name. I'm Roger Melanson. And that dangerous looking hombre to your left is Sam, obviously. Say hi, Sam!"

Sam did not alter his position or facial expression. He remained in full grin mode.

Roger's good-natured countenance disappeared. It was replaced by the look of a man profoundly saddened and weary.

"He's non-verbal, but Sam does say hi though."

Magdalena felt two things in that moment: first that she'd be completely safe with Roger and Sam, and second filled with sympathy and compassion for Sam, and admiration for his father who was still managing a robust kindness for the less fortunate and a positive attitude, even if it seemed to hurt him just a little bit more every time he mustered it.

"I'm on a sacred quest to rescue a trapped prince from an evil wizard." Roger's pained face flipped yet again, buoyed by Magdalena's charm.

"Did you hear that, Sam? We have an actual knight in the car! Well met m'lady, let us ferry you on your way!" Roger turned back to face front and stepped on the gas to get them on their way.

Roger and Magdalena shared good conversation for the next several hours together, never forced, never awkward. Roger and Sam were on their way to New York to Roger's sister's place. His wife was no longer in the picture, but he was very clear that he had no interest in any kind of new relationship, let alone a hook-up. His life was all about Sam now, and he was happy with what he had.

Sam's disability required Roger's full-time attention. Diagnosed at 3, his outward symptoms had already progressed to where it was clear that he'd never be able to live without the care of an adult or a professional. Sam had never spoken outside of guttural sounds and moans, typically to indicate that he was either hungry, uncomfortable, or had gone to the bathroom.

"But he's my son, Magdalena. And he always is going to be my son, as long as I'm still kicking. So what about you? Are you really on a quest to save a prince?"

Magdalena considered how much of her story to tell her new friend and at that moment decided upon the not inaccurate 'being called to University to help with some advanced research'.

"You must be some kind of academic all-star then Magdalena. Me? Could never understand a lick of science. Accounting was and is my game. I know, exciting. But the stuff they're doing now? Fascinates the hell out of me. Especially the research that's going into…" he trailed off.

"Neurodivergence? Autism?"

"Yeah, Magdalena. That," Roger laughed, but it was the kind one lets out to cover up sadness. Loneliness."

"Call me Mags, Roger."

"Alright, then." Roger gave a look to Magdalena from over his shoulder. Loneliness erased.

"Roger, just between us, I'm on the spectrum too. I don't even like saying that when I'm sitting here, but I got the Type I ASD label about ten years ago. That, and ADHD, and a couple of other things."

Magdalena saw Roger's face in the rearview mirror soften and fill with empathy.

"It's hard, isn't it Mags?"

"Yes, Roger, it is. For all of us. Not just the ones with the diagnosis, either. My sister Amy's been a bit of a caretaker for me over the years."

"Live together?"

"Yep. Outside of Tampa."

"You're a long way from home, Mags."

"So are you two, mister."

Shared laughter at that moment, but a shared loneliness. Some feelings just couldn't be escaped at certain moments."

After a bit, Roger told Magdalena to get some rest, and that he'd let her know when they'd crossed over into New York state. She looked over to her right, and Sam was already snoring away in his chair. He was a beautiful child, but even more so at peace and asleep; his face a pale pinkish color in the streetlamp lights that came in through his window. Magdalena put her backpack in between her and the window and rested her head against it. She fell asleep the second her cheek contacted her backpack.

She was met with total darkness, again. Keating was not there in that space. This was not the same as that…nothing place he'd brought her. Magdalena knew he wouldn't be here, and that was okay. More than okay. She needed real, restful sleep, so Keating's not being there was welcome. She knew that outside, in the waking world, she was as safe as houses with Roger and -

Wait. She wasn't alone. From somewhere close there was the sound of a child, sobbing. It was Sam. How could Sam be in here…with her?

He was easy to find. Any person that possessed any fragment of empathy, no matter how small, would have been able to find him.

He was sitting, lotus-style, with his head tilted downward. Gone was his frozen-in-place bashful pose, instead, his arms and hands hung down at his sides.

Magdalena approached him.

"Sam?" she asked.

He looked up at her, shocked that a person was there with him. And then - he looked surprised that he felt…shocked about anything.

"Magda….Magda…." Sam was speaking but couldn't sound out her full name.

She stopped him.

"That's okay Sam. You can call me Mags. Only my best friends get to call me that."

Sam glowed. "Mags. Why are we here?"

"I think it's because we're special, Sam. This is our space. Only we get to come here. Only…some of us, some part of us…gets trapped here somehow."

"I – this part of me – it can't leave. I don't know how to. Where's my Daddy?"

Magdalena knew that Sam - this part of him, anyway, had been trapped here. For his whole life. Was it possible that she could she bring him with her? Pull this part of Sam back into the real world?

She sure as hell was going to try.

"I think I know. But you'll have to be brave, Sam. You'll have to come with me, Sam. Do you trust me?"

Sam lifted his arms, wanting to be picked up.

That was a definite yes. Magdalena picked the boy up, who clung to her in that special way a child does with a trusted adult.

"C'mon Sam. This place is special, but you shouldn't stay here all the time. There's a darker version of this world. And that's where my friend is. He…"

Sam finished her sentence.

"He calls it *das Nichtvorhandensein*. It's not darkness, like here. It's nothing. Shadows of shadows. Absence. "

Magdalena was stunned. How could Sam…unless…

Magdalena realized in that moment that whatever Keating had

done to her, she had just done to Sam. But Sam had reached through her, into him. They were becoming…

No time for that now though. Magdalena held Sam tight, and awoke – both herself, and the boy in her arms.

Magdalena felt the station wagon pull to a stop, and heard Roger say "New York, New York!" and get out of the car. She lifted her head from her makeshift pillow. She heard the door next to Sam open, and then a shocked gasp came from Roger's mouth.

"Oh my God….Sam? SAM!!!" Roger exclaimed.

Magdalena opened her eyes and looked over to her left.

The first thing she noticed was that Sam was holding three of the fingers on her right hand. His legs were moving, but only just - nothing out of the ordinary for a kid his age who was simply just antsy to get out of the backseat.

But then Magdalena looked at Sam's face. It was this face that struck her most of all. His attention was towards his father, at whom he looked intently.

Sam said, "Hi Daddy. Do you know my friend Mags?" Magdalena felt Sam squeeze her fingers. There was pure, unconditional, and eternal love in that squeeze.

Roger looked past his son to her, dumbfounded.

"What...did…."

Magdalena said: "I thought I'd make things a little less hard for you guys, I guess. Good people deserve good things, every so often I guess."

Roger's eyes swelled, and then tears streamed in rivers from both eyes. His face turned a soaring red. A minute passed in silence, until finally, Sam said:

"Daddy, I'm hungry."

Roger could not restrain himself another second.

"MY BOY!!!!!!!!" he cried, and pulled his son from his seat, clutched his body against him. He spun and twirled around in circles as if his son had been missing for years and had been returned to him.

In a way, that statement wasn't entirely untrue.

Magdalena watched the two of them and had never been happier in that moment in her entire life.

She sighed.

"This is already the craziest couple of days of my life," she thought, and felt fear and anxiety and hope and wonder.

What could possibly come next?

"Are you sure about this Mags?" asked Roger. They'd just crossed the border from Rhode Island into Massachusetts on I-95, and like any good father, he didn't know how to shut off his paternal instincts for anyone he cared about. Since the miracle that had occurred in New York the day before, Magdalena Christie became the second most important person in the world to Roger after Sam.

"You don't know these two people at all. What if they throw you out on your ear? Call the cops, or the feds, or....heaven forbid...Mulder and Scully?" He said the words Mulder and Scully with a faux scary-dramatic voice. Also like a good father, he couldn't help himself from inserting a dad joke into every third or fourth sentence.

"Mulder and Scully are going to get you Mags!" joked Sam. Sam had no idea who Mulder or Scully were.

Magdalena looked over at her new buddy and made a face, squinting her eyes and sticking out her tongue. Sam duplicated the face perfectly. They were already thicker than thieves, as the saying goes.

The night before, and immediately after the full hour Roger spent engaged in the first real conversation he'd ever had with his son, Roger managed to divert his attention enough to consider his miracle passenger.

"Not that I'm not eternally grateful, Mags. Even if this wears off in the next ten minutes and Sam goes back to...well, where he was before you two nodded off and met in magic land...but what in God's name did you just do?"

"I found him in the dark...I think."

"Okay, you're gonna have to give me way more than 'I found him in the dark'. Why don't we go get some Burger King and you can tell me over a chicken sandwich?"

"Jesus. Does it have to be Burger King, Roger?"

Roger simply nodded towards Sam, whose eyes had lit up like spotlights.

"Like I said, as long as its Burger King," smiled Magdalena.

The next roadside Burger King and rest area was only a couple of miles down the road. The three travelers found themselves an isolated booth in the corner of the restaurant and hunkered down over their burgers, chicken sandwiches, fries, diet sodas, and chocolate milkshake.

"Okay, Mags. You're more than an academic all-star, obviously. Gimme the full story, not the edited for television version.

Magdalena dropped everything that had happened in the four days since the fifteenth – even the past couple of days with what happened on the Greyhound, to her forty-five minutes with Vic, walking for what felt like forever…to at last meeting Roger and Sam. She worried Sam hearing the part of the story on the Greyhound bus wherein she had psychically destroyed her assailant but Sam was far too concerned with his French fries than anything she had to say at the time.

And surprisingly, Roger seemed unperturbed about that event, instead appearing far more concerned about the endpoint of her journey than anything that had came before the present.

There was a moment of silence as Roger thought about her tale. He sighed, like a father is wont to do when a child lays some heavy, personal news out. He took one last bite of his Whopper with cheese. Roger sighed again.

"I don't know why I order these fucking things."

Sam chirped in.

"Swear jar, Dad!"

"Yup, when we get home kid," Roger didn't take his eyes off of Magdalena.

"They're no good for me but be damned if I can't get enough of whatever that secret sauce is that they put on them. This place - these people that you're going to see? I'm thinking they're kinda like your Whopper right now."

"Rog, that's a terrible metaphor."

He laughed. Genuine, earnest laughter.

"Oh we're on Rog now, eh? Just so. You know, I used to be a writer. Long time ago."

"What happened?"

"Got married to a bitch, it turns out,"

More laughter.

"I was good at metaphors, but apparently, I've gotten a bit rusty. Still, though, Mags. Think you should forget all about these David Keating, Caleb West, and Sarah Fischer characters. I know it seems like this what you should be doing, but I think…" Roger paused.

"What do you think, Rog?"

"I think….that you should let me put you on the next plane back to Florida and forget all about this experiment and whatever it's done to you – and Sam. Whatever experiments he was doing that blew up half of a university campus and somehow turned him into Scanners meets Professor X. How the hell did you even know this guy, anyway?"

"I don't...well, not really. I know him from..."

"Oh, good lord, Mags. Social media?"

"Yeah. Group for neurodivergent people. ASD, ADHD, that sort of thing."

"So that's it then. The connection. Ties that bind, as it were."

"Neurological makeup?"

"Yeah, that's it. Keating's done something to himself that...fixes, or upgrades, or whatevers people with that kind of makeup. To the rest of us..."

"We blow yo' damn minds?" Magdalena smiled, and deviously at that.

Roger did not return the smile this time.

"Mags, this is dangerous. *VERY* dangerous. What happens if the wrong person gets a Mags and Sam upgrade?"

"Keating's in real trouble, Roger. If it's not for him, Sam...me...? We're the same as we were before. I have to do something. And..."

"And what Mags?"

"I don't think anyone else can."

"Because he connected with you."

"Yes."

"There's still more to it, Mags. There is literally hundreds of thousands of people that were between you and him that would be considered atypical as far their neurological makeup, as you put it, that could have sufficed. He's got an emotional connection to you."

"You think he's...."

"Boy's in love Mags. Picked you over all others 'cos he sees something in you that only people in that state of mind ever do."

"Which is?"

"You're his heroine, Mags. Looks like I wasn't too far off when I said knight in shining armor,"

Magdalena had never considered that Keating had caught feelings for her at some point down the line, during their social media relationship. She spoke to a ton of people online - but none of them identified themselves as scientists working on turning themselves into cosmic autistic radio transmitters.

Magdalena finished her diet coke, reaching the end of the beverage and making that horrible wet vacuuming sound as she did so.

Sam pawed at the cup - a gesture meant to get her stop immediately. Definitely still an auditory thing there.

"Okay, well, I'd be a complete jerk if I didn't help you, Mags. I have NO idea what's happening, but this quest of yours just became our quest. If you'll have us."

"Are you kidding? Of course."

"Sam?"

"Rescue the prince. Sure."

Roger gathered up their refuse onto a single tray and stood up.

"We need some more information though. Sam and I had an appointment with his specialist tomorrow anyway - we're gonna have to bump that up to tomorrow a.m. Maybe I'll have Sam call…We should find out *exactly* how Sam here has changed. While we're doing that, you're going to find out all you can about Caleb West and Sarah Fischer - his assistants. They're the ones you're going to meet, right?"

"Yeah."

"Mags those two might be in jail when you - when we get there. If they are, we're gonna have to reassess what the next move is. Sound good?"

Magdalena and Sam both nodded in approval.

Magdalena snapped out of her memory.

They'd arrived at Gordon University.

Magdalena had made it to the site of the explosion. Where it started. At last.

They sat in the visitor's parking lot at the university. A full six days after the explosion, the campus was still in disarray. It was late afternoon, and despite the time of day, there was still the odd news van here and there reporting on the aftermath of the previous Tuesday's events. There was a state police presence as well, not a lot, but enough to put Roger and Magdalena on edge.

Magdalena stated the obvious.

"This is a horrible fucking idea."

"Don't say I didn't warn you Mags. You know what you're doing?"

"I think so. They're in a building called Monarch Hall, second floor. West and Fischer share an office there."

"Alright. Remember, if anything goes south, just leave. This is a public institution, and there's plenty of people around. Just walk away. Sam and I will be here, and you just come back. We'll get out of here, and then we go from there. Otherwise, just shoot me a text and let us know that you're good. Okay?"

"Roger -we're pretty much the same age. You don't have to-"

"Treat you like you're my daughter? Fatherly instinct. I can't do protective without sounding paternal. I hope I'm not being douchey when I do it?"

"No, Rog. I don't even know why I said it. My pops…"

"Sucked? So did mine. Good luck, Magdalena Christie." Roger turned around and stuck out his hand. Magdalena took it.
Sam grabbed the right sleeve of her jacket. His face was already set to "don't go", and the setting was dialed up to eleven.

"Sam, I have to help the man who helped me - and you. I promise I'll be okay."

Sam seemed to acknowledge that in a way, it was important to let her go, even though he didn't want to.

At all.

"Hurry up. We have to play with my toys. Me." Sam let go of her sleeve. "And you."

Magdalena got out of the car and headed off to find Caleb and Sarah.

According to the research she'd done online about Gordon, Caleb West and Sarah Fischer's office was the only one to be found in Monarch. Apparently, both floors were populated with empty classrooms and lecture halls, utility closets, and bulletin boards detailing various events and groups on campus. But, on the C-G University webpage, West and Fischer's shared office was on the second floor. On paper, or computer screen, it was almost as if they'd been exiled to that building.

Magdalena wandered around the first floor looking for any signs of life, but there were none. Not a soul…until she turned one last corner - one that led to a stairwell that led to the second floor. Magdalena nearly collided straight on with another gentleman coming the opposite way. She barely glanced at him, but he was older, mid-fifties it seemed. Probably another professor coming back from visiting West and Fischer.

"Whoa there - pardon me," he said.

"Sorry," she said, keeping her head down. The less attention she got, and the fewer people who saw her, the better she presumed. She kept moving, to the stairwell and up to the second floor.

She could feel the man's eyes on her as she strode away. She did not turn around.

Not that Magdalena would ever know, but the man's name was Allen Potts, a janitor on the campus. Allen was finishing up work, and on his way to meet a couple of documentary filmmakers to give the last of his interviews on the incident from the week before.

Allen Potts would never make it to that last interview.

Magdalena pushed down on the metal bar at the top of the staircase, and then the heavy metal door afterward. Before her stretched a long hallway, at the end of which she could see an office door. It had to be West and Fischer's. As she walked down the hallway, her footsteps echoing the silent emptiness, her anxiety rose. What would she feel seeing two people in the flesh that she'd only seen in a vision?

She reached the office. Printed on the clouded glass on the door were two words:

WEST.

FISCHER.

She knocked on the clouded glass., and Caleb answered the door. He was holding a ceramic mug as he did so.

"Moretti I fucking told you…." he said, and when he saw Magdalena standing there, he dropped the ceramic mug immediately.

It shattered on the ground, spilling earl grey tea and scattering ceramic fragments everywhere.

He was stunned into silence.

From above and behind him, Sarah's head popped into view.

"Holy. Fucking. Shit. It's her."

Roger's phone began to vibrate. He looked down at it and saw Mags had just texted him.

"I'm all good" was what the message said.

"Oh you sweet girl. You are most definitely not all good. Hey Sam?"

"Yeah, Dad?"

"What do you say you and I stay in Boston for awhile. Just in case?"

"Are we the ca - cav-"

"Cavalry, Sam. And yes. It appears as if will be."

"When Dad?"

"When Mags calls for us, kid. We need to be ready."

"Ok, Dad."

Roger started the station wagon and drove off to find a hotel for he and Sam to hole up.

And wait.

Sarah was storing the six VHS tapes she'd already approved of in her carry-all when her doorbell rang. She glanced at two tapes at the top of the bag, titled NEUROTRANSMITTER LEVELS and PROGRESSION/SUMMARY, which were as compelling as they sounded. As in, not at all. They didn't reveal any major insights to their methodology, just a lot of upper-level biochemistry on one and a greatest hits compilation of Keating's milestones as read by Caleb on the other.

Sarah waited for her doorbell to ring again.

Gonna make you wait, golden girl, thought Sarah.

It rang again a full three minutes later - a turbo charged buzzer that let everyone on the first floor below and the third floor above that she had company. Or an Amazon package. Or a crazy girl from Florida.

Of course, it was Magdalena - there was no one else it could be, but she'd half hoped that Moretti or someone from the FBI caught her while she was on route and swept her off to the same interrogation room her and Caleb had shit themselves in on the day of the explosion. That was wishful thinking, though. Instead, she'd arrived right on time, a cosmic-level cue. Sarah stumbled over to her door and opened it. She regarded Magdalena up and down, standing there outside and freezing like someone who'd never experienced an actual winter before. It had started snowing. But aside from all of that, Magdalena looked ready to watch the tape that Sarah had more or less just had a minor panic attack just thinking about.

"Fuck," Sarah said aloud.

"Nice to see you again too, Sarah," replied Magdalena.

Magdalena was wearing a black, loose-fitting cotton shirt, jeans, and a spring jacket - not nearly enough for the twenty-degree day and blizzard they were experiencing in Massachusetts.

"The High Priestess at last. You look like you're dressed for Spring, girl. You watch the weather at all?" said Sarah.

"No, not really,"

"We're getting a blizzard today, girl. This isn't friggin' Florida, you know, and it's almost December."

"I didn't exactly have-"

"Winter clothes. I get it. Florida. Come on inside. I got something warmer for ya I think. Somewhere."

"Uh, thanks?" Magdalena stepped inside.

"Make yourself at home," said Sarah. It was about as unwelcoming as a person could make that sentence sound.

Sarah could see that Magdalena was visibly nervous. Magdalena scanned around the apartment, unsure of what might be lurking for her inside. Sarah noticed this as weakness and pounced. Had to exert dominance.

"Ahhhh. It's just an apartment sweetie. And I'm just a grad student that met the wrong two dickheads. A drunk grad student, too," Sarah stumbled a little and began laughing.

"Sarah, you don't think that's a bad idea? Getting hammered before we try to see Keating?"

Sarah stopped dead in her tracks. "Hey look Magda, can I call you Magda?" she asked.

"No."

"Mags?"

"Still no."

"Well, look. Magda-LENA. First, I'm gonna get you a real jacket. And then we're gonna watch this fucking tape I don't ever want to see again but youuuuuu just gotttttaa seee it so we're going to. And then we're gonna meet Caleb and probably the detective and then see what you have to do with this. Seems like it's all about you for some reason."

"Detective?"

"Oh yeah, Moretti. He's weird. I told you he was weird when you showed up in our office, didn't I?"

"Yes. And hey Sarah? I didn't choose this, Sarah. Think I'd much rather be home right now, all things considered. Can we just watch the tape?"

Sarah frowned at her. "Aw, you're no fun. Ok, fine, cmon."

Sarah threw her other winter jacket from her closet; a gaudy bright blue thing Sarah wore whenever she had a date. Which hadn't been for years, as it turned out. Magdalena hung it on a chair in the kitchen.

The two of them walked into Sarah's bedroom.

Magdalena looked around that area as well, noticing the three-quarters empty bottle of whiskey and the coffee cup that was being used to drink it. The smell of alcohol was overwhelming when she walked in.

"You drink that all today, girl?" asked Magdalena. Magdalena touched Sarah on the shoulder as she crossed the threshold into her bedroom. Sarah wrested her arm away from her touch.

"Sure have. Why, you want some? Help yourself. You're gonna need it after you see this shit."

Magdalena found a chair near the bed and sat down, folding her arms as she did.

"Pass, Sarah. Not a drinker. And nothing you're about to show me is gonna make me start now."

Sarah laughed with the bitterness and resentment of one who knew they'd relapsed and were simultaneously in the presence of a person that thought less of them because they had.

"How about that. Good for you. Me? I had three years on the straight and arrow myself, and then a bunch of people died, my boss turned into a fucking alien, and some psychic girl showed up in my office a week later. Plus a bunch of other shit. Sue me."

"What other shit," asked Magdalena.

"Nevermind. You'll find out eventually."

Sarah put in the videotape, turned, and then sat at the edge of her bed, directly in between Magdalena and the television.

"He's not an alien," stated Magdalena.

"Not to you, obviously."

Magdalena didn't bother asking her to move out of the way at that point - Sarah was drunk and hostile and didn't need any further provocation to continue her ribbing. Magdalena dragged her chair off to the side to get a decent view of the television."

"Buckle up, princess," said Sarah and used a remote to start the video.

Chapter Twenty

"THE FINAL DAY – November 15th, 2022"
(VCR Analog Recording 8):

The final recording begins like the other tapes - with the same few seconds of VHS static, followed by the upwards cascade of black, blank screen. However, once the video starts, there is a far more clinical feel to it to any of the previous cassette recordings. The camera view is of Dr. David Keating's main laboratory proper; the first shot is from an elevated point in one corner of the lab. It's zoomed out, such that the viewer sees the entire room completely with only a couple of areas to the far right and left corners of that are out of view. There are two long laboratory benches that run parallel through the middle of the expanse. These benches are adorned with the equipment one expects to find in a biology or chemistry laboratory - glass beakers, flasks, containers of stock chemical components and reagents, microscopes, analytical balances. Nothing out of the ordinary.

Here and there, periodically distributed throughout the room are more sophisticated pieces of equipment - there are two cylindrical, vertical glass cylinders; chromatography columns attached via silicone tubing to a machine with various instruments, valves, and a digital readout located to one side. These are used for chemical separations.

Against the back wall there is a laminar flow hood, an enclosed environment designed for sterile operations. It is dark and looks as if it hasn't been used in a few days. There is nothing inside, but if the viewer were to listen carefully in this moment, they would hear the faint hum of air whooshing out from the interior of the hood.

Sarah, Caleb, and Keating are all in the laboratory when the video starts. Sarah is fiddling with a stationary camera mounted on a tripod near a desk to the left. She stands back for a second, then looks directly at the camera, which by this point the viewer can deduce is mounted somewhere close to the ceiling. She pushes a button, and the view changes from the upper corner of the room to the camera near Sarah. She looks into the camera once again and verifies that it's recording.

"Cameras are up and running. What else do we need to do?"

She turns from the camera, and the view changes back to the first camera near the ceiling.

The voices are fainter, but Caleb starts speaking.

"David, can you lay down on the gurney here? Take off your sweater first though. And you don't need the sunglasses in here David. We know what your eyes look like."

David holds a single finger up, asking for a moment before they proceed with whatever it is they are planning. David speaks.

"I want to say something first. Sarah, can you switch the camera to the one down here for a moment?"

The camera view switches again to the ground level view. A moment passes. Keating turns around and faces the camera. He takes two steps forward and approaches, faltering for a second.

At first, it appears as if he is showing weakness or sickness from the treatments. He gathers himself and the initial frailty disappears. Keating looks to Sarah, who nods as if to give her approval. Caleb puts his hand on his shoulder to steady him. At last, Keating fully steadies himself and stands straight up at attention.

Magdalena broke in. Sarah paused the video and let out an audible "ugh" sound in disgust.

"Why is he wearing sunglasses?"

"You'll see, can I start it again?"

Magdalena nodded. Sarah restarted the tape.

Keating looks down at the ground, and then removes his sunglasses. His eyes are closed as he looks back up at the camera. He opens them.

There is nothing but black where his eyes should be. The black is reflective qualities, so that the light from laboratory lamps shining above the three scientists can be seen glowing in Keating's obsidian eyes. Because of this, it's obvious that the eyeballs themselves weren't missing, nor had they been removed, or dissolved, or otherwise lost because of his experimentation.

"There have been obvious physical side effects," he says.

Sarah hands him a small device, which Keating reaches over and takes. It is obvious he can still see, despite what has occurred to him. He holds the device up over his right eye, which has a screen that shines with a barely detectable, pale green light.

"Sarah, can you zoom in with the UV lamp?"

She pushes a button on a remote, and the view zeroes in onto his left eye. The device itself looks akin to a cell phone, but as the view narrows down to that section of his face and gets smaller it's clearly a sophisticated kind of camera. It is a handheld version of what optometrists use to image the retina during their routine exams. Keating's cornea remains black even with the UV camera, but the iris appears purplish-red, and the cornea is bright yellow instead of its usual black. There is no retina to be found at the rear of his eye.

"As one can clearly see, the basic anatomy of my eye remains intact - however, the major components thereof have appeared to have been altered in a significant manner," he lowers the camera and hands it back to Sarah, who sets it aside on a nearby bench. Keating is unaware that there is no retina to speak of.

"We have not, as of yet, been able to perform a full medical analysis," states Sarah, "simply because Dr. Keating's eyesight remains largely unchanged, save for the fact that - remarkably his astigmatism and nearsightedness have since been corrected. David no longer needs to wear corrective lenses."

Sarah looks to Dr. Keating, who has put his shades back on while she was speaking. He smiles at her, and Sarah returns the gesture, albeit in a nervous, obliging way.

Magdalena, again:
"Pause it for a second, would ya?"
The tape stopped mid-picture, the sporadic static of a pause appearing here and there on the television screen. Sarah held the remote up and pointed straight at the television screen for an inordinate amount of time to convey her irritation at having to stop the tape without having to speak.
Magdalena either didn't seem to notice or to really give a shit.
"His eyes didn't look like that when I saw him in my dream. He looked normal. Well...as normal as visions can be I guess."
Sarah: "Interesting."
Magdalena turned from the screen to Sarah.
"You don't fucking care at all, do you?"
"Noooope," replied Sarah.

"You should," replied Magdalena.
"But I don't. Can we please keep going? I need to get this over with. Caleb should be calling in an hour or two."
Magdalena nodded.

The recording continues:

"My name, once again, is Dr. David Keating. Over the course of the past few months, I have been my own voluntary test subject in a study to determine both quantitatively and qualitatively, the effects of operamine on the human brain, both from a physical and biological perspective and from observed changes in overall psychological state - even into altered states of consciousness."

"The physical effects have been quite dramatic and pronounced, as you can clearly see, but there is so much more happening than what is obvious to the casual viewer," Keating gestures to his visage.

"We've kept several video journals on strictly analog recording devices. This has simply been for security purposes. Digital can be stolen, duplicated, pirated. VHS analog is not so easily duplicated. The tape you are watching shall be the last video data point of our work. Today, I will attempt to push through the last barrier to a sustained and permanent alteration to my waking consciousness."

Dr. Keating then removes his sweater as he was bid before his speech and lays down on the gurney.
Caleb pulls one strap over Dr. Keating's chest and secures it in a manner that is both secure and tight, but not so uncomfortable or restrictive to the man who lay there as to eliminate all movement of his extremities.

"It's got a little wiggle, room, right, Dave? Not too tight?"

Dr. Keating's head faces straight up towards the ceiling, prior to Caleb's question. Keating tilts it to the left, towards where Caleb stands over him, and a look of affection comes over his face. It's unmistakable, despite the insect-like appearance of the man's eyes.

"Dave?" Dr. Keating asks. "Caleb, you haven't called me that in years."

Caleb seems to accept Keating's answer as acknowledgement that the restraints are fine where they are.

"I dunno, boss. Guess you could say I'm scared shitless about this. Don't want to see someone like you – don't want to see a friend - throw his fucking career or his life away."

The look of affection on Keating's face turns into a frown.

"Caleb. This is a scientific record, please refrain from…"

"I don't give a fuck about the scientific record, Dave. We're using cameras from the early eighties right now. If you had all been truly serious about scientific records, method, data, we wouldn't be using this shit. This is reckless, dangerous, and wrong."

He turns and strides right up to the camera so nothing is seen but his face.

"Up until this time in the experiment, Dr. Keating has received daily dosages of 0.5 CCs of operamine. This volume, at the formulated concentration of 3.5 g/L, delivers 10.5 milligrams of the enzyme into his brain. At 72 kilodaltons, the enzyme itself is too large and hydrophilic to cross the blood-brain barrier, so these administrations are injected directly into the spine at the base of the neck."

Caleb shakes his head and looks down at the ground, and screws his bottom lip to the right side, exposing his left front teeth. It's a gesture meant to display equal parts worry and disgust.

"Today, Dr. Keating has decided to up his dosage of the enzyme considerably. 30 CCs, sixty times that of the normal dosage will now be administered."

Caleb turns to his left and shoots Sarah a look that seems to say:

"We really going to go through with this?"

Sarah recognizes that Caleb is looking at her and purposely does not acknowledge him. It seems as if Sarah has already begun to distance herself from the both of them.

Caleb may have been upset moments before on the playback, but Sarah's obstinance here infuriates him. Caleb stomps out of the camera view, at which point the ceiling camera began displaying the action clicks on.

Caleb walks over to a refrigeration unit and flings the door open. He reaches in, pulls out a rack of small plastic vials, and almost tosses them onto a nearby lab bench. He slams the door closed.

Caleb pulls a syringe out of a drawer. Out of habit, he pulls out a smaller one that was adequate for administering Keating's usual dose. He quickly realizes his mistake, fires the incorrect equipment back into the drawer, and grabs a larger one.

It takes him about ten minutes to pull enough enzyme for the elevated dose, as each vial only had five milliliters of enzyme in them. He quickly cleans up and heads back over to where Keating is laying on the gurney.

Sarah said to Magdalena:

"At this point, I set it so it wouldn't switch back and forth between the cameras. It stays on the ceiling one from here on out."

"Thanks for that, Sarah."

Sarah whispers under her breath:
"Go fuck yourself, Mags."

Magdalena hears her but pretends she doesn't.

Sarah watches Caleb for a second, and then trades her camera remote for a lab notebook. She opens it up to a page that had a green post-it note stuck on the edge of it. She begins writing.

When Keating sees Caleb walking towards him with the syringe, he turns away from Caleb's approach vector to face the opposite direction.

Caleb grabs an alcohol pad/swab from a box, unwraps it, and wipes the back of Keating's neck vigorously with it.

Caleb pauses for a second. He takes a deep breath and takes the plastic tip off the syringe's needle. Caleb wastes no time. He punctures the flesh at the same spot he'd been poking at for more than 2 months. Caleb begins to slowly push the plunger down.

Time itself in the video seems to slow down to an almost unmeasurable speed at this moment - as if the entire lab had somehow been transported across space to the edge of a black hole's event horizon. From the angle above, where the camera eye took in the entire room, the only objects that can be seen to be in motion are Caleb's right hand and the syringe. Even Sarah is completely still. If one were to use a stopwatch to accurately measure the exact length of time it took Caleb to administer that dose, the time would be anywhere from 45 - 50 seconds, depending on who took the time.

Without a stopwatch, the time seems interminable, as if it were 45 -50 minutes.

Caleb withdraws the syringe, and hands it blindly over in the direction of where Sarah is standing. She looks over at the wall clock, quickly writes down a time in her notebook, and sets the notebook down to take the syringe from Caleb.

Meanwhile, Caleb applies a square of gauze to the site where he'd punctured with the syringe, followed by a length of adhesive tape to secure it. He taps Keating on the left shoulder to let him know the injection was complete.

"You know Sarah, you should be the one giving this shot," says Caleb.

Sarah shoots right back.

"Caleb, it's a fucking needle. Not brain surgery."

"Touche," Caleb replies.

There is a nervous laugh between the two of them, and then silence for a few seconds.

Sarah walks over to the same EEG machine seen in the other videos and begins to take periodic readings from it and writes them in her notebook.

Caleb leans against the lab bench with his arms folded. He pulls his cell phone out, clearly to make sure he's ready to dial 911 if and when he needs to. Likely just the 'when' part, however. He knows there have been no toxicology studies, no qualifying data on any of what they're doing other than Keating's previous doses…which didn't come close to what had just been put into his system. There's no precedent for any of this - and, strictly speaking, it isn't even legal. Caleb pauses for another moment, and then speaks.

"Hey. Dave."

No answer.

"David."

Still no answer.

Caleb's eyes widen as marches quickly back over to the prone Keating.

"Yo." Caleb snaps his fingers in front of Keating's face, with no response. Keating's eyes remain closed.

Caleb looks over to Sarah and then nods in the direction of the far corner of the lab.

"Go get the first aid kit and AED. FUCK ME," he exclaims.

Sarah sets the notebook down again and moves quickly towards one of the parts of the lab that is not visible to the cameras.

The playback becomes distorted, and static-filled at this point. It becomes difficult to discern any of the action from now until the end of the recording, but what can be made out is as follows:

Caleb reaches down and with his left-hand attempts to twist Keating's left arm upwards, palm up, to attempt to check for a pulse. Simultaneously, Caleb leans over Keating's prone body to listen and or look for breathing. It is clear he is starting the first steps of CPR. At that instant, Keating's eyes jolt open, as if an electric shock had propped them open.

A split second later, an actual, tangible form of electricity manifests in the form of a blueish-purple light that engulfs Keating's exposed flesh - his head, face and neck; his arms and hands; and two small, exposed areas near his ankles. The glow is not enough to obscure his features from view on the recording, and for a few seconds, Keating appears frozen in place.

Caleb is visibly frightened, and releases Keating's arm before taking a full step back from the prone man. Caleb looks his body up and down, growing more and more terrified as the ethereal indigo glow grows brighter and brighter. Caleb is afraid to approach, obviously thinking that the glow could somehow envelop him as well. He glances at
 his own arm and sees that the glow does not cover him as well without having been in contact with Keating when it first appeared. Keating's arm stabs outward towards Caleb and seizes his assistant at the elbow despite the distance between the two.

Keating yanks Caleb towards him with such sudden, brute force that Caleb is forced down to one knee beside him. Keating then uses this leverage to pull him in closer to him. Keating's lips begin to move, but the words are not discernible on the video.

Magdalena narrowed her eyes as she watched, struck by a dull, aching pain square in the middle of her head. She dropped her head down and brings the palms of both her hands to her forehead.

"This…." she starts, "this is when I saw him…and..I see him now. Again."

Sarah only slightly pays attention to her, focused more on what is happening in the video. Sarah was in the middle of reliving her own personal trauma from that day. She can only manage to remain sarcastic and bitter with Magdalena, purely as a defense mechanism.

"Definitely gonna wanna watch this part then. The purple lightshow is nothing, dude."

Magdalena looks up from her hands as the pain subsides almost as suddenly as it began.

"I can hear him in my mind Sarah."

"Hunh?" says Sarah, irritated again with her houseguest. She can't wait to just finish the tape, rip it out of the VCR, and throw it in with the rest of the ones she picked. She couldn't wait to hand them - and her- over to this Moretti guy or CRUCIBLE or whomever and then leave Massachusetts forever.

And never look back.

Magdalena tilts her head upward at the television screen, as a predator would in sizing up prey. She lets out a slight cooing sound, one that drops in pitch and finally stops. And then Magdalena is whispering, almost inaudibly, and certainly not loud enough against the backdrop of the television and the VHS tape recording playing.

Had Sarah listened to Magdalena instead of what was on the tape, she would have heard that Magdalena's whispered words were perfectly synched to what Keating is saying to Caleb on the tape. The words appear inside her mind, one at a time but rapidly and then disappear. Her utterances continue, as Keating's mind reaches both to Magdalena in south Florida at the time the final experiment occurred and to the Magdalena watching from Sarah's bedroom.

In the playback, Sarah doesn't see what's happening behind her until she's grabbed the AED off the wall in the unseen corner of the laboratory and turns around. She immediately drops the apparatus to the ground when she sees what is happening. Sarah can absolutely be heard on the tape, as opposed to

"CALEB WHAT THE FUCK IS HAPPENING!!!"

Caleb, locked in place next to Keating, can do nothing but listen to what his mentor is saying to him.

Magdalena (whispering):

"I have called her to me, standing there in the undeterminable void. Father called it *das Nichtvorhandensein* when he punished me. She is the only one who can save me. Blue hair. She is covered in glyphs."

The voice that comes from her lips alternates between hers and Keating's imperceptibly. The Sarah watching herself from just two weeks ago has regressed into the shock of the scene. Sarah heard none of what Magdalena is saying just a few feet away from her.

The magenta glow that surrounds Keating grows so bright that it can be seen beneath his clothes. Keating only continues to mouth words into David's ear, as if imparting some of the secrets of the universe.

And then it happens. Bolts of thin, chaotic and organic pink lightning bolts fly in all directions from Keating's right hand, as if the appendage had become a van de Graff generator. One such bolt rockets straight up into an overhead lamp hanging from the ceiling, blasting the plastic casing around it and the bulb inside into pieces, sending them flying and turning them all into a shrapnel. A shard hits Caleb on the back of the head, a wound he doesn't notice.

A quick shower of sparks rains straight down thereafter and falls onto the tile floor.

That same bolt sends such strong current into the wiring of the room that no surge protector has ever been designed that would prevent it from doing its damage. Various equipment around the lab overloads at once, with no less than four or five loud bangs ranging in volume from a firecracker coming from a laptop centrifuge to a shotgun blast from pressurized incubator positioned off to the right side of the screen. Each bang is followed by the start of a fire. Smoke begins to pour from each individual hunk of mechanized metal and plastic that had been set ablaze.

Another one of the initial cotton candy-colored bolts flies directly at Sarah, whose reflexes are quick enough to dodge it. It strikes the wall behind her, scorching a jagged, black burn mark in the wall instead of onto Sarah.

The remaining charges from Keating's hand struck objects off-screen. the impact of which is not readily apparent.

Sarah, having recovered her balance and still without a response from the two other men in the room, reaches into her pocket for her cell phone. She tilts her to the side, closes her eyes, and screams:

"GOD DAMN IT" before throwing it off to her side. There is a laboratory phone halfway between her and Caleb and Keating. She glances at it, determines it's at least worth trying to call in the cavalry with and begins to move toward it.

She picks the handset off the cradle and doesn't get it halfway before she limply drops it on the lab benchtop. The video is still mostly visible, but the static continues to increase on the television.

Keating and Caleb are still in their positions - still acting as if they're finalizing their next play during a flag football game.

Sarah makes for the doors then. She is out of options, or so she thinks. She's overlooked the existence of the lab's two fire extinguishers. She makes it to the laboratory double doors, which can only really be established as such by the viewer by the way Sarah struggles to extend both of her arms straight out in front of her to an object just off screen.

She pulls and pulls, but the doors do not budge. They have been fused shut. Sarah screams violently at the top of her lungs.

"THE DOORS ARE FUSED SHUT CALEB!!!! FUCKING HELP ME!!!!"

Keating stops speaking and falls comatose.

Magdalena stops whispering - but there is a second delay in the VCR tape playback, like a phone caller into a radio station who'd had forgotten to turn his own tv down.

Magdalena: "she will bring us altogether'

Sarah *does* notice this last statement. She dismissed it a second later as nonsense.

In the recording, Caleb stands up, dumbfounded, but shakes his head violently from side to side.

The fire alarm in the recording finally kicks off, making it impossible to hear anything else for the remainder of the footage. The various fires have grown much larger, and the three scientists are trapped inside. Caleb points to one of the fire extinguishers and motions for Sarah to grab it.

Sarah does so, and Caleb jogs over to another one off-screen. The two of them attempt to extinguish fires as they can.

In the ensuing chaos, they pay no attention to the wiring that is connected from Keating to the EEG machine, the machine itself, and its power card connected to the outlet. It burns with a purple light brighter than a blowtorch - an intensity that is impossible.

The EEG machine turns into an amplifier of Keating's mental energy and transfers it straight into the building's electrical infrastructure. This is the conduit that sets off the resulting chaos and destruction throughout the building and the Gordon University campus.

The entire picture flashes a bright purple and everything disappears.

The last thing that is heard is Caleb screaming.

"DAVID!!!!!!"

The recording ended. The television screen displayed a few seconds of complete static, and then changing to the light blue that is shown on a television when there is nothing left on the tape. The timestamp at the bottom disappeared a moment later.

Sarah got up from her spot on the bed and walked straight over to the television set. Weirdo secret government guy Moretti said he was going to need a copy specifically of this tape prior to it being admitted as evidence - what for was beyond her, and why he specifically he needed it for was beyond her and frankly, Sarah didn't really care either. If it ended up in his, CRUCIBLE's, or the Chinese Secret Police, it didn't matter to her.

Sarah pushed the eject button on the tape, and turned to face Magdalena, who remained silent at the conclusion of the tape and hadn't moved, either. Her eyes were closed. Sarah thought, 'oh fucking come on you tattooed wierdo. I don't have time to meditate with you' before clapping her hand to the side of the VCR tape.

"Hey! Wake up. No way that video put you to sleep Mags."

Magdalena opened her eyes.

Every ounce of strength and will flowed down and out of Sarah as if she'd sprung a leak in her feet the size of a sinkhole. Her knees buckled, and her already pale complexion shifted to corpse-level pallor.

Even her hair seemed to wither at the sight of Magdalena.

Her eyes had transformed just as Keating's had. Identically. Both the right and left sides of Magdalena's mouth were turned down in a frown - but not one of sadness or emotional pain, but still of a creature ready to strike after having come within range of its prey. She said:

"Bring me to him. Now."

The voice that spoke was inhuman - sounding like a feminized version of Keating's hybrid alien voice at the very conclusion of the video. What had happened to him, had happened to Magdalena as well.

Sarah dropped the tape on the ground, nearly breaking it. She took one step back, her backside brushing up against the television screen.

"Magdalena…Mags?" she asked, frightened nearly to the point of pissing herself.

Magdalena blinked, slowly. When her eyes opened again, they changed back to their usual color. The whites had returned, her irises had reverted to their usual darkened mahogany. She looked from left to right, utterly confused first as to how she came to be standing, and second what had happened at the end of the video. Moreover, she saw the look of absolute terror on Sarah's face as well as the videotape marked "The Last Day" on the ground.

"What, Sarah?"
Sarah could not answer her.
"Did I miss something?" Magdalena asked.

Interlude:

NICHTVORHANDENSEIN

Time.

I've never truly understood it. And it seems that I likely never will either. I'd hoped that along with the other unexpected 'gifts' my experimental design had bestowed upon me I would finally understand what time truly was. Alas, that seems unlikely.

Escape from this place of nothing, of absence – *das Nichtvorhandensein*, does not appear to be possible.

Father always said I belonged here. He acted as if I already was. I often wondered if he cursed my name out loud from whatever hell he was sent to spend eternity. I know that hell doesn't exist, so he couldn't be in it, or at least a place like it.

The woman – Magdalena Christie, she of beauty I had never beheld at any time in my life, the one I reached to…what can she do? I know vanishingly little about the woman I reached to when I descended to this dimension of absolute nothingness, outside of our internet conversations.

In any event, what have I done to her in order to affect some possibility of her rescuing me?

And since all that I can perceive is an indeterminate void, one that starts at the borders and edges and limits of whatever presence I have manifested here and then stretches into unknowable distances, it seems that I shall remain here until there is nothing left of me.

She has just vanished from my sight, after my calling. My consciousness is no longer in that realm of the natural world, although my physical body must remain. I suspect that I am comatose, again. Would this then be a second, more drastic attempt at suicide? The nurses and doctors and experts would most certainly agree upon that point. I laugh, but there is no echo.

Time.

It jumped around for me, the past bleeding into the present and vice versa. What happened before happens again in the present. It has always been…difficult for me to keep events and days as the linear progression that every so-called 'normal' person must perceive. If only those who do not experience the world as I do, or have, could be shown how it seems and feels to those of the neurodivergent bent – the autistic, the attention-disordered, the mentally ill.

I am David Herbert Keating. And I can still perceive what is occurring in the natural world. But as I do, there is something that perturbs me, in this shadow world.

The third presence. When I called Magdalena here. The uninvited guest…

Who, or what, was it? I have no answers for this.

Magdalena called to me. She was assaulted. A man she called…Scumbag. A fitting moniker. I unlock what is inside of her, and she disposes of him. Not what I had in mind, but the woman did what she must have felt necessary. I admire her strength. Maybe there is hope for me.

But I feel myself fading. Fading…fading. This is non-existence, and somehow, I exist within it. The atheists believe this to be the afterlife, one would think. It is not. I am soon nothing but a vague form, and the thoughts that go with that vague form.

The last perception I have is of Magdalena with Sarah. She is watching the video of the last day, and I can reach to her one last time.

Come to me, immediately, I beg. I can see the physical world no more.

Time.

It has lost its meaning. I do not know long I have been here. *Selbst die Zeit existert in das Nichtvorhandensein.* It could be a minute, it could be a week, it could be a century. I do not know.

This is a world where time, matter, and life do not exist. This is a plane of perfect and unbroken…absence.

And just as that absolute and perfect absence, a flawless diamond of anti-matter, that malicious and suffocating silence, a space where sound seemed as if it had never existed nor occupied now or ever, and those shadows of shadows cast by boundless and cyclopean inversions of the physical universe loomed imperceivable, I notice that they all at last have found their way *inside* and *within* each successive thought I complete one after the other.

*I could see them all swallowing every last bit of me…*until all I could do was repeat to myself over and over again just one sentence. The simplest statement of being. And soon, even that signal transmission began its final decay:

I am David Herbert Keating.

I am David Herbert Keating.

I   m   vid Her   Keat   .

I   id   eat.

                    Id-

And then –
-    The silence broke.
            -   It broke at a million points.
                        - It splintered like glass.
- And each and every one of those fracture points was made by a single voice.
                                    - A single human
                                    voice.
-Thousands. Millions. Millions of fracture points.
                        -Too distant to make out what even a single
                        one of them said.
        - But I listened. I listened to the fracture cascade.
        - The cascade ceased, and there was nothing left but the millions upon…
        -Millions of voices.
                - And I could tell that it wasn't because of their distance from me…
                        - that I couldn't make out…
                        -What they said.
        -It was because they weren't saying anything. At all.
                                -It was nonsense.

A million voices in a cacophony….
        - of echolalia.

        The sound allowed me to complete my base thought again.
        I am David Herbert Keating.
The sonic context, reference point, counterbalance, whichever one prefers is what made my base thought possible again. I was relieved, yet frightened.
        Who or what did those voices belong to?

I repeated the baseline declarative.
I am David Herbert Keating.

And then to my horror, the echolalia ceased, but the voices continued. They had heard my thought, somehow. And each voice repeated the same words over and over again, and over each other, and each over another over another….

Davidherbertkeatingdavidherbertkeating

They grew louder. The voices were coming closer. Whatever or whoever the voices belonged to were coming closer.

DAVIDHERBERTKEATING

Fright. Horror. Fear. I struggled to return to my mantra. I started:
I am-
They finished.

**YOUAREDAVIDHERBERTKEATINGYOUAREDAVI
DHERBERTKEATINGYOUAREDAVIDHERBERTKE
ATINGYOUAREDAVIDHERBERTKEATINGYOUAR
EDAVIDHERBERTKEATINGYOUAREDAVIDHERB
ERTKEATINGYOUAREDAVIDHERBERTKEATING
YOUAREDAVIDHERBERTKEATINGYOUAREDAVI
DHERBERTKEATINGYOUAREDAVIDHERBERTKE
ATINGYOUAREDAVIDHERBERTKEATINGYOUAR
EDAVIDHERBERTKEATINGYOUAREDAVIDHERB
ERTKEATINGYOUAREDAVIDHERBERTKEATING
YOUAREDAVIDHERBERTKEATING.**

And then all I could hear was a million million voices…

                laughing.

And then I heard a single voice among them that
wasn't…

                laughing.

It was father.
He kept saying, shouting the same word over
             and
             over

like when he called my name
when it was my turn for the belt
as if I as a person,
a human that never existed
as if I and this place
of absence were one in the same.

***DAS NICHTVORHANDENSEIN!!!!
DAS NICHTVORRRRHAAAAAAANDENSEIN!!!
NICHT…VOR…HANDEN….SEIIIIIIIINNNNN!!!!***

I found that all I could do was scream.

Part TWO:

M
O
R
R
E
T
T
I

Transcript from:
"Massacre at Gordon University: What Really Happened?"
(2023).
dir. by Fred and Alice Carpenter.
Interview w/ Allen Potts, Maintenance Technician, Gordon
University 1994 – 2023
Current whereabouts unknown.

"Well, those first news reports from the school were broadcast on the local stations here in Mass, up in New Hampshire and Maine...Rhode Island too. Oh yeah - there was the basic cable station NECN - New England Cable News - that did a thing too. Those stories were more or less ya' thirty second blurbs that they cobbled togetha from police scannahs and then phone calls from the TV stations to the school – ya' know?"

"Did you personally give any media outlets any information on what happened at that point?"

"Nah. I was just outside the fuckin' building when the explosion happened, so I spent the first couple of hours or so just tryin' to make sure nobody was hurt out where I was. Hell, makin' sure I wasn't hurt, either. Not a young guy, in case ya haven't noticed."

"So do you think it was just social media like Twitter, Facebook, Instagram, TikTok, and word-of-mouth from people who were there that started all the stories, got the national media attention?"

"Yeah, I suppose. I don't use any of that nonsense myself, so I couldn't rightly say. But ain't that the way now? Broad daylight when all the craziness happened. Kids reach for the cell phones to take pictures before they're safe before they do anything really, so when windahs are blowin' outta buildins and people are dyin' inside 'em, everyone's snappin' friggin' pictchahs instead of running for their lives. So, like I said, I was trying to get kids and people away from the danger. Too busy to talk to some asshole from channel fucking five."

"There couldn't have been that many kids on campus. COVID must have had some impact on Gordon, right?"

"Gordon U was good about testin' when it was bad a couple of years ago, y'know? Social distancing…all that happy horseshit. After the plague died down, the trustees made sure that the only students who were on campus needed to be on campus. The Monarch building, for example. Monarch used to be full up all the time with classes - but at the time of yon purple mushroom cloud, it only served one purpose. Office space for West and Fischer, the fuckin murderers."

"So why were the majority of the students on campus there that day?"

'For labs and independent research kinda stuff. Like what those three knuckleheads were doin' in their house-a-horrahs. You're right, though. It was lucky there weren't more kids there, tell you the truth."

"When did you decide to come forward?"

"When I got my walking papers by the University for even returning your phone call, saying I wasn't interested in speaking to you. Soon as I got those, I was like well fak you guys then. Called ya up, here we are. I got a couple more days of work there after today, and then I'm done.

"Did you tell the university you'd been contacted by our production team?"

"Fuck, NO." Mr. Potts folds his arms. "But somehow, they knew." He leans in towards the camera. "Now what does that tell ya?"

The documentary continues with a voiceover, the same voice that conducts the interview with Mr. Potts. Photos of the aftermath on the campus where Keating, West, and Fischer conducted their experiments are played in sequence as the voiceover continues:

"Social media and the internet made things exceedingly difficult for local, state, and federal law enforcement to contain specific details about the explosions at Gordon University. What is more to the point, and far more important to consider, is how little the university was able to bend the narrative on that initial rush of first-hand accounts that flooded onto the web. What is more to the point, and far more important to consider, is how little the university was able to bend the narrative on that initial rush of first-hand accounts that flooded onto the web. Yet, because of that same deluge of students, faculty, and staff giving their own individual accounts, no one ever considered that a supernatural, otherworldly force was somehow responsible for the multiple explosions, fires, deaths, and injuries on that day. The sheer volume of information worked *against* the truth coming out of Gordon."

"In this era of Q-Anon, misinformation, and conspiracy theories permeating the internet, encountering stories of such an outlandish and frankly difficult event to take seriously would come off as nothing more than another fabricated tale. People decided what happened for themselves regardless of what "facts" were and were not reported by the media or by what some "experts" claimed as truth." "What is most striking about this event then is not so much as the frankly ridiculous theories that would subsequently arise on right-wing conspiracy websites, YouTube channels, and other online outlets about the massacre, but the fact that those with first-hand information and accounts were systematically silenced thereafter. The deluge dried up within twelve hours. Only Mr. Potts was willing to come forward and speak to us."

"How was this silencing even possible? Moreover, *who* was responsible for it?"

Pictures of clandestine government agents appear, from the fifties all the way to the current day. The voiceover continues:

"There were six deaths and eighteen injuries of varying severity that stemmed from surge of mysterious energy and the catastrophic explosion that ensued. Of the eighteen injured, it's since been accepted that seven were direct eyewitnesses of what some would call an extraordinary phenomenon, and what others might even call...supernatural."

Allen Potts reappears. He is nervously smoking a cigarette.

"Do you think you're being watched right now, Mr. Potts?"

"Kid, have you been listening to a single word I said?" *Potts shakes his head, puts the cigarette out in a bottle of water, and laughs to himself.*

"They're watching you, now, too."

"Who, Mr. Potts?"

"Them. The government. The democrat cabal or Illuminati or whatevah. You making this movie is keeping the whole thing going, you know. *They* want it quiet. *They* want it all gone. Let me ask you something. You think all the rumors, all the Facebook posts, all that gossip meant anything? Nobody trusts anyone anymore. But something like this movie you're making? This is going to attract their attention more than anything."

Caleb pulled off his headphones while the documentary continued to play on his laptop. The file for it had been in his regular email, from Moretti. Caleb wasn't sure if "The Massacre at Gordon" was supposed to be a warning of the possible consequences he could be facing or a reminder of the human cost of their actions, or both. He sat there for a moment and pondered it. It was likely both, and then some.

And how in the actual hell did Moretti *already* have a copy of it?

More to the point, who the hell was Moretti really working for?

Moretti had marked the email with the documentary footage attached as 'high importance' – so it had that stupid red exclamation point next to the subject line in his inbox. The subject line read of the email had read "I TOLD YOU SO, KID" in all caps and in bold font. Even a thousand miles away, Moretti was treating Caleb like he was an imbecile.

This entire communication was Moretti's subtle way of reiterating the importance of resolving their shared predicament in the next twenty-four hours, and that what was at stake had exponentially increased while Caleb was on his little field trip to Germany.

Fine, Moretti. I get it, Caleb thought.

The conspiracy nuts were already rushing to get their this-is-the-real-truth videos, blog posts, and whatever out into the mainstream. The production that Moretti sent him however, with its intelligent and thoughtful production and interview with Potts, likely represented a tangible, credible threat to the effort to keep some sort of lid on a situation that had already quite literally exploded.

"The Massacre at Gordon" was trouble.

The implication was impossible to miss. He, along with David and Sarah would forfeit their chance at ever returning to a semi-normal life, should it reach public consumption.

Caleb shook his head and muttered under his breath.

"Fucking *film students.*"

The intent of these two dipshit directors seemed less like an altruistic mission to do a service for the American people, shedding light on a government cover-up and exposing the nefarious machinations of a bureaucracy bent on keeping the population ignorant and more about the directors making a name for themselves.

They were capitalizing on an opportunity.

Fucking. Film. Students.

There was no fucking way Caleb was passing this 'pop-up' documentary onto Sarah. She hadn't been holding it together well since…well since the surgery if he was being honest and seeing this would send her straight past the point of no return. The very last thing they needed is her relapsing and diving to the bottom of a bottle. It had been three years since her last run, but Caleb was still worried that she'd toss that sobriety aside like used latex gloves. Keating's journal entries were far from reassuring, but what was in them couldn't be kept from her.

But shit had changed altogether before Caleb even got on the goddamned plane. The two suits in Heathrow had seen to that, dispelling the notion that Moretti represented the only shadow ops, black-bag government spook organization with a vested interest in their current affairs.

Moretti had sprung both Sarah and Caleb from the eight-by-eight cells like he was the director of the FBI.

But who was it for? For Moretti? Or was it for whomever employed him?

Back in Germany, David's family, the members that were still among the living hadn't been easy to deal with. Keating is an English surname, not even remotely German, so Caleb had been sent there to track down his brothers - Karl and Heinrich Neumann. Their father, Emil, had passed away in 2018. Cirrhosis, apparently.

Caleb knew the basics of how David came to America, and how came to be David in the first place, but none of the finer details.

His mother, Catherine Keating, had met Emil while they both were undergraduates at Humboldt, the institution that produces just about every German luminary the West had ever heard of or cared about. Catherine and Emil were both brilliant, each in their own right, and when they eventually married a few years removed from university, it seemed like brilliant children were on the way.

First came Karl.

Swing and a miss.

Karl worked in a brewery and drank like he worked in a brewery.

Then came Heinrich.

Better, but still, strike two.

Heinrich ended up as an accountant. Or a banker. Something with money.

And lastly, on Catherine and Emil final swing, came Walter.

And at first, it seemed Walter was the home run they'd been waiting for…except.

Walter was different.

This was where things in the Keating-Neumann family start to become hazy. By the time Walter was fourteen, he and his mother had put Berlin firmly in the rearview mirror.
So firmly, in fact, that Walter Neumann in Germany became David Keating in the good ol' U.S. of A. His mother did her best to erase their past.

David had adopted his mother's surname after he and his mother stole away from his father and brothers. Caleb knew there had been some kind of rift, but what that rift was, he hadn't the first idea.

It had been a straight miracle he'd managed to convince either Heinrich or Karl that he was there on behalf of David.

"SEIN NAME IST WALTER!!!" screamed a shitfaced Heinrich directly into Caleb's face) and that he was trying to help him. Karl, the more measured of the two and the one who could speak English, simply stated:

"Walter had always been beyond helping, Mr. West," before agreeing to hand over the computer and the journal David had sent him weeks before.

And after dealing with these two jackholes and their spot-on renditions of what 'belligerent yet obscenely infantile' behavior looks like in an adult human being, Caleb decided it best to refer to them as cousins, rather than David's older siblings.

Caleb wasn't about to share the journal with Moretti before giving Sarah a chance to read it, and at least talk to her about it first.

He was doubly glad to have made this decision once he'd confronted the two spooks prior to boarding the plane.

It was all too much to think about. It wasn't going to make anymore sense until he reunited with Moretti, in the flesh.

Caleb put the headphones back on and continued to watch the documentary. There really wasn't anything else to do other than watch the Carpenters' documentary.

Wait. The couple who put together this stupidity were the Carpenters.

Caleb laughed out loud and sang a quick bar or two.

The Carpenters are walking together on a lawn on the campus of Gordon University, as evidenced by a sign briefly glimpsed in the camera view.

Carpenter begins.

"These witnesses were made up of those individuals who saw the "purple lightning" first-hand. This "lightning" as it was described, leapt from power outlets to automated machines, then to larger pieces of industrial equipment that drew large amounts of current as a course of their operation. Dr. Keating and his associates, Caleb West and Sarah Fischer, were conducting their final, illegal experiments at the same time these witnesses state they saw the phenomenon occur."

Soska continues:

"Not a single one of these individuals could be located by any means at our disposal, much less interviewed for this production. They were professors, and they were students. None have been seen on the campus since that day. When asked, university representatives simply stated unrelated facts, dismissing us with quips like 'all concerned made full recoveries, but those affected will not be returning to the university.' A denial? Perhaps. But a deferral? Most certainly. "

Carpenter finishes:

"Our attempts to interview some members of the student body proved fruitless - responses were limited to either t that they didn't see or know anything, or that they weren't on campus that day. For event so dramatic, it was almost as if nothing of any import had ever happened."

Caleb did appreciate how quickly two married undergrads (more like undersads) from Endicott put together a credible documentary on 'what really happened' at Massasoit. How they talked Potts into talking to them eluded Caleb, however. Potts must have been pissed off mightily to be speaking to those two amateurs in the first place.

But it was like Allen Potts said - they'd definitely landed themselves on a couple of different watch lists by making the film in the fucking first place.

At that moment, the stewardess appeared at the front of the plane and began to approach him.   There were only a couple of other people on the flight, so she'd be alongside him in seconds.

Caleb hit pause on the video and closed his laptop. "Can I get you anything else? We'll be making our approach in about an hour. Last call," the stewardess flashed her toothiest, flirtiest smile at him.

"Oh, no thanks," Caleb responded. He wanted her gone as quickly as possible.

"You know sir, I wasn't going to say anything, but you look familiar to me. Were you on TV?"

The question alarmed him, moreso than any documentary ever could.

We're fucked, he thought.

"Oh, I get that a lot. I've been told I look like Chris O' Donnell." Caleb struck a movie star pose.

"Who's Chris O' Donnell?" she asked.

"The kid in *Scent of a Woman*? NCIS Los Angeles?"

The flight attendant shook her head and shrugged her shoulders.

"I guess I just have a movie star kind of face, then," Caleb said with as shit-eating of a grin he could manage.

The attendant laughed with a rehearsed, customer service-flavored giggle and moved onto the passenger seated four rows behind him. After the brief surge of panic-related adrenaline subsided, Caleb thought of something Moretti had said to him before he'd left the states.

Moretti had mentioned to him that he'd be bound to be recognized in public from time to time, no matter what his 'organization' did to contain the story. Most of the time, the encounter would go like the one he'd just had with the flight attendant - a vague recollection of having seen his face somewhere. Still though, Moretti had advised him on what to remember when it happened. He did this while staring straight into Caleb's soul through blue eyes that were so faded, they bore the same shade as Cirrus clouds on an otherwise clear day:

"I'd keep to yourself as much as possible when you're on this little errand, Mr. West. Talk to as few people as possible. Don't do any fucking sightseeing. Know what I'm saying, kiddo?"

"Fuck you buddy," Caleb said out loud at the memory. Like the first thing he was going to do in Berlin was go to a discotheque. Moretti had thought him a special kind of idiot right from the start.

At the same time Magdalena Christie was nodding off on the Greyhound bus she'd boarded in Tampa Bay, Stephen Moretti left Seattle on a direct flight to Logan Airport, Boston, due to arrive at 2:30 A.M. The flight was seven hours long, and while Magdalena slept, Moretti was wide awake. He stayed that way for the entire duration of his trip to the east coast.

There was already far too much to think about, consider, and plan. This latest assignment, ostensibly a mysterious explosion on a college campus with a few researchers at the center of it all, ordinarily wouldn't have spurred him into such a whirlwind of thought and consideration.

But there was something much, much different about this one. There was more to be done out in Boston than just the assignment.

Much more.

The flight Moretti took to get there wasn't commercial, coach, economy or otherwise. CRUCIBLE special operatives flew the friendly skies via private jets without exception. Never amongst the masses – unless there was special occasion to make to do such a thing. Moretti centered his thoughts by recalling his days in the FBI, and the typical pedestrian inconveniences that went along with flying coach:

Waiting to disembark behind a line of thirty or so exhausted travelers.

Baggage claim, staring a shining silver snake-like conveyor belt and losing oneself in the hypnotic progression of it.

The quiet, dull fascism of being frisked by TSA or scanned by that ridiculous infrared device airport "security" used to find contraband.

Having to make small talk with another human being. This perhaps, most of all. Banter, chitter-chatter, even just an exchange of pleasantries to other people, even if it was just inane bullshit.

Moretti's plane touched down on a secluded, rarely used airstrip at Logan just after two a.m., eastern standard time. The exit door/hatchway opened before him right as he approached them, as if opened by motion-detection automation. Although that wasn't the case, Moretti did notice his escort/handler waiting at the bottom of the stairs that led from the aircraft as if *he* was standing there by a kind of automation, which in a sense he was. It just wasn't motion detection.

He stepped off the plane and into the windswept darkness beyond.

Moretti was immediately greeted by forty-mile an hour gust of sub-freezing air blasted seemingly almost directly into face. Even with his jet-black beard fully grown-in to 70s action star thickness, the facial hair did little to dull the blade of late-autumn New England winds – especially those that swirled out on the unshielded and unprotected East Boston peninsula upon which Logan was constructed.

As he stomped down the stairway from the jet, Moretti made his feelings on his current geography known to his handler:

"I fucking hate New England."

His handler didn't acknowledge the statement, only turned in an about face as Moretti approached, and then strode alongside Moretti in lockstep shoulder-to-shoulder.

It was as futile and childish an attempt at being by-the-book as he'd ever encountered in his life. In this abandoned, forgotten stretch of Logan there wasn't another single soul for a mile in every direction. His handler was impressing exactly no one with his decorum and adherence to protocol.

Moretti would have taken something along the lines of a quip like "New England hates you too, Moretti" or even just a "everybody hates it here." But nope, nothing, not a word from the mid-level moron that got assigned escort duty that evening. Only silence.

Moretti thought to himself:

I fucking hate CRUCIBLE.

Moretti knew that whatever vehicle his lord-and-masters had arranged wasn't going to be anything remotely as slick, high-financed, or comfortable as the private jet he'd just flown into town on. The ride that awaited him would likely be the exact opposite in those criteria of its airborne counterpart.

The dynamic by which the disparity between quality of air travel was driven by one simple principle: the average American and citizenry writ large had to remain entirely ignorant of CRUCIBLE's existence.

That meant that in the air, away from the prying eyes of Tom, Dick, and Harry, it was private jets, military technology, and the fastest transportation possible.

On the ground, it meant camouflage, subterfuge…anything and everything to blend in – but taken a step further than just appearing as either first responders or law enforcement. Special operatives were directed and trained to appear as close to the average American as was actually possible.

When CRUCIBLE did want someone or someone(s) outside of it to be aware of its presence, which was almost *never*, then that party would be made aware via the Constabulary, that group of stereotypical G-men that would appear in circumstances that called for the parties they contacted or communicated with to feel like they were dealing with just that – a shadowy, black ops organization that paid as much attention to intimidation as they did to sound as if they'd been somehow stripped of every human emotion during their training.

His escort, neither a member of the Constabulary nor a special operative but seemingly as robotic and self-important as both divisions tended to be, led them to an even more distant and isolated area of Logan Airport than where the jet had come to stop in its landing. Moretti took note of their distance from the nearest signs of life and operational parts of their airport – at least a mile – and fingered the safety to 'off' underneath his jacket.

Force of habit.

At last, his handler brought him to a carpark a full mile in the cold and dark on foot to where his vehicle had been secured for him.

Sitting under a single streetlamp that cast a moldy, cheddar-colored light was a beige Toyota Corolla, early 2010s model. The car looked as if it spent the better part of its days as the transport for a suburban mother of no less than three

Instead of thinking it, he said it out loud this time.

"I fucking hate CRUCIBLE."

His erstwhile companion seemed to take notice of this comment, casting a suspicious eye at Moretti. Moretti took notice of the man's concern.

"Take it easy, pal. We don't have an 'employee of the month' award. My feelings about our employers should be the least of your concerns."

Despite his explanation, the man seemed to mentally underline the dissention as something to include in his report.

Moretti grimaced at him and approached the vehicle. He glanced over his shoulder once, imperceptibly, to see that Employee of the Month was eying him for more material to suck up to whomever was his superior. Not a surprise.

Before him then, under a single streetlamp that cast a moldy, cheddar-colored light was a **red** Toyota Corolla, early 2010s model. The car looked as if it spent the better part of its days as the transport for a suburban mom of no less than three. This vehicle carried the telltale signs of an additional feature, a total of about five or six that Moretti spotted within less than a second of his initial inspection. The dangerously worn tires, partially caved in rear bumper, passengers' side window that didn't quite roll up all the way, and the drivers seat pushed so far back as to appear like a kind of intermediate backseat all spoke of teenage ownership. These were all marks of the child that inherited the vehicle after Mom was done with it and had moved onto some gaudy, gas-guzzling SUV to parade around in at soccer games and PTO meetings.

It wasn't any kind of specialized training that CRUCIBLE had given to Moretti that allowed him to draw this conclusion.

He'd seen the same thing years before, when he'd bequeathed his prized vehicle, to his son Derek. Car was the same color, too.

The day that Derek had passed his driving test, and was handed a drivers' license, Moretti handed him the keys to his baby – a rebuilt, positively badass in any and every context, 1978 **crimson** Monte Carlo.

"For…for real Dad?" asked an incredulous Derek Moretti.

"For real, kiddo. Please just…just treat her well."

And within two weeks, Derek had already backed into a light pole, the tires looked as if they'd been driven over nothing but miles of broken glass, and one of his buddies had broken off the handle that rolled the passenger side window up and down.

The worst was yet to come, however. Less than a couple of months later…

"Agent Moretti. *AGENT MORETTI.*"

Employee of the Month snapped him out of his lapse into a memory of his son.

"Yes. What? What is it?"

"Is everything to your satisfaction, sir?"

A smug question, and the first hint of an actual personality on behalf of his handler – albeit one emblematic of an individual with a sadly misguided idea of his own importance in the grand scheme of things.

"Keys?"

"In the ignition, Agent Moretti."

"Thank you. You've been very helpful and patient. I'll be sure to mention your performance to my superior."

"Really, sir?"

Employee of the Month's eyes lit up brighter than the lamp above them.

"Of course not. You're an idiot that'll be dead in a year when you encounter an operative fixing to go off grid puts a bullet in your ear. Be glad I'm not one of them, dude."

Moretti didn't bother to look for the man's reaction, instead getting into the car without another thought.

Once inside the vehicle, Moretti took a deep breath.

He was a terrible liar. Whenever he did so to a person, no matter how inconsequential they were or how little he cared about them, it always took him a moment to calm himself down.

The car took three tries to start, and when it did rumble to life the fan belts sounded like trapped cats begging to be put out of their misery.

"They really take this nondescript shit too far," Moretti grumbled, and pulled out to head north to Gordon.

At that time of night, even a city notorious for its simultaneous states of *Mad Max: Beyond Thunderdome* levels of aggression and having more jams than Smuckers like Boston eased up on reducing the life expectancy of its citizen, and a night owl like Moretti could enjoy a hassle-free, even peaceful drive.

It took Moretti only ten minutes before clearing the city limits of Boston proper. Not along after, the landscape around him quickly transformed - from the sight of broken concrete, the smell of lingering and spectre-like exhaust fumes, and the feeling imparted by the cold angular geometry of the tall buildings and countless panes of square and rectangular glass to the vision of a clear, smooth highway ahead, the smell of cold, crisp, clean winter air streaming in through that window that thankfully didn't roll up all the way, and the feeling that the dark, uncertain area rolling towards you is where you've always needed to go, instead of where you've always ran away from.

Moretti smiled in the silence and allowed himself to feel that peace. Once he'd felt like achieved it, he knew it was time to call her.

It was time to call Lourdes.

Moretti fumbled through the right pocket of his favorite **crimson** bomber jacket and fished out his **black** phone. It was a model from the early days of cellular devices and had a flip screen. With the hand he used to retrieve the device, his left still on the wheel, Moretti struggled to get the damn thing open. After at least a full minute of trying to catch the groove in the middle with a finger, any finger, he managed to catch his pinky in far enough to open it.

Moretti laughed to himself. When the "flip" phones came out, it was sold as a convenience feature that made the device easier to keep in pocket and therefore carry. Instead, its *in*convenience in operating for someone driving a vehicle would have been a far better selling point with regards to texting and driving and the like.

Moretti pushed the center "5" button, having set-up one-touch dialing for the one contact that was on the **black** phone. He brought it up to his ear in time to hear the first ring. It rang a second and third time. After the third, Moretti began to feel anxious. Maybe she was just slow to answer. This phone call, they both knew, was inevitable, even necessary if either of them would ever hope to truly be free.

A fourth ring. Moretti's anxiety shifted into the same gear, bypassing second and third altogether.

After the fifth, Moretti began formulating a plan to buy himself enough time to drive north to Vermont to investigate Lourdes' disappearance. He was already on his way, as the highway he drove on was also the same one that would get him to her the fastest. He'd have to-

A click, then a woman's voice. Low in pitch yet infused with the verve of youth and conviction of one who's faced down evil their entire life.

And she was the only one he allowed to use his first name. It'd have sounded strange coming from anyone's else lips, but from her it sounded natural. She asked him how he was doing in Spanish, but she used a phrase that tested whether he'd followed through on a promise he'd made to her years before.

"Cada dia sobre la tierra es una vicotria, Lourdes. How's it been going with you?"

Her response to his question troubled him. He'd vainly hoped to hear something different, something better than what he knew she'd say - as if there was an actual chance that it could happen. No time to get to that problem, not for a while anyway.

Lourdes asked about what the situation was, knowing that it was special – even for a CRUCIBLE special operative.

"Big explosion on a college campus near Boston, couple of researchers messing with things they shouldn't be messing with. Yeah, I know what you're gonna say. History repeats itself, only last time wasn't an explosion, and it wasn't scientists, was it? Ordinarily, I'd sleepwalk through this kind of gig. I get calls for geniuses stepping over whatever line in the natural order's sand CRUCIBLE has drawn twice a year its seems but – it's what we talked about in the church, Lourdes."

Moretti surveyed the mostly empty visitors' lot, then picked a parking spot in a corner furthest away from the campus proper, near a short stretch of road designated for emergency vehicles. The tip of the isosceles-shaped, rotted wood gate hadn't been secured to its anchoring post, merely pushed close enough to it to give the appearance of it being properly closed. Not that it would have kept any trespassers out even if it had.

And why it was placed at the worst possible location for first responders, fire, and police to respond as quickly as possible was beyond even Moretti's formidable deductive capabilities.

The second Moretti killed the engine, his cell phone that hadn't been manufactured a decade prior sprang to life.

"Jesus Christ," Moretti said to his overhead visor, head upturned in pure frustration at the sound of its ringtone. "Can I get a second to get my bearings, boys? Maybe take a piss?"

It seemed his superiors were keen on receiving an update as soon as possible - that much was made clear to him before he left Seattle. Still, it wasn't like he'd simply blow them off until it was convenient to reach out to them - so why call the literal second he arrived at the scene?

It was obvious.

Something else had happened while he'd been on his way there. No other reason. What remained after that conclusion was whether they'd let him in on the nature of the recent developments – or keep him in the dark instead.

And this Sicilian Defense style of thinking was how he was going to have to play this from here on out. He had to stay a step ahead of them at all costs, but there also had to be that fallback in case he faltered.

But it could be done. It *had* to be done. These motherfuckers had owned him for far too long already.

Here we go, he thought to himself before swiping the green "accept call" icon to the right on his phone.

"Moretti."

The voice that spoke on that phone was never a human one – spec ops always interacted with a computer-generated, digital speech generator . This way, the Morettis of the organization would be prevented from ever being able to identify, much less find whomever the individual was they directly reported to in the hierarchy. Moreover, they couldn't even be sure it was a single individual. In the field at least, Moretti's boss was a computer voice reading text instructions delivered on an encrypted line.

There was a low humming noise, followed by a series of three clicking noises.

"Contacts at scene have been altered and are different from initial dossier 41-985032. New personnel are F.B.I. Special Agents Kendrick and Pitcairn, Boston Major Case Detective O' Connell. Immediate objectives unchanged. Assess situation and acquire targets, if possible."

Three more clicking noises. The call ends.

"Yeah, no shit assholes. When isn't it assess and acquire?" But he did have his answer as to whether he'd get an updated version of what he'd been sent to investigate.

And that was a big ol' no, negative, not happening, Stephen Moretti. But instead of becoming frightened at that, he smiled.

His assessment of what was at play with this guy Keating's experiments was correct. One way or another, shit was going to get out so of hand here in Boston that the explosion the day before was going to seem like a firecracker in comparison. He'd been right to call Lourdes.

Moretti got out of the Toyota, locked it despite the obvious lack of any immediate signs of life, and made his way across the lot to the foot traffic friendly main entrance of Gordon University. Prior to reaching the mysteriously wide open and wrought iron gates, Moretti made the decision to walk the campus exterior perimeter for no other reason than to get a lay of the land. When it came down to it, whether one wanted to call it the cliched 'scene of the crime' , slightly less cringe-inducing 'epicenter of the shitstorm', or the passable and accurate 'ground zero for a purple and magenta lightning-fueled psychic detonation', Moretti felt that Keating's laboratory could wait another twenty minutes or so.

The damage there had been done. Moretti wanted to take in the incident's effects from a wide-angle first before zooming in close. He didn't need a long look at the former setting of his mind's eye to see -and hear- something terribly, terribly wrong with Gordon University.

He'd taken no more than ten or eleven steps beyond the gates before it had become apparent that the entire campus had somehow been disconnected, or more accurately, *disassociated* from the physical universe around it. Moretti sensed it the second he moved past the gate at the main entrance, then recognized it that moment or two later.

The university was silent.

As in, absolutely zero sound.

Anywhere.

But the disorienting nature of this subtle warping of the laws of physics wasn't just a matter of the campus being quiet at four in the morning; this was something as unnatural

as it was pervasive. It was as if the idea of ambient noise was forbidden. Unallowed, under any circumstances. No longer a thing, or an option. In essence, it felt like a strange kind of defense mechanism.

Moretti recalled that both the abandoned runway and the carpark at Logan Airport were saturated by the muted screams of Atlantic Ocean gusts, beyond number and beyond mercy, as they struck the few buildings that stood on that forsaken East Boston peninsula. But here, at this tiny college, something had happened just hours before that would have made that infinite sonic army, invisible and invincible, turn tail and run.

Continuing his walk along the edges of the school, Moretti thought of the woods after a heavy snowfall as being like what he experienced…in the way that an aspirin was like morphine in that both were painkillers.

But you gave aspirin to someone with a headache.

And Morphine to someone about to die.

Moretti stopped short, in front of a freshman dorm. Turning to face the building, he saw that every single blind in its windows had been drawn, and each had been snapped entirely shut. This was a place that didn't want to hear, didn't want to hear, and thus didn't want to feel. What had happened less than twenty-four hours prior his arrival had frightened Gordon College into —

"Catatonia," Moretti spoke aloud, barely being able to hear himself say the word.

This was bad. Bad even for a CRUCIBLE assignment. Nope. It was even worse than that. Moretti followed up his previous, elegant, one-word assessment with a cruder one. And delivered in a much louder, from-the-diaphragm volume.

"This place is fucked." Moretti quite clearly heard this proclamation and felt more at ease for having done so.

Coming back around to the gates after a bit less than a half-hour, it was time to work his way into the middle - towards the Science Building where it had all gone down. Everywhere, buildings had been cordoned off, locked down, gone black, and become husks. The campus had been closed to the media by sundown a few hours earlier, and any visitors and staff had been ordered to leave. He'd seen the occasional pair of State Troopers walking the grounds and recognized that as alarming as well.

In exactly zero states did State Troopers walk patrols of crime scenes in pairs. Even the buzzcut dopes with stiffer hats had themselves a little run down one pant leg.

Okay, so alarming, yet darkly amusing. Moretti appreciated the irony.

He passed between two admin buildings, both heavily adorned with cordoning chains and signs, with spotlights aimed directly at those same signs. When he emerged from that walkway, the Science Building stood before him in complete darkness. Not a spotlight, sign, or single shred of tape to be found.

Nobody wanted to come close to this structure, much less stay close to it for any length of time, much less have to fucking touch the thing even for the two or three seconds to put up a sign.

Moretti could feel it too. Something or things had been seen and/or possibly heard, by the eyes or ears of this world, in the halls of the structure waiting for him that was equal parts incomprehensible and horrific, .

And all at once Moretti found himself truly and completely scared for only the second time in his entire life.

The light that did reach the front of the Science Building had originated from multiple yet scattered, powerful but distant sources that had a direct line-of-sight path to it. Their combined brightness added up to little more than casting a few barely discernible shadows, some outlines of the windows as they had been arranged on the buildings' two floors, and the subtle movements of three men standing at the base of its front steps. From this distance, they looked like nervous, agitated ghosts no longer interested in haunting the halls they'd once roamed.

Moretti closed the distance between himself and where the men had gathered like a house cat, maintaining a steady and smooth rate of approach to delay his quarry's eventual notice of his presence. He'd have the full measure of all three before they could even catch their first glimpse.

First was to match names to faces, or even just shadows at that second. The one in the middle, a six-foot-six monster with an indoor voice loud enough to be heard through the sonic muffling had to be O' Connell, the major crimes guy from Boston. He was talking about the Bruins to two relative strangers, even in this situation and under these circumstances. No surprise there.

FBI Agents always seemed to have an air of conformity about them – one that took the form of an asinine kind of restraint. They generally wore conservative attire in the field, but were always quick to flash that oversized, ridiculous white rectangle they called a badge. Anytime one did it was like they trying to indicate much more important they were than everyone else simply with a piece of paper.

The one on O' Connell's left was nearly as tall as him but half as heavy and hadn't stopped glancing every which way since Moretti caught sight of them. He looked like a Pitcairn. The one on the right was average height and weight, but also had meticulously coifed hair. That one had to be Kendrick.

Done. They hadn't noticed him or his approach. Having completed that initial surveillance, Moretti announced himself.

"Gentlemen. Moretti. You must be Special Agent Pitcairn…" He made for this safety pin of a man, the most skittish of the group, sticking his hand out to him. After gasping in surprise at Moretti's seeming emergence from nowhere, the agent weakly raised his own to return the gesture.

"Ah! Agent Morett-"

O' Connell stepped in between the two of them like an offensive tackle picking up a blitz.

"He's Kendrick, asshole. You must be this top-secret spook asshole we've been waiting fah, hunh?"

Whoops. Moretti had incorrectly deduced the human microphone on the left was Pitcairn. It'd be easy to think that a couple of years chasing cults, aliens, magic, and weird shit had disconnected him from "normal" detective work, but it was a guess anyway. Moretti provoked reactions he wouldn't have gotten had he just strolled up on them, and that was the point.

Because O' Connell had just identified himself as a problem to be contended with inside of a few seconds. Moretti began contending by sidestepping him like a first-round cornerback, getting to the metaphorical quarterback anyway to complete the handshake/sack. Moretti knew it'd piss him right off.

"Apologies, Agent Kendrick. Stephen Moretti, Special Liaison." Kendrick took his hand in his. Moretti ignored the man standing no more than five inches behind him and moved on to the real Pitcairn, who looked like he'd been contemplating his resignation for the past several hours. Between both F.B.I. agents, there was no ceremonial flashing of the badge that followed either handshake – interesting. The F.B.I. guys were clearly deferring to –

"Ahem."

At last, Moretti turned around and glanced upward at O' Connell. Moretti's first impression was that his head resembled a tumor. His second was that this man could have been a Kingpin actors' double in a Marvel movie.

Moretti was silent, and simply stared into O' Connell's eyes.

"Don't I get a smile and a handshake, guy?" O' Connell asked, his face a noticeable shade of **red.** Moretti held quiet eye contact for another three or four seconds, then continued with his general greeting to the group.

"Gentlemen, thank you for remaining onsite until my arrival. I know it must have been a bit of wait, but I was coming all the way from Seattle."

Pitcairn volunteered some measure of professional courtesy, or at least tried to out of sheer habit it seemed.

"Quite alright sir, we heard a lot about…"

Pitcairn stopped here, having received an angry glare from O' Connell that instructed him to shut the fuck up.

'So who the fuck are you, Stephen Moretti Special Liaison?" demanded O' Connell.

"What fucked up government shit are you from?" with the 'are' in his last question sounding as if a pirate recently stabbed in the gut had said it aloud.

Moretti continued to act as if the man wasn't there, not really, anyway.

"I just need to be let into the building," he said.

Pitcairn looked to Kendrick, who only shrugged.

"We can provide an escort, give you what we know about-"

Moretti cut him off. "That won't be necessary, Agent Pitcairn. I'm making just a cursory survey for our science office."

O' Connell stepped into Moretti's face. He'd had it.

"That why they had the three of us stand here until four o' clock in the fucking morning pal?" This was the most insufferable of Boston accents, so 'here' came out as 'he-ah", 'four' came out as "fah", and 'fucking' and 'morning' were "fahkin' and 'mahnin'. Nothing worse to listen to on Earth. From the sound of it, Moretti deduced the man was from Charlestown, epicenter of butchered English in the universe.

"A cursory survey?"

O' Connell's breath smelled like a stale chicken parm sub and cherry vape smoke in the grossest possible mixture of those two odors. Still, he did not back down.

"Yes. Tell me, Detective O' Connell. Would you like to disappear forever?"

"PAH-don?"

"You heard me. I bet that despite your personality and face, there are people who still give a shit about you. They'll never receive any kind of closure, I assure you."

O' Connell looked into Moretti's eyes and saw that the threat was no bluff nor was it of the idle variety. He took a step back, having been backed down in swift fashion. Moretti continued the direct eye contact with O' Connell until finally the giant capitulated and looked away.

Once the stare down had completed, Kendrick made towards the front double doors and unlocked them.

"It's all yours, sir."

Moretti strode deliberately past O' Connell and up the entrance steps.

"Thank you, Agent Kendrick. Please ensure I'm left alone while I'm inside. I appreciate it." Moretti shook his hand again and took the keys Kendrick had used to unlock the door in doing so.

"Gonna need these. You don't mind, do you Agent Kendrick?"

"No. Not at all."

"Good man."

Moretti pushed open one of the wooden and glass double doors, walked in, and clicked a wall switch to attempt to turn on the lights.

Power to the building had not been restored, then.

Moretti reached into his jacket and pulled out his flashlight, one of those very breakable plastic ones that came only in outlandish colors - like bright yellow, cartoonish purple, or Halloween orange and cost no more than five dollars no matter what store one purchased it in. Moretti's was baby blanket blue, had bought it the day after he was recruited to CRUCIBLE, and he'd had it ever since. It was simple to use, with one switch - on/off, and when he needed it, that light always came through.

He'd even named it.

Fred the Flashlight.

"Alright, Fred. Showtime. Let's find out what the fuck happened here."

Click. Fred was ready.

He turned back around towards the door and glanced outside. O' Connell, Kendrick, and Pitcairn stood at the bottom of the stairs, gawking after him. Moretti lifted Fred and shone its beam directly into O' Connell's eyes. Among Fred's primary usage as a light source, Fred could also be used to annoy and harass as well. This was a bonus feature, arguably more valuable at that moment. Moretti locked the entrance double doors and disappeared into the darkness of the damaged building.

Outside, O' Connell growled under his breath.

"What if I disappear you first, asshole?"

Sarah wouldn't tell Magdalena what had happened to her during the final moments of the tape, despite Magdalena's constant pleading the moment she'd regaining consciousness. Or rather, snapping out of whatever analog-induced trance she'd been in while the end of the tape played out.

Sarah's obstinance started with the violent side-to-side shaking of her head in response to Magdalena's innocently phrased 'did I miss something'. From that reaction alone, it was clear to Magdalena that the moments just prior weren't simply a matter of her zoning out, but that something far more significant had just occurred.

"What happened, Sarah? Talk to me."

Sarah began backing away from her, as if she was afraid of her very presence. Sarah went into the kitchen, and Magdalena followed. On the third inquiry, Sarah answered by stating that 'it'd probably be safer and best if you didn't know, Mags', using the nickname she'd only given three people in her entire life permission to use.

It didn't help that they'd taken an instant disliking of each other the second they'd met at the University, each for their own reasons.

Sarah's had nothing to do with Magdalena, personally. It really didn't matter who it was, young or old, blue, brown, black hair and no tattoos or twenty, it was what Magdalena represented. Keating had reached out to Magdalena for help, instead of Sarah. She'd interpreted this as a slight – she had only been useful to him to perform the surgery, but after that it seemed she was no longer of use.

Magdalena's was personal, on the other hand. She'd just arrived in Boston after having endured Scumbag and Vic to get there, fighting and struggling until she'd met Roger and only to meet Sarah. Sarah, who had wasted no time in speaking to her in as condescending and disrespectful tone as she could possibly muster.

Now, seeing her again several days after that first meeting, Magdalena found herself having to fight back the overpowering urge to punch her in the mouth. Sarah wasn't just good and wasted – she was two or three drinks away from passing out cold. Seeing her in this condition, Magdalena's resentment skyrocketed to the point of having to hold back from smacking her dead. This complete drunk of a so-called scientist felt like she had the right to decide what knowledge was best for her to disseminate because she had a fucking degree.

Now, seeing her again several days after that first meeting, Magdalena found herself having to fight back the overpowering urge to punch her in the mouth. Sarah wasn't just good and wasted – she was two or three drinks away from passing out cold. Seeing her in this condition, Magdalena's resentment skyrocketed to the point of having to hold back from smacking her dead. This complete drunk of a so-called scientist felt like she had the right to decide what knowledge was best for her to disseminate because she had a fucking degree. Why she felt like that seemed more rooted in some stupid power trip on Sarah's account, and not based in keeping anyone's best interests in mind.

Caleb on the other hand, seemed a little bit more likable than Sarah, based solely on their one and only encounter. The dude looked and acted like the prototypical New England professor/academic - dressed as if he'd just finished an L.L. Bean catalog model shoot, and sported wire-rimmed glasses that constantly fell down his face because he had a narrow, sloped nose that looked as if it could cut a roast. The man-bun he sported was way too much, however. That thing needed to go. Immediately.

Still a bit assholish, though. Between him and Sarah, there was no compelling evidence that said people with advanced science degrees weren't also infused with a healthy (or unhealthy, depending on how one regarded it) dose of arrogance and entitlement.

It certainly wasn't deserved in that moment for Sarah. Since the tape had ended, she'd been frantically pacing around her apartment, calling Caleb over and over again on her cell phone.

It went like this for a solid hour:

Sarah would start with an angry yet desperate plea for Caleb to answer his phone.

"Cmon cmon, pick up you fucking asshole."

Sarah then pulls her index finger back as if nocking an arrow, then slams the tip onto the end button on her phone.

Hits redial.

Dials again.

Phone begins ringing.

Angry yet desperate plea.

No answer.

Rinse and repeat.

"Hey Sarah?"

Sarah ignored her. Dialed Caleb's phone again.

"Sarah, if we're about to meet up with Caleb anyway, why do you need to talk to him so badly *now*?"

Sarah glared at Magdalena as if to say *how dare you interrupt my panic attack*, with one side of her face – eyebrow, cheek, and lips turned upwards in a collective sneer. She turned away from Magdalena to listen for Caleb, like doing that would either improve her cell phone reception or hearing.

No answer from Caleb again. She hit the end button. She whipped back around to face Magdalena again and stomped over to her kitchen counter. She poured another shot.

"Can you please just answer me? Or maybe just say words instead of glaring at me? I'd even take just sitting down and breathing for a second instead of drinking," asked Magdalena.

Sarah tensed up, this last comment about her current relapse upping her anxiety. She threw back the shot in one swift motion and slammed the glass down.

She turned on Magdalena like a cornered, feral animal.

"Because we're not just meeting him, dear. It's Caleb and this other guy…person. Whatever."

"What other guy?"

"An agent. Liaison, he said. Moretti. Some government spook-agency thing. Why do you think we sent you to that hotel?"

Magdalena hadn't really given a shit why they had, but it made sense. She waved her hand in a circular motion for Sarah to continue.

"I don't fucking trust him, why would you, but for some reason he's been helping us. I *can't* tell Caleb what just happened with you because Caleb will be with him, so that's why I gotta get a hold of him. I don't want this…guy knowing what the hell just happened."

In truth, she'd been specifically told to report anything directly to CRUCIBLE and CRUCIBLE only.

Sarah bent at the knees, suddenly overcome with the combination of a perilously high blood alcohol level and current level of insanity in her life. She swayed as she did so, and pointed at Magdalena.

"If I'm not telling youuuu, then I'm trying to protect youuuu, precious Magdalena." Sarah then began to fall forward. Magdalena caught her in time to prevent Sarah from doing a faceplant onto her kitchen floor. Locking her arms under each of Sarah's armpits, Magdalena dragged her over to a chair at her kitchen table.

What Sarah had just said made no sense. If this guy Moretti was helping them, then why would she need protecting from him? Why keep anything from him, either, trust or no? Sarah was probably too drunk to even try to explain or answer those questions. Still, it was obvious that even if Sarah wasn't whiskey-blitzed, she still wouldn't give her the full story.

Which was insulting as fuck.

I fucking hate booze, Magdalena thought to herself, to distract herself from her loathing of Sarah. There was nothing she hated more than alcohol. Her father's alcoholism saw to that before Magdalena had reached her thirteenth birthday.

Childhood trauma notwithstanding, drunks are intolerable to be around for the sober, almost without exception. Alcohol always has a way of amplifying the negative aspects of a person's personality, and Magdalena could tell that Sarah was the type of person that got pissy even at minor inconveniences. Major ones like, well, everything that was happening then turned Sarah into the stumbling bitch trying not to throw up all over her kitchen table at the present.

"I don't need protecting, Sarah. Especially not from a terrified drunk, anyway."

At this, Sarah launched herself straight up, nearly falling over in the process.

"I'm not fucking doing it for you, sweetie. Doing it for David."

So there it was. Sarah wasn't afraid for herself, or Caleb, or Magdalena. She was afraid for her boss. This was her trying to stay loyal to the guy, as misguided as it was. Maybe she wasn't a complete asshole after all.

Magdalena, summoning every ounce of patience and temerity she could, walked over to her, guided her back down into her chair and asked:

"If you're not gonna tell me what just happened, can you answer maybe just another question then?"

"What."

"Who the hell is Moretti? You must know more than he's a 'liaison'"

Sarah closed her eyes. "Moretti is the guy that got us of jail that night we fucked everything up. He showed up, waved a wand, and poof Caleb and I were out of jail. I came here, home, and he went to fucking Germany."

Sarah gestured wildly towards the bedroom.

"My job was to go through all the shit that went down."

"So why is he helping you and nobody else is?"

Sarah's eyes fluttered, and she shrugged her shoulders.

"Be damned if I knew," she said.

Moretti had received full floor plans for the Science Building when he first got the call the day before and was currently using Fred to illuminate the papers he'd printed them out on. He'd printed everything out, despite the strict mandate to never reproduce materials related to an assignment. This was a security measure, but Moretti wasn't about to look at the electronic copy on an inches wide cell phone screen.

And it was fortuitous that he had. His two cell phones powered on, but neither came close to functioning. Strange – it had been clear from the physical phenomena outside that some manner of field had been projected or was still projecting around the campus. But this field didn't seem to affect electric current, and by default magnetism – but higher electronic functions were seemingly kaput.

Moretti thought of the rest of materials that he'd received and was relieved he'd made hard copies of everything. Lourdes would need it all when the time came.

The electronic information was no longer available, anyway. Files transmitted by even the most encrypted satellites, and even those that CRUCIBLE used could still be intercepted, discovered, and decoded by the wrong parties.

CRUCIBLE found their way around that. They simply wiped every trace that could be found of both the transmission and the transmitted from existence. Every dossier was remotely wiped and any electronic device re-imaged remotely one hour after Moretti received them.

And Moretti had found his way around CRUCIBLE. It was an old dot-matrix printer he'd used with a Commodore 64 in his early twenties.

That dossier included briefings on Dr. David Keating, Sarah Fischer, and Caleb West, the three scientists responsible for the mess in Massachusetts. Each of them had interesting histories as far as CRUCIBLE was concerned, and thus had full workups on each.

But not even one of them had any kind of a criminal record, not even jaywalking, so local and even federal law enforcement had nothing really to go on any of them. Which was good.

Moretti thought to himself, swinging Fred from one empty, pitch black office to another, that Massachusetts State Police and the FBI were probably limiting their investigations to charges like manslaughter, criminal negligence, destruction of property and the like. They weren't thinking about what Keating and his assistants were experimenting with. That buffoon downstairs was bullying his F.B.I. counterparts likely so he could ring them up himself, get the collar, and make the Channel Four news. Moretti had to be careful to keep O' Connell in his lane.

CRUCIBLE loved guys like him. He'd been one of those kinds once as well.

Moretti found a clear spot in a first-floor hallway to hunker down and get his bearings. He placed his floor map on the ground, sat down cross-legged and studied the drawing.

"Fred, it looks like our three idiots er, *scientists*, were up the stairs and directly to the left. You ready for all of this?"

Fred dimmed for just a split second, the way cheap flashlights often do, but Moretti interpreted this instead as Fred's 'let's do this, you silly bastard' acknowledgement. Moretti folded up the map and stuck it in his jacket pocket.

Fred dimmed again, as if to ask him if *he* was ready.

"You know it buddy," Moretti replied to his anthropomorphized flashlight.

It dimmed a third time.

Moretti sighed.

"Yes. I know. The **crimson**.. It'll be okay, Fred. It's just for scrying, it's not for…the other thing."

Yet.

Fred returned to normal function.

"Doesn't mean I'm suddenly good with it, either."

Moretti reached the top of steps and looked to his left, in the direction of the lab. The double doors into the area looked as if they'd been blown off their hinges with a napalm bazooka.

"Why do I always get picked for this shit?" Moretti asked, his voice echoing down the hallway and into the room ahead.

He'd been picked seconds after the massive final operamine injection had hit Keating's nervous system and activated enough neuronal cells to be detected by CRUCIBLE. Moretti had just woken up and had fixed himself his customary breakfast of a salad bowl filled with an entire box of Cookie Crisp cereal when the notification came in on his black phone - that stupid fucking black phone –

-MAJOR FLUCTUATIONS IN ALPHA WAVE SPECTRUM –
-NORTH OF BOSTON, MASSACHUSETTS, USA-

Looking at the screen and the words displayed upon it, Moretti reflexively and sarcastically said "Oh phew. For a second I thought it could have been Boston, Turkmenistan. Asses." Why they felt the need to include the Massachusetts and USA part eluded him.

His eyes widened when he read the words 'alpha waves', however.

Moretti pocketed the phone, then trudged up the stairs in his house to his third-floor office and unlocked the door. There was nothing in the space except a cheap desk, a wooden chair, a lamp, and a computer monitor. The walls were blank. The windows had never been opened. Moretti sat down at the desk, took the carryall bag up off the floor and placed it on the desk. He placed the phone next to the carryall and waited.

He'd spent no more than two hours in that office during the three years and change he'd worked for CRUCIBLE. He snorted dismissively.

"Worked".

Moretti may have awoken less than an hour before getting the alert, but the machinery that operated within his thoughts began its initial round of questions. It was what had got him to detective by twenty-seven, detective sergeant by thirty-three, and a straight legend in the Seattle PD by forty. They'd called him a savant, a brilliant criminal mind, born to the profession.

Moretti wished he could cut all the wiring to it and be done with it forever since the talent had surfaced by junior high school

Because when he began the questions, he'd never stop…until there were no more to ask.

"Now. Why are they calling *me* to the scene?"

There were countless Special Operatives between him and Boston that could have been faster to arrive on scene. Obviously more loyal ones as well.

"What did they mean by fluctuations? Intensity? Location? Both?"

Moretti had been doing research on that biophysical phenomenon ever since Burlington – or since he'd been coerced into taking this…position.

Because before he'd even got on the plane to come back to Seattle after what happened there, he knew they were a pre-condition of circumstance that would allow him to escape CRUCIBLE.

Could CRUCIBLE be onto him somehow? It was possible. The questions linked, so Moretti went further. Kept asking.

"Do they know I'd be looking for this type of case, specifically, and that's why they're sending me – to possibly trap me?"

This worried him.

"How could they know? Are they trying to lure the *srorrim* out?"

The low-pitched ring tone that Moretti had come to dread began to emanate from his black phone, the same tone that would ring in the Gordon University parking lot several hours later. Moretti picked it up and closed his eyes as if to meditate. On the fifth ring, he pressed the 'answer' button.

"Moretti." The robot voice began.

Since that day, it hadn't become any clearer to him what their motivations were.

This worried him more.

He stood just outside the lab where Keating and his team had performed their work, in the space where the double doors to the lab should have been. The rumination over yesterday's chain of events occupied his mind as he'd approached the area. This was the flashpoint, the fulcrum upon which all these things were held in a balanced orbit – for now. His methodical recall of recent events was a centering exercise for him, something he'd practiced since he began working for CRUCIBLE. Bring all your thoughts to the beginning before starting again.

The double doors had been pried off and removed completely, it seemed. If they had been pried, they couldn't be opened.

Fused.

The doors had fused together.

Jesus Christ.

Moretti stepped into the laboratory proper.

The smell of burned plastic, rubber, metal, and chemicals still hung in the air, permeated the parts of the lab that hadn't been reduced to char or ash. But the odor of something else hit his senses, overpowering all those rancid remains of fire and destruction. It was…alien. It didn't belong here. It didn't belong anywhere.

Moretti thought:

This area would have been ventilated in the intervening hours, certainly, after everyone had been evacuated and the immediate danger mitigated.

But there was something in here that couldn't be ventilated, couldn't be cleared.

The fear Moretti felt no more than a few minutes before, outside, had returned.

Moretti did a quick side to side scan of the lab with Fred. He shook his head.

"One of these times Fred, I promise. I'm just gonna ignore that fucking phone call."

Caleb had no idea what to expect when he got back to Logan, or who would end up greeting him once he arrived. Or if he was going to continue living for long once on the ground.

Some real time had passed since the explosion – not hours, and not a day or two, but weeks. What was the press saying? What did people think? To what extent was his life just…over?

He hadn't stopped thinking about the woman - Magdalena - showing up at Gordon out of the blue just days after the fire. Like she'd been summoned. Like David said he had done.

Nor could he push Moretti's presence from his mind for very long, either. Just before he'd put Caleb on the plane to Europe, he assured him that he'd take care of any charges -pending, of course, his full cooperation in retrieving anything he could from Keating's family in Germany. Moretti also made it his responsibility to ensure Sarah turned over their full video record of their experiments.

Caleb turned away from that face of his – and that ghost stare of his – to head towards the gate. Before he could scan his boarding pass however, he heard Moretti call to him one more time. The fucking guy had a voice you couldn't ignore. Caleb did try.

"Oh, and hey Caleb!"

And failed.

Caleb turned to face him one more time.

"Don't lie to me son. And I'll know if you're lying to me, Caleb." Caleb found himself nodding like a chastised grade schooler.

Today he wasn't going to lie – explicitly, that was. Caleb didn't think the omissions of materials he was sent to secure in Germany counted in this case - especially to a guy who had been concealing who he really worked for the entire time he'd known him. If Sarah didn't try to hide any of the analog tapes she'd kept at her place, Caleb felt like he'd be okay.

Caleb thought about the small refrigerator in the corner of his basement. The small refrigerator that had been wired to a back-up source of power if something crazy had happened and his house had lost power…to a snowstorm or what have you. The five hundred milliliter Nalgene flask had to always remain between two and eight degrees Celsius. Above eight-point-seven Celsius, and…

The day of the explosion, the lightning, the power surge, and the resulting power surge had destroyed most or all of the equipment and computers in the lab, taking the biological and chemical samples stored there with them. The entire purified store of operamine was among the 'tits up' reagents as well.

Except for the sample that Caleb kept at home.
In the small refrigerator in the basement.
That was always going to be omission *numero uno* to Moretti. To everyone, really. It was his insurance plan, break glass in case of, get out of jail sorta-free card.

Did any of the other facts he'd planned on leaving out of the story he was giving to Moretti really matter after the existence of nearly a half-liter of operamine?

The second omission, of course, was Magdalena. That she was real. Not a dream, not a hallucination, not a vision of a guardian angel.
Caleb unbuckled the safety beat in his seat when the plane came to a stop. He stood up and made eye contact with the stewardess. She smiled at him. He smiled back, thinking it might be the last one he'd ever exchange with another human being. Because…
This wasn't going to end well.
Caleb stepped off his plane, and onto the jet walk. He could feel how cold it was through the porous metal construction of the contraption – one of those aberrantly arctic days that would punch its way into a Boston November like a soccer hooligan at an American football game.
Caleb drifted in behind a tight group of three people who'd seemingly all got off the plane simultaneously, but ahead of him. Peering through the open spaces between their heads out into the terminal, he expected more suited agents like the pair in Heathrow waiting for him there. They'd slap the cuffs on the second he walked out, dragged away to a federal prison for the rest of time.
He emerged from the terminal doorway and -
Nothing. No one. A mostly empty terminal, with no one noticing or even caring he'd arrived.
But his paranoia only barely eased, subsiding in the most marginal of ways and one Caleb couldn't notice – his pupils returned to normal dilation from black hole-sized. Still, it didn't amount to much.

In that space in his mind where the irrational had done the most damage and disrupted the most basic of thoughts, a paralyzing dread snuck in anyway… as if waiting for the opportune moment to strike. Sheer terror would follow, to destroy any remaining grip on sanity.

Every step forward felt labored, and every second that passed seemed to be weighted, as if waterlogged with fear of the next horrible thing to happen. Caleb was certain that the bullet destined for his brain would hit his skull within the next five minutes.

Caleb made his way down to the baggage claim, appearing to every person who caught sight of him, even briefly, to think he'd done an eight-ball in one of the airport bathrooms. He couldn't stop shaking.

When he arrived in front of the enormous silver contraption, Caleb found that despite only having eight or nine passengers, his flight's baggage hadn't begun being shunted out onto the baggage carousel. Caleb pulled out a phone - not his usual iPhone 14, but the burner phone he'd set up to speak to Sarah directly and as secretly as was possible.

He turned it on.

There were seventeen missed calls, all within twenty minutes of each other, and they were all from Sarah. Holy shit.

The calls were all from forty-five minutes ago, while his plane was on final descent, so he wouldn't have been able to answer even if wanted. There was no point in calling until he got back to his car.

His battered brown suitcase pushed its way through the car-wash flaps of the baggage carousel entrance, and Caleb jogged around the entirety of the pathway to grab his bag as fast as he could.

Another passenger from his flight waiting for her bags remarked: "looks like somebody can't wait to get home!"

'Spot on, lady,' he thought, "I simply can't wait to get back to the nightmare my life has become'. Caleb jogged towards the sliding glass doors. Beyond that was the parking garage where he'd left his Toyota for the past week.

Caleb didn't wait until he got the car to call Sarah back. He stepped out of the cold, harsh New England air and into the relative warmth of the parking garage lobby area. He slid his parking ticket into the automated machine, and then dialed Sarah. There was a click, and then the line picked up.

Sarah skipped the pleasantries. "CALEB WHAT THE FUCK?? WHERE HAVE YOU BEEN?!?! YOU SAID YOU WERE GOING TO CALL THIS MORNING?"

Sarah was so loud, Caleb had to hold it a foot or two away from his face.

"Sarah. Sarah! My flight was delayed. My flight - my flight WAS DELAYED! Calm down!"

She was drunk. Fuck.

It took a couple of minutes, but Sarah's voice returned to a reasonable volume and tone. While she kept going on and not making any sense, Caleb finished the transaction with the ticket scanner. He slipped his wallet back into his pocket and then turned his focus completely on the call.

Sarah had been mumbling the entire time.

Yep. Definitely shitfaced. They were so totally fucked now.

"Are you kidding me right now Sarah?"

"What?"

"You've been drinking, haven't you?"

"Yeah, but just a little - I was watching the tapes this morning because -"

"Right. Because we're meeting Moretti and watching the videos of the work we did stressed you out so much that you had to pick up the bottle."

"No Caleb, it's not that. Something's happened."

Caleb rolled his eyes and pushed the '5' button on the elevator control panel. "Oh yeah, something's happened all right. You found the whiskey you keep in the back of one of your cabinets, tied one on."

The doors opened, and Caleb stepped on. Sarah began to sob.

"Caleb, I'm scared. I'm scared about meeting this guy Moretti again. I — I don't trust him. I've been *alone, and I didn't know what to do.* And then...well...Magdalena came here. We watched the last video together."

"So?"

The elevator doors opened onto the fifth floor, the roof of the airport parking garage. Snow gusts immediately hit Caleb square in his face. The sky was charcoal, and he could barely see more than thirty or so feet ahead of him. Caleb stepped outside, and the strength of the wind made it difficult to hear Sarah's voice in the phone speaker. He turned his back against the blistering gusts, dropped to one knee, stuck a finger in one ear, and attempted to listen.

"....stood there....she....possessed or...connected...Magdalena..."

Sarah seemed continue for another thirty seconds or so, but Caleb could barely hear a word. He stood back up, having given up until he could get back to his car. Caleb turned and looked towards his car. As it came into view, he noticed a man leaning against the passenger side of his car. He didn't need to get any closer to know who it was.

Moretti, dressed in a black peacoat and black Fishermen's wool cap.

Dread overcame Caleb completely. Time began to feel...heavy. The seconds like minutes, the minutes, hours. He approached his car. Moretti spoke up, loud enough to be heard over the wind.

"Well, Mr. West. Welcome back to the states."

"Hi, Agent Moretti."

Moretti frowned. "Oh, Caleb. I thought we were past all that. I told you before - just Moretti. That 'agent' shit is for the dickheads that still care about the cause and the true believers. Now," Moretti came fully to his feet and stopped leaning on Caleb's car. He approached, stopping such that his face was only four or five inches from Caleb's.

"Why do you think I'm standing here, getting snow-blind, freezing my ass off, voluntarily ruining my day...instead of where we agreed we were going to meet?"

Caleb shrugged his shoulders.

Moretti was average height but could make himself seem like he was seven feet tall simply by altering his mood.

"I told you not to keep anything from me, kiddo." Moretti took another step forward and was now right in his face.

"Yes, Agent - I mean, Steve. Stephen. Moretti."

"And what did you do?"

"I-"

"You kept something from me. Or should I say, someone." Moretti held up a picture of Magdalena in his right hand, which Caleb could only see out of the corner of his eye. The picture was taken in Boston, not Florida.

"This is her, isn't it? The woman from Keating's vision?"

Caleb said nothing. Moretti shook his head.

"Alright, kid. It's alright. Protecting her. I get it. Get in. Let's go see her."

"I wasn't-"

"Can see it on your face kiddo. You don't think you were, but you were. Might make a decent man out of you yet."

Caleb pulled his keys out of his jacket pocket and made to walk over to the drivers' side of his car. Moretti snatched them out of his hand with an unexpected deftness and speed.

"I'll drive. You've got some listening and reading to do on the way. Get in."

The two of them got in the car. Moretti started it up.

"This thing run decent Caleb? Not gonna conk out on us on the way over to Ms. Fischer's place, is it?"

"No, it's fine."

"Good. Myself? Been driving a total piece of shit since I got here." Moretti stopped and looked at him.

"I don't blame you for keeping secrets. I'd probably do the same. I've been keeping a lot of stuff from you, but that's my job, y' know?"

"Who the hell do you work for, Moretti?"

"We'll get to that. Guessing you ran into a couple of colleagues somewhere along the way. But you gotta start asking better questions, bud."

"Like what?" Caleb asked.

"What you should be asking is *why* I work for the people I do."

Caleb sighed in frustration. "Okay, *why* do you work for the people you do? I really don't know what you or these people want to gain out of this."

"I work for them because I have a unique talent, Caleb. Something that makes me...invaluable to people like them. But they don't know the half of it. And they *can't* know, either. Put your seat belt on."

Moretti threw it into reverse. The two of them drove off.

Moretti stood staring at the gurney Keating had strapped himself to, and two things came to mind:

The black-and-white 1931 film "Frankenstein", the original and only, some would say. Moretti, like most people, hadn't read Mary Shelley's book, and so their exposure to the tale was through movies and television. Moretti remembered his mother popping the VHS tape in when he was 8 or 9 one Halloween, thinking it was better holiday fare for a child than that Michael Myers movie that had just come out.

The psych ward he'd spent six weeks in as a teenager, seven years after his viewing of "Frankenstein" with his mother. His analytical mind wasn't seen or regarded as the precision tool it would be later in life back then. Instead, his alcoholic father thought he was schizophrenic and had him committed.

Moms and Dads could be so different sometimes.

"Ironic, isn't it Frederick?" asked Moretti of his plastic companion. "I got strapped to one of these against my will a few times in junior high, and nothing exciting happened except me feeling forgetful for two days. This guy Keating though? Lights up every goddamn psychic switchboard on the east coast, willingly frying his brainpan in the process.

Moretti looked over to his left and saw that Keating had himself plugged into an EEG machine, which in turn was plugged into the building's power supply. The burnt-out device was only a couple of feet from the gurney.

"So. The good doctor injects himself with some crazy compound X. Something happens inside his skull that fed actual electrical current – and a whole lot of it - back through into the EEG, into the building's electrical system, then the campus systems, and so on.

Holy shit. This was it, then. Keating had force-evolved himself. Into…what?

"Okay Fred, thanks for doing the heavy lifting. I'll take it from here." Moretti shut the flashlight off and stood silently in near darkness for a moment.

"I hate this part," he said.

Moretti took a pocketknife from his bomber jacket and pulled the blade out. He closed his eyes.

And began to chant…

And all at once…

Used the knife to make deep cuts on both hands…

And wiped the blood upon his brow, cheeks, and chin.

He opened his eyes the whites having turned the same color as the blood that covered his face.

He said one word:
"Chichiltic."

Moretti laid down on the gurney, and slid his hands around the wrist restraints, grasping them in each **crimson**-soaked palm....

Moretti had used the crimson to connect with Keating. It was day. - and Keating's mind had been altered…physically…chemically. It was…alien….like an insect. No - not like an insect - like Keating had changed his mind to function like one. Why?

Because he was alone, and he never knew how to reach out. Keating was alone - profoundly alone. This was his way to never feel that way again. He wanted to be like everyone else. He'd never connected, truly connected, with anyone ever in his life. Moretti could feel nothing but pity for him. Keating's was a profound, unending sadness.

And then - a needle.

Directly into the base of his brain. A moment of pain, and then — an expansion. Too fast. Too much. Moretti was only a passenger here, so he only experienced a fraction of what Keating felt, which must have been staggering. The topography of the brain was no longer sufficient to hold what had been laid bare and opened.

Keating -

Split into

Countless numbers of himself.

The countless multiplied again and again until all of him -

His consciousnesses disappeared into darknesses beyond number at the bottom of infinite voids. He followed just one of him as it fell until it reached an end that had no end, and there he saw…a woman?

How was this?

Pretty — late thirties/early forties yet still somehow with the innocence of a child and the hope of the broken-hearted.

What was….where were they?

They sensed him at once.

He could not stay there in the darkness with Keating's consciousness. They knew he was watching them.

But then Moretti felt -

THERE WERE THINGS IN THE DARKNESS.

Fear. He must not know them. They were unknowing. He would become undone to see them. Madness. They were coming.

THEY WERE COMING.

He let go of the fragment of Keating he'd tethered himself to, and was ejected out from…he had no word for it. It was a no-place.

At once the world appeared as if it were made of light, and what was left was:

Energy. Keating hadn't become the energy; he'd left it behind. Somehow Keating's thoughts had become manifest, but uncontrolled. Random. Like - electricity in a field. The sheer power of what he had ascended to was surging through the air, through cables, and wires. But it was cold. Ice. What had held life within it held life within it no more. As Keating departed from the world, the purple and magenta and indigo bolts shot out, unchecked, destroying whatever it touched.

A thousand different directions. Unchecked. Keating's power left here. And Keating himself was....

Moretti sat up.

"Nowhere." He thought he'd heard a word for it in his head, but it sounded made up, foreign. Maybe.

But this was nothing he'd ever seen before. Nothing the world had seen before.

He saw death. He saw destruction.

Moretti clicked Fred on and rummaged through his pocket. He pulled out the black phone and pressed the call button. There was a single ring, and then the sound of the line being picked up. Moretti had to control the narrative.

Starting now.

If CRUCIBLE ever knew...

The robot voice spoke.

"Report, Agent Moretti."

"Bullshit, Moretti. That's not a thing. People can't just cut their hands open, touch things, and see the past," insisted Caleb. His arms were folded, like a petulant child who'd been told he can't get a Happy Meal just because he wanted to play with the toy inside.

Moretti couldn't help but smirk. It was always the scientific types that dismissed things like precognition, psychometry, and ESP as if it was heresy to even say the words out loud. Seeing Caleb's hypocritical obstinance was extra satisfying – the kid had seen Keating's transformation first-hand, was five feet away from Keating's consciousness as it split into an infinite number of fragments - each so tiny as to slip completely out of reality, only to reform again, only in a nothing-space where existence should have been impossible.

And still, Caleb had the absolute balls to tell Moretti that there was no way that his crazy shit could possibly be true. It didn't matter – the point of the exercise wasn't the transmission of that information, but to try and calm the kid down by telling him they really were paddling the same leaking raft.

"Hand me the phone you use to talk to Sarah."

Caleb glared at him, shocked. Moretti couldn't have been able to see him-

"I saw you using it when you stepped off the elevator. It's clearly not your regular phone man. Nobody uses flip phones anymore. Well except us. I have secret friends too kiddo."

Caleb thought Moretti must have had some kind of crazy eyesight augmentation. Moretti just had a pair of IR goggles in his left pocket.

"You're not going to call-"

"I'm not going to use your damn phone, Caleb. Just hand it to me for one second."

Caleb handed it to him. Moretti pulled off the highway, near North Station, and then into a street-level parking spot.

Moretti took the phone into his left hand, then rolled down the drivers' side window. He then fired the thing out in the storm.

"*DUDE WHAT THE FUCK?*" yelled Caleb.

Moretti grunted, then rolled up the window.

"So, Sarah's either an alcoholic or an addict. Which is it?"

"Did your blood power tell you that?"

"Nope. You did. Just now."

"How…"

"You don't need that phone anymore, Caleb. So why get angry about me tossing it out the window, unless you thought something else could happen in the what…half-hour, hour before we get to Sarah's house? Screams addiction, bud."

"Alcoholic. She relapsed earlier. Shit just finally got to her."

"That's too bad," Moretti was angry with himself. He wished he could have sent Sarah, but knowing Keating's family history, there was no way she would have gotten a thing out of them.

They sat there in silence for a moment. The snowfall eased up, so it became possible to see more of Causeway Street.

After another minute or two, Caleb broke the silence.

"You know Keating is right up the str-"

"He needs Magdalena. We'd be wasting our time." Moretti narrowed his eyes. I need a minute to think.

This is the moment, Stephen.
Decide.
You call this in right now, CRUCIBLE takes the three of them in to never be seen or heard from again. You get back on a plane to Seattle. CRUCIBLE adds whatever biotechnology they've developed to their arsenal. But —
You may never get another chance like this again. You're going to have to rely on the kid sitting next to you, a frightened drunk, and a woman you've never actually met in person before. Not good.
Yet there was something about that woman, Magdalena. There was an inner strength within her, so powerful that he could sense it seeping out of her presences' edges - despite her never had called upon it. The woman reminded Moretti of…Lourdes. But likely what Lourdes must have been like before *she became the badass he'd met in Vermont years ago.*
Lourdes had helped Moretti call forth his better, true self then. Decision ma-

"OK. Fuck it," said Moretti. It was the first time Caleb had heard the man use the f-word since he'd met him.

"Is everything okay, Moretti?" he asked.

"Not at all," he replied. Moretti threw the car in drive and pulled out. He continued:

"We're…*they're* called CRUCIBLE, Caleb. And they're the organization that's going to try and kill every single one of us."

"Us?" asked Caleb.

"Yeah."

Chapter Thirteen

The robot voice repeated its command.

"Report, Agent Moretti."

He remained silent.

Five minutes passed, then the automated voice spoke a third time.

"Report, Agent Moretti."

He let out a deep breath. On his last assignment, Moretti had accidentally learned that not responding to the automated voice three times transferred the connection to CRUCIBLE senior. Or whatever. It'd be another ten whole minutes after this last prompt before a person would pick up on the line, however. Which was fine. He'd use the time to process what he'd just experienced. Moretti set the phone down on the ground in front of him and closed his eyes.

Keating's work was going to change the world. How and what would change would be determined by what transpired over the coming weeks. His transformation would erase everything about what it may or may not have meant to be human.

Oh, and opened a pathway to a place that may be outside of the known universe. That too.

He'd manifested his consciousness as bioelectric energy outside of his physical body the day of the explosion. In that metamorphosis, in freeing that which is contained within a central nervous system, it revealed – albeit in a chaotic and unstable manner – that the raw power of that essence is far greater than chemical and electrical potentials.

Moretti had piggy-backed on that transformation, and in doing so gained an understanding of what transpired. It was both the most freeing and most terrifying experience a person could possibly fathom.

Moretti considered that he was likely the only person on earth that would have been able to make that connection as the **crimson.** Lourdes was a big believer in destiny and fate. Moretti wondered what she'd have to say about this.

"Hey Lourdes – this guy Keating? Makes Professor Courtney seem like a vanilla cupcake by comparison – least in just raw brain power. He can-"

"What are you gonna do about him, Moretti?"

"I-I-I don't know yet. He's not an evil piece of-"

"When they seek power for its' own sake, its' *always* evil. They are *always* evil."

"I'm not sure that's why he did it, Lourdes. I need to know more about him."

"So find out. You were meant to be here. You were always meant to be here."

"Puedes ser un verdadero dolor en el culo, Lourdes."

"Buena suerte, padre."

What Keating had become could destroy CRUCIBLE. Evil, good…it didn't matter. Moretti needed him either way.

There was an audible click sound on his phone, and the silence of the laboratory was broken. Moretti had lost himself in thought. The click had snapped him out of it.

"Stephen. This is the second time you've broken communication protocol in a year. A third time will result in your immediate termination."

Moretti knew what they meant by termination, and it didn't mean he was going to have to polish his resume to look for a new job. "I apologize, but the details in Massachusetts warrant direct communication with a ranking agent."

"You cited that exact reason six months ago when the same type of direct contact was made. This dereliction of procedure was tolerated in Burlington when you first started. The incident six months ago did not require-"

The mention of his cry for help, that night in the church with Lourdes, set him off.

"I was fucking surrounded by reassembled ragdoll corpses from a hundred dead people!!"

"This incident does not require direct communication."

Oh, I think it does, whoever you are, thought Moretti, fuming.

"Sir, if you'll allow me to at least appraise you of the situation. Dr. Keating has discovered-"

"I am going to disconnect now, Stephen. Please call back and make your report on the established channel."

Click.

"So be it, assholes. Wasn't about to tell you the truth, anyway."

There was nothing more to be learned here, or to be done. Moretti got up and started to make his way back to where the three stooges, who were undoubtedly still talking about him, stood watch. If it had just been O' Connell standing out there he'd have taken his time, maybe even searched the halls for a vending machine to get a soda, because fuck that guy.

Moretti flipped Fred back on, and the beam fell upon something that very much gave Moretti a bit of pause.

"Oh, Fred. Good job, my man," Moretti said as he approached it, a device that was anachronistic and bizarre to behold, given the level of biochemical technology on display here.

It was an old video cassette recorder camera mounted on a tripod. Like, mid to late 1980's VHS camcorder - the kind that kicked out scratchy tapes with date stamps written in loud, bright white letters in the corner of whatever was being recorded. Moretti walked over to it and stuck his free hand into the empty tape slot.

Interesting. They'd been recording their work using VHS tapes so there wouldn't be a digital record, to copy and/or steal. Which probably meant they'd kept most of their data someplace that wasn't easily found. Maybe these three scientists weren't so dumb after all.

He'd planned on interviewing the other two that were in the lab with Keating, his assistants. Now he had himself some leverage.

Sarah slammed the phone down on the kitchen table, seemingly with enough force to shatter the thing. She hadn't bothered to push the 'end' button before she did, so the scratchy, broken sound of Caleb's voice could still be heard. Magdalena walked over behind Sarah and reached over her shoulder to take the phone away so she wouldn't have a chance to snatch it before she could. She pushed 'end', and then Magdalena pocketed the phone.

"Sounds like he knew you were drinking from here, Sarah."

"Naw, he musta got cut off. I don't know what's happening right now."

No shit, thought Magdalena. This girl needed to stop fucking drinking...like now. And she wasn't going to stop unless she had no other choice.

Magdalena spied the whiskey sitting on the kitchen counter. She grabbed the bottle, ripped off the cap, and dumped the rest down the sink drain. It wasn't much, maybe three or four fingers worth from the bottom. Shaking her head, Magdalena cursed herself for not doing it sooner.

Sarah made no attempt to stop her. In fact, she'd barely noticed. The fruitless phone call she finally got from Caleb drained her aggression completely, washed her belligerence away like a bedsheet stain. All that was left was despair. Defeat. Self-pity. Her head was down, her gaze fixed upon her kitchen table. Magdalena watched as Sarah began tracing the darker grains of wood on its surface with her finger, left to right.

Only a matter of time before she passed out. Magdalena had to keep that from happening, somehow.

She searched Sarah's kitchen cabinets for her drinking glasses. She found where she kept them, all two of them, and selected the bigger of the two. She filled it with ice, then water from the dispenser on Sarah's refrigerator.

Magdalena set the glass down just ahead of a pattern Sarah was tracing, then sat down across from her.

"Drink some water, Sarah. If Caleb and Moretti are on their way, you're gonna tell me what the fuck happened during the video. The short version."

Sarah discovered the glass, then looked up at Magdalena. She nodded her head in agreement, resigned to not having real kind of control or influence over the situation. Sarah didn't begin talking straight away, however. Her blood alcohol was in the high .2's and rising still.

A minute passed. Nothing. At last, Magdalena snapped.

She grabbed Sarah's wrists and pulled them close to her.

"WE DON'T HAVE TIME FOR YOUR BULLSHIT, SARAH," Magdalena shouted directly into Sarah's face. Sarah's eyes popped open, frightened. Magdalena calmed herself and continued.

She needed to know what had scared Sarah so much, including whatever she might have done to Sarah (or whatever Sarah did to her) while they were watching the end of that tape. Sarah was withholding that information "to protect her", but from what?

Sarah took a big gulp of water and finally began to talk.

"I don't know. It's the same thing that happened to David during the treatment with the enzyme."

"Which was?"

"Your eyes turned black. As in all black, and shiny, like polished, uhh, what's it called?" Sarah could not think of the rock's name.

"**Obsidian**?"

"Thass it!" Sarah was having trouble speaking clearly "There wasn't any white in your eyes."

Magdalena felt her mind immediately drifting, like it did whenever she lost control of her attention for the umpteenth time on any given day - but this was not symptomatic of attention deficit or mild autism. She was recalling her vision, the incident in the bus, and then all of the thoughts and feelings that came with both.

"Then you say, 'breng mee too hem now'", Sarah, barely hanging on.

"You mean bring me to him, now?"

Sarah nodded.

And then Sarah's eyes cleared. She sat straight up and yanked her arms out from Magdalena's grasping hands.

"You didn't sound like you, though. You didn't even sound human. You sounded like….an insect. But not just one. Two voices. Speaking at once. Like a hive."

Magdalena could understand why she was so frightened. But Sarah looked over, wobbling, staring out her dining room/kitchen window, worried far more about not so much as what she had said happened, but by what it meant.

"What, Sarah?"

"What's happened to you shouldn't be happening, Magdalena. We dosed Dave for months with shit from honeybees. I cut his brain up to alter his brain structure. Made mushroom bodies!"

"Hunh?"

"Nevermind, you wouldn't understand."

Sarah plopped down again and continued.

"He'd been changing...but not fast enough…for him. He wanted to jack himself up. Caleb went along with it, so I got outvoted. And then Davey Gravey turned into a fucking light show. Explosions. But before all of that, his eyes and his voice were different, not overnight, but worse and worse until they were just like yours did when you watched that part of the video."

"So he have passed something onto me?"

"Seems that way, sista," Sarah waved her right arm and hand in the air to pre-emptively dismiss whatever it was that Magdalena was going to say next.

"Don't want someone else to end up like him. You should go home, Magdalena."

A minute or two of silence passed between the two of them while Magdalena attempted to think of what to do next. Sarah's eyelids began to droop, her last semi-lucid moment for the day having passed. Whatever adrenaline surge she may have just experienced had run its course - recalling Magdalena turning into an insect-eyed mutant only did so much. Magdalena needed one last question answered before she could let Sarah pass all the way out.

"Sarah, who is Moretti?"

Sarah smiled and grinned like an idiot. She began to sing "Secret Agent Man" by Johnny Rivers, only most of her words were gibberish.

Magdalena slapped her across the face.

"Sarah. Moretti. Who is he?"

Sarah's face turned to sheer evil - her face and features melted in a frown, and she almost looked as if she was going to try to hit her back.

She kicked out her chair and stood up again, almost falling over the table face first as she did so. Instead, Sarah went to her bedroom and came back with her laptop. She opened the top, the monitor clicked on, and Sarah pressed a single button - it called up a saved email she'd received. There were several audio files and two video files attached. The video files were named FischerS and WestC. There was also some text in the body, which Caleb had written. It was only two sentences:

Moretti gave me all of this, to prove he was trying to help. I still don't trust him.

The email was dated the day after the explosion.

This wasn't what she was looking for - but Magdalena knew Sarah was useless. Hopefully what was in these files was what she was going to say about this man, anyway. She clicked on the video file marked "FischerS".

The thumbnail image was of a man, mid-fifties sitting behind a desk looking at a two-way mirror. The camera was ceiling height, looking down on the man. He turned up to face the camera directly.

Magdalena immediately knew who it was. She'd sensed him, his presence that day that seemed so long ago, when she last slept in her own bed and had been pulled into an endless void. The eyes that seemed to look right at her from the computer screen were the same as the unseen ones that watched from the darkness as Keating made his contact with her.

Moretti was the one who was there in the vision, somehow watching them.

So that meant Moretti knew who she was.

Which meant -

Magdalena wondered how much time she had before he'd be knocking at the door. She had a vague idea that it couldn't take more than thirty or so minutes before they'd be there. She looked up from the screen to Sarah.

Sarah was passed out cold on the floor snoring.

Moretti slammed on the brakes, the one thing a driver should never do in a snowstorm, and the car immediately began to spin out. He turned in the direction of the skid, the one thing a driver should do in the event of losing control of a vehicle in a snowstorm. The car straightened out and Moretti pulled the vehicle onto the shoulder. He flipped the hazard lights on and brought Caleb's car to a complete stop.

Before tearing into the idiot riding in the vehicle with him, he counted silently in his head:

One Mississippi…

Two Mississippi…

Three…

A large white van with the name of a cleaning company written in dark green on the side rolled past.

Right on time, Moretti thought. He closed his eyes and gathered himself. He turned and looked and saw the kid there in the passenger side. He was crying.

"You have got to be shitting me, kid," said Moretti. He didn't yell. Wanted to but didn't.

Moretti had given him the short version of what CRUCIBLE was, and how much danger they all were in. He told Caleb that now, since he hadn't handed everyone over to them, they were already operating under the assumption that he'd gone 'rogue' as it were. They were all in it together from there on out. They'd just pulled onto the highway going north to Sarah's apartment as he finished.

Ten seconds later, Caleb had simply stated, as if it was a matter of no consequence at all:

"Not all the operamine was destroyed. I still have a sample at my place."

"Why didn't you mention this to me sooner, Caleb? Wait. Don't answer that," Moretti said. He could see the kid had lost his hold on his emotions and making him say what was immediately obvious would have been cruel. Caleb didn't trust him. Plain and simple. And he couldn't blame him for it, either. It was actually smart to not tell him about it, from Caleb's perspective.

If only he'd have been able to tell him he really wasn't one of the bad guys from the start, this might have been avoided. Moretti put his hand on his shoulder and squeezed it.

"Hey. Caleb. Come back to me, dude."

Caleb looked at him.

"It's alright. But you have to tell me now. Is there anything else you're holding back? What did you get out of Keating's family?"

Caleb told him about the dark web email exchanges with Sarah, and the files he'd sent therein.

"But the physical copies were destroyed. I saw to it myself," he finished.

"Okay. I believe you," replied Moretti.

"Moretti. There's something else I found out. David had kept it from Sarah and I…somehow. He'd said he had surgery, but it wasn't that."

"What was it?"

"Tried to kill himself, Moretti. Swallowed a bunch of pills and put himself into a coma. He'd given up on life."

Moretti said nothing at first, then smiled.

"Power for its' own sake," he whispered.

"What?" asked Caleb.

"Nothing:" he replied. Moretti took a deep breath.

"Alright, kid. Ready?"

"Ready?"

"We're going to your place. Now."

Moretti pulled back onto the highway, got off at the next exit, and then found their way to head back south the way they had just come.

"Where am I headed?"

"72 West -"

"NO, Caleb. We can't flip on the GPS right now, or probably ever. Just tell me the directions. Left, right? What? How far?"

"Take your next left. We're getting on Storrow Drive West. What do you mean, ever? Is CRUCIBLE following us?"

"Local and state cops, too kid. They'll be the first to give us problems, I'm sure of it."

"How can you be sure?"

"Look behind us, Caleb."

Caleb contorted his body to turn around all the way to see who was following them. He recognized the man in the passenger side of

Crown Vic twenty feet off their bumper immediately.

"It's the asshole who arrested and questioned me, uh.."

"O' Connell."

"He looks pissed, Moretti. Why isn't he trying to pull us over right now? Why isn't he-"

"Waiting until we get off Storrow, kid. Then it's game on. There's a manila file folder sitting on your backseat Caleb. Grab it. Not much time, so move."

O' Connell had picked up the radio in the vehicle he rode in and was speaking into it.

Caleb unbuckled his seat belt and lunged over for the folder. He also noticed a yellow plastic flashlight just next to it.

"What about this flashlight, Moretti? We gonna need it for anything?"

Caleb couldn't see Moretti's face from the awkward position he was in but if he had, Caleb would have seen Moretti's smile in full bloom, teeth and all.

"Yeah, but do me a favor first."

"What?"

"Shine it in O'Connell's eyes for me?"

"*WHAT?*"

"Just do it, kid. He'll know I put you up to it."

Caleb did as he was bade, and when he looked to see how O' Connell reacted, Caleb started laughing immediately. He twisted back into the passenger seat.

"How'd he take it?" asked Moretti.

"His face is red. Like, stoplight red. Oh, and he definitely said your name. Four or five times, actually.

"Excellent," Moretti said. "Put your seat belt back on, Caleb. Once you do, read that file, and *don't* look up once you start.

"Why?"

"Because you'll probably shit your pants. Now read."

Caleb looked down and opened the file.

Moretti yanked the steering wheel hard right at the same time he pulled the emergency brake. The car and everything in it jolted starboard, but the vehicle did not skid as it changed course. Moretti had timed the maneuver to jump off at an exit ramp on Storrow well before the one for Caleb's house.

The vehicle O' Connell rode in had no chance to make that kind of turn. Instead, the driver skidded to a stop just past it.

The move would buy them five, maybe ten minutes of drive time before they'd get picked back up by either the cops, the feds, or CRUCIBLE. Moretti was unfazed. All that mattered was getting to that sample first.

Magdalena decided she couldn't just leave Sarah on the floor to sleep off her whiskey drunk, especially since she had rolled over onto her back only a minute or two after she'd noticed her laying there. It was impossible to determine what BAC she'd cranked her body and brain to, but if she hadn't drank in years like she'd claimed, coupled with the fact she might have weighed a hundred twenty, hundred thirty pounds swimming with her clothes on, it was likely she'd topped off in the point-three's. Sleeping on her back was dangerous.

Magdalena remembered one time she'd found her mother on their living floor one afternoon after school. She'd been in the exact same position Sarah was in, also drunk as shit. Magdalena had wanted to leave her mother there, for the hope that at some point she'd choke on her own vomit. She didn't abandon the woman however, instead dumping a bucket of water on her face to rouse her to get her up on the couch.

The memory came and went, despite its trigger being an almost exact re-enactment of that afternoon all those years ago. Maybe it was because she didn't hold nearly the same amount of resentment for Sarah as she did her mother.

Magdalena did consider that maybe that was why Sarah rubbed her the wrong way. Sarah even *looked* like her mother. She stood up, walked over to Sarah's supine body, and then began to drag the passed-out wreck to her bed. It didn't take long, only a minute or two.

Funny how history liked to repeat itself at the worst possible times.

She laid Sarah on her side and threw a blanket on her. Magdalena returned to the kitchen, and back to the laptop. She sat down and was about to hit play on the file she'd brought up, but suddenly felt the urge to take the device somewhere other than the kitchen to watch the video. There was no reason for it, other than just a feeling, an unconscious drive to do this.

There were two other doorways in the kitchen other than the one that led to Sarah's bedroom. One was clearly to her bathroom, as evidenced by the towel rack on the interior side of the door that hung open. The other, a doorway with no door, led to a room that appeared dark, as if the windows in there not only had blinds drawn, but blackout curtains over them to ensure that no light whatsoever penetrated into the area.

Magdalena hadn't noticed it when she first arrived, but now that Sarah was conked out and not a menacing, panicked drunk stomping around her kitchen, the room stood out in ominous contrast to the remainder of the otherwise well-lit apartment.

Magdalena grabbed the laptop and walked towards the room, stopping at the entrance. It was weird - an intense smell of incense hit her as soon as she stepped inside, like it had been burning in there non-stop for the past week. The smell of Sarah's whiskey breath and the whiskey itself must have overpowered it, but again, with Sarah sleeping there was nothing to interfere with her sensory inputs. Magdalena fumbled around on the wall to her right. She couldn't find it at first, but then eventually found it, underneath a wall hanging or tapestry. She turned the light on.

"Holy. Fucking. Shit."

What Magdalena saw before her was the absolute last living room design/set-up she would expect from a career scientist and purveyor of all things rational and logical. Instead, what lay before and around her resembled the tearoom of a gypsy or a fortune teller - but only had been recently transformed to look as such. There was an end table adjacent to a couch immediately in front of her, so she set the laptop down on it to just try and take in the sheer bizarreness of her new surroundings.

First:

It wasn't blackout curtains or blinds like Magdalena had assumed that kept the area totally shielded from the outside world. Instead, there were heavy Afghan weaves that had been nailed to the interior window edging so that they covered every centimeter of glass in the room. Each of them looked as if they'd been purchased at a musical festival vendor's tent. Despite their obvious hippie-jam origins, they were effective. No light could enter the space, period.

Next:

The overhead light that she'd just turned on had a light green scarf pinned to the ceiling over it — but in contrast to what was on the windows, the material the scarf was made of was so thin that the light penetrated it quite easily. Everything in the room looked as if it had been tinted a lime color.

There were two couches in the room and a recliner. The couch in front of her, which stretched away from her, was completely covered with various books on mysticism, fortune telling, the supernatural, ESP, and of all things, reincarnation. Magdalena walked over to

Sarah's living room table, knelt down, and saw that Sarah had herself a tarot card reading in progress. She glanced over at the recliner, and naturally there was a DIY book on performing tarot card readings sitting on it. Sticking out from the middle of it was a piece of paper, the top of which was printed with the words "Barnes and Noble". Obviously, the receipt, but Magdalena was curious as to *when* she'd bought this book. She reached over and pulled the slip out.

Sarah had bought the fortune-telling set up the day she'd arrived.

Suddenly, Madame Fischer's Tea Room, Est. 2023 made sense. Sarah had no scientific explanation for Magdalena being a living, breathing person so she'd turned to the mystic arts faster than planning a junior high Saturday sleepover once someone discovered the existence of Ouija boards.

She took a quick look at the spread on the table. In between incense burners and candles, were the tarot cards. Next to the deck, a total of six had been pulled and spread out in the shape of a hexagon, arranged in such a way to have a single point on the closest side and one on the opposite side of the table from where Sarah sat. All of the cards were still face down, except for one.

It was The Hierophant. Magdalena picked it up and regarded it for a moment. She had no idea what it said about one's future, but for some reason she felt like she wanted to keep it. She stuck the card in her jeans pocket.

Focus, girl, she thought to herself. She'd been sidetracked, and rather easily at that. Magdalena stymied the frustration that usually came with her capacity to be distracted to her own detriment and got back to the laptop.

Opening it, her eye caught an audio file before it relocated the thumbnail of Moretti she'd just seen. She double-clicked and listened.

It was a voice she didn't recognize, male but high-pitched, and the cadence made it sound like it was read from a prepared statement. Or a documentary.

"In contrast, the six other witnesses who confirmed the stories of purple and magenta-colored shockwaves did not report any major injuries. From these six, only two spoke directly to any members of the press. Both reported purple, violet, and/or indigo electricity coming from all of the electrical outlets and from any devices that were plugged in, operating or no, in whatever room they were in.

The first explosion occurred in the basement of the Science Building at 11:17 am EST, with two more to follow within the next ten minutes. The second and worst of the explosions occurred in a building immediately adjacent to the Science Building. There were no human occupants inside, but the structure was designed to house campus utilities, where a number of pressurized, flammable gases were stored. Forensic analysis indicated that a tank containing hydrogen gas ignited, completely destroying the building and injuring multiple individuals in proximity to the explosion.

The final explosion occurred in the wastewater treatment and utilities building. Three university employees lost their lives."

Magdalena felt a tear run down her cheek as the last few seconds of the file played out. There were only a couple more seconds left in the file.

"Interviews with some of the first responders revealed that the metal double doors to Keating's laboratory could not be opened for a full three hours after the mysterious and disastrous power surge wreaked havoc on the campus. The doors had been fused shut and required sophisticated rescue equipment to open.

One member of the fire team spoke to our crew.

'It's crazy. You know that steel melts and fuses at over 3000 degrees Fahrenheit? Wonder what could have done something like that in there. But damned if I knew how anyone could have possibly survived in there.'

…how indeed."

Magdalena knew how. It was him. Keating. He'd somehow been able to keep himself, Sarah, and Caleb from burning to death.

What had Keating become?

```
FILE 653XWU-Keating-4RE-Moretti
Section C: Psychopathology: Keating, David H.
```

Part 1:
Post-Traumatic Stress Disorder(complex)

Keating was diagnosed with PTSD as a result of several severe, frequent traumas endured throughout his childhood and early adulthood. Father had developed alcoholism prior to Keating's birth; Keating witnessed repeated physical violence/abuse of mother and two older brothers Subject was exposed to repeated incidents of emotional abuse as well, as well as neglect. Actual extent is unknown. Mother relocated to the United States with Keating under an assumed name.

Additional reports obtained show that subject was hospitalized on multiple occasions, although none of the hospitalizations were ever connected to abuse causations.

Mother deceased, suicide, June 1st, 2010. Resultant PTSD (complex). Relevant criteria include commonplace experiencing of physical violence from age five onward until relocation; abandonment/neglect i.e., left at home alone for weeks unsupervised, brought to inappropriate locations such as bars, pornography stores, and parties by father; witnessing of physical violence to mother; various incidences of neglect including a specific event of wearing feces covered clothing to elementary school. Reference attachments 4 -9 of reports from attending therapists.

Behaviors/symptoms include hyper-awareness;
severe restlessness and obsessive thoughts;
insomnia; major depressive disorder; inability
to form lasting and healthy relationships with
others; extreme isolation.

ACES score: 8 (indicative of severe and
multiple childhood traumas; refer to
Appendices 2, 3, and 4 for further details on
this diagnosis.

Caleb looked up from the report. At the moment he did, Moretti blasted through a red light at a four-way intersection.

"JESUS CHRIST!!!!" exclaimed Caleb, not just for the reckless driving, but for this unknown side of the man he'd worked under for years.

"Keep reading, kid, and don't look up. Focus."

Caleb looked behind them and saw that they still had no one behind them.

"Looks like we're still good for now, though."

"Definitely not, kid. By now CRUCIBLE has eyes on us from above."

"In a fucking snowstorm? That's impossible."

"VERY possible, and actually advantageous. I told you. The technology they possess will rock your world, dude. Even in…our context."

"They don't know why we're headed to your place, Caleb. CRUCIBLE is patient. They'll wait until it's time. Now *focus*."

Caleb found that he could do anything but continue to fucking focus, but he tried anyway. The next few pages went on about Keating's abuse at the hands of his father and then his brothers. Caleb knew firsthand what kind of twisted assholes they were but had no idea they were Bavarian pretzel twisted.

Here was a photo of a child's torso, badly bruised and with visible lacerations. He kept flipping through to the next part.

Part 2:
ASD 1/Adult Attention Deficit Disorder

Subject Keating diagnosed in late twenties
with high-functioning autism and Attention
Hyperactivity Deficit Disorder. Attending
physicians and neurologists were contacted and
confirmed diagnoses persisted to current day.
Standard battery of tests performed to assess
pathologies.
Subject displayed extreme aptitudes for
specific disciplines, to the detriment of
others. Subject subsequently demonstrated
genius-level intellect in chemistry, biology,
biochemistry, proteomics, and zoology.
Stanford-Binet and other intelligence tests
indicated an IQ of 170 to 180.
Subject presented with combined ADHD type -
demonstrating difficulty with impulse control
and maintaining concentration for even short
periods of time. Easily distracted and could
not maintain attention on anything other than
subjects that interested him. Subject
repeatedly showed irritation, especially when
forced to remain in one location for extended
periods of time. At time of report, subject
currently taking multiple medications to treat
condition.
Autism displayed is typical of Asperger's
Syndrome. Often overlapping with ADHD
symptoms, the subject displayed sensory
processing issues, specifically to do with
loud noises and physical touch (comorbidity
with abuse and neglect). No medication
prescribed for this specific pathology.
Coping strategies and meetings with
specialists were suggested, to date subject
had not done either.

Current Medications:
Adderall (20 mg/day); Lexapro (25 mg/day);
Hydroxyzine (150 mg/day).

     Caleb did not continue reading, although there were another ten to fifteen pages in the file. He didn't have to. Everyone had their secrets. Caleb knew that. Keating's were different. He had an idea about the spectrum and the ADHD stuff. No clue about the rest of it. And the intelligence? The guy had been alone his entire life. Never part of anything, or ever really being to share himself with anyone.

     All Keating wanted was to be loved. Like everyone, really, but Keating never could connect. Not with him or Sarah, either. He —

     Caleb's mind took another step forward. Magdalena. He'd reached out to her, specifically, because they had something in common. The neurodivergence. Had to be. She probably had shit go down in her home life too, but likely not to the extent of Keating. He'd read somewhere that childhood trauma affected brain development - physically, not just on an emotional level.

     But how did he know —

     Another step. The back-up laptop, the one he used for social media. He'd sent that to Germany, but he had no clue why he'd done that. The reason was obvious, now. He thought that might protect her, should something happen.

     And then — one last step.

     Their minds must have been essentially identical. That must have afforded Keating the ability to connect with her mind, to pull her consciousness in to his. In fact, the neurodivergent and trauma-related aspects of his brain
chemistry must have been the least-affected by their experimentation. Maybe, it was the thing that made everything possible — the abilities, that was.

     And he had communicated with this woman, and she hadn't rejected him. In fact, they'd become as close as social media would allow. Keating had connected with someone, and she was beautiful and kind and caring and —

     - just like him.

Caleb closed his eyes. He imagined Keating trading messages with her at some ridiculous hour of the morning, neither able to sleep, neither knowing why they were the way they were, but they'd found each other.

Caleb could feel the car dart this way, screech to a halt, then speed up again. Moretti must have been driving his car like they were in a Fast and Furious movie. He laughed to himself. Here he was, reading about the atypical neurology that Keating had kept from him all these years, and now he himself was laser focused on the subject at hand.

"Find something, kid?"

Moretti, sitting in the seat next to him, might as well have been a mile away.

"CALEB."

Caleb opened his eyes.

"He met her over social media. She's neurodivergent, autism-spectrum and ADHD, just like David. She's probably got childhood trauma, too. The combination of both altered their brain development and chemistry in similar ways. It allowed for the connection Keating made. The neurology and…"

"And?"

"The love."

Moretti looked at Caleb with something that looked like pride.

"Nice job, kid. Welcome to the game."

"Moretti."

"Yeah?"

"If Magdalena is able to start doing the things Keating could, destroying the sample now could be as bad as keeping it."

Moretti shook his head.

"The plan stays the same."

"Okay. Take the next left. Can co-pilot now."

Moretti looked in the rearview and frowned.

"This is about to get real."

"*About to get real?* Are you joking?"

Caleb's phone rang – his real phone.

"Give it here. It's for me," said Moretti.

It was O' Connell.

Moretti answered the phone. Caleb pointed frantically to the right. Moretti cranked the wheel taking that sharp turn. Their tail, of which O' Connell was riding shotgun in, was back and took the same turn.

"O' Connell. How may I assist you?"

Angry, barely intelligible screaming came from the phone. Moretti had a grin on his face that would have made the Cheshire Cat envious, and the more O' Connell yelled, the wider it got. Caleb had no idea what to make of this - they clearly had a dislike for each other, but this was Moretti breaking the same law he was supposedly protecting. It was disconcerting, and yet, pretty fuckin' damn funny.

"Uh, hunh," Moretti said, not listening at all to the jumbled parade of f bombs and threats.

"Okay...sure. Well, yes, I see how that could be a problem. Listen, O' Connell, I'm afraid I'm going to have to go."

The yelling continued. Moretti rolled his eyes at Caleb and made the mocking 'flapping gums' hand gesture to Caleb.

"Okay sounds good buddy. Listen you go ahead and call whoever you gotta call, but me and the kid here got some shit to take care of. We'll meet you there, okay? Kisses!"

Moretti tossed the phone into the backseat.

"How far away are we kid?"

"Five minutes. Take your next left."

"There a back way into your place? One the cops won't already have blocked off?"

"We're taking it."

"Atta boy."

"How are you gonna shake O' Connell again?"

"Got something up my sleeve, kid. Get ready to jump out of the car."

Caleb fumbled for his housekeys, found them, and unlocked his back door. Everything had become a fever dream. It was the same state of unreality he felt when his friend and mentor began emitting purple electricity from his entire body. It was like being a passenger at the back of a bus, with a scratchy analog television showing him what was going on in the front, where real life was happening.

Once inside, he locked the door behind him. Caleb scanned his kitchen for something more to secure it, spied a metal stepstool, then quickly scrambled over to grab it. The door opened into the house, so he jammed the stepstool underneath the doorknob so as prevent the door from opening even if unlocked. It wasn't much, but what the fuck else was he going to do?

He crawled over to some nearby cabinets and propped his back against them, sitting on the floor. Caleb looked towards the ceiling.

"Fuck," he whispered.

He'd been running flat out for the past ten minutes through the woods behind his home after having been shot at by police. In that moment, Caleb wished they'd hit him. He felt like he deserved it. He recalled what had transpired later in the evening, on the last day of the experiment.

Caleb had no idea that anyone had even been harmed at all - let alone been killed – by what happened that day. Sitting in a processing area at the Massachusetts State Police barracks in Salem, two monsters of human beings appeared from a metal door at one end of the room. The smaller of the two, a man of six-foot-five and two hundred pounds of fuck you ordered him to 'get the fuck up, stupid'.

The larger of the two spun him around and slapped handcuffs on him, running down the list of charges for which he was being arrested.

One crime had jumped out at him like a slasher in a sleazy horror movie.

"Eleven counts, manslaughter first degree."

And thus, the slasher plunged the knife into his throat. People had died because of what they'd done that day. And as far as being at least partially responsible for that happening, Caleb knew he was guilty. He was brought to a holding cell, where one of the troopers opened the door and the other shoved him inside – without taking the cuffs off.

"Should be charged with murdering those people, you sick fuck," one of them had said.

He'd remain there until he was brought up to an interrogation room later.

And now, while sat on his kitchen floor and heard multiple gunshots outside, he knew more people were going to get hurt.

Glass breaking.

Movement in his living room, then footsteps.

"Caleb?"

"Kitchen," he replied.

Moretti appeared a second later from the hallway that opened on to where he sat.

"Okay, kid, where is it?" asked Moretti. He looked at Caleb like a father who'd just found out his son had kept drugs in his bedroom someplace.

"Basement. I'll get it."

"Kay man. Quick as you can."

Caleb got to his feet and within seconds, the world begin to spin, as if on a rocket propelled merry-go-round. He felt Moretti grab him by his shoulders but didn't 'see' him, despite his standing right in front of Caleb no more than a foot away.

"Kid, you okay?"

Caleb regained himself. Moretti's face came into focus, the round dark brown eyes looking directly into his.

"Yeah, fine. Don't feel too good, that's all. Lemme go," Caleb mumbled as he pushed past Moretti.

Moretti watched him as he went, a look of genuine concern etched into his face. After Caleb disappeared down the stairs on the other side of the kitchen from the hallway, he split back to the living room.

Caleb joined him a minute later.

Moretti glanced briefly from the windows towards him.

"What are you going to do?"

The second he asked his question, two police cruisers pulled up, flashers on, joining the Crown Vic that had O' Connell and his partner and the one that had been stationed out front before any of them had arrived.

That vehicle had been driven into at speed with Caleb's car by Moretti, who'd leapt from the drivers' side a second or two before impact. The cars formed a line, blocking their return to his car and their way out.

Caleb froze from raw fear, and sheer panic.

Moretti saw this.

"CALEB! WHAT ARE YOU GOING TO DO?"

Caleb snapped out of his momentary trance. He popped off the cap to the bottle and dumped the contents onto the floor.

"Is that going to-"

"It's ruined. They won't be able to get shit out of it, even if they knew to look. I can piss on it if it makes you feel better."

Moretti smiled.

"That won't be necessary. What about the inside of the bottle? Residue?"

Caleb considered his question, then turned his back to Moretti. He unzipped and began pissing in the bottle.

"Ooookay," Moretti said, turning his attention back outside.

"When I'm frightened, I usually have to take a piss Moretti. Why I just suggested it."

"Get an attitude too, it seems," he replied.

"No, it's just right now. I deserve to get shot. A bunch of people died because of us. The sample's gone." Caleb finished and then threw the now half-full bottle off to the side.

He turned back to Moretti.

"Lemme go out there, give myself up. You run, go get Sarah and Magdalena."

"Not happening, Caleb. We're both getting out of here. Just gotta stall shit for brains out there."

"Moretti-"

"Caleb. Quiet. I get what you're feeling right now, but stow it because heroics ain't gonna bring those people back. We've got more to do."

But this brought Caleb exactly zero relief.

"Is there anymore of it, kid?" Moretti lowered his voice and returned his gaze to the windows.

"No," whispered Caleb. His reply was barely audible.

"IS THERE ANYMORE?"

"NO!" he shouted back.

Then came the sound of a bullhorn. Sarcastically polite yet antagonistic banter via cell phone conversation was no longer a viable means of communication, so out it had come.

"Stephen Moretti, agent of whatever the fuck!!! Don't know what the hell you're up to but we're bringing you in! Walk out slowly, with West, hands in the air!!" It was O' Connell doing the talking, obviously.

"Stay away from the windows, kid. He's got local cops with him - and I can't vouch for their restraint or their trigger fingers."

"So what do we do?"

Moretti simply turned to him with a half-menacing, half-reassuring smile.

"Wait for the cavalry, kid. In the meantime, we stall. It won't be long."

"Cavalry? Who the hell is the cavalry?"

Moretti looked at Caleb as if to ask him, sarcastically, if he really didn't know.

It took a second, but Caleb filled in the blank.

"You're kidding? How the hell is that going to work?"

Moretti answered him by putting a finger over his lips to hush him. He then strode right up to the front door, opened it, gun in hand.

"Didn't you say stay away from the windows?"

"I meant *you* stay away from the windows, kid. They ain't gonna just shoot an agent," he replied. Moretti took a step outside and yelled out at the assembled law enforcement outside.

"This isn't going to go down how you think its going to, O' Connell. Take my advice - pull the cops back now!"

Moretti closed the door after his statement.

"Oh, that'll work," commented Caleb.

Moretti sighed. "Listen kid, you might know the secrets of science and everything in a chemistry, but this is my territory. I had to give him a warning, even if I know he ain't gonna listen."

Moretti leaned to his right and looked out of the window again.

"Yup. You see right now, O' Connell is calling in his backup. There are five cops out there including him, and there's two of us. We're both what we in the biz call 'armed hostiles', and they're not coming in here until backup arrives. The problem is…" Moretti nodded, as if what he was seeing play out was exactly what he expected.

"He's being told right now that it's going to be awhile and to hold his position." Moretti saw O' Connell drop his car's radio disgustedly.

"Hunh?"

"CRUCIBLE, Caleb. CRUCIBLE. They're the only ones who are coming, and they're coming because they think O' Connell and these men are going to get in the way of their getting what they want."

Caleb supposed this was genius on his part, but who could tell? He kept talking about these guys like they were the evil Men in Black, but at this moment, he was counting on them.

"So your secret friends show up. What then?"

"That's the hard part, kid. I don't know what we're gonna do until we see they do when they get here."

Five minutes passed. Caleb watched them tick by on his wall clock. They felt like an entire day to endure. Fear…terror…both felt like time travel, especially when they came from the possibility that one could lose their life at any second. He was trapped in his own home, with a guy he'd known for all of two weeks, with police officers and detectives crouching behind squad cars, guns pointed in their direction. Caleb was not looking forward to whatever the "hard part" was that Moretti referred to.

And then, Moretti stated as if nothing of any import was happening:

"Here we go." Moretti waved Caleb over to him. "Here, check this out. Stand near me. You need to see this."

Caleb walked over to him, and sure enough, a white van had parked behind the police cars. On the side was a sign that said "Savoy Cleaners" written in lime green, like a mom-and-pop version of Servicemaster from the 50s. A shitfaced gorilla would have been able to tell that it was as fake as a "meet hot singles in your area" dating website inside of a few seconds.

Two men stepped out, one each from the driver and passenger side, and two more from the back of the van. They were all dressed up in uniforms from the fictional company. The two closest of the regular police officers approached them immediately, waving their hands.

What followed next could be filed under "it didn't look like that on the X-Files".

The men in the uniforms pointed - *with their index fingers* - at each of the officers out there, including O' Connell, as if accusing them of something. that Moretti seemed to be fond of in the most ironic sense. As they pointed at each of them, the officers simply dropped where they stood to the ground, as if they'd fainted. One of the officers' sidearms went off when its owner hit the ground, but the bullet struck O' Connell's car and not another person.

"What the…." Caleb managed to say. Moretti finished for him.

"Fuck? That's what you meant, right? We need to talk about your mouth, young man. Let's get in the habit of saying hell there."

Caleb just looked at him.

"They have darts, about three inches long, implanted in the palms of their hands. When they pointed, the darts launched. They operate like sophisticated drones – the projectile seeks the point on the target that shows the highest fluid velocity, which is always an artery. They all just caught one right in the jugular."

"So what, it knocks them out?"

"Well yeah, but the compound that gets released is much more than just a sedative. They found it in….Iceland maybe? I forget."

"What?"

"It causes amnesia, Caleb. I was making a joke."

Caleb stared at Moretti stone-faced.

"Which I'll never attempt again, apparently. Anyway. There's a suggestion component to the chemical as well."

Caleb couldn't believe it. CRUCIBLE really was like evil Men in Black, come to life.

Moretti frowned at him, as if he could see the thought formed in his head

"Except it's not Men in Black, kid. There are five cops that just got darted out there. Two of them are never waking up - the stuff causes comas, too. It's roughly fifty/fifty. The ones that wake up are only going to be able to say something to the effect of that they don't recall what happened, and that's when CRUCIBLE won't even have to make it go away. The local authorities will do that for them."

"What's going to happen if we go with them?"

They kill me for not doing my job, and they take you in to question, torture, extract everything you know, then kill you too."

"WHAT?"

"Need you to relax. We're gonna walk out there now, and we're gonna make it like we're surrendering to them. Just don't say a word. Period."

Caleb experienced no reassurance from this.

"Hey. Caleb."

"What?"

"It's gonna be fine. You wanna know why? Because I can't do this CRUCIBLE shit anymore. I'm done. And those guys out there are gonna kill you, Sarah, Magdalena, and Dr. Keating eventually. You made something they want. Became something they want to be. And they're not going to stop until they get both."

Moretti pulled a second gun from behind his back and handed it to him.

"Can you shoot, science boy?"

"Yeah."

"You're a terrible liar, Caleb West, but it's shit or get off the pot time. Them or us. Which is it gonna be." Moretti did that full eye-contact thing he did, and Caleb felt his spine straighten as he returned his gaze.

"You ready?"

Caleb nodded.

Moretti saw that he was.

"Follow me."

Moretti strode to the front door, opened it, and stepped outside. Caleb trailed right after.

It had grown darker in the time they'd been inside, shrouding everything in shadow. The snow had all but stopped. The world outside held that muted quality to it, the one it has after a heavy snowfall.

Caleb had a front yard about a hundred feet square, one that was populated with small shrubs and a couple of small pines here and there. A five-foot wide path wound from the front door to the wood fence, where the police vehicles and the "cleaning" van were all parked.

Two of the CRUCIBLE agents paired off to their left, the other two towards their right. They simply stood there, just beyond the fence, waiting as Caleb and Moretti slowly approached. The slider door to their van was open, an obvious signal to them that the back of the van was where their unconscious or lifeless bodies were going to be tossed.

Within a moment, Moretti and Caleb had closed to fifteen feet from where their opponents stood. All four were emotionless, standing there, staring. They could have been androids for all Caleb knew.

The one closest to them spoke.

"78 slash 22, Moretti, Stephen." The man turned to Caleb. "West, Richard Herbert".

"Please raise your hands. You will come with us now."

Moretti began speaking, saying something about their being part of the 'constabulary' and to identify themselves. Caleb knew it was a distraction.

"78 slash 43, Rivera. He is Williams. The other two are Poulin and Shriver. Do not resist. You are being watched, Moretti."

Caleb looked down towards the ground and saw two of the police officers, just the local ones, strewn about like it was kindergarten naptime.

Why hadn't they darted us already? he wondered.

Because they can't risk putting you into a fucking coma, stupid. They can't risk frying your brain, dude.

"Oh, I'm sure that I've been watched for…"

Caleb looked at the agents, and at that instant noticed that all four had their eyes on Moretti. None of them considered him to be a threat.

Fuck that, he thought and pulled the gun Moretti gave him. He had the weapon out and pointed at the agent closest to him and they still hadn't looked at him.

Caleb fired twice, one shot for each of the Poulin/Shriver pairing. At that range, all Caleb really had to do to hit his targets was account for the weapon's kick. He had fired guns before at a range with a few buddies, so his technique was just good enough.

The first shot hit the agent square in the chest. The second hit the other agent just above his left thigh.

Caleb glanced over at Moretti, who didn't hesitate once he'd heard Caleb fire.

Moretti pulled his gun from mid-air, or at least it looked that way. His firearm had been in a forearm holster and watching him pull and fire was like watching a trick shooter at a carnival or rodeo. He pulled his trigger twice, once at 78 slash 43 Rivera and the other at Williams, crazy secret organization code unknown. Both were headshots. Rivera's brains splattered in an eruption of skull, bone, brain, and blood; Williams' painted the side of the van in loud crimsons and shiny blacks, visible even in the widening shadows of the coming night.

The agent that Caleb had failed to kill instantly pointed at him.

Caleb saw a hole open up in the flesh of his palm. A shiny, silver point appeared and begin speeding towards his head.

"Oh my god oh my god oh my god oh my god…" Caleb thought. He heard Moretti fire a third time. A split second later he heard a metal on metal "ting" noise. The silver point vanished.

Moretti had shot the dart out of the air.

Caleb fired at the fourth agent again, and hit the man just below his nose. He saw his teeth fly out of the side of face before he fell dead.

Moretti holstered his weapon, this time in his waistband, and folded his arms. He looked over at Caleb.

"Thought I told you to wait on me, kid."

"They all had their eyes on you, Moretti. I saw my chance."

Moretti walked over to him and clasped him on the shoulder.

"A scientist with balls. Now I have seen it all. Let's go."

"But what - how -"

"WE HAVE TO GO CALEB. NOW."

Moretti gently pushed him towards the van.

"In there?"

"Yup. CRUCIBLE will think their agents have us, and so we won't catch any heat driving it, least not right away. Not much time though."

Caleb and Moretti spent the next minute or two wiping what was left of Williams' brain off the side of the van.

Moretti pulled away from the scene, rolling out of the driveway before flipping on the headlights and onto the main street.

"There's bound to be trouble in front of or around Sarah's place. Call them now and warn them. Tell them we're on our way and to get ready."

Caleb laughed to himself.

"Oh this'll be great. 'Hey guys, just survived a police standoff and a shootout, committed a few more felonies and killed a couple people. Be there to pick you guys up, though, so pack a sandwich and wait for us by the door!"

Moretti laughed. "Pack a sandwich. That's good, kid."

"Thanks, pop."

Moretti felt a twang of pain at that, one that Caleb could see on his face as it struck.

"I'm sorry, Moretti. I didn't-"

"No worries, Caleb. Glad we made it this far."

Caleb felt said for the man at that moment. Something had happened. Something bad. Maybe he'd ask him later about it, if they got the chance.

Caleb reached into his pocket and pulled out his iPhone. He dialed Sarah's number.

It only rang once before someone answered - except it wasn't Sarah that picked it up. It was Magdalena.

"Hello?" she said.

Caleb looked at Moretti, who could hear the voice on the phone and thus also knew that it was Magdalena that had answered. Moretti inferred this - he knew what Sarah sounded like, and that voice wasn't hers. He opened his eyes in surprise, but then made a circular motion with his fingers and nodded as if to tell him 'talk to her, kid'.

"Magdalena? What - where's Sarah? Did something happen?"

"Caleb, uhh...Sarah's....."

Caleb listened, and as he did Moretti could see the frown on his face grow deeper and deeper.

"Sit tight, Magdalena. We're on our way. We need to figure out how to get you two out of there,"

More talking from Magdalena.

"Uh, okay? What do you mean you'll see when we get there?" But Caleb pressed the off button.

"Moretti. We've got a problem."

"We have several, kid." Moretti looked over at Caleb, who looked positively baffled. "What is it, man?"

"Well, first...Magdalena wanted me to tell you 'don't call me Mags, Stephen.'"

And with that, Moretti did something he hadn't done in quite some time. Moretti laughed his ass off.

After thinking about what she'd learned from just the one audio file, Magdalena checked her cell phone to check the time. It had only been a few minutes since Caleb had called. She was relieved she hadn't wasted too much time investigating Sarah's interior décor and on the audio.

She needed to know who this Moretti was. Magdalena clicked the thumbnail picture, leaned back, folded her arms, and watched.

A black screen came up first, followed a title card, of sorts:

Suspect Statement: Caleb West
Joint Initial Statement received by Det. Sergeant Matthew J. O'Connell, Boston Police Department & Special Agents James Kendrick & Carl Pitcairn, F.B.I.
Observed and Reported by Special Agent Liaison Stephen Moretti

Magdalena's first thought was a question: what the fuck was a special agent liaison? The screen disappeared, and then the video started in earnest:

The camera shot alternates back and forth between two rooms, each on either side of a one-way mirror. Clearly the interrogation room at a police station, although which one or where is not indicated. It couldn't have been just a local station because this type of set-up for witness and suspect statements wasn't typically found therein. It had to be a large municipality or city (likely Boston), or a State Police Barracks.

Moretti sat in the observation room, relaxed and placidly watching the proceedings in the adjacent room. He looked early to mid-fifties. Black hair and facial hair, easy on the eyes. The guy looked like he came from the same factory as Jeffrey Dean Morgan or circa late seventies Burt Reynolds.

He leans back in the chair and folds his hands behind his head and smiles. Something in the other room has entertained him, somehow.

Magdalena cocked her head to one side, perplexed. How the hell did this guy manage being in her vision with Keating? The only thing he looked like he was skilled at or had some latent ability for was driving a sports car and picking up divorced women at a local bar. But, as the camera sat on him for another few moments, she noticed that his chill countenance disguised his seriousness. He was watching everything, learning whatever little piece of information he picked up on, and carefully considered it all as he absorbed it.

There is an audible 'click', and the picture display switches to the room on the other side of the two-way mirror. There in the other room are O' Connell, Kendrick, and Connor...and Caleb. Caleb is seated on one side of a long table that runs from just below where the camera was situated near the ceiling all the way to the far end of the room. Two of the officers are seated, and another was walking around the room like a neighborhood-designated asshole dog, the one that pissed on everything and everyone as so much territory. At last, he sits on the table smack in between the other two officers and Caleb. The interrogation was all his to make and that was that.

The video clicks over to Moretti, briefly.
"O' Connell. Being a prick is written into your DNA," the man says to an empty room.

The audio and video had been set-up so that the video display switches between the two areas when a voice or speech is detected. This is obvious when the screen clicks back over to the interrogation room the moment Moretti finishes his derogatory.
One of the officers directly behind O' Connell, whose faces weren't more than eight or nine inches away from his perspiration-soaked back, timidly ran through a bunch of preliminary questions. These were basic, like Caleb's name, where he was from, and so on. Caleb answered them all politely and directly, even eagerly, despite having to ask the man to repeat himself several times because of the human soundproofing that sat and glared at him for the duration. Caleb's expression said 'I'll tell you everything' even to the untrained eye. One didn't need to be an expert on body language to know he hadn't planned on obfuscating anything, at least not then.
O' Connell eventually loses his patience with the superficial questions, leans forward, and snatches Caleb up out of his chair by his shirt collar. Caleb is terrified.
Immediately, a sound is heard over the loudspeaker in the

interrogation room as it begins to hum. The camera clicks over to Moretti, who looks ready to jump through the glass.

"Let go of the kid *NOW* asshole," he states.

Then, silence.

The camera clicks back over to the other room, and O'Connell has already obeyed. But instead of staring at Caleb, he is staring at and through the two-way mirror.

After O' Connell determines he's sent enough of a message to the man sitting on the other side simply with his dramatic countenance, he turns back to Caleb.

"Hey. Junior Frankenstein. What the fuck do you think you idiots were doing in that lab of yours? Tell me and the boys here. And don't dumb nothing down, eithah," O' Connell warned, the word 'either' coming out as if it were spoken in another language.

Caleb holds as little as he can back in his description of their experiments. He speaks fast, barely stopping to breathe as he does. It's clear by his body language and vocal cadence that he *wants* to tell someone, has been wanting to actually, just about anyone in authority about what they'd been doing. He thinks this will somehow absolve him, yet he leaves out the more involved, scientific details.

Caleb never considers for a second that he's speaking to officers of the law - not career scientists. It's not long before he begins talking about "normalizing alpha waves through neuron modification" and "reorganization of occipital lobe structure and function", and within just a couple of seconds his interrogators are completely lost.

Caleb is also clearly frightened. Once he begins talking, he doesn't stop. It's not long before he gets to the incident from earlier that day:

"'Caleb…' – Keating grabbed me, pulled me in close to him as the fires were going up all around us.   I looked at him, and at that moment the fire alarms went off, so even though he was right there I could barely hear him. He yanked me down close to him, and he began telling me what he was seeing."

"You mean what he saw," Connor interjects.

O' Connell turns on Agent Connor this time. Connor looks as if the glance alone had made him piss his pants.

"Sorry. O' Connell. Continue," he says, clearing his throat.

"Thank you for that permission, agent. Keep going, shithead," commands O' Connell.

Caleb continues. He makes it clear that at that point, what Keating was saying to him was said while in a fully conscious state — which should have impossible considering the circumstances. It wasn't a fever dream, or a hallucination. He wasn't mumbling and it wasn't incoherent. So, it wasn't what he saw then, but:

"What he was *seeing*, officers, but what he was describing wasn't anywhere in the lab where we all were. . Keating wasn't telling me about a dream - and he wasn't talking about his own laboratory going up in flames around him. I'm telling you - his *consciousness* was in two different planes at the same time. At that point there were extreme, if not poisonous levels of the compound acting on every cell of his nervous system"

The two F.B.I. agents exchange a 'this guy's totally batshit' look, one that Caleb manages to catch. It upsets him even more than he was already. He'd hoped for understanding and instead received mockery. Caleb finally falls silent, his shoulders slumped in despair.

O' Connell:

"Alright then. I'll bite. What was he *seein'*?" he asks, sounding like uttered like every stereotypical Boston townie dickhead.

Caleb didn't look up at O' Connell but went on all the same.

"He spoke about being everywhere and nowhere, being one consciousness and being an infinite number of them. He said he couldn't control his change anymore, so he needed to fall into the dark. Other stuff too, but I don't recall anymore."

Magdalena, watching the video, can tell that Caleb left quite a bit out here, and that he most definitely could recall all of it.

"Sure about that, shitstain?" snorts O' Connell.

"Y-yes," Caleb says.

O' Connell flips the switch, leaps into Caleb's face and screams into his eyes.

"WELL I DON"T FUCKING BELIEVE YOU, YA CRAZY FUCK!"

O' Connell is about to continue yelling when Kendrick, who has been silent the entire time writing furiously in his notebook taps O' Connell on his elbow. O' Connell turns to him. Kendrick taps his watch.

O' Connell is disgusted, but knows their time is up.

"Okay pal. This is how it's gonna go. We're gonna figure out how many more things to charge you and your psycho surgeon girlfriend with and make no mistake there will be a LOT of things. Then we're going to come back and show you to your nice cell. Down the road, they'll see how fucking crazy you and her are, and you'll spend the rest of your days on benzos and anti-psychotics and playing with crayons."

O' Connell finishes by whispering to Caleb:

"You fucking people oughtta be ashamed of yourselves."

The three interrogators get up, gather their things, and leave through the door into the room behind the two-way mirror. When the door closes behind Connor, who is the last to leave, Caleb immediately breaks down and begins to sob.

The camera flips to the observation room, where Moretti had been seated.

Magdalena grew impatient. So far, nothing in this video really seemed to impart any insight into who Moretti really was... other than he didn't have a lot of love for the guy named O' Connell. Magdalena only half paid attention as the officers then went back and forth on what to do next.

The officers speak to each other for a moment. By the end of their tete-a-tete, it's decided among them that interrogating Sarah was likely only going to yield the same mad scientist bullshit. She was off the hook as far the fifth degree went and thus allowed to sit in her room and wait to be brought to holding.

Moretti, for his part, insists on speaking to Caleb by himself. O' Connell disagrees, even going so far as to get into Moretti's face. Moretti smiles and does not back down. O' Connell flinches - an almost imperceptible wince, followed by the tiniest of steps backward.

"I'll talk to you outside, pal. Think we need to get some things straight while you're lurking around my precinct."

"No, you won't. And no, we don't." Magdalena laughs at this. It always came down to dick measuring contests with these guys.

O' Connell and his cohorts leave the room. As soon as the door slams shut, Moretti shakes his head.

And then, it happens. Why Sarah gave her the laptop, with this video on it.

Moretti looks up, and directly into the camera. He walks over to it, stops, and then finally sighs.

"Hi Magdalena," he says. "Mind if I call you Mags, though? Pretty long name you got there."

Her heart dropped into her stomach at the sound of her name from the man in the video from over a week before.

Moretti continues speaking into the camera.

"Bit later on, I'm gonna be taking the video files from this session with young Caleb here off the State Police's hands, and I'll be giving a copy of it to Sarah. Can't do it right away though," Moretti smirks here. "Caleb doesn't think you're real -doesn't think any of it's real despite what he just said- and Sarah hasn't even heard your name yet."

Magdalena started wondering how he managed to do what he did, finding his way to that netherworld. Moretti begins speaking again. He's anticipated those very thoughts:

"Was at the laboratory on the campus a few hours ago, and well, let's just say for now I can do some cool tricks too."

His face goes deadly serious at this point.

"I represent some *very* bad people, Mags. They'll be coming for you soon. But…I think I'm going to help you and David out. But I'll need you to help me too." Moretti looks away from the camera and at the two-way mirror.

"See ya soon. With any luck, I'll be with the kid here. We'll get David out of there, Mags. Promise."

Magdalena hit pause and sorted what just happened on the video out in her head.

This video was recorded the morning after the explosion. Moretti was there, on the campus, the night before. Whatever it was he could do, it allowed him to experience that vision on the other side of it, almost like a mirror. Moretti knew that she was real because he actually saw her.

Caleb thought she was a hallucination at that point, which explained why he didn't mention her at all to the cops while he was being questioned.

Sarah was clueless to all of it, because she'd been running around the lab putting out fires instead of listening to what Keating had been saying, and Caleb hadn't had a chance to tell her yet about what he had said.

And as for herself, Magdalena wouldn't arrive there until a couple of days later.

Son of a bitch. Moretti's fucking actually checks out.

Magdalena turned up the volume a notch on the computer and mustered as much focus as she could on the computer screen while Moretti spoke to Caleb.

"Hey kid. You okay?"

Caleb looks up, tears completely covering his reddened face. It is clear he is not. Moretti sits down and regards him for a moment.

"Nope. This isn't going to do, Mr. West. I'm gonna need to focus as best you can here because I'm gonna need your help."

Caleb seems to relax, but only a little.

"My help?"

"Yup. My name is Moretti. Stephen Moretti. Only one person's allowed to call me Stephen, though, and you ain't her."

Caleb sits and says nothing, intent on what this strange man has to say.

"You see, I work for a very special group of people who are quite interested in your work. Well, you and Sarah and Dr. Keating's work. Credit where credit is due, as they say."

"Mr. West, what would you say if I told you that the alpha wave pattern and signature of every man, woman and child on this planet is as unique as their fingerprint, and not just a bunch of squiggly lines at a super low frequency?"

The color faded from Caleb's face as his despair yielded to the scientific machinery installed on Caleb's hard drive of a brain. Here, somehow, was a man that spoke his language.

"Well, it's a theory that's long been bandied about by…"

"Not a theory Mr. West. One hundred percent verified."

"But how - who -"

"I told you Mr. West. A very special group of people. Anyway, that alpha wave pattern can be detected and recognized in certain situations, such as when an individual is under stress or is highly emotional. Now, most people, even when they're facing life or death circumstances, can only be detected from a couple of miles away - mmmmm, like twenty or so I think is the limit."

Caleb is dumbfounded.

"When you and the Get-Along-Gang went for broke yesterday, Dr. Keating's alpha wave pattern *could be detected from our group's satellite.*"

"That's impossible, Mr. Moretti."

"Just Moretti, Mr. West. No mister. My son's buddies used to call me Mr. Moretti. That honorific doesn't apply here. Well, to me anyway."

"Sorry."

"No worries, son. Now, the people I represent want to know everything about what happened here. And I do mean everything. That means data, files, samples of any reagents and/or biological components, and so on. Those dopes…"

Moretti nods back towards the door the other officers left through.

"Do not give a rat's ass about any of that. What they do care about is ensuring that you and Sarah do not see the light of day for a long, long time, kid."

Caleb grows upset at this last statement.

"But we're not gonna let that happen, are we? Just so long as you work with me and get me everything I need. Then, once that's done, my organization and I will make this all go away…if you'll pardon the cliche. Can you do that for me?"

"Sure. Sure! Is this group you work for, like some kind of government think tank or something? I'd love to be able to work with them."

"Mmmm, you don't want that Mr. West. Just do this, and you and Sarah get to move on with your lives - it'll be someplace far away from here, but you will get to move on. Do we have a deal, kid?"

"Yeah. Of course. Anything."

"Good. Knew I could count on you kiddo. Now let's go grab Sarah and get you guys squared away. Got assignments for you two already. Fun, fun!"

"You mean, we're just gonna go now?"

"Yep."

Moretti stands up, and Caleb follows suit.

"What am I doing?"

"You? You're going to Germany, big guy."

Caleb is silent as the two exit the room.

"I'll take that as a yes, sounds good, Moretti," he says, the door closing behind them.

The video ends.

Magdalena closed the laptop and sat for a moment. Her mind had ceased to function. It was all too much. too soon.

She wanted to run but could not.

She wanted to scream, but her voice would not respond.

She wanted to cry, but she had forgotten what crying even was.

And lastly:

A mental picture of Roger, and little Sam.

Roger: "I told you this was a bad idea, Mags."

Sam: "Promise you'll come back?"

Magdalena leapt up and fired the laptop across the room like an expensive frisbee.

She took several large, deep breaths. And then, a phone ringing from the kitchen. Quickly, she walked into it and saw Sarah's normal iPhone lighting up. She guessed there wasn't any need for subterfuge and burner phones anymore. Magdalena picked it up.

"Hello?"

Caleb:

"Magdalena? What - where's Sarah? Did something happen?"

"Caleb, uhh...Sarah's unconscious. She'd been drinking all day, and now she's out cold in her bed."

Caleb said that he and Moretti were on their way, and she needed to just hold on a few minutes. He implied that the apartment was likely surrounded at that very moment.

She glanced around the room, and spotted, of all things, one of those magnets that listed the numbers for local police, fire, and ambulances.

Ambulances.

Magdalena smiled.

"Caleb, I have an idea. You'll know when you get here."

Magdalena hung up. She then dialed 911.

Caleb and Moretti had ditched the dummy cleaning company van down the street from Sarah's apartment and approached on foot. Moretti surveyed the surroundings and noted that the conditions could not have been any better for them.

Completely dark.

Poorly lit side street with terrible access to the main road.

And the snow had picked up again, back to blizzard levels, dropping a now surreal amount of snow on the area.

And finally, the blinding red and yellow lights of the ambulance Magdalena had called to Sarah's apartment.

Absolute stroke of genius on Magdalena's part, thought Moretti.

Moretti already liked this girl, from the little snippet of wit he already got and her demonstration of being able to think on her feet. They were going to need a hell of a lot more of that before this was finished.

Calling the ambulance bought them all time. When CRUCIBLE sent in their clean-up crew to Caleb's place, it effectively took the local and state police out of the game for a while. Undoubtedly, there was a whole menagerie of police, fire, and first responders in force there now, sifting through the mess there. They'd be scratching their heads wondering what the hell had just happened, why there were four dead nobodies in coveralls with no identification and science fiction level weapons in their hands. One of them, of course, no longer was in possession of a face to identify. That was about as messy as Moretti had ever left a scene in years.

CRUCIBLE would have tugged on the right strings in the interim, thus calling off any more immediate interference from any more of their constabulary.

They also would have known the second Magdalena called the ambulance in at Sarah's place, and there wasn't a whole lot they could do with that. They'd have to wait and bide their time, and simply observe.

Moretti had no doubt they had people lurking - and that's where the outside elements were fortuitous.

Caleb and Moretti found a collection of garbage cans on the side of the building adjacent to Sarah's to hide. They paused there to plan their move.

The kid was doing well, for his part. He knew he'd fucked up, and he'd been making amends ever since. It was all one could do, and if anyone knew about that, it was him.

Life was funny like that.

"So what, when they bring Sarah out in the gurney, we jump the techs and take the ambulance?"

"Yep."

"Sounds easy."

Moretti looked over at his companion.

"Well, compared to…"

Moretti smiled. "Actually yeah, pretty easy. But that's when you usually mess up kiddo. And we gotta be fast. As soon as we jump out, they'll pounce too."

"So they're basically hiding, waiting for us?"

"Yep."

"This sucks, Moretti."

"Welcome to my world, kiddo."

"I been here awhile now, sir."

Magdalena had just told them that the ambulance was for Sarah, who'd given herself a Bon Scott-level case of alcohol poisoning and wasn't responding. Which, conveniently enough, wasn't far off from the truth.

Ambulance proven again to be genius. Maybe it was luck that she'd thought of it, but regardless she'd had the presence of mind to think of it.

"Caleb, didn't you say she had a bunch of stuff going on upstairs? ADHD and autism you said, just like David?"

"Yeah, why?"

Moretti pondered this for a moment, and Caleb, sensing this, filled in the gaps for him.

"Her stress reaction mechanism worked in her favor, Moretti. She probably had more norepinephrine and dopamine in her system at once than she'd ever had in her life. People with ADHD and similar conditions take medication to release those very same neurotransmitters to regulate their attention and focus. All of this probably turned her into Neo at the end of The Matrix."

"Hunh?"

"She's built for working in crisis mode, Moretti. Her and David. With the childhood trauma *and* the spectrum stuff, their nervous systems function on a far different wavelength than most people."

"No shit?"

"No shit. Hey, I thought you knew this stuff. What was with the speech back in that interrogation room you gave me? Alpha waves and satellites and all that? Was that bullshit?"

"Not bullshit. Totally true."

The back door to Sarah's apartment opened, and out came one EMT, carrying the front of the gurney. Sarah was secured with three belt straps and an oxygen mask and was still out cold. The second EMT appeared, carrying the back

end. Magdalena was behind them.

Moretti squinted, and saw that Magdalena was holding something that looked like…

Caleb made out what it was first.

"Is that a fucking rolling pin?"

Moretti couldn't help but laugh, again. It was like something out of a Tom and Jerry cartoon, when that racist caricature of a maid jumped up on the table swinging one around while Jerry wreaked his havoc in the kitchen.

Magdalena looked frantically around the area for them as she followed behind. She meant to bean the rear guy as soon as she saw them, it seemed.

"Don't believe that a rolling pin was mentioned as part of the plan, Moretti."

"Yeah, but…a fantastic addition. Let's go."

They reached the back of their emergency vehicle. The lead EMT opened the rear doors of the ambulance, and Moretti was on him like Batman. Moretti laid into him with a sucker punch before the poor guy knew what was happening.

Moretti wheeled around and saw that Magdalena had already dispensed with EMT number 2.

"Stephen," she said.

"Mags." he replied.

"Cool moment, guys," Caleb finished. "Can we fucking move?"

Caleb and Magdalena pushed Sarah and her gurney up into the vehicle. Moretti kept watch, looking for any sign of trouble.

There was nothing.

Magdalena and Caleb jumped into the back, and Moretti slammed the doors shut. He sprinted over to the drivers' side, hopped in, and hit the gas.

Still, there was nothing.

Caleb directed him to head north - the quickest way out of metro Boston and into the first couple of suburbs.

They'd be able to ditch the ambulance somewhere up there, and then head out on foot to a place where they could figure out what to do next.

They were five minutes gone from Sarah's when Caleb negotiated his way up to the front to take shotgun.

"Take it easy kid. And get a seat belt on."

Caleb buckled in, took a quick peak in the rearview and then out his passenger mirror, and eased in.

"Hey, pretty easy, hunh? CRUCIBLE didn't even show."

"They showed, Caleb. They're waiting for something."

"Waiting for wh-"

Neither Caleb nor Magdalena nor Moretti nor Sarah (who would only be told later what had occurred that knocked her out of her drunken stupor so suddenly) knew what hit the ambulance, at least at first. There was a high-pitched, whistling sound. Then a brief, overpowering smell of combustion, and finally a deafening soundwave that felt and sounded like being punched close-fisted in both ears, stomach, and teeth all at once. Its origin was a point located mere inches underneath the vehicle.

The rocket struck the undercarriage of the vehicle with such force the ambulance flipped over and into the air like it was a matchbox car.

Medical supplies and equipment went flying, becoming as much of a danger to anyone of the four passengers inside the vehicle as the impact of the ambulance's spectacular crash. Sarah had been strapped onto the gurney, which was secured to the floor of the rear of the ambulance. Magdalena was the least secure, but even she'd been smart enough to buckle in as soon as they'd gotten into the vehicle. Her harness simply wasn't as tight.

Had Caleb given Moretti any kind of argument on the seat belt, his chances of surviving would have been zero. The ambulance's rotation stopped, and it fell to rest on the drivers' side of the vehicle (a bit more than spinning one-eighty on its axis), but the vehicle kept moving forward as its momentum carried it another twenty yards or so. Moretti's thoughts during this last part of the crash:

Hit us with an RPG.

Loud and scary but shot underneath us.

Sending a message.

If they wanted us dead at any time, they'd have done us all back at Fischer's place.

They know more than they should.

The lights in the interior went out as the sound of crunching metal and glass was all that could be heard.

And then there was nothing but darkness and silence.

Interlude:

D
E
R

G
E
I
S
T
L
O
S
E
N

And when there was nothing but darkness and the infinite voices of somethings speaking and singing and , taunting and trilling their aphasic nonsense not-words I forget who I am for how long I don't know
am I even
am I still or
am I a 'them'
I am splitting we we them us I grasp at you and you

There is so little of me left that hasn't descended into madness
And with that little that is left I hide myself away

and I wonder

Did you forget about me?

Have I been forgotten, down here, in the world below the world, devoured and consumed, descended, and subsumed?
All I ever wanted was a place at the table, a chair upon which I could sit and sup, speak and break bread and drink from my cup.
I longed to belong, to come in from the cold, to be welcomed as one among the others, no better, no worse, mostly the same and not that much different.
It was all just to pull myself close,
The surgery and doses,
But now I am alone, devoured
By the creatures known only as *der Geistlossen.*
I am glad you are gone from here, even that mysterious eavesdropping other, for when I caught sight of the first of their infinite number, I realized that I looked upon a creature that should have remained unknowable to me, unknowable to anyone. Yet here I am, my being and my presence dissolving, corroding into…
…more of them.

I did not see the first at a distance, my dear. When I was able to see it while hearing millions mocking, it was already within me, inside my thoughts, in the space between each individual thought. As it touched each one in sequence, it turned it, polluted it, and corrupted it. One became two, then four, then eight.

Then the hordes appeared, and I was overrun. These notions I have now I have hidden from them – they consume the rest at the moment, but it won't be long before I will no longer be capable of even this.

One cannot "know" them, as one would with a piece of knowledge, or a thing, or a fact. You can only regard them as what they are *not*, which is of a mind that is capable of "knowing". I am reminded of my Wittgenstein, from his famous 'what one cannot speak of, we must pass over in silence' – they are only knowable as the things that disappear from one's regard as they consume my mind. They are mind-less. They are *der Geistlossen*.

At once, they stop.

At once, they detect another presence. It's a shadow, in a world of a shadows, so there is only the traces of the outlies of it. Distant, but I You are here…but you are not here by choice, it seems. Something has happened, I can feel it. Unconscious. But it doesn't matter to them, they will find you and feed all the same.

Most of them depart to search for you.

I wait…

I reach out…

And I see your shadow, only a fragment of you is here, most still within the world of things.

With all the strength I can manage, I force you back out, my angel. My Magdalena.

-WAKE-
And your shadow here returns to the world.
And I return to what's left of me. But I – will fight them.
For I have not been forgotten, it seems.
Please I do not want to be alone anymore.
The strength of mind is no longer mine.

I split myself up and put myself back together for you for everyone.

I would prefer to be nothing than be alone.
Now I can never be nothing with *der Geistlosen* turning me to an infinity of cruel homunculi.

Please…save me.

Part THREE:

A S C E S

N
O
I
S
N

Chapter One

WAKE....

The word echoed in Magdalena's head as she opened her eyes. It was dark, but not pitch. There was a faint red light, from a few feet away. The knowledge of where she was returned a second later. She was in the back of the ambulance, still belted into her seat. Something had struck the vehicle, from underneath. It sounded like a bomb.

"Was I-" she groggily said.

Sarah screamed at her, snapping her out of the post-unconsciousness haze.

"FUCKING OUT COLD? YES!!! NOW GET ME THE FUCK OUT OF THIS GURNEY!!!"

The back doors opened, and there appeared Caleb and Moretti. From the way that they were oriented relative to she and Sarah, the ambulance had turned onto its side.

No, that wasn't accurate. The ambulance had *flipped* onto its side. What the hell were they hit with?

"They're alive!" yelled Caleb.

"Always wear your seat belt," replied Moretti.

Things moved so fast, too fast for Magdalena to keep track. Caleb and Moretti pulled them from the back of the ambulance and the four of them were out in the cold. Moretti pointed and yelled for them to follow.

They were slow, but it wasn't long before they found cover. Whoever had attacked them did not stay to finish the job.

Why?

Moretti lowered his head and looked at the snow-covered ground at his feet. He took a deep breath, then let it out. He watched as the moisture from his exhale formed a cloud in the air in front of his face, then as it disappeared.

Hours had passed since they'd been ambushed. But now, as the hour approached midnight, even the snow had decided it was too cold to keep dropping at the rate it had been at all day. In fact, it had ceased entirely. They wouldn't last out here for very long.

Moretti had no idea what to do next.

Earlier that evening, while in the thick of the snowfall and a car chase with one of the biggest assholes in law enforcement, he had notions of being able to pull it all off, with the endpoint of putting Magdalena Christie in the same room as David Keating. What happened then, between those two, had always been uncertain and out of his control. One hopes for the best outcome, even if it meant great sacrifice. Always prepared for and to do whatever it took. Making that meeting a reality seemed an impossibility at that moment.

As Moretti sat on the log he'd found, contemplating the day and losing hope, he caught himself and stopped his line of thinking. He'd been in impossible situations before.

There was always a way.

It was, after all, a miracle that Caleb's plane got into Logan airport before the blizzard had really kicked into high gear, he was well and truly divorced from CRUCIBLE win or lose, and (c) he and all three of his erstwhile companions had managed to walk away from an RPG strike unscathed. The second and third things had nothing to do with the snowfall, but miracles were miracles and Moretti thought a few more couldn't be off the table just yet.

He clicked on the wideband emergency radio he'd ripped out of the ambulance. It had been reporting out 'four fugitives responsible for murders of two police officers/ on the run/somewhere in the Somerville/Medford/Malden areas' for an hour, and when the device came to life, it was still cranking out the same alert.

Okay, so more than just a few miracles.

He laughed to himself, and then pulled Fred out of his red bomber jacket pocket. He held the flashlight up in front of his face like the host on Antiques Roadshow, as if appraising yet another forgotten piece of attic or garage clutter. Fred wouldn't have fetched a cent on that show that served to delude elderly people into thinking the artifacts from their time – and therefore they as well– still had calculable value to the world. But to Moretti? Well. Some things you can't put a price on. Fred had saved his life, once upon a time. It was freezing that night too.

"Of all the seasons and places for this shit to happen, it had to be New England in fucking winter, Fred. AGAIN. I bet you had something to do with this?"

Fred did not answer. He did not have anything to do with their current circumstances, and if he did, he wasn't spilling the beans.

"Not talking, hunh? Ah, I wouldn't either. Least we still got each other, right buddy?"

From behind him, Moretti heard a rustling of branches. He wheeled around and clicked Fred's 'on' switch. He did not turn on.

"What the…" Moretti quickly inspected the device. Fred's bulb had been partially smashed when the ambulance flipped. He felt demoralized by this. The feeling told Moretti why CRUCIBLE had waited to strike.

They wanted to send him a message.

It said:

"We could kill you all at any time, but now we want to see what you'll do next."

Nobody in the ambulance was seriously hurt - but they could have very easily terminated all four of them and chose not to. They needed something.

They knew about Magdalena.

As if on cue, she emerged from the rustling Fred could not shine light upon.

She walked over and sat down next to him.

"You usually talk to flashlights, man?"

"Nope. Just this one."

"So he was your friend then."

"Kinda. You usually talk to mutant scientists on different planes of existence?"

"Nope. Just this one."

"So he's your friend then."

"Kinda."

They both laughed.   Moretti knew he'd liked her.

"What do they even want with him Moretti? With me? No wait. Lemme answer that. They want to use us as weapons. That's always the answer in the movies."

She was sharp, this one. She was fully aware that she was part of CRUCIBLE's equation now, too. And quite possibly a better prize than Keating was. Magdalena was upright and had been bestowed abilities that would have made their radar, probably *already had* made their radar. They just couldn't pin her down until tonight. When she'd emerged from wherever she'd been tucked away. Made sense. But still, something else wasn't right.

"Maybe not you, or him, specifically. They want what you have though, and they don't want anyone else to get their hands on it."

"I don't even know what *that* is, man."

"Magdalena. It doesn't matter, really. In the end, as it always is, the people in power want more power, and they want to stay that way. I didn't try to pin down what their endgame for this whole brou-ha-ha. Don't even want to, really. It's not good, whatever it is."

"Power for power's sake."

The statement hit Moretti like an uppercut. It was as if Lourdes was sitting next to him, Magdalena a…mirror of her.

Moretti began to consider the real possibility that this was supposed to happen, and happen in exactly this way.

"Something like that," he replied.

"So how'd you even get involved with them? You don't seem the type. You seem like a pretty decent guy."

"That's a story for another time. Answer a question of mine first Magdalena, and I promise it'll get told."

"What?"

"Why did you come? A thousand miles, all the way from Florida It couldn't have been just because of some crazy dream."

"But you know it wasn't a dream. You were there, man."

"Well yeah, but the question still stands. You could have just as easily ignored it. I know it's crazy to consider now that you're in this, but this kind of stuff happens *all the time*. Most people stick their heads in the sand. Why'd you come?"

Magdalena's face sank into sadness, visible even in the shadows of the unlit night sky. Moretti's question had forced her to recall a feeling she'd never wanted experience again. Her expression alone was enough for Moretti, but she answered anyway.

"Because I didn't want the rest of my life to just pass me by, Moretti. I'm a nobody. I've been a nobody. If I didn't come, I'd have stayed a nobody until the end of my life. You know what the highlight of my day has been for as long as I can remember?"

Moretti shook his head.

"Going out to my sister and I's front porch and watching cars go by."

Moretti smiled and put a hand on her shoulder.

"Nobody is 'a nobody', Magdalena. You got people that love you, of that, I'm sure. Your sister, for one. You try and tell them that you're 'nobody' and they'll get pissed at you first, then spend the next few minutes convincing you otherwise."

He paused for a moment, then continued.

"But that isn't really what made you come, Magdalena. I'm sure there's more to it than just some plucky 'I'm gonna do something with my life, I'm gonna be somebody' nonsense. I've known you for two hours and I already know you're better than that."

Magdalena only looked at him, disbelieving. Nobody had ever said anything like that to her ever in her life.

"It'll come to you. You tell me when it does, okay?"

"Will I get my story then, Moretti?"

"Call me Stephen, Magdalena. And yes. Promise is a promise. I keep mine."

"Call me Mags."

The two of them sat together, in the dark, in silence, in peace for another half-hour.

Sarah and Caleb came bumbling through the trees, apparently trying to make as much noise as possible.

"These two with you, Stephen?"

"Nope. Must have followed us here." Mags and Stephen shared a laugh. Caleb and Sarah stood in front of them.

"We have to run. There's no way we're ever getting close to that hospital now." said Sarah, still buzzed, pissed off she had to be here with these idiots.

"They'll track us down eventually Sarah. We need a different plan," rebutted Caleb.

"You and your plans. You and David got us into this shit, and now look at us. We're totally fucked." The two of them began to bicker like children over mutually coveted toy.

Magdalena and Moretti looked at each other as if to say, 'how the hell did these two get to be a part of Keating's team'. They let the two scientists go for another minute or two before Magdalena had finally had enough.

"Will you two just shut the hell up?" Magdalena stood up, with newfound authority. Caleb looked over to Moretti, who gave him an expression that said 'hey kiddo, she's the boss now. Don't look at me.'

"Alright then, genius. What are we going to do?"

Magdalena already knew what they were going to do, or moreover, what she was going to do. And she couldn't possibly have hated it anymore than she did at that moment. She pulled out her cell phone, saw that it had enough signal to make a call. She dialed a number and waited. The line picked up.

"Hi. Yep. You were right." she said.

Roger had the feeling he was going to get a phone call from Magdalena that morning, just minutes after he and Sam had awoken. He didn't know when it would come, just that it would come that day and he damn well better be ready.

For Roger and Sam had played Monopoly the night before. They'd ordered pepperoni pizza, and drank Pepsi, and stayed up late watching a cheesy on demand movie together until Sam had fallen asleep with his head on his chest. Roger dared not, would not move a muscle, even as so many tears of happiness and joy had run down his cheeks, chin, and down to his neck and shoulders that he looked as if he had just stepped out of the shower.

That strange and wonderful blue-haired, brown-eyed woman had handed them heaven as if she carried it in the back pocket of her jeans.

That being said, it was safe to say that Roger was prepared to drive through hell to save her from the demons that resided there.

The 'all-hands' alert came that evening. It came via the local evening news and when it did, Roger wished he had something more on hand than the aluminum softball bat he kept in the back of his station wagon. The situation was so dire, the news began a half-hour early.

"Channel Four here to report a hard-to-believe, incredible scene unfolding now in Watertown, just west of Boston. I'm Rick Williams, and we'll go directly to Paul Carlyle who's there at the site of a deadly shootout in a moment. Two police officers and four civilians are reported dead at the home of Caleb West, one of the researchers directly involved in the disastrous explosion at Gordon University just a few short days ago. Paul, what can you tell us?"

Roger checked his phone quickly to pinpoint where Watertown was and saw it was just a few miles from the hotel where he and Sam had holed up since they'd got to town. He could be there in twenty minutes, tops, but Roger already knew that wasn't where he'd be going.   Everything was important, though.

No word from Magdalena.

Roger continued watching. Paul Carlyle was stationed down the street from Caleb's house. Unbeknownst to Paul, the spot where we stood was no more than ten or fifteen feet from where Caleb had leapt from the passenger side of his own vehicle at just under thirty miles an hour. If he'd known what to look for, Rick would have seen the trail of Caleb's body in its roll at a forty-five-degree angle to the right and in the opposite direction of the tire tracks leading up the house.

Roger saw the odd track. It was the first thing he saw. Roger assumed it was Caleb driving, and someone else had leapt from the other side of the car. That person knew how to jump from a moving vehicle and had executed the move almost perfectly.

He was close enough. Moretti had given Caleb a crash course three minutes before the jump, and Caleb had pulled it off. Six of one.

Roger began paying attention to Carlyle again.

"Moreover, Mr. West is believed to have been assisted by an unknown, rogue element within the federal task force assigned to investigate the explosion – speculation at this time points to an operative acting on behalf of a possible terrorist organization. This individual or individuals are presumed to have been aiding West and Fischer since the explosion."

The television cut to a split screen between the network anchor and the reporter.

Williams began speaking.

"And Paul, we're hearing now that you have new information?"

"That's right, Rick. We've just received word that Fischer, West, and this element have taken a Florida woman hostage." Magdalena's picture appeared on screen.

"This person has been identified as Mary Christie, forty-one years old and a resident of Sarasota. Ms. Christie works part-time as a waitress at a local Chili's. She's been described by her live-in sister as having a high-functioning form of autism-spectrum and a more severe affect of attention deficit disorder. It's unclear if she has any further connection to Fischer, West, and their accomplice but Rick…one wonders whether…

Roger heard a ringing in his ears as he felt all of the blood in his body drained into his feet.

Magdalena. She was with them now. The entire state was looking for them. Where could they possibly hope to run now? In that moment of worry mixed with panic, Roger thought of Sam and turned around to check on his boy.

Sam, for his part, had sat quietly on the edge of the bed, watching along with his father. He looked unperturbed by what had been reported. He looked up at his father, almost bored with what he saw. To Sam, it was no different than watching part of an action movie, only with someone explaining everything that happened from behind a desk or standing in the street. Sam let out a mighty yawn.

"Gonna take a nap Dad. Wake me up when Mags calls?"

"Hopefully she's okay, son. This is much worse than I thought it would ever be. We'll wait for as long as we can."

Sam rolled over onto his side. As he twisted his body to lay down, he replied in a 'daddy, stop being so silly' voice.

"They're all fine, Dad. The ambulance they were in got into a big accident, but they got out. Looking for a place to hide."

Roger took a step towards Sam, frightened, and interested at the same time.

"Who's fine, Sam?"

Sam let out the irritated 'ugh' that only a child out of patience with a parent can make.

"Mags, Caleb, Sarah, and Moretti."

Moretti. He must have been the 'rogue element' mentioned on the news.

"Are they-"

Sam had already started snoring.

"Safe?" Roger finished.

He felt more troubled than before. His son was connected to Mags on a level he didn't have any understanding of – until just now. Heaven, it seemed, did come with a catch.

Roger sat down in the recliner chair in the corner of their room and placed his cell phone on the arm. Unable to sleep, he simply waited for the call to come.

At some point, he had drifted off. Roger awoke with Sam standing in front of him, pointing at his phone.

"Mags!"

Roger looked down at the number - the call was from a number he didn't recognize. It was Mags though - he was sure of it. He pressed the answer button.

"Magdalena?"

She answered him, sheepishly. She told him he was right - but being right wasn't important to Roger. He pivoted off that line of conversation immediately.

"Doesn't matter. Where are you guys, and what do you need from me?"

Magdalena gave him the short version. As she did, Roger took to his phone, and figured out a rendezvous point. He told her where, and that he was on his way.

Magdalena hung up.

She looked at Moretti, who seemed to perfectly understand the implications of what she'd just done.

"Thank you, Mags. I'll do my best to protect them as well."

Magdalena nodded.

Sarah:

"Who the fuck are Roger and Sam? They sound like characters from a Disney movie,"

Magdalena didn't hesitate. She slapped Sarah dead across the face. Sarah was stunned into immediate silence.

"They're the cavalry, bitch. Be thankful we've got them, or we really would be fucked, as you said."

Caleb cut in. "Had 'em in your back pocket the whole time, didn't you Mags? Can I call you Mags?"

"No, Caleb, but it's nothing personal."

"And yes, I did always have them there. I had no idea how *any* of this was gonna go – they were there at Gordon the day I showed up."

Moretti continued to marvel at this girl. Caleb had been coming into his own the moment he stepped off the plane that day, but Mags had survival instincts written into her DNA. And wasn't already there had been burned in since. Moretti imagined that Mags already had herself a pretty tough life to impart that kind of toughness.

"So what, they'll just come get us?" Caleb asked.

"Yup. They..owe me a favor."

A thought struck Moretti at that moment. They. Roger had a kid with him.

"Mags, how old is Sam?"

Roger did give thought to leaving Sam behind in the hotel. Going to rescue Caleb, Sam, Moretti, and Mags was dangerous, would make him an instant criminal, and knowingly putting his son's life in jeopardy went against every parental instinct he had. There was no way any person who considered themselves a decent parent would even think to bring their child along.

But before he could give the notion any more thought, Sam had his jacket, winter hat, and scarf on and was ready to go.

Roger could only shake his head and get himself ready to go as well. Leaving Sam behind at the hotel wasn't an option he ever had.

"You know Sam, this isn't a movie. There's going to be dangerous people and we could get very hurt," he stated as he put his scarf around his neck.

"I don't want to stay here, Dad. I want to see Mags."

"Yes, but Sam. I'd be a really bad Dad if I knowingly put you into this kind of danger." He hunkered down in front of Sam.

"I love you, son. I can't lose you. Not now. Now that you're…"

Sam put his arms around his father. "I love you, Dad." He let go and smiled.

"I love Mags too."

And there was no arguing that. Roger loved her too, and knowing that, it wouldn't have been right to keep Sam from being able to at least see her one more time before whatever it was . Who knew. Maybe...Sam could help. Maybe he was meant to help.

Magdalena, Caleb, Moretti, and Sarah found the access road on the east side of Prospect Hill Park, without encountering any ground-level signs of CRUCIBLE or other authorities along the way. The going was tough in the pitch blackness in that area of the park, as the snow-covered and unsure terrain severely restricted their movement. It only worsened as they progressed further away from the more well-traveled areas that park visitors frequented during the day.

Caleb stated at one point, "had to be this shit-ass park, didn't it?"

Sarah asked, "why'd we hide in a fucking forest, anyway?"

Moretti didn't bother to explain anything at either of their questions. Magdalena remained silent the entire time.

This only made Sarah repeat her question, only this time, she grabbed Moretti's right shoulder to demand an answer this time.

He stopped in his tracks and turned to Sarah.

"Sarah Fischer. *Doctor* Sarah Fischer?"

"No. Just Sarah. I'm not a doctor."

"Could have fooled me," mumbled Caleb under his breath. Sarah shot him an evil glance.

"I'm sorry we don't have a lot of time to explain my why and wherefores as to selecting our current surroundings, suffice it to say that it both gave us time to collect ourselves and cover to hide from the multiple authorities that are hunting for us."

"But why didn't we just find an empty building, or a house or…"

"*Because*, that's why, Miss Fischer. There're more than just police that are after us. People with more than just spotlights and squad cars. Buildings and houses are easily searched. We'd have already been found if we done that. A place where there was a thick enough wooded area was the only option. Now press on, young lady."

"I'm not-"

Caleb and Magdalena glanced over at Moretti while he explained their circumstances to see that he was using up his last little bit of earthly patience with her to do so. He'd reached the end of it when he explained the forest aspect of his plan.

Caleb put a hand on a Magdalena's shoulder, and nodded as if to say, 'I got this".

"Just let it go, Sarah. Moretti knew what he was doing."

"So we're trusting him and Magdalena now?"

"Yes. Now please. Let's just keep quiet and get to the place we're supposed to go." The erstwhile band of outlaws stumbled their way through the dark and the woods and the brush for another half hour.

They were running out of time.

And then finally, when they reached the rendezvous point - a turn off on the access road behind the park that led to a dirt utility road - their hope of escape seemed to evaporate in the frigid and black nighttime air.

Chapter Seven

O' Connell had never been more bent on "accidentally" killing a perp in his entire career as he was with "Agent" Stephen Moretti if that's what his real name even was. The animosity began upon their first encounter at Gordon University and had only grown since that interaction.

After waking, confused and disoriented but with full knowledge of what had transpired, he scanned the scene for anyone that didn't belong. He knew there'd be people there to look after their psycho science-fiction cleaning crew. O' Connell shooed away medical attention and shoved an idiot reporter who'd found her way through the police lines to get an exclusive before he picked out them out.

Standing off the side, in the spot where the van had parked, were three individuals who *definitely* looked like they'd stepped out of some silly-ass B movie. These nobodies wore expensive suits, had body armor on underneath those expensive suits, and conversed as calmly with each other as if they were at a museum instead of bloodbath crime scene.

"Hey! Agents fucking X Y and Z!"

The men in the suits took no notice of his calling out, so O' Connell wasted no time getting directly in their faces.

"Hey. ASSHOLES. You wanna tell me what the fuck is going on here? One second, I'm in a stand-off with an agent liaison and his little science buddy. The next, I'm getting shot with knockout darts coming out of people's hands like Scorpion, Mortal Kombat style. I wake up and the guys who shot me are fuckin' dead, the scene is in full chaos, and then there's you Area 51 dickheads surveying the scene."

None of them responded.

"Hey!" O' Connell shoved one of them. "I'm fucking talking to you pal!"

One of the other two whom O' Connell didn't accost spoke into his collar, into a communication device hidden there.

"We have one who remembers. Detective, Boston Police."

The other of the two who had not been on the receiving end of O' Connell's 'Boston Hello' spoke into his collar as well.

"How should we proceed?"

They reminded O' Connell of 'agents' from that Keanu Reeves flick *The Matrix*, or whatever the fuck it was. Except, no shades, and infinitely more aggravating to deal with.

The third, who had since regained his balance: "Understood."

The first one stepped forward into O' Connell's face.

"Detective Jonathan James O' Connell, Boston Police Department. Seventeen years on the force, several instances of unnecessary force, netting two suspensions. Yet, you not only made detective, but detective lieutenant. You must have some invaluable skills in addition to the connections needed to have risen to this level."

"The fuck did you just say to me?"

"Where do think they would they be headed?"

"What, you mean you assholes don't know?"

"We'd like to hear your assessment."

"This some kind of test, Agent X?"

"Data verification. So yes. A kind of test if that makes more sense to you."

"They'll be looking for Fischer if they haven't already found her or stashed her someplace. Where they go after that? Probably into hiding. Half the Commonwealth's looking for them by now. I pass your test?"

"Agent Moretti spoke very poorly of you in his reports to us, Detective O' Connell."

"Oh, he's *your* Agent Moretti. I fucking knew he was some kind of black hat motherfucker. How the hell else could he just waltz out of my precinct with-"

"Detective O' Connell if I may, none of that matters now. Moretti was acting on orders from his superiors to allow both Sarah Fischer and Caleb West to gather information for us. He used that directive for his own ends and has since become an independent actor."

"Independent actor. Yeah, you could say that."

"We do say that. We represent interested parties who require Agent Moretti neutralized, West and Fischer acquired, and Christie re-purposed. Your assistance could very well prove invaluable in achieving these objectives."

Christie? Who the fuck…whatever. Who cares. Moretti neutralized meant Moretti dead. Sold, he thought. O' Connell scanned them. Nothing. No tells. He thought himself a poker player of the highest caliber, but he failed to get any kind of a read or an indicator as to what they were after - or why. Whatever the fuck those kids were doing at

Gordon was bigger than just a lab accident, anyone could see that. O' Connell was only now getting an idea of just how big.

Fine. He'd help them. Frankly, he didn't give a fuck about any of the science fiction bullshit. He just wanted Moretti. Humiliation was one thing. Killing cops was another.

"What fuckin time is it anyway Agent X?"

"Eleven-fifteen, Detective O' Connell. Your assessment was correct, although that occurred hours ago."

"If you knew, then why didn't you-"

"An attempt to intercept them was made shortly thereafter. They escaped on foot. Their current location is unknown."

"They'd be headed for a wooded area nearby. A location not easily searched."

"We know. We are aware of where they will eventually be headed. We intend to intercept them at that location."

O' Connell was confused, but the instruction seemed clear.

"Why didn't you just say that. I'll call in…"

"You are not to call in any local support or law enforcement, Detective O' Connell. Instead, you'll accompany us there and assist."

Weirder and weirder and more wrong by the second. This stunk to high heaven.

"Where are they headed?"

"Massachusetts General Hospital, Detective O' Connell."

"You mean-"

"Yes. They mean to rescue Doctor Keating somehow."

"Well, I can tell you right now there's no fucking way Moretti'd be that stupid to-"

"Detective O' Connell you may either accompany us and assist, or you may stay here and continue scratching your head wondering what the fuck just happened for the rest of your days."

"What's in it for me, then?"

"Consider this a tryout then, Detective O' Connell. We're always looking for a few good men for the Constabulary."

"That what your agency's called?"

"All in good time, detective. All in good…time."

O' Connell looked at the three of them, unflinching, and then turned to go back to his car. On his way over, he spotted Kendrick and Connor. They'd looked about as confused as two people could possibly look before they saw him. They were a jarring counterpoint to whoever the hell the other three were supposed to be. Kendrick saw him as he opened his car door.

"O' Connell! What the hell happened here?" yelled Kendrick, jogging over to him.

Connor was content to project incredulity, remaining in place and raising both his hands, palms pointed upward to the night sky in the universally accepted sign language for 'what the fuck?'.

"Not now Kendrick."

"Who the hell are those guys?"

"I said not now." O' Connell grabbed two reloads for his sidearm and his cell out of glove compartment.

"O' Connell, if these guys know something, you're obligated to share any vital-"

"Kendrick," O' Connell said, standing up and closing the car door.

"I'm not obligated to do shit. Call in whatever you gotta. It won't matter. Whoever those guys," O' Connell nodded in their direction, "are, they're in control. And I'm going with them. I want Moretti. They're giving me Moretti. Let you know what happens when I can."

Kendrick was speechless, unable to answer.

O' Connell cringed at his reaction. FBI's finest, and the guy didn't have any kind of an answer.

"Look. If it makes you feel better, tail us if you want. I don't recommend it, but you guys do…you."

O' Connell returned to the agents, who beckoned him over to their…Geo Storm? He overheard one of them speaking into his collar communicator.

"He'll be coming, then. Yes. All six. We only need the one, however. O' Connell to assist in clean-up."

The agents got into the vehicle. The driver simply said to O' Connell:

"Get in."

Wait. Did he just say, 'all six'? thought O' Connell.

The CRUCIBLE constabulary agents (Whitman, Price, and Hadat) and O' Connell left the scene, pulling down the road that led out of Caleb's property. Kendrick and Connor waited a moment, and then followed after them.

Kendrick and Connor pulled up to the first stop sign, just behind the Geo Storm. The two of them were having a laugh about the car O' Connell was in, when a woman appeared and then tapped on the passenger side window. Kendrick rolled down the window.

"Ma'am we're in a bit of a -"

Kendrick never finished. The woman pulled out an outlandishly large, silver .45 equipped with silencer, and proceeded to empty the clip into the car, splattering Kendrick and Connor everywhere inside the vehicle. She reached into her pocket and pulled out a small device. She thumbed a button on the device and flipped it into the car. A second later, there was a small explosion inside the vehicle, with everything inside turned aflame.

The woman walked away and spoke into her collar.

"Containment achieved. Situation alpha neutralized." The woman disappeared into the night on foot.

The access road that Roger specified as their pick-up point lay on the other side of an eleven-foot-high chain link fence that stretched for forever in either direction. At the top of the fence was a coil of razor wire.

Caleb absently pushed on a section of chain-link directly in front of him. Flimsy, but its give didn't matter.
This was by design - flimsy chain linking was harder to climb. Caleb pushed on one of the center poles. Solid.

"We'll never get over this. This fence was built right."

Magdalena was puzzled. "How the hell do you know about chain link fence Caleb? Thought all you knew how to do was sin against nature."

"Installed chain link fence while I did my undergrad. Uncle owned a company. And I didn't see nature trying to stop us until the last day, Magdalena."

"Thought all you college types worked part-time at Starbucks?" she retorted.

Caleb smiled. "Could have done that. Didn't."

"Why?"

"Because I fuckin hate people."

At that moment, Sarah failed yet again to stifle her misery reflex, deadpanning a line she'd seen on a British sit-com.

"So what now, Captain Wow?" she said.

She then put her hands on her hips in as comical a fashion as possible. She *was* actually trying to be endearing, having felt a bit left out of Mags and Caleb's witty banter. Sarah was still a bit drunk, and this gesture seemed like it could mean her lightening up a little.

Moretti, Caleb, and Mags exchanged looks. All at once, they'd had the same thought - knocking her ass out there and then. They could leave her right out on the road, once they'd managed to get out there, to maybe slow down their pursuers. She'd be alright.

Sarah saw this and felt defeated. She fingered the burner phone in her pocket. Maybe she'd use it after all.

Caleb and Magdalena waited for Moretti to speak.

He shook his head and held his arms close to his body.

Magdalena looked to her left, then to her right. She wheeled around to look behind them. The sound of dogs could be heard, faintly, in the direction from where they came.

"Looks like we gotta climb, world's most expertly constructed fence or not."

Moretti answered immediately. "Nope. Razor wire on top. No climbing."

"Can't we like, throw a coat over it or something? Climb over the coat?" The dogs sounded closer, even after just a few seconds.

Moretti:

"I have no doubt we could do that, Mags, but I guarantee at least one of us is gonna get caught on that shit. And then there's the helicopter."

"What helicopter?" asked Caleb.

As if on cue, one appeared in the night sky, shining a spotlight in a searching pattern.

"Well Jesus fucking Christ. Anyone just happened to have wirecutters in their back pocket then?"

Moretti brought his right hand to his forehead.

"Left them at home. Mags, how long before they're here?"

"Roger said no more than an hour. That was an hour ago."

Moretti looked as if his train of thought was now actually causing him physical pain. The fence was in place so the town and the state didn't have to spend money on having a nightwatchman. There wouldn't be any unexpected guests on this side of the park, then. The park he'd picked because it was the furthest they could reasonably make it to on foot from the overturned ambulance. There actually had been two others to choose from, but this was the logical choice. In making that call, he may very well have fucked them all over. It was sound reasoning at the time.

CRUCIBLE had meant for them to get away. The fuckers wanted to see what would happen when, not if, they got to Dr. Keating. They were counting on his abilities being enough to get them back into the city, and to the hospital where he was still unconscious.

CRUCIBLE was sitting back. Watching.

"What?" asked Magdalena.

Moretti turned to her, and for the first time in the short while that she knew the man, she saw a look of genuine worry.

"Moretti they'll be here -"

And then -

All at once.

A voice, clear as day. Not out loud, in her mind.

It was Sam.

"MAGS!!!" it was as if he was shouting, like he already could see her. She answered in her mind.

"Sam?"

"Dad said to walk a hundred yards to your left. And hurry."

Magdalena smiled. She announced the instructions to the others.

Moretti looked at her puzzled, but just for a second. He'd realized what was happening.

"You guys apparently don't need cell phones?"

"Apparently not."

Sarah, Moretti, Caleb, and Magdalena did as they were bidden. After following the fence for a few minutes, they saw them.

There, with a section of fence having been plowed down, backed over by a heinous looking station wagon were Roger and Sam.

Roger rolled down his window. "You know, you didn't mention any of this in the car ride up from North Carolina, Mags."

Magdalena looked to Moretti, who was now smiling.

"I wasn't worried. Were you?"

"Not for a second," Moretti lied.

Moretti never considered that it could be anything other than his abilities as an agent that CRUCIBLE counted on to get them back to the hospital.

Fortunately for the six of them, Roger had not damaged his vehicle too badly, nor had he popped any tires in knocking over a section of fence for them to cross over, a fact he immediately bragged about as they pulled out onto the main road.

"She's a beaut, ain't she folks? Me and Carla have been through some times, haven't we old girl?" Roger stroked the dashboard a little too affectionately for everyone's comfort.

"Dad, stop touching the car. Gross."

"You never mentioned her name before, Rog," added Magdalena.

Roger glanced behind him and frowned. "Don't listen to Sammy and Mags, old girl. Daddy loves you."

Moretti, who'd taken shotgun, stuck out his hand.

"Stephen Moretti. You must be Roger."

"Yessir. You one of the good guys?"

"You could say that."

From behind the two men, Magdalena spoke up. "Yes. He is."

"Good enough."

Moretti opened his mouth as if to speak and Roger stopped him.

"I know to keep the lights off big guy. We lucked out not having one of those traffic copters up there missing a whole section of chain link laying on its side while we waited. We knocked a section out further down than you in case we were spotted. And Sam here...well. Sam knew how to get a hold of Magdalena on their private channel."

Moretti:

"Interesting." Moretti turned around and saw Sam and Magdalena looking at each other. They were having a silent conversation.

"How long had you been sitting there Rog?" asked Moretti, taking his eyes off the real time telepathy he witnessed to regard their rescuer.

"Dunno...maybe ten minutes."

"How come you-"

"Had to make sure it was really you and not cops posing as you."

Moretti considered this for a moment. He then asked:

"Military, Rog?"

"Iraq. Just after 9/11. Met his mom there, believe it or not."

"Still together?"

"Nope. Not my type, come to find out." Moretti and Roger exchanged a knowing look. The car fell silent for first time since they'd all piled in.

Caleb cleared his throat to break up the moment.

Moretti seemed to snap back into the here and now. He turned stuck out his hand out to Sam.

"Hi Sam, my name is Moretti." Moretti looked to Magdalena, who nodded approval.

"I'm curious, too," she said, knowing that there was more behind his friendly handshake than just a introduction.

Sam smiled and stuck out his child-sized right paw. Moretti made contact and again fell silent.

The station wagon found its way back onto a section of road called the Fellsway, a state road that claimed to stretch east to west but did neither in reality.

"Where to, kids?" Roger was now a father of five it seemed.

Mags answered for Moretti, who was still shaking hands with Sam.

"Mass General. Got a hot date with a biology professor, Rog."

"I was afraid you were gonna say that."

Moretti wasn't certain what would happen, if anything, when he shook Sam's hand. He expected nothing but was prepared for something that resembled his experience when he used the **crimson** to connect with the events in the laboratory from hours before. It was a form a presence scrying – he didn't just see, his entire being became manifest in what he beheld. The gurney in which Keating laid in while the laws of the physical universe vanished along with his consciousness…consciousnesses…whatever – became an anchor for that to work.

Sam had been touched by Magdalena. Just a few moments before, Sam spoke to Magdalena through a kind of short-range telepathy, although what the actual range of that was yet to be determined – or tested. So what had been passed from Keating to Magdalena had done from Magdalena to Sam. What then, was the boy capable of doing?

Moretti thought there had to be some kind of law of diminishing returns at work. There had to be. What Keating had done to himself couldn't just be passed on, like a cold or the flu, with the same potency or effects.

Could it?

The answer to Moretti's questions came the second his hand contacted Sam's.

Moretti's mind flooded with all of Magdalena's, Sam's, and Keating's contacts from the past two weeks all at once, but not in such a way as to overwhelm him.

Sam streamed it to him in such a way that it felt like a soft download. His mind felt like a laptop, and Sam had delivered a ZIP file, then unpacked all within a manner a second or two. Everything, from the Greyhound bus – Jesus Christ Mags, did you have to make the guy pull his own eyeball out – to her pulling a trapped part of Sam's psyche from within a prison in his own mind, it was all there.

Moretti let go of Sam's hand and smiled.

"Nice to meet you, Sam, and thanks for bringing me up to speed."

"No problem, Stephen. I get to call to Stephen, too though. Okay?

"Sure, kiddo."

He turned around and faced forward.

They had become an actual hive mind. If they were allowed to, they'd become…

"Ascendant, Stephen," Sam said from behind him.

The implications of what could happen. It would change the planet. What it meant to be human.

Dr. David Keating, in trying to "repair" his neurodivergences and mental illnesses, had instead fast-forwarded evolution by about a million years or so, and unlocked the next stage of human evolution - in those individuals with neurodivergent conditions.

Homo sapiens as it was currently constituted, could become a thing of the past - just another entry in a biology or an anthropology textbook, alongside neanderthals and cro magnons.

And CRUCIBLE was going to allow Magdalena to reach Keating? For what? To see what kind of weapon they could forge from their meeting?

Moretti smiled.

CRUCIBLE had no idea what they were truly up against.

Chapter Ten

"So you guys have a pretty good idea of what we're up against then, I take it?"

Detective O' Connell, whose default setting in dealing with anyone other than his Captain was bullying, had felt his balls immediately shrivel up into his stomach when he sat in this car with the men he'd previously labeled as Agents X, Y, Z. He attempted to get names - asked them as part of a weak introduction he'd made. His inquiry was met with silence. The aforementioned ball shriveling had initiated at that moment.

"We do, Detective O' Connell. My name is Whitman. Behind you are Price and Hadat."

Their names sounded familiar, but he couldn't place them. Individually they were unremarkable, but together…they sounded made up. They definitely weren't their real names. Not like it mattered.

O' Connell wondered if he'd get a made-up name too if he passed their 'test'. The three of them still freaked him out good, however.

In a matter of moments, the ridiculous vehicle the four of them rode pulled into the entrance ramp to the parking garage at Mass General. Whitman rolled down and pushed the glowing green button on the right side of the ticket dispenser. An edge of their parking garage ticket was pushed out of a thin metal slot. He extracted it from the machine and stuck it into the lapel of his suit coat.

Like he - or one of his team - were really going to end up paying it. Maybe their parking was validated wherever they needed, one of the many perks of being a black ops government agent.

Yeah, right. Along with memory erasing knockout darts that may or may incur permanent brain damage in those poisoned with them. O' Connell mused that they probably had juicy pensions, fat 401Ks, and laser pistols for sidearms like they were all crewmembers on the U.S.S. Enterprise.

"You guys are actually going to pay for parking?". Thus far, they were rolling like they were the same as any other visitors to the institution - checking up on Uncle Joe after his open-heart surgery, picking up a friend after needing to go to the emergency room, or whatever. They'd made no calls since leaving West's house, hadn't even spoken into their collar-communicators. They didn't even try to find a more remote spot in the Mass General parking garage in the compact hybrid car they rode over in - they parked immediately next to the elevators and garage foot exits.

And then it occurred to him.

This whole routine had been camouflage, subterfuge perfected to high art. There was no announcement to their presence because they'd just arrived looking like anyone else - the whole obvious government agent attire notwithstanding. You knew they were there only when they wanted you to know - and that moment would invariably be too late for you to do a thing about it. You'd see them with zero time to react.

His train of thought kept going. The skirmish at West's house.

He thought about that cleaning crew from earlier. Moreover, the vehicle they showed up in. A van like the ones industrial cleaners typically utilized would look the same from the front as a S.W.A.T. team van. Square front, large windows, not a civilian or a pedestrian kind of transport. O' Connell had assumed nobody in that team had seen them drive up, period. Now, he was sure one or more of the officers had seen them and were fooled into thinking the cavalry had arrived. Didn't give them a second look. He remembered being angry with the local force earlier for allowing them to approach so closely.

He regretted being so focused on fuckface Moretti now.

They'd picked that fucking look so they could get all the way to their position outside West's house before they could react in any kind of significant way. They…knew. Somehow. What the fuck was their actual plan?

O' Connell had the sudden urge to kill them all on the spot, but he was in the front passenger seat. He didn't turn around, but suddenly he was sure there was something pointed at his head at that very moment and had been since they left.

Fuck these guys.

Whitman turned to him.

"Detective O' Connell, we need you to assist us in one very specific way. If you can cooperate with us, we can assure you of a great many things that would benefit your career."

"Kinda like you scratch my back you-"

From behind them, either Price or Hadat cut him off mid-cliche.

"Yes, Detective O' Connell. We're familiar with how cooperation works. We're not aliens."

"Cooperation? Fuck you guys. This is coercion. When I-"

Now, the other agent.

"You will do nothing that is not part of our plan Detective. Failure to follow our explicit instructions here will not end well for you. It's all or nothing."

Back and forth now with these assholes. This deal was getting shittier and shittier.

"We understand you had difficulties with Agent Moretti. He made that much abundantly clear in the few reports he did give us while assigned here."

The one speaking continued.

"He is no longer part of organizaiton. Which makes him a civilian. His involvement here is therefore illegal. He is now a traitor to the United States of America. And should be dealt with as such."

And there it was. They wanted him to do their dirty work for them. Take out Moretti. These guys were unbelievable. First, they nearly kill him. Then, they recruit him. This was bullshit, despite his enthusiasm to do just what they wanted.

"Nah. There's something more. If you guys wouldn't be able to handle him, you would have just called in backup, like maybe Agents L, M, N, O, P."

"What?"

O' Connell, realizing that his escorts/captors would have no idea what the alphabet soup meant, shook his head.

"Nevermind. Why didn't you just take your own four-man team? Why me?"

"That's classified, Detective O' Connell."

'Yeah, I thought as much, fuckface' thought O' Connell.

Whitman turned to his colleagues. He nodded and took up the rest of the briefing/speech/pitch.

"Detective O' Connell, you were shot with neurotoxin that should have erased your entire memory of the incident earlier. It is powerful enough to leave some individuals permanently affected by the chemical. It has the potential to kill as well. Unfortunately, two members of the local police department were affected in such a way. It wasn't our intention, we assure you. We use it as a tool to...limit knowledge of our presence whenever it becomes necessary to have one."

O' Connell's anger rose. These motherf-

"You were unaffected. This is quite rare - only about one percent is unaffected by the neurotoxin. Because of this unqiue aspect of your constitution, we feel as though you have...potential for our organization."

Neurotoxin. He was unaffected. O' Connell suddenly felt like Superman, and as he felt this validation of his capabilities his anger over the fallen officers vanished.

O' Connell's outlook had changed on a dime. Yeah, these guys were spooks, but this was his chance to blow this proverbial popsicle stand. He always knew he deserved more than he had already. Something greater.

"Alright, I'm in. What's the plan, Whitman?"

"You and I will station ourselves on the fourth floor. Price will take the third floor. Hadat will wait just inside the main entrance and signal when they've entered the building."

"Wait a second...."

"What is it, detective?"

"Whitman. Buddy. what about…you know. *All the other fucking people in the building?*"

"Detective O' Connell. Massachusetts General Hospital has been emptied except for Keating and three security guards for three days. We've anticipated this series of events for quite some time. All the cars you see," Whitman waved in the direction of the parking garage behind them "were parked here for the public front."

Holy shit. These guys can just do this. And no one – not the public, nor the Commonwealth, knew? Or said anything?

"Who the hell are you guys?" asked O' Connell.

"We're CRUCIBLE, detective. Welcome."

O' Connell couldn't parse which he felt more of – complete terror, or the power to do anything he chose.

"Empty?" asked Caleb. "They emptied one of the most prestigious and well-known hospitals and the largest in Boston out just for David?"

"Yes," said Moretti. "They would have done so probably in anticipation of what's about to transpire."

"Okay, how the hell has that not been all over…" Moretti turned around and glared at Caleb.

"Thought we'd been over this, Caleb."

"Sorry, Moretti. I've been thrown more major hooks in the past couple of weeks than most people get hit with in a lifetime. My full comprehension of this shit may wane from time to time."

Moretti only intensified his glare.

"Jesus, man. I'm here. Focused."

He turned around and faced front again. He began mumbling something to Roger, softly, so no one else in the car could hear.

Prior to this admonishing, Moretti had spent a solid five minutes breaking down everything he'd deduced about their siutation. He needed everyone on the same page going into this…whatever it was, and the time for playing it close to the proverbial vest was long gone.

Keating turning himself into ground zero of a kind of hyper-evolution, a touchpoint for those with altered neurobiologies to change into an ascended species of *homo sapiens*.

The attack on the ambulance only being a message, and not a bonafide attempt on their lives. This was met with incredulity from everyone in the car at first. It did sink in not long after, especially when he gently explained that they weren't shot dead on the spot when they'd made for the woods.

CRUCIBLE actually *wanting* Magdalena to reach Keating. Just to see what they could do.

Ending with clearing out Mass General just to make that happen.

What Moretti said to Roger:

"How much further?"

"About five minutes."

"Kay. Caleb and Sarah know the area best, so they'll both

come with. I'm betting Sarah knows at least a little bit about how the hospital is laid out from memory – otherwise I'd leave her behind with you and Sam."

"You mean Sam's not going in with you?" Roger gave him a sarcastic grin.

"No, he's not coming, wisenheimer. Park a mile from the main entrance and the four of us will walk the rest of the way. You can stay here with the little guy while we either save the day or destroy humanity. Or both. Either way."

Roger's eyebrows furrowed in concern. "Did you say destroy humanity?"

"I did."

"Now who's the weisenheimer, Stephen?"

A shared smile this time.

"Mags." Moretti called to her in the backseat. No answer. "Mags?"

Moretti had to twist his body completely around to see Mags, who had taken up the right rear seat directly behind him.

"Oh, this can't be good," he said.

Sarah and Caleb looked over at Magdalena. Caleb's jaw dropped open, speechless at the sight of her. Sarah, who sat next to Magdalena, reacted in opposite fashion.

"*OH MY GOD WHAT THE FUCK!!!*" she yelled. Sarah began shoving her way left as if Magdalena had just displayed all the symptoms of having contracted full-blown Ebola.

Magdalena's eyes had darkened to the color of tar nad pitch in noonday sunshine, a glimmering kind of obsidian that appeared as if she had put black contacts in her eyes. Blood ran out of her right nostril in a constant flow, and saliva bubbles and foam had gathered in a sizable mass, covering her most of her mouth, lips, and chin.

Sam didn't flinch at all. Moreover, he didn't even look over at Magdalena. Since his how-do-you-do with Moretti just after they'd all piled into the station wagon, he'd been filling in his puzzle book like he was doing the New York Times Crossword. He did sense the collective's panic at Magdalena's current physical state, however. He sighed like a put-upon parent of a misbehaving child, put down his book, and reached over from his car seat to touch Sarah on the shoulder to attempt to either calm or reassure her. All under control, kids.

"Don't sweat it, Miss Fischer. She's in the *Nichtvorhandensein*.
With Walter. Just for a second, though. He's not feeling so good and
won't be able to get back unless she touches him."

Sarah listened to Sam and paused for a moment. Silence
followed in her pause, which she then broke with the following
question, asked of everyone else in the car:

"Does anybody have any idea what the fuck this kid is talking
about? The Nicked-von-what?"

Moretti recognized the German word immediately. Not what it
meant, but part of it appearing in his thoughts while on his brief visit
there. It was German, of course, and he kicked himself silently for not
recognizing it as such.
Because of course, anything associated with a nightmare for Keating
would use the language he'd used to name them all as a child.

What the hell did it actually mean, though?

"The *nichtvorhandensein*, Sarah," corrected Roger. "Although
I've never heard the word used outside of a philosophy textbook, to be
honest."

Moretti looked at Roger.

"The short version then, *herr* Melanson."

"English, either absence or non-existence. German, both."

"That doesn't make sense," chimed Caleb, channeling Ron
Burgundy. "Can't have one without the other, bro."

"Told you, *bro*. Outside of a philosophy book, I've never heard
it. You know how the Wittgensteins and Heidiggers of the world
rolled. Loved their contradictions. It makes sense that your guy there
would use it though – least from what y'all have said."

"Perfect sense, Rog. We all get it, right?" replied Caleb.
Silence.
Roger continued.

"Kay, slightly extended short version then. Non-existence that
has a kind of 'other' state of being. Outside of knowing, there's
unknowing, and if it can't be known in any way then it can't exist. But
the unknowable still has to occupy some…space. In some way."

Moretti's brain was pushed to its limits trying to comprehend
what Roger had said.

Sarah seemed to make the thought experiment work. Alcohol
and philosophy – like peanut butter and chocolate.

"David's consciousness splt into so many discrete subunits of itself, identical to the original yet fragmented until each became incapable of…knowing. Ha. So what was left? Descent into…whatever the hell von Nichtenberg is."

"I fucking hate this," finished Caleb. At least Sarah figured it out.

"Mags can't stay for long. There's things there," Sam added.

Moretti knew there were things there too.

"Dave told me. She won't be ready for them yet."

Moretti asked.

"What does Dave call the things, Sam?"

"*der Geistlosen*," Sam replied in perfect German.

Moretti looked over at Roger.

Roger looked back at him.

"The Mindless," he said.

The next three minutes lasted three hours, each punctuated by the deafening silence within Roger's station wagon.

Sarah kept Magdalena's airways open. Her heart sounded like a death metal beat, but it stayed constant.

It wasn't like she had any real medical precedent to go by on this one, anyway.

As Stephen went into his monologue on what was what – Magdalena pressed her face on the glass and stared out the window. Moretti had a calculator for a brain – a trait she envied but ultimately couldn't follow. None of what he said mattered to her, really.

All Magdalena could think of was when she was going to break the news to everyone else that she had absolutely no idea what the hell it was that she was supposed to do.

She had once seen this journey as a way out of her meaningless life - or at the very least something to break up the monotony and routine. And as the best case, an opportunity to rise above her disabilities. That's what she'd said to Stephen out in the woods. She didn't want to be a nobody for the rest of her days.

Truth was, she didn't care the slightest bit about any of that now. She wanted to go home. She wanted to see Amy.

Wasn't going to happen.

But there was Roger and Sam. Roger was kind, decent, and a loving father to Sam. He'd loved him unconditionally as any parent could on the planet – in fact, he'd loved him even *more* because of Sam's condition. Since she'd touched Sam, their physical resemblance to each other was uncanny, even for father and son. Still - it wouldn't have mattered to Roger, either way, if she had never crossed paths with them. His love of his son wouldn't have broken even under the weight of a planet.

It's because his heart was broken beyond repair by another; he'd lost most of the love from his life and Sam is all that remained of it. His love was more defiance than desperation, however. It was a show of emotional strength, a demonstration to show someone just how unworthy they were to be Sam's -

Magdalena found herself wanting to find out where his ex ran off to and pay her a courtesy call upon completion of this thought.

Stephen was a protector, through and through. The man may not have been the best with expressing his emotions – even in the short time she'd known him Magdalena could tell this much was certain. But where Stephen lacked in sensitivity, he made up for in sheer balls. But he wasn't the kind that drove around in pick-up trucks five times the size of an aircraft carrier and called people "snowflakes", but that rare kind that also possessed a functioning brainstem. Moretti knew he could dismantle you – he didn't need to advertise it.

But at one time, he probably did. He may not have driven a truck, but it was a safe bet he had an ego that wouldn't have fit inside this station wagon. He's lost, too. Somebody's already beat him and took something from him he'll never get back. He doesn't take a single thing for granted.

Who – or what - the hell was capable of pulling that off?

And then, Magdalena thought of her own father, who'd resigned his position without a second thought before she'd even reached fourth grade. Bob Christie didn't even say goodbye to her and Amy. Just one day…gone.

A single tear rolled out of her right eye.

Then another.

Then out of her left eye.

Silently.

Because when you cry out loud, you wanted comfort. Soothing.

Magdalena stuffed her hands into her jacket pockets in that instant. It was a form of *self-soothing* she used because she knew the people sitting near her, Sarah and Caleb, weren't going to fill that need for her. In the left pocket however, was a piece of paper – actually more like cardstock - she couldn't recall shoving in there. She pulled it out to see what it was. One quick glance at it reminded her of where she'd got it, and so she put it back as quickly as she could before Sarah could take notice of it.

Caleb appeared to take an interest in Magdalena's activities in that instant and saw the entire series of events.

"Whatcha got there, Magdalena?"

She had to come up with something quick and convincing, so she went with a true response altered by only a minor detail.

"Lucky tarot card I keep with me, Caleb."

Caleb scoffed.

"You keep a lucky tarot card with you. For real?"

"Yes, for real, jerk. It's the Hierophant card."

"Why that one?"

"Symbolizes wisdom, I guess. I like the design, too."

Caleb's eyes squinted, as if hearing the word had brought an incomplete memory to mind and he was attempting to recall the missing parts. He started talking about some complicated science jargon and then-

DARKNESS.

Like all the lights in windowless room had shut off at once.

An image in her mind appeared.

Sam, holding open his puzzle book to her. There were no puzzles in it. In it, only two words were written, one to a page.

Be

Careful.

The image vanished.

The second it disapated, they were upon her. They had been waiting.

**CAREFULBEBECAREFULSAMROGERSTEPHENCALEBDA
DDYWHEREISMYDADDYCAREFULBEBECAREFULCARE
FULDOESNTLOVEYOUNOBODYCARESROGERSTEPHEN
CALEBEVENCALEBWOULDBEAFATHERNOTYOUNOTY
OUNOTYOUSADSADSADSADSADSADSADPATHETICSADB
ROKENIMBROKENIMBROKENIMBROKENSADSADSDUN
LOVABLEROGERSTEPHENWOULDNTLOVEYOUFOULF
OULFOULFOULFOULBROKENBRO
KENYOUWILLALWAYSBEBROKENMAGSMAGSMAGSMAG
SBROKENMAGS**

Magdalena found that the only thing she could do was scream.

But

Despite how loud it was she could still hear —

a boy, crying silently. How could she hear
because she had just been crying silently.

She could hear him, through her scream and over the sound of millions of mockeries of everything she was — who she was. They could destroy her if they wanted. But she WOULD NOT ALLOW THAT CHILD TO SUFFER FOR ANOTHER SECOND. Every aspect of her being coelesced to a fulcum, a diamond point, microscopic and cosmic at once. It was a single word.

NO.

The creatures fell silent. Her will had forced them into a retreat. But she could feel them, regrouping. Magdalena looked down and saw him.

It was the boy.

It was Keating.

All that was left of him was a child. They'd devoured everything else about him and left him that way.

Weeping, silently, alone in the darkness.

She reached down and touched his cheek, gently, with the backs of her fingers. One drop ran over the top of her index finger and into the crevasse at the middle joint. Magdalena closed her palm, then opened it. Like a magician, she had made it disappear.

"David?"

The boy ceased his sobbing. He looked up at her. He had sandy brown hair, and the very brightest blue eyes she'd ever seen.

"Ich heiße Walter. Wer bist du?"

She didn't know any German, but it was obvious he'd asked her what her name was. She attempted to replicate what the boy had just said.

"Ich heiße Magdalena."

"Magdalena?"

She nodded.

"Magdalena." A spark. He remembered. The boy lifted his arms up, wanting to be held.

She held out her arms, and just as she was about to wrap them around him -

Chapter Eleven

Roger had pulled over into an empty spot, about a half a mile up the street from Massachusetts General Hospital. He didn't have a GPS or a cell phone to direct him, relying on Caleb's directions. He threw the station wagon into park.

The moment he did, Magdalena's voice spoke.

"We don't have much time."

Chapter Twelve

"JESUS FUCKING CHRIST!" Magdalena had once again frightened Sarah to pieces.

"I said she was coming right back, Sarah," said Sam, disgusted. Then, to Magdalena:

"He wasn't Dave anymore, was he?"

"No, Sam. He was your age. His name was-"

"Walter," Moretti finished. "Long story, Magdalena, but suffice to say he-"

"I'm already familiar with the basic jist, Stephen. Time's short. Let's not fuck about."

Moretti turned around to regard Magdalena. She returned his gaze with one of her own, equal, and of the same shape.

"I figured it out, Stephen. It came to me. I came to it - him," she said.

"And?" he asked.

"Nobody is going to suffer as long as I can do something to stop it. Ever."

Moretti nodded.

"Promise is a promise." He took a breath. "*They* promised me they could save my son if I helped them. I didn't know what to do. So I helped them. He died anyway. Here I am."

"Fuck them."

In that brief instant, Moretti saw Lourdes sitting there in the backseat instead of Magdalena.

Like a mirror, Stephen. This was meant to be.

"All these accidents that happen…then the riddle gets solved."

"Hunh?"

"Line from a Bjork song, Mags. *Joga.* She was her best friend. Called Joga her hierophant. My son loved Bjork. Now I do. Go figure."

Caleb interrupted them.

"Uh, hi. Caleb West, representing People's Republic of Normal here. What's the plan?"

"We can start by getting the fuck out of the car," said Sarah.

Caleb looked to Moretti, who nodded. Caleb reached over Sam to open the rear passenger door.

"Kid, why the hell you still in a car seat? Don't need that crap anymore. You roll with your big bro Caleb, you roll like big bro. Sam laughed. "Once this crap is over, you and I are hitting the arcade," Caleb added negotiating his way over his new buddy.

"I've never played any video games, Caleb."

Caleb stopped short, turned, and looked positively offended.

"You've. Never. Played. Any. Video. Games."

Moretti interrupted.

"CALEB."

Caleb quickly scanned up and down the street. Not a soul in sight.

"Nothing, Moretti. You said they wanted us to come. If that's true, I'm not gonna get-"

Roger interrupted.

"CALEB."

"Pneumonia the second I step out of the car." Caleb rolled his eyes at Sam, who laughed again.

"Kid, you and me. Arcade. ASAP."

Caleb hadn't been fully clear of the door before Sarah pushed him out of the way and made towards the sidewalk on the other side of the car.

"Dude, where the hell are you going?"

Sarah stopped short, irritated.

"Duuuude, I have to take a piss. Like now. You wanna come with?"

"Well no, Sarah, but you know...fugitives? Police? Secret government agencies bent on...whatever it is they're fucking bent on?"

Sarah lifted her arms and pivoted in a semi-circle.

"Look around, Caleb. The only people out down here are either homeless and hiding near a steam vent or driving snowplows. The authorities still think we're fumbling around the woods someplace."

"Well jeez Sarah, while we're at it, you think maybe there's a couple of bars open right now?" Caleb's face lit up, mocking Sarah.

"Fuck you Caleb."

Caleb regretted the comment as soon as he'd said it.

"I'm sorry, Sarah. You did fall off the wagon today. I'm just – doing a really shitty job being concerned for you."

Sarah's anger was causing steam to rise off of her skin then.

"Really, Caleb? You're concerned. Now. After all of this. Were you concerned when David started changing? When his eyes turned into bug eyes? When he started doing the horror movie Professor Xavier shit?"

"Sarah I…"

"No, Caleb. You don't get to do *shit*, now. You've been along for the ride this whole time. I wanted to stop the day after I cut him open." She shook her head. "God, I *knew* this was ALL bad. But I still went along that far, and now I somehow gotta make up for all that, too. And the only reason why I did do that was because you two assholes helped me get sober. And then you let me…"

"I'm…I'm sorry Sarah. I thought you…"

"You thought wrong." Tears were running from her eyes by the time she got to the word 'wrong'.

She finished: "I'm going around the corner, and I'm gonna squat in an alley and piss in the snow, okay?"

"Alright, Sarah. I'm sorry for everything. Again."

Sarah turned and walked away.

"Fuck ALL of you," she said, not under her breath. No one heard her.

Roger got out and took stock of their surroundings. He had an idea they'd be their getaway car, so he wanted to get a look for himself. Know the battlefield, so to speak.

It was wide open in almost every direction. These people – whoever they were, could be anywhere.

This was a horrible place to stop. To their immediate right was a Starbucks, one with a golden steaming kettle above the door. Even this late at night, the kettle had steam coming out of the top, and quite a lot of it as well. Roger looked past it just to left and saw a massive structure that might have been the most hideous building he'd ever seen in his life. It was concrete and brick and looked as if it had been built using a mixture of Duplo and Lego blocks with abhorrent results.

"Hey Caleb – there has to be someplace better than out here to stop." He pointed to had to be the worst architectural eyesore he'd ever seen.

"I mean, what the hell is that building there?"

"It's Boston City Hall, Roger."

"You're kidding."

"Yup, it's pretty heinous. We're not happy about it, either Rog. This is Boston, though, so the general attitude is 'fuck you we're not changing it'."

"Alright man, well look. We're exposed out here. Like, really exposed."

"In an alley, they take us all down at once. Then they force Magdalena at gunpoint up to the hospital, take notes, and if it gets out of hand, they shoot her and Keating both. The end."

Roger was taken aback.

"Got good in the spy game in the past few hours, dude?"

"Nope. Just kinda, walked it through in my head I guess."

Sarah had since disappeared around the corner in the shadows between the building with the more obnoxious than usual Starbucks and City Hall. She'd found an alleyway in between the sandwich place and a copy store that further down that row of storefronts.

She'd have to be quick.

Sarah pulled out the cell phone she'd set to off since the wee hours of that morning and turned it on. It rang the second the four bars appeared on its analog screen.

It was a man who'd called her. O' Connell would have told Sarah the guy's name was Whitman, but Sarah wouldn't have cared much. She wanted out. Now.

"Miss Fischer. We were hoping to hear from you. Your life - and ours just got that much easier. The boy with your group?"

"The boy?"

"Come come now, Sarah. Catch up."

Sarah felt like she had just been punched in the gut.

"You mean-"

"Samuel Melanson. Tracked him along with Magdalena Christie. Christie appeared again on our tracking early this afternoon – at your domicile I believe. Young Samuel, however, didn't appear until late this evening."

Moretti had been wrong. They weren't sending a message. They were-

"Had to draw him out somehow, so we forced Magdalena's hand, so to speak. The four of you had no choice but to call his father to rescue you."

Sarah was stunned into silence.

"I'll take that as a yes, Miss Fischer. Thank you for your assistance. Oh, before we let you go. Your continued cooperation will need to extend into remaining quiet about our arrangement, and these insights I've shared. Do you understand?"

Again, Sarah could not find the will to speak.

"DO YOU UNDERSTAND, MISS FISCHER? I WILL NEED YOU TO SAY THE WORD, PLEASE."

"Y-yes."

"Leave your phone on, Miss Fischer. Do not hang up."

Sarah would have given anything to hear that abrupt click just one more time.

"Good. Leave your phone on so we can track you as your group approaches."

Sarah walked back to Roger's car as briskly as she could. When she returned, Caleb was rambling on to Roger about City Hall Plaza.

"So everyone once in awhile, they have concerts and shit, but mostly the whole area really conveys that Leningrad mystique, don't you think?"

"Caleb, this city fucking blows."

Caleb took notice of Sarah returning and broke off his conversation with Roger.

"Hey Sarah, listen I know I already said I was sorry, but like, I know I fucked up. I'm sorry."

She looked at him, her features melted from pure emotion. She looked defeated.

"I'm sorry, too Caleb. For everything."

Caleb was puzzled.

"Wha?"

Moretti watched their exchange from the front seat.

He thought:

Sarah just warned them we were coming. That's what wasn't right about all of this.

He was wrong.

Chapter Fourteen

"So, this is the famous Dr. David Keating?"

Whitman had just opened the door that led into Keating's hospital room. The space was dimly lit by a single, soft yellow lamp in the corner opposite from his bed.

"Yes."

O' Connell looked around. There was no sign of any breathing apparatus, heart monitor, EEG, or really anything. The man was just laying there, as if he was simply asleep.

"Uh, correct me if I'm wrong Whitman, but isn't there supposed to be I don't know…shit to keep this fucking guy alive somewhere?"

"He was removed from the ICU this afternoon and brought here, detective. All of that would get in the way of our work here tonight."

"Won't he-"

"He'll live, detective."

At that moment, a single chime rang out from Whitman's suit jacket. "Excuse me. I have to make an urgent call. It'll be just a moment. Do not approach Dr. Keating, O' Connell."

Whitman returned to the corridor outside and left O' Connell to stand there like an idiot.

"Hey he's not gonna like, sit up and make my head explode is he? Like that movie with the…"

Whitman popped his head back into the room.

"It was called *Scanners*, Detective O' Connell. And possibly. We're not exactly sure. Best to remain quiet."

O' Connell couldn't believe what he'd just heard. *Not exactly sure?*

He was only there to settle a score with Moretti, and nothing else. And certainly not babysit Keating while fuckface took an urgent call. His first lesson in Crazy Shit 101 with CRUCIBLE had already taught him more than he ever wanted to know about mad scientists, brain-wiping dart guns, and other related batshittery.

Tonight was purely going to be the Moretti gets what's coming show. That fuck who shined a flashlight in his face back at the University and spoke to him like he was a first- year rook. That greasy guinea pissant that breezed out of his station with *his* prisoner. He was resposnible for all of this getting set off, and he was responsible for cops lying dead in the snow.

He was about to leave when Whitman returned. Quick urgent phone call it seemed.

"I, was, uh, gonna set-up shop outside in the hallway, that is, unless you need me for anything else in here. Ambush them as they come down the hall."

"Unnecessary, Detective O' Connell. The elevator we took up to this floor is the only one functioning. The stairwells are are secured and locked. I recommend you take position in such a manner as to-"

"Hey pal? I've been a cop for -"

"Seventeen years, Detective O' Connell. I'm well aware of a great many details of your career and life."

It was a retort O" Connell wasn't prepared for. The statement of how long he'd been on the force was his fallback whenever anyone tried to tell him his job, even if they were right.

It meant he'd been investigated. His life had already been sussed out in one of their dossiers somewhere. They'd shaken him out, examined, and drawn conclusions about who he was and what his tendencies were.

The intrusion into his own personal life, this *violation*, shook O' Connell. Of course, he'd made an entire career out of surveillance, investigation, and the systematic prying into other people's lives. He'd just had his first taste of being on the opposite side of the ninety-watt lightbulb. When Whitman had said they knew 'a great many details', he probably meant that they probably even knew which way, over or under, that the rolls of toilet paper hung in his bathroom.

Jokes on them, he thought. *Toilet paper sits on the sink next to the can. Who needs a-*

"Detective O' Connell." The fact was that the toilet paper sat uninstalled in the dispenser on the bathroom sink, and that he'd never installed a single one in his life.

"What?"

"Stand in front of the elevator. Shoot Moretti when you see him."

"How do you know-"

Whitman simply stared at him.

"Alright, fine."

A thought occurred to O' Connell as he walked away. They could have stationed any of their agents at the elevator to put a couple in Moretti as soon as the doors opened. Why had they picked him?

It never occurred to him for a second that there was no neurotoxin on the dart that hit him at Caleb's house.

Only a tranquilizer.

O' Connell muttered to himself as he reached the elevator.

"Doesn't matter, man," The freaky-deaky shit was going down inside the room, and frankly, the less he had to do with that, the better. He only wanted Moretti, and they were giving that asshole to him.

And at last, he had an epiphany.

"The Running Man. That's where thy got their fake names. These fucking guys are named after last year's losers." He looked back down the hallway to Whitman, who nodded to him and disappeared into Keating's room.

"Can fucking say that again. Alright then. Come to papa, fuckface," he said, pointing his gun squarely at the doors.

"I'm waiting."

Chapter Fifteen

The wind whipped across the empty plaza before him. In summer, it was so many people, nine-to-fivers, tourists, retail slaves, suburbanites in the city for a day trip to shop, or eat, or take in Boston for a day. As Moretti cast his gaze from its furthest edge and scanned it from right to left, all he saw were thin drifts of frozen snow forming crystalline ghosts, fleeting, disappearing upon darkened and broken concrete. This was a city where the forgotten dead were cast to haunt, seconds at a time, disapating into the mercy of oblivion, only to be cruelly pulled back into spectre form again and again.

He wondered if death would be as cruel when it came for him.

He shook his head.

"God I hate Boston," he said.

Magdalena touched him on the shoulder.

"Penny for your thoughts?"

He turned and smiled at her.

"They're not worth that much, Mags."

"Ready?"

"Nope. You?"

"Not a chance."

"Mags, what, uh, do you…"

"Physical contact, Stephen. That's it."

"That's it?"

"Yeah."

"Okay. Then what?"

"And then….we'll protect you, instead of you protecting us."

"I don't need protecting but thank you for the thought. Do you have any idea who we're up against? What they're capable of?"

"Also doesn't matter. They don't know what we're capable of."

"Mags?"

"Make them order a tuna on rye this time. It's my favorite sandwich."

"Gross, Stephen."

"I know. But I friggin love 'em for some reason."

"Alright, I'm gonna go say goodbye to Sa-"

"No, Mags. Do not do that. Let's go."

"Why can't I…"

"Because it's cruel, Magdalena. Goodbyes are cruel. Let the next time you see the kid be wordless, and let it be an embrace. Now. No time to fuckabout."

They walked over to Caleb and Sarah.

"You three stay here. Two seconds."

Moretti then walked over to Roger, who'd returned to his car and was already fiddling with the car radio. Roger was the first good man he'd met in his travels in far too long. Good father. Kind. And had his head screwed on straight. At that moment, there was nothing he wanted more than to be just sitting with him and just…talking. About nothing and everything all at once.

Roger rolled down the window.

"So this is it big guy?"

"It is, Roger."

Roger stuck out his hand.

"Sorry I didn't get to know you more. Have a feeling we'd have some stories to share."

"Thought we'd share more than stories."

"We make it out of this, we make it a date?"

Moretti felt a stab. He thought of Kafka. You are the knife I twist within myself. That, my dear, is love.

"Sure, Rog."

"So what do me and Sam do now?"

Moretti looked down the street towards the hospital. After about a quarter of a mile, the street sloped downwards and vanished, meaning that Mass General was at the bottom or near the bottom of a hill.

"You wait until the four of us disappear down that hill up ahead. Keep an eye out for anyone coming up behind us, and if anyone does, ping my phone."

"You're going to have it on now?"

"Yeah. No point in the subterfuge now."

"Stephen. This is a trap you're walking into; you know that right?"

Moretti only nodded.

"Okay, then what."

"Once we're out of sight, you and the kid get out of here as fast as possible. Then -"

"Already had a rental ready. Will they come looking for us?"

"They don't even know you two exist, Roger. And if whatever is supposed to happen happens, I think our team gets an upgrade. Should be okay from there. I hope."

Roger nodded towards the backseat. "We already did, amigo. Take care of yourself, Stephen. And take care of Magdalena. Bravest kid I ever met."

"Me too."

"Must have had a good father."

Moretti laughed. "No Rog. Magdalena is the way she is because hers was a fucking bum. Hundred percent."

"I'd adopt her tomorrow, but I think I'm a bit too young."

"I'm not. Don't worry. She'll know she's loved before the end, Roger."

Roger smiled and rolled up the window.

They exchanged a silent nod, and Moretti joined the others.

There were no cars, no traffic of any kind as the four of them walked down Cambridge Street towards Massachusetts General. The sidewalks had not been cleaned. The streetsm only enough to allow them to trudge slowly upon. The fluorescent yellow of the streetlamps made their shadows look blue on the muted white of the snow on the ground.

They reached the point where the street began to angle down. Moretti turned around, and waved to his lookout, and then continued on with the others. It was a matter of another five minutes before they reached the street entrance to the hospital.

They stopped there.

Moretti spoke.

"Whatever happens, you do what I say, and do not ask any questions. Do you all understand?"

"Yeah," said Sarah.

"Yes," said Caleb.

Mags only nodded.

Moretti drew his gun.

"Okay. Time waits for no man, kids."

Roger did as Moretti asked and watched the four of them walk off to meet whatever fate held in store for them. The talk radio station was set to a political station, not news. He was sick of hearing about how they were all criminals.

Roger silently began to rehearse how he was going to tell Sam that all four of them were gone.

Meaning that they were dead.

All things considered, Moretti, Caleb, Sarah, and most importantly, Mags being well out of sight when everything went down was the best way for their little adventure to end. Mags would be forever an angel to his son, a memory that would fade over time, as all memories do, but Roger knew that her coming into their lives and what she'd done was a miracle.

Before they'd made it a hundred feet down the street towards the hospital, Roger found himself shedding tears from the corners of both eyes.

"Hey Dad?"

"Yeah, Sam?" a shaky and broken response from Roger as he wiped his eyes dry with the sleeve of his jacket.

"Did they go to the hospital already?"

Sam had paid no attention to his surroundings for quite some time, it seemed. Roger was thankful for this - there were no protracted goodbyes, no wailing, no insistence on going with them. His boy hadn't noticed until they were already gone. Moretti had seen to that - and that realization revealed that Moretti must have been a father as well.

He knew.

"Yes, Sam."

"Cool. I hope they're okay."

That was it for Sam's thoughts on the matter. Cool. Hope they're okay.

Going well so far.

A few moments later, Roger was just able to see the outline of Moretti waving to him. Time to go. Roger silently prayed that things would remain 'cool'. He threw the car into drive and began to pull away.

Cool vanished from existence in an instant, never to return. It was replaced with alarm and fear on the part of Sam, and he made their presences known in the next instant.

"Where are we going Dad?"

Roger's only thought was:

fuck.

"We're going back to the hotel, buddy. It's too dangerous here for us to just wait, so we need to go."

"We need to stay and wait for Mags, Dad!"

"Buddy, they'll be fine without us. And when they're done, they're going to call us to come get them."

"You're lying. I can tell."

"Sam, we need to go. I don't have time to argue with you. They'll be okay."

"No, they won't. Mags and Dave might need me."

And then - the car shifted gear back into park, without Roger having ever touched the shifter. The key turned back to the off position.

Roger lost all coherent thought at this display.

Telekinesis.

fuck.

He had to say something.

"Sam, listen, we can't-"

Sam stopped him mid-sentence.

"Dad. Somebody's here."

Roger looked to his left and saw nothing but the lower half of a person standing just outside the drivers' side. The closest streetlamp was behind the man, so Roger did not see much of him.

The man knocked on the window.

"Sam, just be quiet and let me handle this, okay?"

Sam was silent.

Roger rolled the window down.

He turned to his left and made to address whoever this person was.

"Is there something I can-"

The man produced a gun from behind his back, and without saying a word fired a bullet into Roger's temple. Sam watched his father's head kick obscenely to the right, blood and matter spraying the front seat as a homicidal Jackson Pollack would.

Roger slumped the rest of the way down, with what was left of his head eventually coming to rest in the passenger seat.

The man dropped the firearm as soon as he had fired it, and just as quickly produced a small, silver ball from his pocket. He clicked something on its surface and tossed it into the car. The device released a blue-gray gas in the interior, filling its space within a matter of seconds.

Sam could not manage a cry, nor a whimper, nor any real reaction before the gas rendered him unconscious.

Agent Singer spoke into his collar.

"Target acquired. Primary mission objective complete."

A nondescript SUV pulled up alongside. Singer pulled Sam out of the station wagon, placed him into the backseat of the SUV, and got in.

The vehicle drove off,
leaving only the sound of the wind gusts,
blowing across the city of the dead.

The four of them turned right off of Cambridge Street and ahead of them stood the main and emergency room entrances to Massachusetts General Hospital. Caleb, Sarah, and Moretti had seen it before – Magdalena had not. The three of them looked at her, expecting her to panic at the size of it and having to scour the building looking for Keating.

She was stone-faced.

"Magdalena, are you going to be able to f-" Caleb started to ask.

"He's on the fourth floor." She pointed to a spot on the building above them.

"There."

"Okay, then."

"Alright, let's get this over with guys. C'mon," Sarah began to start waling ahead of them.

Moretti grabbed her by the shoulder.

"Hey. Sarah. What did I say?"

"Right. Sorry. Agent Moretti."

He locked eyes with her and telegraphed his knowledge of her betrayal. Sarah said nothing.

"Okay then, Fischer. Suit yourself," he beckoned for her to lead them in.

"We're going in through the ER entrance, people."

The automatic rotating glass door still operated and turned clockwise to allow them entry.

Not a single soul.

"We're screwed. We're totally screwed. I'm gonna get one of those darts and my brain is going to explode and-"

"Shut the fuck up, Caleb," commanded Sarah.

"You shut the fuck up, Sarah! How about you go crawl into another bottle you-"

"Quiet, the both of you. It doesn't matter. If they wanted us dead, we'd be dead. We're not. We need to find an elevator."

Magdalena chimed in. "The only people in a position to compromise their asset are the ones standing right next to him. They're waiting."

Moretti smiled.

"Correct."

Sarah saw a chance to avoid the main event and took it. Her and Caleb could make sure no surprises were waiting on the third floor. She offered it up to the group.

"Why don't Caleb and I take the third floor. You two go on the fourth. Make sure there's nothing waiting for us down there."

Caleb immediately disapproved of her plan.

"No fucking way, Sarah. I'm sticking with Moretti."

Sarah immediately got into Caleb's face.

"I might not be able to stand the sight of you at the moment Caleb, but it's better than being anywhere near these two. You and I are sticking together, period."

"Go ahead you two. Stephen, we're wasting time."

Moretti watched Sarah's reaction to Caleb's complaint with added attention. He'd told them no more than ten minutes previous to follow his instructions *no matter what*, and here she was, putting her fellow mad scientist in his place at the mention of a strategy only slightly different to the one she'd just proposed. Moretti agreed just to ensure Caleb would be out of harm's way.

"Fine. Let's find a way up."

It took a solid twenty minutes of searching the ground before the four of them found a working elevator.

Moretti picked up on this.

"Only one working elevator."

"Why don't we try some stairs instead of coming up the way they want us to come? Anyone?" Caleb was noticeably frightened. He'd acquitted himself well thus far, but this was different.

Moretti responded to Caleb's idea by pushing the up button adjacent to the double doors.

"Stick to the plan, kid. You and Sarah get off at three. Mags and I will go four."

A moment later, the bell rung, and the doors slid open.

"This looks like us, gang."

They boarded, and the car began its slow rumble up to the third floor. Caleb and Sarah stepped off, and the doors began to close behind them. At the last moment, Caleb spun around, panicked.

"Hey what should we do if we-"

Moretti made no effort to respond, let alone stop the doors from closing.

Sarah pulled at Caleb's elbow. "Come on."

In the elevator, the car had barely begun its short ascent to the fourth floor when Moretti pounced on the emergency stop switch. The car slammed to a stop, between floors.

Moretti turned and faced Mags.

"I'd be proud if you were my daughter, Magdalena."

"Wha-"

Magdalena had no idea how to react to this. It was the last thing she'd expected to hear out of this man.

"Your brain, your mind is turned upside down and rewired overnight. The next day, you get on a Greyhound to place you've never been. Waking up and being assaulted. You kill a man, though you didn't mean to."

"I don't think he-"

"Definitely dead, Mags. Another guy tries to rape you. You don't kill him. You luck out with Rog and Sam. On and on and on, and you stayed the course. Now, look at you. I would be proud if you were my daughter, Mags."

"Sam-"

"I told him and Roger to head for the hills once we were out of sight. They're safe. But yes. Sam gave me the full download, even though I'm not like you."

Moretti held his arms out to take her into an embrance.

Magdalena leapt into his arms.

They stayed that way for a full minute before they let go of each other.

"Okay," Magdalena said.

"That's the last fuckabout."

Moretti flipped the switch, and the elevator rose to the next floor.

On the fourth floor, O' Connell had been watching the elevator lights intently. When the car didn't immediately get to the fourth floor, he knew Moretti had stopped the car.

"Motherfucker," he said aloud. "He knows." O' Connell walked straight up to the doors and pointed his gun right at them. He firmed his stance.

"C'mon, asshole."

Sarah and Caleb wandered around the third floor for all of thirty seconds before they ran straight into a Constabulary. Caleb gasped when he saw the man standing directly in their path, thinking they were both dead. He looked and dressed exactly like the two men he'd encountered in Heathrow.

He grabbed Sarah by the shoulders and attempted to spin her around in the opposite direction.

"SARAH! RUN!!"

Sarah stopped. She didn't run.

"Caleb! Stop. It's okay."

The agent made no threatening moves. He only nodded.

"Miss Fischer. Glad to see you made it. Well done. This is Mr. West, I take it?"

It took a full minute for Caleb to process what had just occurred. When he did, he walked to a position in between the agent and Sarah, blocking her view of him.

He'd never felt as angry in his life as he did in that moment. He did not hesitate. He smacked her across her face.

Caleb didn't see him with his back turned, but the Constabulary had pulled pulled a silver gun that looked more like a flare gun than an actual firearm out and pointed it at his head.

"The fuck did you do?" he asked.

Sarah waved him off.

"I saved our lives, you fucking asshole."

"SARAH!!! WHAT THE FUCK DID YOU DO?!"

Sarah ignored him and walked around him towards the agent. Caleb stood there, dumbfounded, too terrified to move.

He heard the two of them talking behind him but was unable and also unwilling to listen to what they said to each other.

They appeared next to him. The agent put his hand on Caleb's shoulder.

"Come on, son. It's over. Let's get you out of here."

They walked to a nearby stairwell, unlocked at that floor. Caleb could not think, could not speak. The emotions of what had just happened were nothing he'd ever experienced in his life.

It wasn't supposed to end this way. Not at all.

They walked to a nearby stairwell.Agent Hadat pushed open the stairwell door, and the three of them disappeared behind it.

The doors opened on the fourth floor only halfway before O' Connell caught sight of Moretti. When they'd opened all the way, O' Connell shot him point blank, twice, in the chest. He flew backward into the back wall of the elevator compartment.

Magdalena screamed.

"MORETTI!!"

"Hey. Bitch. Whitman's waiting for you down the hall." O' Connell waved his pistol in her face.

"NOW, before I change my mind and put an end to all of this here and now. I don't give a fuck about whatever these black hats want with you."

Magdalena slid past O' Connell, making no eye contact and remaining silent as she did. That scream - the word 'Moretti' - was the only sound she'd make.

She tried to use whatever...power...she thought she might have had.

It was quite easy she found. Maybe it was because she was close to Keating, maybe she'd just never tried to do it, maybe she'd simply never had a chance.

She touched Stephen's mind.

"Stephen?" Faint. Fading. He was dying.

Proud...

"STEPHEN!" the force of her will pulled him back into life, past when he should have already been gone.

"Ya. I'm tired kid. Let me go."

Magdalena could see her. She could see Lourdes. Of course. Stephen loved her.

"I don't love her, ya dope. She's a good friend. And I trust her with my life...and death."

She vanished from his mind. Then, Stephen appeared.

He smiled. "Like I do with you, Mags. Go get him kid. FUCK THESE GUYS."

Magdalena fell to her knees as he vanished from her mind.

Chapter Twenty-One

O' Connell began shouting at Moretti's prone body. He fired again, this time taking off his right hand.

Moretti reached into his red bomber jacket.

O' Connell laughed openly at him.

"Go ahead, you fuck. Try and pull on me.

Moretti had dropped his gun when he'd first been hit. Instead, he pulled out Fred, the yellow flashlight he'd used to piss off O' Connell when they'd first met.

He pointed Fred up at O' Connell's face and clicked the on switch.

Fred turned on, blasting its light into his face once again.

Moretti managed three last words.

That a boy."

A third shot, this time to Moretti's forehead. O' Connell holstered his gun, stepped to the side of his body, and pushed the "L" button for the lobby.

Magdalena willed herself to her feet.

She willed herself to the door of Keating's room.

She opened the door.

Magdalena's eyes caught sight of Keating's physical body laying on the only bed in the room, then the man who waited there for her. He stood in a darkened corner, oppostie from Keating.

"Ah, Miss Christie. Sounded like you'd arrived by the sound of it. But then it seemed like it was taking you a bit too long to come down the hallway, and well, I got worried. Thought my errand boy had gotten a little trigger happy out there. And I did hear three gunshots."

Magdalena said nothing in response.

"And yet you are unharmed. *Molto bene.* Detective O'Connell really had a..thing for Agent Moretti. He'll be a wonderful cover for us."

Magdalena could not respond. Of course they'd used that stunted ape to do their dirty work.

Whitman advanced a step.

Magdalena took a step back in retreat.

"What's the saying? Yes. Does the cat got your tongue? Never made any sense to me. Regardless…I'm not actually here to interfere. No need to fear, my dear. In fact, there are many interested parties curious to see what happens next with you and the good doctor here."

Whitman nodded, then glanced in several different directions at a number of different points in the room. As he did so, a tiny red light would turn on, indicating they had begun recording and/or transmitting.

Proud…

Magdalena smiled.

"Okay. Lights, camera, action, Agent Smith."

"Miss Christie, my name is…"

"*Shut up.*"

The man's head tilted to one side.

"I'm sorry?"

This idiot has no idea what's about to happen to him, she thought.

And if CRUCIBLE was content to sit back and watch, collect their data, and then assess or whatever it was that they did…

...then this asshole was fucked.

She felt strength surge into her legs. Magdalena strode right up to the man, got into his space, and put her face inches from his.

"SHUT. UP. You're already dead."

And then she saw it in his face, and it filled her with delight. She grinned wider than the Cheshire.

'It' was fear.

He smiled as well in a desperate attempt to hide it. The attempt failed.

"Good! Compliance. Well then. On with the show, please."

Magdalena turned from the man and stepped over to Keating. "I'm here."

A twitch in his right eye.

"You're not alone."

She bent over and put her arms around him. She whispered into his ear.

"You're so far away, Walter. Come home."

And all Magdalena did was embrace Keating, laying in his bed. What had been missed by a fraction of a second before was not missed a second time. Because there was only one thing that would ever bring him back from that world.

And for roughly five minutes, absolutely nothing was caught on any of CRUCIBLE's cameras, because nothing appeared to be happening in the hospital room.

Sometimes, love could be unknowable in this world.

In the *Nichtvorhandensein*:

Walter looked up to see his father and brothers stnading around him in a circle, with their backs to him. He was frightened. The Mindless had...

wait.

He'd called them something else before. The boy couldn't remember the word anymore. Der Geesh...something. But they were Mindless. His abusers.

295

They had always been mindless.

"My name is David," he said aloud.

The three of them spun around on him. They attempted to begin their nonsense chorus, their violence of thought and…

"SILENCE," David commanded. He could feel her. Magdalena. He could feel her arms around him. He could feel their –

connection.

David threw his arms out at his sides, as his features, his face, his entire shape cast itself into every color at once, white was just a word, because love

was light and

light

was

all colors, known, unknown, and a third kind:

of the Divine.

"I AM ABOVE YOU NOW. HERE YOU WILL REMAIN, FOR THIS IS ALL YOU WILL EVER KNOW.

I WILL IT TO BE."

And for that one time, love was known in that world, as light where no light could exist.

In the hospital room:

Keating arms wrapped around Magdalena. His eyes opened and looked into hers.

"Hi," he said.

"Hey. We've got company."

"Indeed. And we're also on Candid Camera, as well."

"Hunh?"

"Nevermind. Show's over."

"It never started for them, David."

"Good. Let's keep it that way."

From around the room, each of the tiny red LED lights shorted out all at once, followed by a short spark of electricity.

The man in the corner – he went by Whitman in their silly little organization, real name was Carter Drummond – pulled the same shiny silver flare-gun looking weapon on them both and made to shoot them both.

He could not pull the trigger, however – his finger had frozen in place.

Magdalena and David released each other. David sat up. They turned to face their attacker. Whitman had only enough time still in control of his own thoughts to see that that both of their eyes had turned as black as anthracite. David was about to pop the man's mind like a helium balloon when Magdalena stopped him.

Magdalena told David through their direct mind:

No, let me. I owe a friend a favor.

She then raised her left index finger aloft in the air as if she had a counterpoint to make in an argument with someone…

…or if she were ordering a sandwich at a deli counter.

Whitman also raised his left index finger in the air, as if the two of them were playing Simon Says.

Magdalena said aloud:

"I'd like a tuna on rye, please."

Whitman then repeated the words.

And in the floor above and the one below, the sounds of his screams echoed in the hallways and in the rooms and in the ears of those still left to hear them.

O'Connell watched as the light for the floors in the elevator compartment moved from '1' to 'L'.

"Jesus. Finally. Get me the fuck out of this Looney Tunes show."

The doors opened and standing there in the lobby to greet him was Agent Price.

"Oh. Hey there. Was just going to-"

Price pulled his silver sidearm and stuck it in O' Connell's face before he could say another word. However, unlike his two counterparts, Price actually got to use his. He pulled the trigger, but instead of a projectile, a concenrated burst of sound emanated from the barrel. The sound had been tuned to a highly specific frequency that targeted the amygdala and hippocampus of its target, causing both to expand at a rapid rate within seconds.

O' Connell's head exploded like a cherry red party favor, his lifeless body falling on top of Moretti's.

Like in that movie, what was it called again?

Chapter Twenty-Three

Magdalena had found herself enjoying the first minutes without any immediate fear, dread, and uncertainty since…well, since she'd gone to bed the night she'd had her first contact with David. It felt alien, unknown. She laughed to herself, remembering one of her favorite Bukowski quotes: "I've had so many knives stuck in me, when they hand me a flower I can't quite make out what it is."

David finished putting on his clothes, the same ones he wore when he'd been strapped to the gurney. He stopped, suddenly.

"Magdalena, something's…" started David

"Wrong," she finished.

The two of them immediately reached out with their minds for Sam.

His presence…his being…was gone. Sam had gone…*dark*.

Chapter Twenty-Four

Magdalena and Keating left the hospital together and did not encounter any resistance as they exited, not that anything remaining there *could* resist either of them.

Within just a few minutes, they approached Roger's vehicle. What remained of the scene seemed to issue a warning from just the visual for Magdalena to go no further. It went unheeded. Once Magdalena caught sight of the interior of the station wagon, she ran towards the now- abandoned scene.

"MAGDALENA! WAIT!"

She arrived at the vehicle, at the open drivers' side door. She saw Roger's lifeless body, tilted over towards the front passenger side.

David attempted to catch up to her and physically pull her away from the horror – but her rage, her raw anger – it frightened him far too greatly. It reminded him too much of someone else he'd just left in the darkness.

David finally came up alongside her and took her hand in his.

"There's nothing we can do, Magdalena. We need to go. Now."

Mag at first began to sob, which then gave way to open weeping.

"Sam…" Magdalena felt her knees buckle, and almost give out completely. David took her by her waist and pulled her along.

"We'll find him, Magdalena. I promise."

"How can you promise something like that?"

"We did talk to each other, Magdalena. And I bet I know something you don't know."

Magdalena and David then fled the scene by foot, disappearing into the freezing night.

University of Alaska, Anchorage.
May 2024

Caleb sat behind his desk, surveying the lecture hall in front of him. The thirty or so students in his undergraduate Biochemistry class were busy scrawling away on their fourth and final exam of the semester. The worried and concerned looks on his students faces told stories of struggle, despair, focus, and deep thought. One kid in the corner appeared totally lost, even going so far as to look to vainly at his classmates as if they could transmit the answers into his head. Another looked angry she even had to take the exam in the first place. Still another had a look as if he'd aced it, but he'd never got more than a B- on anything. Over on the other side –

Caleb caught himself mid-projecting.

It was always the quiet times that did it.

It had been months since Boston, but this was not nearly enough time to quell his feelings of sorrow, regret…and anger. It felt as if they'd never diminish. He-

An unfortunate student, looking up from his paper, made eye contact with him. Caleb bore the same intense gaze that Moretti once had. The poor kid was likely trying to recall the Michelis-Menten equation. Instead, he looked as if just he'd pissed his pants.

Caleb looked away.

Still another twenty minutes to finish their exams, and then it would be over. Sarah had flown in from San Francisco to see him the night before, for whatever fucking reason. For her…cooperation…she'd been assigned to a VP position with a large pharmaceutical company. Didn't matter which one.

They hadn't seen each other since the hospital.

And as for Caleb? CRUCIBLE had tucked him far, far away, where he could do the least amount of harm should he choose to follow in his mentor's footsteps. Not Keating.

Moretti's.

No word from Magdalena and Keating. They'd vanished. Not a surprise. Magdalena was going to come for Sarah, eventually. CRUCIBLE probably knew this and had twelve fucking plans in place for when it did.

And Magdalena knew this as well.

Massachusetts General was just the beginning.

After midnight became midday and the entire world saw it happen and then forgot that it had, Sarah and Caleb were unceremoniously loaded into a black sedan by Constabulary agents.

Caleb assumed he was about to be shot and dumped in the Charles. Instead, the sedan brought them out to what was ostensibly a real estate office out in Quincy, a suburb of Boston to the south. How quaint. CRUCIBLE HQ was a fucking Re/Max franchise.

By that point, Caleb didn't care if indeed that was what was about to happen. All he could think about was his promise to the kid.

They were going to go play video games together. Caleb was going to show Sam Tempest and Centipede and Mortal Kombat, skee ball and spending a ridiculous amount of money for tickets to exchange for some plastic piece of shit toy. Something a kid like him should have done a hundred times already.

Yeah, it wasn't Xbox One, Playstation Twelve or whatever. That wouldn't have mattered to Sam anyway. Sam deserved to just be a kid.

David – Walter – deserved to just be a kid.

Magdalena too.

And the three of them *already had challenges coming into this shitshow called life*. It was cruelty. All he wanted to do was show the kid the world outside his father wasn't all like that. Jesus Christ. How many of the world's problems would be solved if most of humanity's childhoods weren't robbed, taken, stolen, deprived, or polluted in some significant way?

He just wanted to be done with it all. He wanted it to end. But that possibility was never going to happen.

The clock finally struck one o' clock. The students, browbeaten and defeated, submitted their exam books on his lectern. At last. He could go home and get as drunk as a skunk. Oh wait. Sarah. First her. Then drunk. With any luck, he'd have the balls to finally swallow a bullet.

The last student had shuffled through the exit door, and as she exited, she said:

"Have a good summer, Professor F."

"Ah don't gimme that, Melissa. You aced it and y'know it too."

The door didn't get to closing all the way before a hand grabbed it and pulled it back open. In the doorway was Sarah. Now Samantha Samson.

She looked smart in a power suit, five-hundred-dollar hair styling, and as confidant as Tom Brady.

"Professor F, Caleb?"

"Joke the students have. I'm supposedly one of the toughest graders. Professor F."

"I'm not one for nicknames."

"I know, Samantha."

"Oh, right. Forgot. Hello Professor Fant."

All these accidents that happen.

The way Sarah had rephrased her greeting for maximum sarcastic effect set off a cascade of recall in Caleb's mind.]

The tarot card that Magdalena had in her pocket on the way to Boston General. That Bjork song Moretti was talking about. And now…the fake name he'd been given by CRUCIBLE. They were all connected to…

"Son of a bitch," replied Caleb.

"Oh, please Cal – Noah. It's Noah, right? Thought we'd be past name calling by now."

Caleb started laughing. Hysterically, even.

"Yeah, sure. Name calling. EXACTLY, Samantha Samson. You're their little pet, walking around with Sam's name around your neck like a fucking albatross."

The confidence, power suit, hairdo…wilted in the instant Caleb started cackling.

Sarah's face flushed with embarrassment, and with anger.

"Came to hand you your first assignment, asshole."

"Aww, Sarah. Samantha. What happened to being past name calling?"

Her face returned to its original skin tone. She smiled.

"I have your first assignment, Noah."

She tossed a leather attaché onto his lectern.

"I flew here to hand it to you, personally. Goodbye, Noah. I doubt you'll becoming back."

"So why would I even take the assignment in the first..."

Sarah only looked at him.

"You shouldn't have left me, Caleb."

Samantha Samson turned and left, slamming the door behind her.

I think I like my new name, thought Noah.

Noah picked up the leather attache case and walked it over to the trash and threw it in.

Noah walked over to the chair where he'd draped his favorite maroon bomber jacket and put it on.

Then the riddle gets solved.

E P I L O G U E
C h r i s t i n a

Plattsburgh, New York. December 6th, 2023

Ed Grady and Barbara Melanson (nee Quinn) walked out of the conference a little bewildered, a little unsure, and a lot worried. They'd been called in for a special meeting with Christina's second grade teacher, a special needs counselor, a neuropsychic evaluator, and three other educational professionals who were all there to provide their "input" and "feedback" as to Christina's condition.

Christina was diagnosed as neurodivergent the previous November, which meant I.E.P.'s, support systems, learning strategies, and endless meetings as the one her mother and her boyfriend had just finished.

Christina was just outside on a playground near the exit doors when they appeared from within the building. She had been pushing herself on a merry-go-round with her own feet. She wasn't unhappy that she was by herself, though, quite the contrary.

This was the happiest part of her day.

She'd managed to get the merry-go-round going pretty well all by herself - actually, much faster than her classmates had at recess. A few hours earlier at recess, they'd all jammed onto the thing like sparrows on a power line. Too much noise, too many arguments from too many kids about which way to go. Christina thought it funny, watching from a distance. Merry-go-rounds could only spin in two directions, clockwise and counterclockwise…and they still couldn't make up their minds on which way to go.

But now, it was just her, and she knew which way she wanted to go. And she was spinning around at the speed she wanted to - just right for her comfort level. The playground of her school was built on the west side of the building. At this time of late afternoon, the sun shone so brightly it brightened the color of every object, each part of the building, and the schoolyard three shades lighter.

She could take it all in at once, if there was nothing else to distract her, nothing else to upset her.

She saw her mother and Ed, which shook her out of her euphoria, and she immediately applied her Chuck Taylors to the ground as brakes. The moment was over. She could tell by the looks on their faces that they didn't have a good meeting with the school adults. They never had good meetings.

It made her feel horrible, a burden just for existing.

She thought of her brother whenever she had this feeling. She wished she could see him again.

There were two people standing on a corner across the street watching her as she played.

It was, of course, Magdalena and David. Only, Mags to her friends, Magdalena to all others no longer went by either. That person no longer existed.

She thoiught of herself now as simply…Mary.

Christina looked over at them, standing there. They were both laughing, but they didn't look like they were laughing at her. Somehow, she could hear what they were saying from where she was as if they were right next to her.

David had said:

"So you're sure you're not sad to not be the queen bee, at least not anymore?"

Mary: "If it means I get to play on merry-go-rounds instead of chasing down assholes in black suits and sunglasses, I think I'm good."

"That's not what our first priority should be, Mary."

"That's too bad, David. Because its' mine."

David frowned at her, but his companion had turned away so that she never saw the expression.

"What would Moretti have-"

"Moretti's dead, David. So leave it."

Silence followed this exchange. They remained still and didn't approach the playground. Instead, they stood together and watched as Ed and Barbara collected her and left the school grounds. The three of them got into Ed's Honda Civic, parked nearby. The adults took no notice of the two strangers standing there, absorbed in themselves and how they were going to deal with their problematic daughter.

Christina never took her eyes off them as she and her guardians moved from playground to car. She liked them both. They were like her, somehow. She had pretty black hair and lots of tattoos. Christina wanted tattoos like her. And then, Christina felt something strange. The woman started speaking to her, but not with her mouth. In her head.

"You're not supposed to get any tattoos until you're older, Christina. But maybe we can make an exception in your case." She felt and heard and saw Mary's face - in her mind – smiling at her. Christina physically looked over to the side of the street where she stood and saw that Mary's actual, physical expression was blank.

"Hi Mary! My name is Christina!" she found she could speak without opening her mouth too.

The man appeared in her mind then, too. "Hi Patrica! My name is.."

"David! You're really smart, Dave. What's an ameeeno acid, anyway?"

David physically laughed as well as in her mind.

"C'mon *Dave*, talk to the girl,"

David asked: "Christina, how would you like to be a queen? To not ever have to feel bad about being you ever again?"

The question made Christina feel the joy she felt on the merry-go-around all over again. Suddenly, she very much wanted to go with the two people across the street instead of with her parents. She was a burden to them, but to David and Mary, she was something else entirely.

"Can I be a princess first though? I want to be a princess first."

The two across the street both physically smiled.

"You can be anything you want to be, my dear. And we're here to help you do that, okay? But not right now. Soon though." Mary said in their thoughts.

"Yaaaaaaay!" said Christina in her mind. David and Mary felt her joy.

"But we have to find my brother, too. Where is Sam?"

"The three of us will find him, Christina. All of us. Together."

The Civic drive off down the street. The connection between the three of them broke.

Once the Civic was out of sight, Mary turned to David.

"So you're sure she can find Sam?"

"She's the only who can, Mary."

Mary began to walk in the same direction the car had drove off but stopped after taking a few steps. David was not following alongside and had remained in the same spot as they had been in for the past hour.

Mary turned around and saw a peculiar look on his face – something akin to the Dalmatian on the labels of some vinyl records she'd seen as a kid. David looked as if he were listening to something, but it was a sound apparently only he could hear.

"David? Is everything alright?"

At the asking, he seemed to snap out of whatever state he was in and returned Mary's attention, but with a look of genuine concern upon his face.

"Uh, yeah….yes. Just felt...weird there for a second." David waved a dismissive hand towards Mary.

"Go on ahead. I'll catch up, I'm just a bit dizzy is all."

"You sure, Dr. Keating? Not gonna drop down into bottomless voids again, are you?"

David smiled.

"Nope. One's enough for me. Go on. We both know where they're headed. I'm right behind you."

Mary smiled at him, turned, and continued on her way.

She got all the way to the end of the block, about a hundred yards away, and stopped one more time. Mary turned around.

David was gone.

Ed, Barbara, and Christina had been driving for twenty minutes and were almost to their home. Barbara dropped her cellphone into her purse and pulled down the blinder on her side to adjust her looks. She caught sight of her daughter in the backseat.

Barbara began screaming, a screeching, ear-splitting sound. Horrified, Ed screeched to a halt, and turned to look at what had frightened his girlfriend. He was stunned into silence at what he saw.

Christina's eyes had turned completely black, without a trace of pupil, iris, or white. She smiled at them both. She then spoke, sounding like a pilgrim or explorer after discovering a shining new continent, a philosopher after discovering a profound truth, or a scientist proving a breakthrough theory.

I know.

If it makes you feel any better, I cried too.

A lot.

I write under the name w.p. Quigley, as a tribute to both e.e. Cummings, and H.P. Lovecraft, my favorite poet and author repsectively. But.

Ich heiße Walter.

And part of me still sits in the dark.

-w.p. Quigley
April 2021 – July 2023

Know the signs

Physical Abuse.

Neglect.

Sexual Abuse.

Mental Injury.

Reporting child abuse and neglect is everyone's responsibility.

Children need adults to pay attention to these signs.

If you suspect that a child is being abused or neglected, contact your <u>local department of social services</u>.